PRAISE FOR ELISE K. ACKERS

'Elise K. Ackers is certainly one to watch' Chanticleer Book Reviews

'One of the best books I've read this year! For those who love Nora Roberts' Rachael Johns, bestselling author of *The Art of Keeping Secrets* and *The Greatest Gift*

'An amazing new Australian voice' Cathryn Hein, bestselling author of *Rocking Horse Hill* and *The Country Girl*

'I … will read anything this author writes' Arijana, Goodreads

'Ms. Ackers' writing was mesmerizing' Jacek, Goodreads

'Romantic, refreshing and perfect. Ms. Ackers is a master wordsmith' Ashia, The Romance Reviews

'An author who's definitely leaving her mark on the Australian industry' The Never Ending Bookshelf

'This is a prime example of what happens when it all goes right' M.A. Grant, author of *First*

ALSO BY ELISE K. ACKERS

Small Town Storm

The Man Plan

Unforgettable

Midnight Mask

Dear Stranger

With Benefits

Summer Return

Autumn Vows

Winter Beginnings

One for the Road

The Road Less Travelled

ONE FOR THE ROAD

Elise K. Ackers

Web: www.elisekackers.net

Cover design: Elise K. Ackers

Cover images: Amsterdam Love Locks by glynlowe and Young Woman by lekcej.

For those amazing people who were my whole world for thirty-seven days.

1 HELLO, MY NAME IS …

Temptation called Adaline forward with a finger curl and a smile. The man who'd introduced himself as Jack was working his way down the passenger list, speaking briefly with those he would show the world, and it was her turn to stand within the blaze of his attention.

She stepped forward, introduced herself and heaved her suitcase onto the scales. Next to his ironed uniform and fresh appearance, she was the kind of rumpled mess that could only be achieved by a long haul flight and a sightseeing binge. She was tired, wired, and in good company with a room full of travellers who looked little better than herself. Nevertheless, she smoothed her hair and straightened her T-shirt.

'Adaline Sharp,' Jack repeated, checking his list. His affected Australian accent hinted at how long he'd been far from home. 'Solo. Aussie. One bag,' he checked the scales, 'fifteen kilos.'

It was a good thing he hadn't weighed her emotional baggage. Her crap was well in excess of the allowable limit.

It was also what was going to keep her immune to him.

Jack no-offered-surname, tour manager and authority on all things Europe, sighted her passport and payment receipt, marked a box alongside her name and waved her to a nearby seat. A bright-eyed brunette was quick to take Adaline's place.

All around her people were talking, snapping pictures and fumbling with luggage. London's Royal Central Café was overrun with beginnings. These were the faces of Adaline's future – friends yet to be made, acquaintances to be tolerated. Leading roles and support acts for all the adventures to come. Assuming she ever opened her mouth.

Adaline dragged her suitcase between her feet and gazed around the room, wishing to be noticed as much as she wished to be invisible. Weeks of research had done little to prepare her for the reality of being here. She envied those who introduced themselves to strangers as if change and adventure were commonplace. For her, those things were as foreign as this country.

She'd left her comfort zone somewhere over the Indian Ocean.

One guy, a head taller than those around him and halfway through his second beer, spoke at a volume which could rival a megaphone. Another wore a shirt which read, 'I have more issues than Cosmo'. He was shaking hands, introducing himself and making people laugh. Three women who looked to be younger than Adaline, maybe just eighteen, sat at a table pointing and whispering. Every so often they giggled into their hands and pouted for pictures.

Fifty-odd people had come together from all over the world. Groups of threes and twos mostly. A group of six. Others solo like herself. She could guess where some called home; half a dozen wore thongs and board shorts, one had a USA flag keychain dangling from a backpack. Three Chinese girls sat in a tight triangle, bent over their phones, knees touching. The next two in line to see Jack were from New Zealand, Adaline could hear their conversation and recognised the clipped vowels.

She wondered if either of them was *clairebluesky*, a friendly Kiwi who'd written to Adaline a few times on the online tour message board. Claire had said she'd be travelling with her best friend and these girls were clearly comfortable with one another: they were jostling to weigh their bag first, elbowing each other and snickering.

Jack ticked them off then waved them away with a smile. When they were seated he stood and banged three knocks on the tabletop.

'Can everyone hear me?' he asked, turning a slow half-circle to encompass the room. 'Thank you for being so quick to check in. I have a few things to mention, then you're all free to go.'

His age surprised her. He looked to be in his mid-twenties. The longer he spoke, the more Adaline was sure she recognised a Queensland twang. His hair was a chaos of finger-length black. He was tall, his posture was assured, and his close-lipped half smile was warm, but Adaline wondered if he had the personality to rule a coach full of eighteen to thirty-somethings. It was easy now because everyone was excited. How would he be in a week when tempers were up and people were dragging their feet? When people were late to the coach, sick, or ignorant of local customs? Shove this many people together for fourteen days, there were going to be problems. Was it typical for tour managers to be so young? Adaline shrugged her lips and pushed her hair away from her face. Maybe it made him more relatable to the group.

Jack spoke about spending money. Passport control. All the key stuff that affected their departure.

Adaline stared at the nondescript floor tiles between her and Jack and struggled to believe this was her reality. It was all finally happening. Only days ago she'd been ghosting around her house, dreaming of this moment. For months, her departure date had been a mirage and it felt like she'd been thirsty for years. But now she was liberated. Free. Out of reach and for the first time in a long time, answerable only to herself.

Why then did a part of her want to run to the nearest cab and speed back to the airport? However overwhelming, however surreal, for the next two weeks this was Adaline's life. Didn't her flighty feet realise there was nothing to run home to?

She blinked hard and looked up. Her gaze found the guy sitting opposite her, the one with the Cosmo T-shirt, the chair beneath him turned around so his elbows could rest on the back. His brown eyes were darker than his brown sun-bleached hair, and they were watching her. His lips curved.

She nodded once then looked away.

Jack spoke for about twenty minutes. He promised more information when they were underway, then finished with a threat.

'We leave at seven sharp. Be at the coach fifteen minutes before to load your bag. Don't be late. We have a ferry to catch so we won't wait for you. There are three coaches leaving on tours tomorrow – make sure you get on the right one. Memorise this face.'

All the women surely had.

Jack clapped his hands and smiled. 'Have a great night. I'll see you in the morning.'

The mood in the room shifted. It became fuller, more excited. It reached for Adaline with seeking fingers but, overwhelmed, she turned from it.

She was out of practice. With people, with herself. She'd been so good at this once – meeting people, connecting with them, but there were parts of her now that felt rusty with disuse. Use or lose it, she thought. So had she lost it? Would it – would she – come back?

What if this grand plan to get behind the steering wheel of her life turned out to be an even grander mistake?

Overcome by doubt and fear, she spent the night alone in her hotel room, clutching her bed sheet to her chest. She gave herself pep talks and concentrated on her breathing as floors below her people sat together, ate together and forged new friendships.

They were all nomads now, and some were doing it much better than others.

* * *

Conversations were at fever pitch. Names and countries were on everyone's lips and people kept checking the time. The early risers ate pastries and drank from takeaway cups they'd purchased across the street. Those who rarely saw the dawn side of nine a.m. made their way onto the coach and went back to sleep. For Adaline, adrenaline was better than coffee. It rode her bloodstream like electricity and made her stomach dance.

Last night had been a waste. She was starting the tour at a disadvantage.

All around her she recognised new acquaintances. People who hadn't been sitting together last night were huddled together this morning, not quite at ease yet, but no longer alone. The solo travellers had found each other and smaller groups had blended into larger ones. Adaline was surrounded by people who'd managed to get out of their own way and she envied them this, but she reminded herself that it was within her power to be like them.

She was ready now. A slow starter, she thought. First day nerves but she'd arrived – in body and now in mind. She was going to be in the moment. She was not going to dwell on thoughts of home. If she'd wanted to stay in that rut she could've saved thousands of dollars and not left the country. Here, now – that's what was important.

A tall, severe-featured man wearing a Gateway jumper stowed Adaline's suitcase in the coach undercarriage. She thanked him as she imagined her doubts being similarly packed away. Easing through the bodies to the front coach door, she made eye contact with everyone who looked her way. A dozen smiles later, she climbed the steps.

Jack was sitting on the driver's seat, facing the steps, elbows on his knees and clipboard in hand. He asked her name, put a mark on his list, then smiled his curious close-mouthed half smile. 'Welcome aboard.'

It hadn't been jet lag. The man was an artist's dream. Everything from his pronounced brows to his wide, full lips would make a sculptor's fingers itch. Denim blue eyes, a jaw that seemed to flare out near his ears – Jack was both masculine and beautiful. There was a faded scar under his right eye, his only obvious imperfection, and Adaline's curiosity stretched beyond the length of it. She wondered what had happened and who or what had affected his otherwise perfect face. She wondered if Jack knew that it improved him.

His smile widened and for just a moment she felt like the only girl in the world.

Someone stepped up behind her and the spell lifted.

'Uh, thanks.' She hurried away. A net, she thought, moving down the aisle. His smile was a net. Hearts would break.

The coach was luxurious, designed for long days on the road. There was a small toilet off the middle stairs and a powerboard charging station above it. The windows were spotless and the corn yellow palette outside the coach continued in the curtains and seat covers. Over a dozen people were already on board, slumped in their seats, mouths open. Adaline chose a seat in the middle and settled in to watch everyone else join them. Some were polished, ready for the day. Others looked like they'd been wrestled into their clothes. She tried to pick some of the accents of passing conversations but it had never been a strength of hers. There were some obvious indicators – a maple leaf sewn onto a backpack, a Southern Cross tattooed on the back of a leg – but otherwise, Adaline could only guess who belonged to what flag. For some reason it had seemed more obvious last night in the cafe. The differences between one passenger and the next kept her amused right up to the moment the last one boarded and the engine rumbled to life.

The seat beside her was taken by a short, curvy girl with dyed blonde hair. She wore a top that showed too much cleavage for this hour of the morning and earrings that almost reached her shoulders. She cast one look over Adaline, snapped her seatbelt over her body then turned to face her friends seated across the aisle.

Adaline blinked at the girl's back. She'd been one of the whispering, pouting girls last night and this was not the social start Adaline had hoped for.

The door hissed shut and about a minute later the coach began to move. People cheered.

Adaline crossed her arms under her breasts and shifted to face the window. The streets of slowly stirring London rolled past. Adventure lay ahead. The excitement within the coach felt like static electricity on her skin, and the collective mood helped untangle some of the knot of nerves in her stomach. Things would be easier once she was on the road, surrounded by distractions and opportunities. Everything would feel further away. How could her problems possibly compete with the beauty and history of Europe, or the energy and passion of the people she would meet?

A soft tapping sound made Adaline first look up at the overhead speakers, then towards the front of the coach. Jack had stood from his seat and was facing the group. He tested the microphone again, murmured something to the driver – the severe-looking man who'd taken Adaline's bag – then made a grave announcement.

'Okay, we're not even an hour into the tour and we've already lost a passenger.' He waited as people made soft exclamations and checked for their friends. 'One of our solo travellers appears to have slept through his alarm. I really can't stress this enough: we will not wait for you. We can't. Our schedule's too tight and no one would thank you for being the reason we miss a ferry connection or excursion.' He waved a hand in a helpless gesture. 'I hate to make an example of the poor guy, but this is what happens. If you're late, we leave. Please be on time, for your own sakes.'

Looking appropriately stern, Jack moved on. 'Now, I'd like you all to meet Danya. He's our driver, he's a whole lot of fun, and he wants to have a few words.'

The next voice was louder than Jack's and thick with an accent Adaline couldn't place. 'Hello, I am Danya. I drive. Welcome and happy morning. I just say, keep coach clean. I clean every night then party with you. Less cleaning, more party.'

People laughed. In seconds, Danya had made himself one of them and contradicted the unfriendly expression many had seen before they'd left. He looked old enough to be nudging the tour's age ceiling – easily thirty-four, possibly thirty-five, and his succinct, no-nonsense way of speaking was somehow charming instead of brusque.

Jack moved the microphone back to his mouth. 'You laugh now, but this coach will be one of the few constant things in your life for the next two weeks. You'll become really fond of it, I promise you. And as someone who's toured with Danya before, you want him partying with us. He's insane.'

Adaline glanced out the window when the scenery changed. The buildings, streets and chaos were gone. Even though they were mere kilometres from the city's heart, expansive green fields stretched away from both sides of the coach.

Doubtlessly noting people's shift in attention, Jack leaned forward to better see the inexplicable space. 'Those of you from big cities, anything strike you as odd about what you're seeing now?' Adaline glanced back at him, curious. 'You may be wondering why such prime land isn't built out and the answer may surprise you: you're looking at mass graves. In the seventeenth century hundreds of thousands of people died in plague epidemics. Some of the bodies were dumped around here. People were carted out of the city dead or dying, hauled into the pits and buried – sometimes alive.' He paused, marking the sombre fact. 'Many of you may not know that the London fire, although devastating, is attributed to bringing the plague to a long overdue end.'

Adaline gazed at the blur of green, imagined the screams of horror and despair, the crackle and spit of hungry flames, and closed her eyes. She had known about the fire, but not the mass graves. There was so much about this world she didn't know. There was so much to learn and understand.

Struck by this sad tale and intrigued by the history of it, she wondered if Jack was full of such stories and inclined to share. If so, would the passing days take her closer to the front of the coach where she could better listen? Or would she be drawn to the back, where even now people were laughing raucously, having not heard nor appreciated Jack's glimpse into the past?

'Okay,' Jack said, 'I can see I've lost a few of you already. But if I could have your attention for a few more minutes... Hands up if you're from the United States?' Adaline straightened in her seat and glanced around. About fifteen hands went into the air. 'Australia?' Hands went down and other hands went up. Adaline counted nine, including herself, then Jack put his hand up, making it an even ten. He continued to call out country names until everyone had raised their hand, even Danya, who turned out to be from Ukraine. There were New Zealanders, South Americans, Chinese, Canadians, Mexicans, Swiss, Italians and Thais – a very mixed bag.

'Great,' Jack said, 'now here are some fun facts: there are forty-eight of us. Thirteen are solo, four are related, eight are dating, and four are married. One of you has done this tour before, and tours such as this typically split into four groups: culture vultures, foodies, adventurers, and of course, the party crowd.' Loud whoops from the back made him laugh. 'Who all seem to have found each other. I'm about to play your day song. Love it or hate it, this is going to start every morning on the coach. Fun, right? Anyway, that's all from me —' more cheers '— yeah, yeah. We'll be at the Dover ferry in about two hours, depending on traffic. Keep your passports handy, we'll be going through customs.'

Jack sat and people began chatting to one another. Lady Gaga began singing *Just Dance*. Excluded from nearby conversation by the blonde girl's back, Adaline focused on the view and thought of Paris.

2 RORY

Rory slapped his cards down on the table and pointed at the player to his left. 'Bullshit,' he declared.

Pies, the bullshitter in question, laughed. 'We're not playing bullshit, mate, we're playing poker.'

'I'm calling bullshit on your hand. You're counting the deck.' The four other guys at the table shifted in their seats and arrowed suspicious glances at their friend. That they didn't think it impossible made Rory more certain. 'I don't know how you're doing it,' he said, 'but I know you are. I want my pounds back.' His phone rang in his pocket. 'And I'm out.'

He stood, shook off Pies's attempted grab with a laugh, and walked away from the game. He answered the call as he approached the back rail.

The chalky white cliffs of Dover had long since sank into the horizon; there was only blue now, above and below. The ferry's engine noise made him think of an army of air compressors and the churning sea was like every storm in Rory's memory – combined.

'Mum!' he said, attempting to make himself louder.

'Hey, sweetie, how's Paris?' The connection tripped then steadied.

Rory pushed the phone hard against his ear. 'We tried to talk it out, but in the end we called it quits. We're gonna stay friends, though.'

'Hilarious. I wonder how much that joke cost me?'

Rory grinned. 'We're not there yet. We get there this evening and it's only —' He pulled the phone away to check the screen, '— a little after ten a.m.'

'Oh!'

Static ate the rest of her reply.

Rory imagined her sitting at the kitchen table, jabbering away about the different timezones, and felt a blunt ache in his chest. It was just after eight o'clock in Sydney. She would've had dinner by now and maybe she was in her pyjamas already. His dad would be on the lounge, probably pretending to read but really just waiting for his turn on the phone. Junk, his kid sister, would be doing whatever fifteen-year old girls did behind closed bedroom doors.

All so far away.

'Mum? You're breaking up.'

'—ondered — saw on the news ... — and your itinerary — ... We're... —ittle worried.'

Rory glared at the thrashing water. 'I didn't catch that, but I'm fine.'

He guessed something had happened in Paris; a protest, maybe, or wild weather. Whatever it was, he was out of its reach, but Monica Frost always imagined her loved ones in the middle of trouble – she was a worrier.

'I'm on the ferry,' he shouted down the line. 'I can't really hear you, but I'm fine!'

Thinking it would be quieter inside, Rory turned from the back railing and hurried towards the external door. He wrenched it open and tripped over the raised door jamb as he passed through.

'— your dad, but he said —' Silence, then a burst of mechanical noise.

The call disconnected on Rory's curse.

People looked up from their books and their families, from all the things they were doing to distract themselves, and stared. He waved a hand in apology.

He typed a quick message – another reassurance – then pocketed his phone.

Jack had said the sea crossing would take one and a half hours, and Rory imagined he'd whiled away an hour or so with the Australians he'd met last night. He hadn't paid attention to the time they'd left port, he'd been too busy matching Pies joke for joke, but he figured there was still enough time to get something to eat and find a few more people from his coach.

The group seemed good. Dinner and drinks after the pre-departure meeting had been fun; he'd shared a table in an English pub with a few Canadians, two Mexican sisters and five Aussies, and he'd laughed so hard his sides had hurt. It had been worth the gruelling morning, dragging himself on to the coach after three hours of sleep. Coffee had made it all possible.

Rory went in search of more.

The ferry turned out to have many things to pass the time. There were restaurants and bars, spacious seating areas and cash points. Overhead signs pointed to a duty free supermarket and bureau de change, and the wide, well-lit aisles accommodated thousands of people crossing the channel; some in seats, others on the floor leaning against walls or backpacks. He could tell the people just starting out. The practiced travellers seemed to have less bones in their body; they'd tucked themselves into all manner of positions in unironed clothes and worn, practical shoes.

Rory found the cafe and joined the end of a short line. In front of him, two girls were squabbling about seating arrangements.

'Turns,' the shorter one was saying. She had an asymmetrical black bob that played up her strong jawline, thin eyebrows, and an opinion she wasn't backing down from. 'I get the window next, or you can make a new friend.'

'But I didn't see anything,' the other girl complained. She had a rounder face and a wide, unsmiling mouth. Her waist-length brown hair was highlighted by streaks of red, and half a dozen wooden bracelets rattled on her wrists.

New Zealanders, Rory thought, registering their accents, and possibly from his tour – they seemed vaguely familiar.

'Tough,' the first girl said. 'New rule: if you're gonna sleep, you don't get the window.' She threw a hand out to emphasise her point and almost clipped Rory across the face. Rory leapt back, stumbled, and crashed into the person behind him. He made the global, wordless warble of a falling person, the person behind him yelped, and the girl who'd caused it all cried out an apology.

When he recovered himself, he turned to make his own apologies – and stopped.

The girl – *the girl* – from last night was pushing her long brown hair back from her face. Strands of it were stuck to her lipstick and tangled in one of her earrings. She blinked and there was a flash of green on her lids, a compliment to the moss colour of her eyes. She had long lashes, a pointed chin, and a small, slightly upturned nose.

'I'm sorry,' Rory pushed out, inexplicably as dazed as she.

'My fault,' said the girl ahead of him in the line. She leaned around him, her hands held up. 'Sorry, sorry. I almost hit him, so he hit you. My bad, all of it. I'm Claire.' One of her hands came down for a handshake.

The pretty girl with her hair in disarray was the first to recover herself. She took Claire's hand and shook it. 'Ada.'

'Ooh, from online – hey!' Claire thrust her hand into Rory's next. Taken aback, his voice cracked when he introduced himself.

'This is Jenny,' Claire said, bumping her friend, who nodded then turned away to order. 'Are you on our tour too?' she asked him. The girls appeared to have recognised each other's names.

'Yeah.' Rory glanced at Ada. She smiled back at him through hands that were trying to fix her hair. 'Gateway?' he said, 'Jack?'

The girls nodded. Jenny asked Claire what she wanted from the cashier, and Claire turned away.

'I like your shirt,' Ada said. She finished smoothing her long fringe across her high forehead, and when she dropped her hand from her face, she looked somehow transformed. Elegant, he thought, like the girl next door who'd been embraced by Hollywood.

Rory looked down at his T-shirt, needing to remind himself. He'd dressed in the dark this morning. The faux blood stain on his right side made him look like he'd been mauled, except there were small black letters across his chest which read, 'I'm fine'. It was one of his favourites, but not what he would have picked for this introduction. 'Thanks,' he said.

She heard the doubt in his voice and hastened to reassure him. 'Really. It's funny.'

They smiled at each other.

'I'm going to buy you a coffee,' he said. He reached into his pocket and pulled out a crumpled note. 'For stepping on you and wrecking your hair. Which looks fine now,' he added quickly.

'You don't have to do that,' she said, although she looked delighted. 'I'm set for a drink.' She tapped the water bottle poking out from under the flap of her satchel bag.

'A muffin, then. A pastry.' Rory turned to see what was for sale behind the thick glass divider. 'A biscuit – what is that, is that shortbread?'

She laughed and something inside Rory shifted. He looked back at her and wondered how he might make her laugh again.

'I'm fine, thank you. And that is shortbread, that's what I'm here for.'

When it was Rory's turn to order, he got her two pieces.

They sat together at one of the cafe tables, her with her snack and him with his double-shot cappuccino. Claire and Jenny sat at the neighbouring table with their coffees and deeper introductions were exchanged.

'You're from Adelaide,' Rory guessed, when Ada said she was from Australia.

Startled, she nodded. 'How did you know?'

'You lot use your vowels differently down there, it's easy to pick.' He touched his fingers to his chest. 'Sydney.'

Ada looked intrigued. 'Okay.' She propped her elbows on the table and leaned forward. 'So which one are you?'

'One?'

'Of the four. Foodie, culture nut, adventurer?' The corners of her mouth lifted. 'Party boy?'

Rory smiled. 'Can I only be one?' When she shrugged, he felt compelled to explain himself. 'I'll probably float across all of them. I like a drink as much as the next person but I'm here to see and do everything I can. Preferably not with a hangover.'

Claire, who'd been listening, spoke up. 'We have coach-free days. We're staying in lots of places for more than a night. Those are the nights I'm drinking.'

'It'd be better to drink the nights before long drives,' Jenny said. 'Then you can just sleep.'

'Hung over on a bus? No thanks.'

Rory wondered if the pair ever agreed on anything. Either way, they'd picked their category. 'What about you?' he asked Ada, who was watching the girls with amusement. She considered this for such a long time, Rory

11

almost asked the question again.

'I don't know,' she said at length. 'This is my first big trip, I guess I'll find out as I go.'

'What are you like at home?'

'None of the above.'

Rory didn't get a chance to pick apart this curious answer because Jack came out of nowhere and rapped his knuckles on the tabletop.

'Head to the stairwell in five, people.'

Ada thanked him and he left to find the others.

Lucky for Rory, the girls knew which stairwell to return to. He downed the last of his coffee then followed them to the port side where they joined the queue of people waiting to return to their cars or coaches.

Back in the cavernous undercarriage engine noise and conversation was amplified. Rory thought of an airport as he walked between cars and stepped around backpacks leaning against wheels. He followed Ada up the middle stairs, all the while gathering his courage, then swung into the aisle seat beside her when she sat.

Some of the boys at the back whistled and whooped. Ada looked back at them and laughed. She seemed happy for the company, so the little knot in his stomach loosened.

'This will be nice,' she said, smiling at him as she pulled her belt over her lap. 'My last neighbour sat with her back to me the whole way.'

'I saw. But don't get too excited, you might miss her before too long. I'm a talker.'

She made a show of settling in. 'Good. Talk.'

And they did, non-stop for half an hour until they were interrupted by the opening notes of the French national anthem. Everybody straightened in their seats or turned to the front. Jack let the music play through the speakers for a moment, then turned it off.

'Welcome to France!' People cheered and he laughed. 'Okay, we've got a while before we get to Paris, but I just wanted to let you guys know what you're up for. We'll be going straight to the Gateway village. We'll unpack and have a quick dinner, then we'll do an evening tour of the city.'

More cheers and exclamations.

'Settle in,' he said, 'get to know your new family. I'll talk a bit about French history when we get closer —' a few people at the back groaned '— and I'm passing back the room sheet now. Four to a room: all guys, all girls. No mixing. Those who've paid for the double rooms just need to tick beside their names.'

He turned the microphone off and conversations resumed.

'What are you most looking forward to?' Rory asked Ada, settling back in and giving her his full attention again.

She smiled. 'It's already happened.'

Rory frowned. 'We haven't done anything yet.'

'We've started,' she explained. 'We got on this coach and drove out of London.'

'You're easy pleased.'

She laughed and Rory felt that curious realignment again. 'Maybe I am,' she said.

'After leaving,' he pressed, 'what's next on your highlights list?'

She thought about it, then smiled. 'Greece.'

'Me too, the Greek islands.'

Ada reached forward to take the clipboard from the guy sitting in front of her. The room sheet was a series of boxes grouped into fours beside larger, bolder numbers. Room numbers, he supposed. The name of the Gateway village was printed across the top of the page and the couples had their pick of the double boxes along the bottom. When Ada unhooked the pen from the clip, her fingers shook.

Rory lowered his voice. 'You okay?'

She jolted, as if she'd forgotten he was there and he'd startled her. 'Yes,' she said. Then she dropped her voice too. 'The girls put my name down.'

Ada's name was written under the names of the two girls from the ferry, Claire and Jenny, and a third name, Beth, and there was loopy handwriting under it which read, "Hope ok!"

'I see that – nice.'

Ada stretched up in her seat. Claire was looking back, trying to catch her eye. Ada beamed at her and Claire waved.

Rory waited until Ada was settled into her seat again before venturing, 'Relieved?'

She passed him the clipboard, put her face in her hands and laughed. It was a dizzy sound. 'So relieved.'

'I find it hard to believe you were always picked last at school.' Their fingers brushed when she passed him the pen.

'Ah, but you have to participate to be picked, don't you?' Ada didn't explain this. By the time he passed the clipboard back, she'd moved the conversation on. 'Do you speak any other languages?'

'I'm fluent in sarcasm.'

Ada nodded. 'That counts.'

Somewhere deep inside Rory's body, something important lost its balance.

* * *

Rory sat with Adaline again after the short break at a petrol station west of Amiens. Adaline was so happy about this, she thought her seatbelt might be the only thing keeping her from floating away. She was thoroughly charmed and she hadn't laughed this much in a long time. The weeks ahead didn't seem so anonymous when she had a boy at her side determined to introduce her to everyone who spoke to him.

Rory had made an impression on the group; he'd gone out to dinner, knocked pints together and generally put himself out there. People were drawn to him. This meant that their every conversation was shared with the people around them. People leaned over seats to offer their point of view, or leaned into the aisle to listen, and Rory included them effortlessly. They talked about London. A Mexican girl named Rosa had done a hop-on hop-off tour with her sister, Letecia. A Canadian guy named Chris had done a Beefeater tour of the Tower of London. Two girls from Australia, Rachael and Holly, had done the Tower Bridge Experience and were still freaked out about the things they'd seen. Actors had lunged at them in the dark and the stories had been chilling.

Adaline listened with rapt attention.

She'd landed the day before the tour, which had only left time for a spin on the London Eye, an aimless bus ride around the city, and a few hours walking around the Thames. Everyone's stories were glimpses of a world she hadn't had time to properly explore.

Rory trumped everyone with his adventures on the Underground. She laughed uproariously when he told them all about vaulting himself onto an overcrowded train, and looking for platform nine and three-quarters at Kings Cross, and she listened closely when he recounted a darker moment on an empty platform the night before meeting up with the tour. He was an expressive storyteller, gesticulating wildly and adopting different voices when he spoke of other people. He was a people person, an entertainer. He was so engaging in fact, that she forgot to look out the window for almost an hour.

When Rory smiled, it was with his whole face. Deep lines appeared at the back of his cheeks and under his eyes, and the brown of his eyes seemed to lift a shade. It was as if laughter lit him from inside. He had brown hair gelled into haphazard peaks, green sunglasses hooked around the back of his neck – which he wouldn't wear because they were speaking – and the most expressive mouth Adaline had ever seen. She kept catching herself staring.

It was Jack's voice that broke the spell.

Jack launched into the promised history spiel, filling the coach with dates and names, and battles and milestones, but Adaline struggled to hear. Everyone around her was still talking, more interested in each other than the past. Jonno, another Australian, was re-enacting some fan responses to wax models at Madame Tussuads, making everyone laugh. Rory bumped her shoulder, his eyes shining. She offered him a tight smile then sat higher in her seat, bringing her ear closer to the overhead speakers.

Rory watched this, then turned away. 'Give us a sec, mate,' he said to Jonno. 'I want to hear this.'

Ada glanced at Jonno, who looked surprised.

'Really?' he said. 'History's your thing?'

Rory shrugged. 'Isn't it everyone's thing? We all have one.'

'A thing?'

'A history.'

Adaline smiled. People sat back in their seats and Jack's voice moved to the fore. He spoke for twenty minutes in a storyteller's voice that rivalled Rory's; about why the world was in a longstanding love affair with Paris, about what great works it had inspired and how it had endured the war. He listed modern cultural references then went into detail about the great masters who'd called the city home. Adaline listened and imagined herself amongst it all.

'If you look ahead,' he said, 'there's your first look at the Eiffel Tower.'

Adaline launched forward in her seat. She got a tantalising glimpse of the famous spire then the coach accelerated into a tunnel. She turned to Rory, incredulous.

He cracked up laughing. 'Your face,' he managed, and pointed at it.

Adaline shook her head, her mouth open. 'This is the closest I've ever been to Paris, and I'm under it.'

'So are six million other people,' he joked, referring to the catacombs packed with bodies. He smiled. 'C'mon, you're in a Parisian tunnel. That's something.'

When they emerged from under the city, Jack stood from his seat and turned to face the group. 'Everybody ready to get off the coach?' There were a chorus of yeses before he said, 'If you look ahead, there are your site reps. Wave 'em in!'

Four people in pale yellow shirts and dark pants were standing in the middle of a round-about, shaking their arms above their heads. One was swinging from a flag pole, another had hoisted herself onto the back of a tall, broad-shouldered guy who was still managing to laugh and wave despite his passenger.

'Dinner's in twenty minutes, everyone. Meet at the big white tent – you'll know it when you see it.'

Rory blocked the aisle so Adaline could step out when it was their turn to step off the coach, and he lifted her suitcase free of the pile Danya was building when she pointed it out to him. In the new environment, Adaline felt suddenly shy. She thanked him quietly, returned his broad smile, then stepped away. Claire and Jenny were standing with a blonde girl on the path between a row of wood cabins. Adaline hurried to join them.

The new girl introduced herself as Beth. As they struggled up the path with their things, Adaline learned that she was as a thirty-year-old physiotherapist from Texas. She was shorter than Adaline and her hair was as curly as Adaline's was straight. The gorgeous ringlets sat just above her shoulders, and teamed with her large star earrings and printed pants, made her look fun and youthful. She was travelling with her brother Daniel and she had the whitest teeth Adaline had ever seen.

Her Texan drawl was something straight out of a Hollywood movie. 'Oh my gosh, the hottest guy in the group only has eyes for you!'

A few steps ahead, Claire glanced over her shoulder. 'You think Rory's hotter than Jack?'

Beth's brows lowered. 'Jack's the driver?'

'That's Danya,' Jenny said, shifting her pack higher on her back. 'Jack's the tour leader.'

'Oh, the broody, handsome one. Yeah, he's pretty good. Intense eyes.' Beth looked back at Adaline. 'But yours is yum. That smile, wow.'

'He's not mine,' Adaline said, but privately she agreed. Rory did have a killer smile. She flexed her fingers around the handle of her suitcase. There was a tickle of warmth low in her belly. How long had it been since she'd talked about boys like this, with girls around her age? It seemed like a lifetime ago.

It was only day one and already it was the highlight of Adaline's year.

Beth was looking at the numbers on the doors now, dragging one of the largest suitcases of the whole group.

'Do you have a family in that thing?' Claire asked. Like Jenny, she carried her things in a big red backpack with chest and waist straps.

'Just about,' Beth said, stopping in front of a cabin with a big four beneath the external light. She unlocked the door and everyone followed her inside.

Jenny shrugged out of her pack and dropped it on the floor. 'I've got to pee.'

Behind her, Claire threw her pack down and scrambled toward the only other door in the cabin. 'Me first!'

Jenny grabbed at her. 'Claire!'

Claire giggled and muscled her way into the tiny bathroom. She slammed the door on Jenny's curses.

Jenny scowled and turned back to the room. She arrowed a look at Adaline. 'What?'

Adaline shook her head. She parked her suitcase at the end of one of the bunks. 'Nothing. I'll say it later. If you have to pee so bad, I don't want to make you laugh.'

Jenny stared at her, then grinned. 'I like you.'

Fifteen minutes later, the girls re-joined the group. Adaline felt grimy from a day on the road, but there hadn't been time to do more than change into fresh clothes and reapply deodorant. Looking around, she saw many new shirts and a few dresses.

A site representative was standing at the mouth of the enormous dining tent and everyone had gathered in front of her. There were two tiny lines above her mouth, a drawn-on imitation of the quintessential French curled moustache. She wore a red beret propped at a jaunty angle and big black combat boots. She checked her watch then smiled.

'Bonsoir!' she cried, throwing her voice over the many conversations around her. 'My name's Cassie, welcome to Paris. I'm going to give you guys your first French experience, is everybody ready?' She smiled through the chorus of yeses and applause. 'Good. Now I know some of you might be hungry, so I took the liberty of making you something.'

Cassie moved closer to the trestle table at her back and with a flourish, pulled a silver lid off a serving plate. Adaline's eyes rounded. Dead snails – dozens of them – were piled in the middle.

'Escargot!' Cassie exclaimed, shouting to be heard over squeals and groans.

When the noise died down, she became serious. 'I hope there's enough for everyone. Frank and I spent hours down by the creek finding these guys, but some were too fast for us, you know?'

More groans. A few of the guys laughed.

Adaline swallowed. She pressed a hand to her abdomen and wondered if she would be brave enough to try one.

'Can I get a volunteer?' Cassie asked, plucking a shell from the plate and holding it high.

More murmurs, then Rory moved forward.

'Yeah, I'll step up.' He turned to the group and bowed when people applauded, then took the snail with a grin. Cassie offered him a container of toothpicks. He lifted one free. Adaline smiled when he caught her eye in the crowd.

'Good man,' Cassie said. 'Now what I need you to do is give it a bit of a jab. A really solid one, that's the way. Just making sure it's dead.' She laughed when someone shrieked. 'Now give it another jab, scramble it around a bit then scoop it out.'

The shapeless thing that lifted free of the shell did not look like food, but Rory fearlessly dropped it onto his tongue and began to chew. Adaline's stomach lurched unpleasantly then her hand flew to her mouth when his face screwed up.

'Not cooked!' he managed.

This caused the longest screams yet, which fast became indignant shouts when Rory began to laugh and shake his head.

'It's fine,' he said breathlessly. 'It's cooked, I'm kidding. Tastes like garlic.'

Not to be outdone, the guys stepped forward. And not to be denied another laugh, they helped hand out servings to the girls. Cassie offered everyone serviettes, people got their phones and cameras ready, and the theatrics began.

Adaline stared at the dead creature in her hand. At her elbow, Beth stared too.

'I already want to spit,' she said to Adaline.

Adaline forced a grim smile at the phone Claire was pointing at her, and stabbed. Four times, just to be sure. The moment the snail was in her mouth, she gagged. She thought of the slow, slimy creatures that left shining trails on the concrete path beside her house, of their rubbery bodies and the crack of splitting shells when birds thwacked them against a brick wall. Her jaw wouldn't work – wouldn't chew – so she swallowed it whole.

Beth bounced from foot to foot, which made her large earrings snag in her curls. She rolled her neck from side to side, closed her eyes and followed suit.

Adaline almost fell on the cup of water that appeared at her elbow. She gulped it down, trying to wash the taste away and drown the memory, and Rory grinned.

When she was done, he leaned towards her ear. His breath warm on her neck, he murmured, 'You cheated. You didn't chew at all.'

She turned her face to answer. 'You have an antennae between your teeth.'

He drew away laughing. 'It's actually called a tentacle.'

'What, you read that on snail facts dot com?'

'It was required reading, didn't you?'

A group of boisterous Australians appeared either side of him, shouting at him and one another. They'd downed their snails and seemed to want to congratulate him on leading the charge. Rory winked at Adaline, then gave them his attention.

Beth, Claire and Jenny were grinning when she turned back to them. Jenny still had her snail on the end of her toothpick – it looked ridiculous and gross sitting aloft like that.

'Where's *my* water?' Beth teased.

Cassie spared Adaline from answering. 'When everyone's whet their appetites, file on through for your early dinner. Those with dietary requirements will find their plates on the table in the far corner. Everyone else, it's buffet, help yourselves.'

'Bear in mind,' called Jack, lifting his arm high so people could see him in the crowd, 'the faster you eat, the sooner you see Paris.'

He was lucky to survive the stampede.

Adaline sat with Beth, Claire, Jenny, and a couple from New Zealand, Maree and William. Conversation was easy and fun; everyone talked about the escargot and commented on one another's accents, and there was a strange, almost instant kinship between the six as they better introduced themselves and sampled food off one another's plates. Maree was twenty-eight and looked every bit a model in an electric blue peplum dress. Her black hair was bundled in a high knot and she had three piercings in her right ear. Three crystal studs winked and flashed beneath the food tent spotlights, often catching Adaline's attention throughout dinner. Maree's boyfriend William was as casual as she was elegant, in a much-loved T-shirt and old joggers that didn't look likely to see the end of the tour. He was fair-haired and regular – he looked a little like a lot of people, and was the same age as Maree.

Rory sat at a table across from Adaline, seemingly embraced by the group of five Australians. They were the loudest table, without question. Adaline often looked his way when raucous laughter pitched above the general bedlam.

Everyone ate quickly, and those who went back for seconds were frowned at. Adaline found she could hardly concentrate through her excitement, so she was relieved when Jack stood up and called for attention.

'Everyone on the coach in fifteen minutes!'

Everyone was on the coach in ten.

3 TEASE

Adaline was first on the coach and she took the window seat behind the driver's seat, inarguably the best one for the night tour. From there she had uninterrupted views left and ahead, and a decent view to her right if she leaned around Beth. Rory winked as he moved through to the back, and Maree and Will settled into the seats behind. Jack boarded last. He checked the mounted navigator, spoke briefly to Danya, then pulled the microphone onto his lap. His seat folded down over the stairs. From where she sat, Adaline could see the small gravy stain on his breast pocket and read some of the larger script on his paperwork. He'd come armed with information.

Many seats behind her, one of the Australians made a loud joke and people laughed. Rory countered, and people laughed harder. It was universal, Adaline thought. Be it on a bus in Paris or a classroom back home: the mischief-makers always sat at the back.

She'd wanted to sit with Rory again, but Paris had won out. He wouldn't be able to keep his friends quiet for hours, and might not even want to. Adaline on the other hand, wanted to hear every word of Jack's driving tour and see as much of the city as she could without someone dividing her attention.

Danya closed the doors and reversed out of the coach parking area. Jack waited until they were off site before he began his spiel, and it didn't seem to bother him that a few weren't listening.

'People, I'm going to put the first day sheet on the message board at reception. If you need to know where we're going and when, what meals are included, etcetera, all the information will be on that. Anyway, welcome to fair Paris, the capital of France. Paris is famous for architecture, food, and shopping, but it's also one of the world's great art repositories. Picasso, Dali, Van Gogh, and Rodin are just some of the featured masters. There are stacks of museums to choose from if art's your thing.

'For the foodies on board, I hope you brought your stretchy pants. We all know what a patisserie is, but just a few tips; a boulangerie is a bakery, and a fromagerie is a cheese shop. Go nuts. If you try any particularly crazy macaroon flavours, tell me. I love those things.

'For those wanting to know about the nightlife, speak to me after – I can suggest some great spots and tell you how to get there and back.'

He spoke about shopping options next. Uninterested in haute couture fashion and hip concept stores, Adaline looked out the window. The city lights crept closer and the butterflies in her stomach bumped against one another.

When the coach rolled into town and the Seine uncurled beside them like a silk ribbon, Jack's commentary changed. He began pointing out landmarks and explaining why they were significant. He dropped in fun facts to break up the history, and added valuable context to the world around them. They drove past green metal stalls selling old books, trinkets, and souvenirs, the river at their backs. Past the lights of the Latin Quarter and the majesty of the outer walls of the Louvre.

'Notre Dame Cathedral,' Jack said, 'coming up on your right, inspired Victor Hugo's *The Hunchback of Notre Dame*. That's French Gothic architecture you're looking at, isn't it gorgeous? If you want to go inside it's free, but the queues are always long so take that into account when you're planning your day. Over fourteen million people go inside every year.

'Just in front of it – that statue there – that's Charlemagne. He's the guy who said, "Live by the cross, or die by the sword".'

Jack went on to explain the metro system, prompted by the sign on the street corner. Shortly after, he pointed out the bridge where Big proposed to Carrie, and the building where the 1789 revolution began. They passed the Musee Rodin Gardens and glimpsed a copy of *The Thinker*, then Jack talked about Napoleon's military history and Louis XIV's extravagance.

Adaline tried to take it all in, but it was detail overload.

'This city was taken in World War Two by the Germans,' he said, 'and we're about to drive past one of the most important relics of the invasion. If you look out to your left and count sixteen windows across, you'll see it. Count carefully, people, if you miss this, you may as well've not come to Paris.' He led the group in a slow count as Danya navigated the bumper-to-bumper traffic. Adaline read the sign over the grand, double-height arched entrance – *Cavalerie* – and wondered what the building had been used for during the war.

'...fourteen, fifteen, six— oh no, the blind's drawn!' People began to grumble, but Jack's tone stayed light. 'Just kidding. Look to your right. There it is: the money shot! What you all came here for!'

Adaline turned and forgot everything.

Proud and marvellous, perfectly framed by the beauty and character of its city, was the Eiffel Tower. The people walking between the tower's great legs were so small they seemed like fuzzy stains on an otherwise flawless landscape. People laughed, pleased with the trick, but Adaline wished she'd known to look sooner. It was better than she'd imagined. Better than any picture or print of it she'd seen, and it was so close.

Jack spoke about the design competition which had borne its concept, about the public reaction to the tower and the wild things people had done on it. Some of the stories she knew, but there were others she wished Jack would elaborate on. As it was, even with the microphone he was struggling to be heard over everyone's chatter.

'Did he say ten minutes?' Adaline asked, turning to Beth.

'Ten minutes, what?'

'A proposal every ten minutes?'

Beth shrugged.

Danya's near-constant abuse of the drivers around him was also distracting, but despite that, Adaline was glad she'd sat at the front. What was laughter and banter to this? Did the people at the back know what they were looking at? Did they understand why some buildings mattered more than others, and could they hear and repeat the melodic pronunciations of each?

Danya dedicated the next fifteen minutes to circling the Eiffel Tower, giving everyone the opportunity to gawk and take pictures, then he drove to the Arc de Triomphe, which sat at the heart of the busiest round-about in the city. Twelve streets merged into an indeterminate number of lanes. He blasted fast tempo trance music through the speakers, making everybody laugh, and plunged into the chaos. They circled twice then drove to the Louvre, where the coach inched through an arched road barely wide enough to accommodate it. Adaline held her breath.

'There it is,' Jack said, 'the pyramid. Isn't it awesome? Six hundred and sixty-six panes of glass. If anyone plans on visiting the museum, speak to me after, I know a sneaky way in that skips the massive queues.'

Then it was over. They were taken back to the village without any of them having set foot in the city they'd come so far for. Jack assured them they would have plenty of time tomorrow, but that was little comfort to most, and no comfort at all to Adaline.

Had she been told this before boarding, would she have struck out on her own? Jack's knowledge had enriched the driving tour, but she'd have traded it for the feel of Parisian grass beneath her feet, or the evening breeze on her face full of scents of the city.

Her disappointment had quietened her by the time they reached the village. Beth hadn't pushed for conversation, she'd been distracted – often glancing back to check how her brother was getting along with the boys at the back – but she'd given Adaline's wrist an understanding squeeze, which had been nice.

Jack met her eyes as she stepped off the coach, and her crestfallen expression seemed to puzzle him. 'Problem?' he asked kindly.

Adaline stepped aside so people could continue filing down the stairs. 'It was all a bit of a tease, wasn't it?'

One side of his mouth lifted. He towered over her, taller by at least a foot. She caught the faint smell of spice and cinnamon when he leaned down. 'You can go back in, if you like. I can call you a cab and give you an address card.' She straightened, and he held up a hand. 'But could I offer you some advice?'

Adaline waited.

'You've had a huge day. If you kick on, you're just going to wipe yourself out for tomorrow. We get two days and two more nights in there. I promise you, you'll have time to see what you came here for.' He paused when a group turned from the cabins, laughing and teasing one another. They walked down the narrow path Adaline had taken to get to the dining hall, which she knew also led to the bar. Rory was amongst them. 'Stay here tonight,' Jack continued, 'chill out with your tour mates and recharge. Tomorrow's going to be a huge day too, and a late one if you're joining us for the picnic.'

Dinner under the Eiffel Tower, of course she would be there. Adaline watched the group until they were out of sight, then sighed at her feet. She looked up at Jack and at the amusement in his eyes. She laughed at herself. 'Sorry.'

Jack smiled. She supposed it was a smirk, but there was no condescension there. 'No worries. I get it. I had a first time here once, too.' Someone called his name, and he looked over Adaline's shoulder.

Adaline turned. Danya was standing on the coach steps, a bucket and cloth in his hands and an impatient look on his face.

'I'll let you go,' she said, turning back. 'Thanks for the advice.'

'That's what I'm here for. Goodnight.'

''Night, Jack.'

Adaline turned away. She glanced at the path that led to her cabin, then walked the one that led to the bar.

A lot of cabin lights were on. Within walking distance of their beds and with nothing else to see tonight, it seemed like a lot of people had decided to turn in early. Others were readying themselves for a long night under the stars. Adaline could hear them laughing and clinking bottles together, toasting to Paris and friendship, and silly things like escargot and Louis XIV.

Sleep did have its appeals, but this small exercise in freedom was a more powerful lure. She would be in charge, of everything from how much she drank to how late she stayed up. She could leave after one drink or she could leave after five. She wasn't responsible for getting anyone to bed and there were people on this tour who seemed interested in things she had to say.

Adaline was suddenly grateful that Jack had talked her into staying.

It was a modest set-up. Two site reps were serving drinks over a nondescript counter to people who were content to sit in spindly wooden chairs on the grass nearby. Rory was standing with his new Aussie friends, drinking a beer whose label she didn't recognise. Beth's brother Daniel was also amongst the crowd, drinking with Maree and William, and the two solo Canadians.

Maree waved when she spotted Adaline. 'Get a drink!' she urged, her accent making her E sound like an I. Her electric blue dress was at odds with the casual surrounds, apart from the denim and creased cotton, but she had a beer in one hand and her shoes in the other.

Adaline ordered a beer too, ended up with the same one Rory was drinking, and joined one of the circles of people exchanging names and stories.

She met Chris and Hamish from Ontario and Saskatchewan; spoke with sisters Rosa and Letecia from Mexico, the girls who'd done the London hop-on hop-off tour; and only needed to spend five minutes with the blond-haired Daniel to know she would be avoiding him for the rest of the trip. A discreet glance at everyone else confirmed they were picking up a similar vibe from the nineteen-year-old American; he was short-tempered and ethnocentric, and his manners were appalling. He spoke over people, mocked their opinions, and drank fast. He'd downed two vodka and Red Bulls before Adaline had finished half her beer.

Hamish had been this morning's late riser. He'd caught the high-speed train from London to Paris and had arrived at the campsite in time for the escargot experience. Adaline listened to his retelling of the moment he'd woken and realised he was late, laughed and commiserated, then drank quietly when the conversation edged into politics.

She dragged a seat alongside Rory when she couldn't take anymore of Daniel's far-right rant, and Rory's broad smile made her wish she'd sought him out earlier. Without a word, he knocked his bottle against hers, raised it a fraction then drank. She drank too, smiling around the mouth of it.

'You about done with Paris?' he asked. 'Ready to continue on?'

'Hardly. I can't believe we didn't get off the coach.'

'We wouldn't have got you back. I can just picture you running off into the Latin Quarter, arms above your head and screaming.'

The image made her laugh.

He re-introduced her to the five Australians who'd adopted him; Matt, Jonno, Chris and Scott, and their apparent leader, Pies. Everyone was trying hard to learn people's names, but there were so many.

'Pies?' she repeated.

'It sounds even better when you scream it,' Pies said. He had small, bright eyes, a round, friendly face, and a rum and Coke in his hand. He rolled his eyebrows suggestively.

Everyone laughed and the conversation moved on.

Adaline stayed for two drinks then went to bed. It flattered her that the boys urged her to stay, but Paris won out again.

She climbed between the unfamiliar sheets of the bottom bunk, feeling both exhausted and energised, and smiled at the wall. She thought it would take ages for her racing mind to settle, but sleep claimed her almost at once.

4 BAGGAGE

By rolling all of her clothes into tight scrolls, Adaline had managed to pack a week of outfits into one carry-on sized case. The task had been made easier by the destination – sunny Queensland called for bikinis, flip-flops, and little else. But she'd added some day dresses, shorts, singlets, and two dressier outfits for nights on the town, just to cover all bases. There were rainforest tracks to explore, scooters to hire – it wasn't going to be just beaches and booze, not for her.

This was her first trip without her parents and she was feeling a lot of things at once. Excited, of course. She'd studied hard, excelled in her exams – that hadn't been easy with all the things she'd been juggling – and she'd graduated high school at last. Leavers was her reward – a week on the white sand with her favourite people, getting a tan and forgetting all the textbook things she'd crammed into her mind. She was also feeling free. Unburdened by consequence, and young, young, young. The next week was going to be all about her.

She couldn't even guess what that would feel like.

Beyond her closed bedroom door, the arguing continued. It had been going on for the better part of an hour. Her father had looked at her mother the wrong way and she'd changed, like a bumped radio dial – distinct one moment, mindless white noise the next. Simon hadn't managed to smother the rage in time, now it had a foothold and dozens of seeking, clawed fingers in every pleasant moment of the morning. Georgia had been allowed too much momentum. Simon couldn't hope to calm her down before her own exhaustion reduced her boiling blood to a simmer, and that could take until noon.

By noon, Adaline would be hundreds of kilometres from here, higher than birds and clouds, well out of range. Just thinking of flying made her feel like she could, but the sense of levity was fast replaced with pity. Her fingers slowed on the zipper of her case. She and her father were a team, a united front. A kind of suburban bomb squad trained in all manner of explosive situations. Together they could diffuse Georgia, sometimes within moments of her mood turning sour. Alone, Simon would need to lay low, to not poke the bear. A simple enough thing to do except *everything* seemed to poke at Georgia. A passing comment, an inadequate response, failure to meet an unspoken expectation … It was endless.

Beyond the door, things escalated. Something fell. Glass broke. Voices pitched and dropped, then everything was horribly silent.

Adaline closed her eyes, imagined a dozen walls and moats within her, then joined the fray. She left her bag – a proverbial red flag – on the bed.

There were pots and pans on the kitchen floor. A length of paper towel was slumped over the back of one of the dining chairs and the two steaks Adaline had marinated after breakfast were staining the living room carpet, looking from a distance like bloodied tongues.

Georgia's fingers were stained with red. Tomato, pesto and garlic flavoured the room. She was breathing hard, her face flushed. Her tangled brown hair was defying gravity and her clothes were stained and crumpled where she'd gathered them in her fists. Shards of ceramic waited for her bare feet to find them.

Adaline hurried forward. She guided her mother out of the kitchen, left her standing in the tiled hallway, then cleaned up the broken plate with a dustpan and broom. Georgia watched her, uncharacteristically quiet.

'Where's Dad?' Adaline asked her, glancing over her shoulder, checking she hadn't moved.

Georgia didn't hurry to answer. Fine-boned and a fraction shorter than Adaline, Georgia Sharp was a monster in a sparrow's skin. Sometimes the monster growled, other times the sparrow sang. There was no telling what would come out her mouth from one moment to the next. She was a trick of nature, beautiful but deadly. Her skin should be acid yellow like that of the poison dart frog or conspicuous like the crown-of-thorns starfish. Her alabaster skin did nothing to communicate her toxicity.

Adaline cleaned up the mess, but left the steaks for her father – she didn't have the time it would take to remove the stains from the carpet fibres.

When her hands were clean and free, Adaline approached her mother and repeated her question. This time she got an answer. Georgia's voice was dreamlike. 'He's packing a bag.'

Adaline thought of her own bag waiting on her bed. 'That's me Mum, I leave soon. Just for a week.' She ventured to touch her mother's hand.

Georgia didn't allow it. 'What will I do?' she asked.

Adaline didn't know if the words were song or poison, not yet, but Georgia's eyes were pinched in the corners so things weren't looking good.

'Do?'

'Without him. Without you. I don't know what to do around here, I don't know what to think.' She clawed at her face. Her narrow, freckled face with dimples as rare as ball lightning. Streaks of red marked her skin like war paint.

Adaline handed her the paper towel roll then stepped around her to find Simon.

He was in the bedroom he shared with Georgia, and he was indeed packing a bag. He looked up when she entered, and answered the questions that must have filled her eyes.

'I'm out, sweetheart. I can't do this anymore. I'm going to find some place to stay in town, I'll call you when I'm settled.'

The few things in Adaline's life that were settled toppled through a sudden trapdoor. She took another step closer.

'She's already calming down.' Adaline's voice was wheedling. Her heart began to tick faster. 'Give her half an hour and she'll have forgotten the whole thing.'

'But I won't have.' He lowered an armful of socks and underwear into the bag on the bed then crossed the room to collect a dozen T-shirts from an open, half-empty drawer. These disappeared into the bag also. Twelve shirts for twelve days?

'Please,' she began, then stopped. The words on her tongue tasted sour and she could imagine the sharp corners of each letter pressing into her flesh. *Don't do this now.*

'Everything will be fine,' he said, but his lack of eye-contact made the words worthless. 'You're in charge for a while, though.' He moved the suitcase to the floor then finally looked at her. 'Call me if you need anything.'

'I need you to stay!' Hysteria. She didn't even sound like herself. She sounded like Georgia. 'I'm catching a bus to the airport in fifteen minutes, I can't be what she needs right now!'

Simon hung his head and sighed. Stooped like that, defeated and bruised from words that packed a punch, he seemed a decade older than forty-one. His skin looked like her uniform dried on the line, slack and creased, pegged in place. There was a brush of grey against his temples and when he looked up, there was a broken marriage in his eyes.

'I can't ever seem to be what she needs, love. I'm sorry. Go, stay, organise whatever you need to.' He hesitated, then offered her a smile he'd learned from Georgia, that Adaline had seen a hundred times before the hammer fell. 'She's different with you. Better. This will all be for the best, I'm sure.'

He left.

Adaline didn't.

And this 'best' he spoke of never came to pass.

5 TROUBLE

Jack ran. Away. From the questions, from the complaints, from the lost property and the obscure food allergies, until he was dragging air into his lungs so loudly that it was impossible to think of anything beyond putting one foot in front of the other. He passed the cabins, one side of the small buildings lit with dawn light, ran alongside the coach, then began his favourite circuit on the main road through the village. He had the world to himself at whatever speed he wanted it, and he wouldn't have to smile or speak for three more hours.

It didn't get much better than this.

Jack wiped his brow and hit play on the soundtrack in his mind. An electric guitar accompanied the drum beats of his foot falls, then he imagined a piano riff and a wordless opening vocal – a high, warbling note that trailed off into nothingness. He began to run faster, energised by the remembered tune.

He passed the toilet blocks, rounded the wide corner … then it was all over.

The real world serenity and the hard rock music in his head were interrupted by a woman jogging towards him. Small, trim – her brown hair tied up high. She wore fitted black pants that finished just below her knees and a Taylor Swift concert shirt, its sleeves pushed up to her elbows. Her joggers matched the red accents of the shirt and the flush of colour on her face. She was beautiful. Make-up free, dressed for purpose not appearance. Her hair swung like a kite tail and her legs looked strong enough to carry her to Spain. Jack found he didn't half mind the interruption.

He imagined half a dozen ways to introduce himself before he realised he already knew her. Her name escaped him, but her face didn't. She'd spoken to him last night after the city tour, and her disappointment had charmed him.

She flared her fingers out in a small wave then curled them back into a loose fist. Before Jack could return the greeting she moved past him, the drum beats of her feet out of sync with his own.

Jack kept running. The distance between them grew at the same rate as his curiosity.

He'd been doing Gateway tours for three years. He'd taken travellers from London to Santorini and everywhere in between. Partied with almost every nationality and warned countless thousands to not be late to the coach each morning. He'd collected European sunrises and sunsets, heard and tried dozens of languages – yet somehow this was a first. In all this time, he'd never been on tour with a dawn jogger.

Jack turned around and ran after her.

He considered keeping his distance – using her compact, firm body like a lure on a greyhound track – but he found he wanted to be closer. Beside her, even.

Jack pushed himself to close the distance between them. He knew the moment she realised he was pursuing her; he saw it in the hitch of her stride then the deliberate drop in speed. He fell into step with her.

'Mornin',' she said. Her eyes were curious but he couldn't tell if she welcomed the company. He'd been too busy being surprised that he would want company to wonder if she did; now he felt a curious wish to convince her.

'Bonjour,' he replied.

She smiled and returned her eyes to the road.

Trite one-liners crowded on his tongue. Do you come here often? Fancy seeing you here. I knew you were trouble – an obscure Taylor Swift reference. He swallowed them all.

She didn't save him. She let the silence stretch between them, seemingly comfortable with it. He'd missed the opportunity to ask if he was intruding, and maybe she was too polite to indicate he was. They followed the wide arc of the road, him on the outside running the greater distance, and measured their strides to comfortably pass over the speed bumps.

'Adaline,' he remembered, stumbling across the connection in his mind. Adaline from Adelaide – he'd enjoyed the repetitive sound when he'd checked her in at the pre-departure meeting. He'd thought of it again when she'd spoken to him last night.

'Jack from the world,' she returned.

'From Cairns, actually.' She increased her speed on the long straight and he matched her. 'Born and raised.'

His muscles warm now, Jack's stride became fluid. Energy was a song in his bloodstream, its own kind of soundtrack. This, this was why he dragged himself from bed each morning. This was how he had the energy to face all the challenges of his job; the expectant faces, the kilometres of exploration and the reams of paperwork. He started his day on purpose.

'How long've you been on the road?' she asked. They passed the reception building, its door closed and lights off. The day sheet hung from the notice board.

'Three years working, one year before that backpacking.'

'Four years,' she said. 'That puts my four days to shame.'

It did, but everyone started sometime. Guessing her age, Jack might have even started later in life. 'You'll be able to brag about two weeks soon enough.'

'True.'

He increased his speed, pushing her, testing her limits. She kept up easily. They didn't speak for an entire circuit and didn't hesitate to begin a second lap. In the quiet between them Jack found time to wonder at his sudden generosity. He was usually so jealous about his free time, unresponsive to those who would intrude on it. Fifty-odd people wanting a piece of him week in, week out was exhausting. Privacy was a luxury. He shared his breakfast table, his knowledge, sometimes even his sheets. Jogging was his only respite and yet he'd relinquished it readily to keep this quiet girl company. Why?

She dragged her pale orange sweatband across her forehead. Her eyes lingered on a cabin long enough that he could guess it was hers, but she didn't slow as they approached it. He hoped she agreed that their silence was a comfortable one.

They completed one more lap of the sleeping village, then stretched beside the coach. He leaned against its side, his heels planted and his leg extended, and tried to think of a parting comment that would charm her. That would bring her back.

'I could show you the skyline tomorrow,' he said, switching legs. Beside him, she switched too. 'I know it's the city of lights, but it looks pretty great at dawn, too.'

She wore her interest like clothes, her face was expressive and as readable as the Gateway logo splashed against the side of the coach.

He took it one step further. 'We do three nights here, but no mornings.'

Her nod was as good as a contract – he doubted anything could stop her from securing that extra experience. The thought of another morning at her side was a pleasant one. He was already vaguely impatient for it to start.

Despite her obvious enthusiasm, she was non-committal. 'Maybe,' she said, straightening from her stretch and shaking her arms at her sides. 'I'll see how I pull up. Thanks for the company. You kept me from being lazy. Breakfast at nine, right?' He nodded and she smiled. 'See you then.'

They parted without ceremony. She strode away, tugging the loosened band in her hair free then re-securing it, and he watched her go. She walked past the cabin she'd looked at earlier, her eyes on it again, moved around a corner, and was lost from sight. Jack turned curious eyes on the cabin door, then turned away to retrace his steps.

It had been months since he'd trod the narrow forest path that followed

31

the curls of the creek. He wanted to make sure it was passable and that the small hill it led to still delivered on the promised vista. He jogged down the road, his body warming again, stepped off their circuit, and donned his explorer's cap.

* * *

The first optional excursion was a day exploring the rooms and gardens of the Chateau Versailles. Jack told everyone the highlights of its bloody, fascinating history as Danya drove from the village. A dozen hands raised when he asked who wanted to be dropped off.

Adaline's methodical approach to her itinerary meant she'd read up on what could be seen and done. She knew what compromises she would make ahead of time and approximately how much time she was willing to give to each activity. It was her way of seeing what would most resonate with her, and for as long as possible. The Chateau Versailles had enchanted her; the countless images on the web, its spectacular history and extravagant gardens, but it hadn't been able to compete with the Louvre, or the love lock bridge, or the many other things in the city that she wouldn't forgive herself for missing. She stayed on the coach as others marched off and watched them join the ticket queues with a small degree of regret.

She would have to come back to Paris.

Lisa, a Swiss solo traveller with a blunt blonde fringe and pale blue eyes, waved to her from the back of the line. The girls had sat together on the ride to the Chateau and bonded by comparing their countries' winters. Conversation had been stilted at first, until Adaline realised Lisa never contracted her words. The odd formality had taken some getting used to. Adaline waved back and the coach pulled away.

Maree leaned over the back of the now empty seat beside Adaline. 'Where are you going today?' she asked. Her oil black hair was carefully braided into a high knot and her heavy eyeliner accentuated the width of her dark eyes. She was all style in a printed summer dress and large gold hoops – Parisians, Adaline thought, would approve.

Adaline smiled up at her. 'The Louvre.'

'Jack said tomorrow's a free-entry day, did you want to go with us then? We're going to walk up the Champs Elysees after and climb the Arc de Triomphe if there's time.'

Adaline considered. She'd planned to see the love lock bridge and Notre Dame Cathedral tomorrow, but those could be visited today. It would be fun to have company, to be able to turn to someone and share a moment with them. Adaline imagined herself writing to Maree in five years saying, "Remember when we saw The Mona Lisa together?". Wasn't that why she'd come with a group, and not struck out alone?

'I wouldn't be a fifth wheel?' she said.

Unseen on the seat behind her, Will made an amused sound at the back of his throat.

Maree looked over at him then back to Adaline. 'You'd be a seventh wheel, actually. Claire, Jenny, Rachael, and Holly are coming too.'

Adaline had got to know Rachael and Holly this morning when the two Australian girls had joined her table at breakfast. Rachael was all curves and smiles, with unruly curls and a fondness for sarcasm. Holly, her best friend, was impossibly thin, soft spoken, and always looking on the bright side. Her pixie cut added an ethereal quality to her, and the outrageous feather duster earrings that bounced against her collarbone were fun. Adaline had liked both girls immediately.

'I'm in,' she said. She shifted in her seat so she could see William. He was wearing jeans and a plain collared polo, and he'd pulled an All Blacks cap low over his eyes. His dark blond hair was just long enough to stick out the sides. She smiled at him. It would be something else to be in Paris with someone you loved. Adaline envied the couple the romantic possibilities available to them. 'What will you both do today?'

Maree looked down at the boy she'd spent ten years with. 'I'm not sure,' she said. 'Got anything planned?'

Will blinked up at her. 'No.'

Maree's voice changed. 'Really?'

Adaline curled her fingers over the headrest. The conversation had taken a turn – she wasn't sure what direction they were facing anymore.

'Jack's the tour manager,' Will continued. 'I'm just along for the ride.' He waved a hand up at Maree. 'You want to do something, we'll do it. Paris is your thing.'

This casual reply did not fill Maree with ideas. Instead, Will's lack of direction seemed to stymy her. She floundered, looking equal parts disappointed and cross.

Adaline spoke before Maree could further change the mood. 'I know something really romantic you could do. I could take you there. You've probably heard of it: the love lock bridge?'

Maree took a moment too long to take her eyes off Will. 'I haven't heard of it,' she said to Adaline.

'I have,' Will said, surprising them both. 'People put padlocks on the sides of it. They engrave 'em 'n shit, then chuck the keys in the river.'

The girls stared. Maree's eyebrows nudged her hairline.

'What? It collapsed a few years back, it was on the news.'

'You want to go?' Adaline asked the pair.

They looked at each other and nodded.

'Okay,' Maree said, 'the love lock bridge it is.' She flashed a measured smile at Adaline, then dropped back into her seat. Adaline turned to face the window and wondered at the suspicion that had crept onto Maree's face. Clearly this morning wasn't going to plan for her; she'd expected Will to take the lead, to suggest a stroll beneath the Eiffel Tower or the like, but he was content to just follow.

Adaline would take them to the bridge then lose herself in the crowd. They would have the rest of the day together, arm in arm. It would be wonderful despite this clumsy start – a miscommunication they would laugh about in the future. And if not, Adaline wouldn't be around to pick up the pieces. That role could go to someone else.

The coach stopped beside an enormous tiered fountain in the Place de la Concorde, one of the main squares of the city. Water jetted from the mouths of fish and tumbled down the stone basins, but whatever atmosphere might have come from the falling water was lost amidst the traffic noise. The roundabout was choked with cars, coaches and bikes. People called to one another and tourists posed for pictures.

Everyone hastened off the coach as Jack called directions to their backs. She smiled at him as she bounced down the stairs, and passed him without a word.

This morning had been surprising. It had been a treat, certainly, sharing the road with a man who somehow looked better when dishevelled and sweaty, but it had also been oddly private. She'd gotten the sense that he didn't typically share his mornings, that they were his only reprieve from the constant demands of his job – so when she'd got back to her cabin, she hadn't mentioned her unexpected company to the girls. Adaline doubted Jack would appreciate a dozen single ladies lining up to join him tomorrow. It would only mean sharing himself further, being on the clock longer.

She didn't expect that of him, and he'd recognised that quickly. He'd just been himself. So much so, that he wanted to be himself with her again tomorrow. The thought of another dawn at his side moved a thrill down her spine, but caution warmed her. No expectations, she thought. She'd go, or she wouldn't – she'd decide in the morning.

She held her phone up to the vista and took a photo. Moments later, she was standing with some of her new friends, arms around them, smiling for pictures. She took photos for Beth and Daniel, laughed through star jump poses with Maree and Will, then found herself in the arms of the first friend she'd made.

Rory lifted her onto his shoulders as if she weighed little more than a sack of flour and laughing, threw his arms out. She did the same and dozens of people took a photo of them, the Eiffel Tower at their backs.

She was still laughing when he ducked to his knees to let her down, and she hugged him when he straightened. Her heart was beating fast.

'That'll be a good one,' he said when she drew away. 'What's your surname? I'll tag you.' One of the Australians – Chris, she thought it might have been – handed Rory a phone and clapped him on the back.

Rory thanked him and checked the photo. He laughed and showed her. It was brilliant. Full of youth and abandon. Their mouths were open with laughter and they'd turned their palms up the same way.

'Sharp,' she said. He closed the window and opened Facebook.

'Don't know how we're going to top that one,' he said, grinning. Then he paused. 'Wow, your last post was almost a year ago.'

Adaline flushed. 'So?'

'So nothing,' Rory said. 'Now you've probably got heaps to say. I mean, you're in Europe.'

She smiled and rubbed at the back of her neck.

'What're your plans?' he asked, pocketing his phone. 'I'm heading to the catacombs with a few people if you're at loose ends.'

'Is it possible to be at loose ends in Paris?'

He smiled.

'Thanks,' she said, 'but I've got a few places in mind and I'm leading the charge.' She nodded at Maree and Will, who appeared to have collected a few extra people. She wondered how they expected to be alone at some point when they acted like social Velcro.

Rory nodded. 'Tell me all about it tonight. I'll split a bread stick with you.'

She watched him walk away, smiled when he turned back to look at her, then checked directions on her phone.

She was enchanted long before she reached the Pont des Arts bridge. People bought locks from street vendors – large ones with Eiffel Tower engravings, unassuming ones with bare faces. They wrote their names with thick markers and confirmed the custom in fractured French. Lovers held one another as they walked towards the place they would declare themselves.

The bridge was a thing of beauty even from a great distance. Swollen with people, lined with heavy expressions of love.

Everyone walked slower once they got there. Flanked by hundreds of thousands of expressions of love, Ada wanted to sink to her knees. It was beautiful. Most were padlocks, but there were others; bike chains, combination locks. Big, tin hearts rusted from ceaseless weather and time. All of them with words, some of them with pictures. Warren & Salma 5/7/15. Together forever, Tiff & Toby <3. M & S. Brittany & Curtis, July 6 2015, this one professionally engraved. Others marked an independent moment, a solo success or promise; Gabriella 2015 will be back; Jayson Everley; Y Fernanda Chile 2016.

A man played the accordion, a jaunty tune interrupted by the occasional trill of coins dropping into his cup. Men claimed the benches, selling locks of all colours and sizes arranged carefully on a canvas sheet. Another man sold water. He waited for customers, tossing a bottle end over end to keep himself occupied. An artist moved his canvas prints around the bridge, constantly dissatisfied with his position, mindless to the photos he obstructed.

Couples posed. They fastened their locks to the sagging wires of the bridge's panels then threw the keys into the Seine. Friends locked their friendships together. Some people lingered much longer than others and Ada wondered who their minds were with. One woman counted panels, then knelt to search for a lock once placed. She compared where she stood with a photo on her camera, then found what she sought and sighed. Her expression softened.

It was an extraordinary place. On one side, the Louvre, on the other the Institut de France. Connected by what had to be the most romantic few metres in the world. A pilgrimage for lovers and dreamers wishing to physically represent the whispers of their heart.

Ada bought a lock, wrote her name on the back, and fastened it to one of the more crowded panels. Paris would know her again. This was the first of many locks she intended to place here.

She lobbed the keys into the grand river, and felt as if she fell with them.

Maree and Will were posing for a photo a dozen metres along the bridge. Adaline watched them a moment, then turned away. She walked for hours. She explored the riverside arrondissements, ate fresh fruit from a street vendor, and treated herself to a gelato in the shadow of Notre Dame. She moved through the long queue for the famous church with Rachael and Holly, then struck out alone again when the girls lingered in the many naves.

The foreign graffiti made her smile. The Opera House was as wonderful as she'd imagined it, and she thought of phantoms and love stories as she crossed town to the Musée d'Orsay. Full to bursting with inspiration and admiration, she was back at the tower with an hour to spare.

She dozed on the grass and thought of home. And when that upset her, she thought of being lifted towards the skyline of Paris, of throwing her arms out as if she might embrace it all.

Pride warred with her fatigue. She felt strong and brave, reckless and independent. Against all odds, she was here. Adaline settled further into the Parisian grass. She was here, and no one could take that away from her.

* * *

Dinner was an underwhelming affair. The Gateway chef must have assumed most people would stay in the city to eat, or that people would be saving their appetites for their picnics. The white rice, curried chicken and steamed vegetables were food court quality, and despite the group's reduced numbers there was barely enough for seconds.

No one was late to the coach.

The picnic baskets had been assembled on a trestle table outside the food tent as they'd eaten, so it was an easy exercise to grab one between two on the way. Ada sat with Rory on the ride to the train, and whooped and screamed when he carried her on his back, racing another pair through the tunnel to the platform. She sat with him on the train where they reorganised the contents of their rattled basket, and was at his side again at the feet of the Eiffel Tower. They shared a wheel of cheese and complained good naturedly about the quality of the wine, and threw themselves into the conversations around them whenever they weren't wholly absorbed with one another.

Adaline was sure there wasn't a better group of people to be found. Everyone was talking fast, about ridiculous things and poignant things; leaning across one another to share food and stories from the day. Adaline shared her experiences and indulged the punchline of every joke. She volunteered nothing of her life in Adelaide and was vague when asked about it directly, but no one seemed to mind; their real lives seemed so intangible against this backdrop, it was hard to focus on them. Paris was too mesmerising, too all-encompassing.

They broke the spell only long enough to speak of what they were looking forward to the most. Rachael was counting down to Verona, she had her sights and her savings set on the city's chic boutiques. Holly and Lisa thought Rome would be their highlight. Claire and Jenny – like Ada and Rory – were most excited to see the Greek islands, and Will and Maree were looking forward to Venice, although for different reasons. Maree longed for the romance of it all and Will had heard that the Venetian campsite was typically the wildest.

'This is so romantic,' Maree said on a sigh. She smiled up at the butter-coloured light coating the tower and leaned back on her hands. The dress she wore seemed uncomfortable. It was too formal for tonight, too form-fitting, and was all the more out of place because Will, at her side, wore the same jeans and faded T-shirt from today.

Rachael and Holly agreed with her comment around mouthfuls of cheese, and Lisa nodded then flopped onto her back.

'So I shouldn't mention the thousands of bodies beneath us?' Rory teased. 'Kilometres of graves, the dead left to rot.'

Rachael threw a breadstick at him and Will laughed. Maree looked more displeased than the jibe warranted. Adaline drank from her plastic cup and felt herself withdraw from the girl.

'Let's toast to something,' Rory said, turning to give Adaline his full attention.

She swallowed and raised her cup. 'Okay.'

Silence stretched between them as they both waited for the other to speak.

'What do you want to toast to, Ads?' he prompted. The nickname made her smile, which seemed to encourage him. He raised his cup a fraction higher.

'Oh.' She scrambled to think of something clever or poignant. 'How about … to freedom. And change. And adventure.'

Her toast wasn't going to win any awards, but it was honest. More honest than anyone around her could guess.

He tapped his cup against the side of hers three times. 'And to new friends.' Rory tapped her cup again, then included the others in the toast. After much stretching, touching of cups and laughter, everyone drank.

The tower began to flash like fast winking stars, and the moment was complete.

6 PORTRAIT OF AN UNKNOWN WOMAN

Jack moved alongside Adaline, and neither spoke. They just nodded at one another and fell into a fast rhythm. This was interrupted only once when he nudged her down a different path to the one she was aiming for.

Through trees, across a creek and up a slight incline, he showed her the little known spots, the places only the regulars would know about. Dawn was approaching, and when they crested a small hill and glimpsed the skyline, they slackened their pace to a brisk walk.

She was breathing hard. Jack had pushed her, perhaps to see what she was capable of, so the cool of the foggy morning was welcome on her flaming skin. She slowed further, then stopped, hands on hips, air dragging through her mouth. Jack had moved ahead but returned to her now, his denim blue eyes bright with exertion. He circled her as he slowed his heart rate, then rolled into an effortless walk.

'How was last night?' he asked.

She turned on her heels, watching him as he moved. 'Wonderful.'

'Wasn't sure you'd show this morning. There was a lot of wine in those picnics.'

'I'm a good sharer.' She pushed her hair back from her forehead and fanned herself. As she turned to look at the city skyline, she said, 'Did you go out last night?'

'No. Paperwork. A lot of people kicked on late though, there will be a few sore heads today. Wouldn't be surprised if a lot of them miss breakfast.'

Adaline nodded, not knowing how to contribute to the conversation further. She'd turned in shortly after getting back – an early night by some people's standards – so she wasn't sure what had happened after ten-thirty.

They stood in silence as the sun broke over the horizon. She smiled at it, grateful that she'd seen something so beautiful whilst others slept.

When she looked over at him, Jack took that as a signal to lead the way back.

They were out of the village, having left through an unfenced section beyond the creek, so they had to be careful with their footing on the uneven ground. Jogging ahead, he gave Adaline ample opportunity to admire the strong lines of his torso and the tight curves of his backside.

Just as they had done the morning before, they stretched against the coach then said their goodbyes.

Adaline got far fewer questions when she returned to the room this time. Her clothes told everyone all they needed to know, and no one thought to ask if she'd jogged alone.

* * *

The seat Rory had been saving was claimed by Pies's unwelcome backside. Before Rory could object, Pies informed him he didn't care, and his voice made Rory think of gravel in a bucket. Rory flexed his fingers around the fruit he held then resumed his watch of the little cabin with its light on.

Adaline had missed breakfast and she was about to miss the coach. She'd been the first out of bed according to Beth, her American roommate, but according to Claire the Kiwi, she was the last of her group to shower. Rory struggled to believe a mild hangover could come between her and the Louvre, but time was running out. Danya had turned the engine on and the coach was idling. Jack was making slow progress along the aisle, answering questions and suggesting things to see. The clock above the driver's seat read one minute past ten – so they were all late.

Danya stood from his seat to see his colleague. 'Jack,' he called. 'Jack, we go?'

'Yeah,' Jack said. He pointed to Hamish. 'Just a sec.'

Danya sat and Jack proceeded to tell Hamish about Rodin's Gallery in more detail than was strictly necessary, given the Canadian's vague interest.

In the seats in front of Rory, Claire and Jenny were murmuring about Adaline. Claire had just decided to ask Jack to wait so she check on her, when the cabin door flew inward and Ada appeared on the threshold. Her hair was wet and her satchel bag was unzipped. A cardigan dangled from the mouth of it, centimetres above untied shoelaces. Eyes wide and face flushed, she legged it towards the coach.

When she ran out of sight, Rory straightened in his seat to see her step on. Except she didn't.

'No,' Danya said, without inflection, without expansion. He stared down at the girl who loved Paris, then through the many heads between Rory and Danya, Rory saw Danya duck his head in a shrug, and smile. 'Okay,' he said.

Ada appeared in the aisle, grinning broadly, seemingly half amused and half relieved that Danya hadn't chosen to make an example of her. Jack looked up, they smiled at each other, then Hamish's verbal tour came to an abrupt end.

'Let's go!' Jack called to the front. He paused as Ada took a seat beside one of the younger Americans, then moved past her to claim his spot at the front. The door hissed shut and the coach began to reverse.

Rory pushed the pieces of fruit into the elastic seat pocket in front of him and settled in to half listen to Jack's latest spiel. When they arrived at the roundabout they'd parked at yesterday, Jack had to bang the microphone against the wall to get everyone's attention. 'Okay people, back here by five if you want a ride back to the village.'

'Take rubbish!' Danya barked as people passed – too late for they'd already left their seats.

They were free. Paris uncurled from where Rory stood on the pavement, beautiful in every direction and full of secrets he wanted to know. At his side, Pies rubbed his eyes with the sides of his thumbs. An arm's length away, Ada was determining whose itinerary best matched with her own. Her eyes were bright and full of interest and her hands were flying as she talked. To Rory, she was as interesting as the obelisk at her back. As vivid as the Parisian fashion. As lovely and deep as the Seine. The desire for her company rivalled his interest in the city. He wanted to see the Paris she saw, at her side, with her commentary and her questions. He wanted to know her curiosities and be there when she got the answers.

'I'm in for the Louvre,' he said, stepping forward.

Ada turned and the welcome in her smile was as warm as an embrace.

Rory was sure he'd follow that mouth wherever she took it.

A few others wanted to see the Louvre too, so within ten minutes they were on their way – Ada walking confidently in the lead, somehow already orientated on streets so far from home. Her head swivelled almost comically as her eyes sought out beauty after beauty. Her hair had dried a little fluffy and the ends kicked out in almost-curls; Rory thought he preferred it to the way she'd styled it yesterday; straight and perfect, and too serious for the girl he was getting to know. This slightly wild hair suited her more.

Rory caught up with her and gave her the fruit. He'd intended to say something casual, but when she thanked him with too much gratitude, no words came. He mumbled something nonsensical at his chest and dropped back.

Their small group of eight shared their wish to see the infamous museum with thousands of others tourists. The vast expanse between the building's wings was full of travellers, historians and gypsies. Women dressed in black, bent at the waist and clutching infants to their chests, approached tourists with creased letters from their English husbands. They asked for money in wheedling voices and took their sob stories elsewhere when people recognised the con. Policemen on rollerblades glided through the crowds.

Guidebook pages fluttered in the breeze and the sheer volume of them sounded like a rumbling conversation.

The lesser known side entrance Jack had told the Gateway group about skipped the enormous queues and got them inside within twenty minutes. Beyond the cashier, it was like standing inside a drum; footsteps and chatter crashed and swelled around the lobby. The glass pyramid ceiling opened the space to the soft blue sky and dozens of escalators and stairs moved an endless crowd out of sight. They joined the throng filing into the Denon Wing.

They stayed together at first, waiting politely when someone lingered over an artefact or information board, but within the hour the group splintered. Rory tried to keep pace with Ada, but he got distracted in the Egyptian section by towering columns, seated gods and impressive busts. He circled sarcophagi in small glass rooms and itched to touch ancient papyrus. He wondered at the colours and the language, then much later, found himself looking up at the serene face of the Venus de Milo.

He didn't join the long queues waiting to stand opposite Leonardo da Vinci's Mona Lisa, instead he walked to the front and saw the painting at an angle. Seeing it was seeing it, he reasoned; and it was beautiful, but the many posters and perhaps just the enormity of its reputation meant he was surprised by its intimate portrait size.

When he turned away, Rory saw the back of Ada's head. She was looking up at an oil painting no one else in the room seemed to be aware of. Easily ten meters wide and perhaps seven meters high, the colourful scene should have captured everyone's attention but the competition in the room was too high.

He moved to stand beside her.

'Wedding Feast at Cana,' she said, when her eyes focused on his face and she recognised him. 'Jesus's first miracle.' She pointed to the lower corner with the hand holding her phone. The screen displayed a Wikipedia page. 'Turning water into wine.' She dropped her hand and scanned the many painted faces. 'Over 130 people,' she murmured.

'It's big,' Rory supplied. He glanced over his shoulder at the large room that barely contained the crowd that wished to be in it.

'The biggest painting the Louvre's got.'

'I like it,' he said, turning back. It was complex and richly detailed, full to bursting with religious symbology, and it had put that dreamy look on Ada's face.

She took her last fill of it then led the way back into the crowded corridor. 'You know,' she said, talking over her shoulder as they were jostled and apologised to, 'if I'd seen that two days ago it would've been my favourite painting in the world.'

He waited until he could walk beside her again, then asked, 'What did you see yesterday that trumps it?'

'La Solitude. I can't remember the artist, I wrote it down somewhere. It was at the Musee d'Orsay.' She laughed. 'I think I gaped up at that painting for a good fifteen, twenty minutes. It was beautiful.'

'Must've been.' He wondered what it looked like. He was curious to know what had stirred her so deeply. 'Remind me to look it up.' Although he doubted he'd forget.

She shrugged. 'If you remember, you remember. What haven't you seen yet?'

The next hour was a blur of rich conversation amongst world-class backdrops. He made her laugh in front of Da Vinci's Portrait of an Unknown Woman and found an excuse to touch her in front of the crown jewels in the Gallery of Apollo. Both hands on her shoulders, he turned her away from a painting she was familiar with and asked her to describe it to him. Later, he asked her to describe a painting that appeared to move her. She spoke about art with feeling and although she knew next to nothing about the great masters or their works, her words were saturated with appreciation and awe.

Rory was sure, years from now, her words and expressions would be more memorable to him than some of the masterpieces she had stood beside.

When they left the Louvre they walked the Avenue des Champs-Elysees with Maree and Will, then climbed the narrow winding stairs of the Arc de Triomphe. Wind whipping through their hair, they pressed themselves against the viewing platform bars and tried to see all of Paris that they could. It was better, he thought, to climb this instead of the Eiffel Tower. From here he could see the monument that made the skyline so recognisable.

He told his new friends about the catacombs as they walked a slow circle around the platform, seeing the city from every degree, and he listened to Ada rave about the grandeur of the Notre Dame Cathedral. Will didn't have many stories; he'd seen a guy drop his gelato and step in it and he'd liked fumbling over the pronunciation of the Metro stations. There'd been a small protest in République, but the signs had been in French so he couldn't tell them what it was about. Maree was full of stories about people; she'd seen a couple get engaged under the Eiffel Tower and a family picnicking on a disused mooring platform on the Seine. They'd had cheese and wine, and long, crusty bread. The little girl had been wearing a classy looking sunhat and sunglasses Maree guessed were worth more than all the clothes she'd brought on this trip.

They walked back down the famous shopping strip, gawking in windows and turning their faces to the sun, and the whole time, Rory could barely stop himself from reaching for Ada's hand.

He curled his fingers against his palm and waited for the next opportunity to help her through the crowd.

7 TONGUE-TIED

Dinner that night was the first opportunity for everyone on tour to dress up, and in doing so, people were transformed. Gone were the creased old favourites that everyone wore on the coach and the sensible shoes that accompanied the day, the guys were in collared shirts and most of the girls were in dresses. Adaline couldn't turn in any direction without copping an eye full of cleavage and some of the guys had even deigned to shave. There were others who hadn't so much as run a brush through their hair, but almost everyone had made an effort.

The noise on the coach was the loudest yet as they drove to the inner city restaurant. People were leaning across the aisles and turned in their seats, laughing and chattering, more confident than ever. What a difference two days together had made.

Seated beside her, Rory had an audience again. He spoke to half a dozen people about little known facts of the Moulin Rouge, retelling the stories Adaline had told him before boarding. He'd wanted her to tell them but had settled for giving her the credit. As she listened, knowing he was telling the story better than she ever could, she watched the bright lights of Paris slide past her window.

It had been an exceptional day made better by his company. Paris had been funnier than she had imagined it would be because Rory had such a unique, off-beat way of looking at the world. He saw the silver-lining in everything and was always building towards the next punchline. His energy was magnetic.

As was his charm.

She stole a glance at him as he scrolled through one of the Mexican sister's photos – they'd gone to the Rodin Museum and he was curious about what he'd missed. His hair was spiked and pulled back from his forehead. His deep blue dress shirt was accented by a thick black tie, but everything was made less formal by his grey Converse sneakers. On others it would look unfashionable, but on Rory it looked ironic.

She liked it, but said the opposite. 'I can't believe you're wearing a tie. Are you accepting an award tonight?'

He handed the camera back. 'I wouldn't say no to one. And I love this tie. Check this out.' He nudged the loop up.

Adaline's eyebrows drew together. 'What's that?'

'A lid,' he said. He used his fingernail to lift the circle of plastic, then pulled the tie away from his chest. The material around his neck was elastic. He held it under her nose and she blinked hard.

'Is that vodka?'

The tie was an elaborate flask. He grinned and put it back together.

'You're an evil genius,' she murmured. His explosion of laughter moved a thrill through her body. 'I mean it! Who thinks up this stuff? How much does it fit?'

'Six shots. Two of them are yours if you don't rat me out.'

'Three.'

'Shit – fine. Deal. It's not like I have a leg to stand on.'

He was fun, she thought, collapsing back into her seat. Unpredictable, yet harmless. She'd never seen a smile quite like his before – so wide that his cheeks folded like ripples around his mouth, and there was such life in his eyes. He was everything she was trying to find in herself, everything she thought she could be were the burdens of life back home less oppressive. She, too, was wild and magnetic – or she had been once, years ago. She supposed now she was caged and tame, full of the same unspent potential as a creature in a zoo.

A long-buried feeling stirred. Desire, keen and warm. Her eyes dropped to his smiling lips, then curiosity nudged into play. Was there enough of her left in this near-shell of a body that he would want her in return? Was she exciting enough, attractive enough, outrageous enough to tempt this larger-than-life man at her side?

They'd spent so much time together and it had been so easy. They'd touched and glanced and teased smiles from each other. Would he accept her hand now if her fingers trailed over his palm?

The smile slipped from Adaline's face. Suddenly the warmth inside her was too hot.

Suppose he did take her hand. Suppose he kissed her tonight. Then what – tomorrow rolls around and they regret it? Or worse yet, they don't and want to do it again? In what capacity? She wondered if Rory would consider an exchange of affection as a kind of contract, if he would want her exclusively. She wondered if it would mean spending every excursion with him, sharing every meal with him. If it would mean watching her words and placating his hurt feelings when she wanted time apart to do her own thing and be her own person.

She looked away and concentrated on her breathing. She did this until the flutters in her chest settled and she could no longer feel the tickle of nerves on her skin. But when the panic subsided, claustrophobia took its place.

No. Desire was one thing, obligation was another. She'd crossed oceans to out-manoeuvre those clawing fingers.

Rory, for all his playing, was not a player. He would respond to her advance with need and expectation; a need for more, an expectation that he would have a place at her side. Adaline didn't want and couldn't tolerate either. Not on this tour, not beyond it. These fourteen days were a reprieve, not a time to substitute one responsibility with another.

She decided she would never reach for him.

It seemed both sacrifice and favour.

Unaware of Adaline's emotional assault, Rory traded sarcastic jibes with Will. Their faux national rivalry was amusing but it was clear to everyone listening that Rory had the faster, cleverer wit. It was a verbal tennis match that had Will scrambling all over the court and Rory bouncing on his feet.

She smiled when he looked at her, and second-guessed herself all the way to the restaurant.

Danya made the arrival announcement, and as Adaline followed the queue out the door, she saw why. Jack had stepped off first and was standing a few meters up the footpath, one hand pressed to one ear, the other holding his phone. He looked handsome in his bottle green collared shirt and black jeans, but not happy. His brows were drawn together.

He looked up, saw her, and waved her towards him. Adaline hesitated. She exchanged a curious glance with Rory, then stepped away from the group.

When she was at his side, Jack told the caller she'd arrived and held the phone out to her.

'It's your mum,' he said. 'She called the head office and they forwarded the call. Take as long as you need, but keep the group in sight.'

Adaline curled her hands against her chest and stepped back.

Jack's expression changed. 'Adaline …'

'No.' She could feel her heart beating against her wrist. Behind her, people laughed and teased. Cameras clicked.

Jack covered the mouthpiece. 'Just no? Should I tell her you'll charge your phone, that you'll call her back? She sounds upset.'

'Tell her anything you want. Just … no thank you.' Adaline turned and began walking away. Her back to him, she said, 'But I wouldn't give her your number if I were you.'

Adaline re-joined her friends and kept her head down. No one appeared to have noticed her strange exchange with their tour manager, they were singing a song about Rotorua and coming home, off-pitch and out of time, and loving the mess of it all.

Fingers touched her elbow and she pressed her eyes shut.

'What was that about?' Rory. So serious, so apart from the larrikin on the coach minutes ago.

'Nothing, just a misunderstanding. Jack's fixing it.' Adaline opened her eyes and straightened. She wouldn't wear this tonight. Like a jacket, she would shrug it off. She turned towards him and smiled.

Rory measured her expression, then took her elbow again. People began to file past them, following Jack who'd taken the lead and started off down the street. When Rory and Adaline were the last of the group, Rory tugged her into the shadow of a doorway.

He offered her his tie.

Adaline's laugh wobbled, then strengthened.

They each drank a mouthful then hurried after the dinner party. The vodka made her throat feel hot. By the time they were on the stairs leading to the restaurant, her stomach felt warm – the pleasant kind of warm that she wanted to nurture like a log fire. After a glass of terrible house wine, she became aware of her cheeks. After a second glass, she began to laugh louder than the others at her table. She and Rory followed the smokers outside between the mains and dessert and together they drained the last of his clever flask.

After that she didn't think much about her mother at all.

8 SONG BIRD

Adaline woke to breaking porcelain. The child in her cowered, but the premature adult steeled itself. It was going to be another one of those days — Georgia angry with a world just woken, angry with her daughter, angry with herself. She would be in the kitchen, Adaline thought, a second plate or mug in hand, waiting, anticipating a reaction she could overreact to.

There was little point in trying to wait it out. Georgia would have her sparring match one way or another, better it be away from the trinkets Adaline loved and the room Adaline had gone to great lengths to keep for herself.

Adaline pushed the bed covers away, swung her feet to the floor and readied for battle. Shoes for the minefield. A ratty old jumper for the cold words, so big in the arms she could pull the sleeves over her fingers. She bookmarked the textbook she'd fallen asleep reading last night and tucked it out of sight, then she strode to her bedroom door.

I didn't cause it, Adaline reminded herself. I can't cure it. She opened the door, stepped out into the hallway and had her last bolstering thought before the blow: I can't control it.

Georgia was exactly where Adaline had imagined she would be, in the middle of the kitchen with a plate in her hand. But the plate was already broken. Smaller shards were balanced on top of it.

Georgia shot out her free hand. 'Careful!' She saw Adaline's shoes and appeared relieved. In fact, with her styled hair, neat make-up and pretty summer dress, she appeared more than relieved. She appeared happy. Crouching over the mess, she smiled up at her daughter. 'I broke a plate. Your pancakes were on them, so … there's that, too.'

There they were, in pieces, as gold as varnished pine, soaked in rich maple syrup. There were banana pieces amongst the porcelain and Adaline spied a smudge of cream on the inside of Georgia's wrist.

Incredibly, her mother laughed. 'Figures,' she said. Maybe it was a trick of the light, but the brown in her eyes mirrored the shining syrup on the floor. She smiled, and those rare dimples hooked Adaline through the middle. Adaline moved closer, dropped to her haunches and reached for a piece of the breakfast her mother had made. She tossed it into the bin Georgia had dragged close, and it landed on the top of the rubbish with a wet slap.

'Thanks anyway,' she said.

Georgia nodded. 'I just felt like pancakes and I know you love them. We had everything we needed in the fridge.' She paused. 'We don't now, of course. It's all on the floor.'

Adaline spoke fast, anxious to keep the mood light. 'I can make us something else. Or I can go to the shops?'

Georgia straightened. She licked the cream off her wrist then settled her hands on her waist. 'Let's go out for breakfast. Buy a whole stack of these. Eat 'em till we're sick.'

Adaline agreed, scarcely believing the moment. Together they cleared away the mess, then each went their separate ways to get ready to leave. Adaline barely stepped beneath the shower spray – every moment away from this Georgia was a moment lost. Left to her own thoughts, Georgia could turn. Sink. The song bird could be caged and exchanged for the beast.

But Georgia was still smiling fifteen minutes later when they stepped outside. She sang along to the radio in the car, encouraged Adaline to put her window down to let in the floral summer air. She was buoyant.

She was the woman who made all the other days worth it.

Georgia called Adaline 'Lynn' as they walked from the carpark to their favourite café, a nickname saved for the sunniest of days. She looped her arm through Adaline's and lifted her lovely face to the sun. 'It's going to hit thirty degrees,' she said, her eyes closed and mouth curved. 'Let's go to the beach. Get tans, read books, swim in sea.'

Georgia loved the coast. It was always her first idea on good days like these. Far more content to be idle than her young daughter, who was always restless, always looking for productive ways to fill her time, Georgia could happily lose the larger part of a day sunning herself on the sand. She said it recharged her.

It could have been hailing and Adaline still would have agreed.

After they ordered mixed berry pancake stacks and large hot chocolates, Georgia put her menu aside and stared at the girl across the table from her who felt she hadn't been seen in months. Georgia was wearing the earrings Adaline had bought her for her fortieth birthday – ladies in old fashioned swimming costumes diving into an invisible sea.

'I'm sorry I'm such a shrew,' she began. 'I wish every day was like this.'

This was dangerous ground. A corridor lined with innumerable triggers.

'Me too,' Adaline returned, then she moved the conversation along.

They spoke about silly things. Inconsequential things from Facebooks feeds to television shows. Pop stars they both liked and upcoming concerts neither of them was confident enough to pre-book. The café was full of elephants, crammed in booths, balanced on countertops, but well behaved enough that they could be spoken around. Referred to in the vaguest of terms.

They left clutching their stomachs, sugar singing through their bloodstream, making everything fast and bright. Everything was funny. Georgia lived for the moment, not trusting the future, and Adaline did anything and everything to please her, to prolong this north star of days.

It lasted sixteen hours and thirty-two minutes.

9 THE HEAD IN THE JAR

Adaline skipped breakfast the following morning in favour of crawling straight onto the coach and sleeping through the group's eventual departure. She woke hours later in a new landscape. Everything was green and blue. Hills rolled away in every direction. The countless rows of grape vines reminded her of dreadlocks and the old stone farmhouses were postcard perfect.

Cold Chisel finished singing about cheap wine, then ACDC continued the theme with *Have a Drink On Me*. Conversations were a low buzz around her, below notice and of no importance. Her memories were too loud. Her flashbacks seemed to have lost their volume control. Jack insisting she speak to her mother. Rory being so kind but so curious. A song about hurrying home and dancing girls keeping pace with frenetic beats and rhythms. The night had been full of noise.

How dare her mother.

Adaline shifted against the window. Her muscles ached from being too long in one position and she was overly aware of her tongue. Thirst was as nagging as her thoughts of home.

The song ended abruptly.

Jack tapped the microphone then his voice dropped from the speakers. 'Wakey wakey. We're only a few minutes from the Chateau. The room sheet's making its way back – we've got six to a room this time, people. Tonight we'll be partying in The Cave with another Gateway group. The theme is underwear on the outside, so make sure you pull on your tightie-whities and your G-bangers and get in the spirit.

'Tomorrow's a free day. You've got until dinner to pay for an optional picnic basket – one between two – and two hours between now and meeting me out the front for the optional wine tasting. Do as little or as much as you want —'

'Take rubbish!'

'And take your rubbish off the coach when we stop.'

Adaline couldn't see Jack from her seat but she could hear the amusement in his voice.

'This is a free night for Danya,' he continued. 'Once he cleans the coach he gets to party with us, and he's hanging out for a drink so let's help him out.'

The coach eased slowly around an elbow bend. Adaline watched a bird land dexterously on a naked stretch of wire and longed to be as free. A French bird in a French vineyard, with no mind to phone calls or secrets. With fresh air in its lungs and any compass point of its choosing. And the sky.

The room sheet appeared in front of her face. She took it from the girl sitting in front of her, then took the pen that appeared next, but a moment later she passed both on without making a change. One of the girls had listed them all together; Claire, Jenny, Rachael, Holly, Beth and Adaline.

Adaline smiled and settled back into her seat.

Another elbow bend in the road and they were there.

The coach rolled between the enormous sandstones gates of Dionysus Chateau. Trees flanked the driveway, leaning over the gravel and creating a beautiful arch. Rich green lawns rolled away from the road and Adaline caught a glimpse of brilliant blue. When the trees cleared she saw it was a pool, and looming above it was the handsome sandstone palace she would call home for the next two nights.

Gateway site crew were waiting for them again, waving cheerfully. Other travellers had joined in the fun and were gesticulating wildly. Adaline saw the pale flash of a bare arse.

Minutes later after a few more directions and promises of good times ahead, Jack let everyone off the coach.

Adaline had just found her suitcase when Jack approached her.

'Hey Adaline.' With one hand, he lifted her suitcase clear of the others and put it at her feet. 'You're on kitchen duty tonight. You'll need to get there by five, which means missing some of the wine tasting. That okay?'

She smiled her thanks as she lifted the handle up and tilted the bag onto its wheels. 'It'll have to be, won't it?'

He smiled back. 'Pretty much. See you later.' He walked away, doubtlessly to find whoever else was on duty tonight.

Adaline waved at Rory, then fell into step with her roommates.

Claire nudged Jenny aside so she could walk beside Adaline. 'Hey, if you want me to stop putting your name down … I mean, I don't want you to feel like you have to room with us.'

'No, I appreciate it, really!' She bumped Claire's elbow with her own. 'I was hoping it would be the six of us.'

Adaline was fast developing a kinship with these girls. Add Maree and Will, and Rory when he joined them, and she felt like they were a great little group. It was a shame Beth came with Daniel, but he seemed determined to befriend the Australians which felt like a blessing.

Inside the chateau the walls and floors betrayed years of hard wear. The foyer was expansive and draughty, and the staircase grand. When Adaline climbed them to the dorm rooms on the first floor, she walked in grooves created by the thousands who had come before her. It was both charming and grandiose – something out of an Austen novel.

The dorm room was modest. There was a small sink and mirror in the corner and three bunk beds against two of the walls. Beneath the narrow window with a perfect view was a wall-mounted coil heater with a thumb-thick layer of dust beneath it.

'We won't be in here much,' Holly said, placating everyone's unspoken judgment. 'Rach, top or bottom?'

Rachael dropped her bag to the floor. 'Who's going to drink more?'

'That's a really good point,' Claire said, turning to Jenny. 'Because getting up on that top bed isn't going to be easy after we've drunk this region dry.'

Everyone laughed then started comparing their drinking plans.

Jenny and Claire had gone to bed with their makeup on last night and hadn't thought to clean their faces yet. Smudged mascara circled their weary eyes and their skin was patchy where foundation had rubbed off. The excessive amount of hairspray Jenny had used made her hair look crunchy now. The fact that either of them could entertain the thought of another night at a bar mystified Adaline. Just the thought of alcohol made her stomach roll.

Rachael, Claire and Beth got the bottom beds, and the others were left to wonder how they would later scale the ladders without falling on their butts. Adaline couldn't imagine drinking so much that she'd struggle, but then again, who could say? Maybe her mother would call again.

The woman had no limits. No compunction or sense of boundaries. She was the whole population of her world except when it suited her to remember her daughter.

How sad that Adaline would prefer be forgotten.

She pushed her suitcase onto its back and shoved it over to the foot of the bed.

'You can have the bottom bed if you want it,' Beth said, misreading the cause of Adaline's sudden frustration. 'I'm probably only going to have one or two drinks.'

Adaline shook her head. 'No. I'm sorry. I was thinking about something else. I'm not fussed where I sleep.'

Jenny smirked. 'Tell some of the guys that and you'll have a very good night.'

Adaline grinned. 'That's not what I meant. I don't think I'll drink much either, so I'm good with the top bed.'

'Why aren't you drinking much?' Claire asked. She pulled her toiletries bag from her backpack and lobbed it onto her mattress. 'Afraid you'll jump

Rory?'

Adaline had to shout to be heard over the laughter. 'No! I'm not planning on getting wasted, okay? That's not my goal for the night.'

'You have a goal?' Holly had scrambled up onto her bed and was watching everyone from above.

'Okay, let's leave her alone,' Rachael said, sounding more amused than stern. 'So what's everyone's situation?' She touched her fingertips to her breastbone. 'I've got a boyfriend —'

'Who's not happy,' Holly interrupted.

Rachael glanced at her. 'Yes, well. That's a story for another time. Anyway, two years strong. Not sure what I'm going home to job-wise. Thinking I might apply for university. I'm hoping I figure a few things out on this trip.'

Holly went next. 'Boyfriend in Rome. Pete.' Her face softened when she said his name. 'I'm leaving the tour early to meet up with him. We've been together for a year, but … um. So I haven't met him in person. We met online. We're going to see if … how things work out when I get there.'

Claire had been unpacking as she listened and went third, folding shirts and placing them on the bed as she told her story. 'There's a guy back home I like. I'm almost done with a hairdressing apprenticeship and Jenny and I are looking at moving in together when I start earning a bit more money.'

'This is kind of our test-run,' Jenny added. She sat on Claire's bed and began loosening her long hair from its messy plait. 'Seeing each other all the time, sharing everything. If we're tearing each other's hair out by the end of this tour we're going to rethink it.' She grinned at her friend. 'Anyway. I work full time, can't wait to get away from my mum and I'm very, very single.'

Beth rubbed her forehead and gazed out the window. 'I don't know if I'm single or not.'

The girls glanced at one another.

'I'm all messed up about this man. He's … a fair bit older than me. We had a fight before I left. He thinks I should love someone younger, I think he's an idiot. I'm only on this tour because of Daniel. My parents didn't want him to do it by himself so I'm kind of chaperoning.' She put her hands on her narrow hips and offered a tight-lipped smile to her audience. 'I'm having a great time. I mean, I'm in France, aren't I? But a part of me just wants to go home and put my life back together.'

Adaline nodded. 'Well, I'm kind of on the run from my life. I'm looking into uni courses but I don't know what I want to study yet. No plans. No guy. No idea.'

The six women looked at each other and smiled. Because nothing else needed to be said for the moment, nothing was. They were becoming more three-dimensional, Adaline thought, more complex than the wide-eyed creatures she'd known before today. Their reasons for being here varied from experiment to obligation, but it sounded like all of their lives were in a state of flux. If they'd omitted as much as she had, Adaline wondered how they were all holding themselves together so well.

'Let's go outside and do absolutely nothing,' Rachael suggested. She held up a container of sunscreen, and like the Pied Piper's mice, everyone followed her out of the room.

* * *

For the next few hours Adaline dozed on the lawn by the pool, listening to boys playing football and groups chatting and laughing in the sun. She stirred occasionally when someone crashed into the water, and thought about the amazing places yet to come. In a week she would be in Venice, in less than two weeks, Rome. How surreal that this was her new reality. It was sad to think that Paris was behind her. All that waiting to get to that lovely city and too soon it had slipped into the past. Too soon all of this would be in the past.

She wriggled deeper into the grass, as if to better anchor herself in the moment, and with her eyes closed, she concentrated on the world around her. The soft tang of chlorine mixed with the delicious scent of warm earth. She could smell her sunscreen. She could feel the occasional breeze try to lift her shirtfront and the soft tickle of her hair moving on her forehead. She was basking amongst the Bordeaux wine region of south-west France and everything else was far away.

Adaline sighed and vowed to come back to this place time and time again in her mind.

She was just starting to think about returning upstairs to get a book when a number of things happened at once. There were fast, heavy footsteps in the grass and shouts of caution and worry. Her eyes opened as a body appeared above her – airborne, falling and reaching. She braced. Something small hit the body, then whoever it was crashed onto the ground and rolled. Cheers and laughter, a smattering of applause from nearby and Rory was getting to his feet, football under one arm and a broad smile on his face. Adaline pushed herself up from the grass and stared, open-mouthed, as he dropped the ball onto his foot and kicked it back in the direction it had come from.

'You okay down there?' he asked her, still smiling.

'You … just dived over me.'

'Would you rather I let the ball hit you? Okay, don't look at me like that, it was a dare.' He offered her his hand. 'It's time for the wine tasting anyway. Consider me your wake up call.' He pulled her to her feet and put his arm around her back until she was steady. 'At least we'll get about half an hour, right?'

She looked around. Everyone she recognised from their tour was also getting to their feet or crossing the lawn, heading towards the ostentatious

ONE FOR THE ROAD

double front doors of the chateau. 'What do you mean?' She brushed herself down, pushed her sunglasses on top of her head and followed the crowd.

'We've got kitchen duty.'

'You too?' It seemed such a remarkable coincidence that she wondered if Jack picked pairs who got along. 'That's lucky for me.'

'Don't be too sure, I'm not the best in the kitchen.'

'Hell, neither am I. They have chefs for that. I think we just peel vegetables and set tables.'

Rory pulled her against him when four people charged through the assembling crowd. They laughed and shouted as they ran, three of them pursing one.

'Thanks,' Adaline murmured. He nodded and let go.

Jack stepped through the doorway then, his eyes on his watch, a clipboard under his arm. As he rolled his shoulders back and lifted his pointed chin, Adaline was struck by the thought that France suited him.

'Hey, all. How many've we got here …' He did a head count, checked his list a few times, then stuck his thumb up in the air. 'We're good to go!'

The group walked down the driveway, through the sandstone gates and along a path lined with wildflowers, terracotta pots and stone walls. It was early evening now, they'd wiled away the afternoon in the sun and Adaline could have happily turned in for the night. Her body was weary and warm, yet in so many ways, today had only just started as she'd slept through most of it.

She tasted two of the samples passed around in plastics cups, snacked on some of the finger food and listened with half an ear as a man whose French name she'd loved but already forgotten explained the wine making processes and traditions of his family's label. When Jack caught her eye and tapped his watch, she slipped away from the group and stepped back through the door which led to the road. Rory joined her a moment later and together they walked back to the chateau. He kept her laughing the whole way and she was clutching at the pain in her side when they arrived in the kitchen.

A short, narrow-faced man in a Gateway polo top looked up from where he stood by the industrial sized stove. He pointed a spatula at them. 'All right, lovebirds, the fun ends now.' Smiling, he joined them by the door. 'Welcome to my kitchen, my name's Latte.'

Rory held his hand out. As Latte shook it, he introduced himself as, 'Skinny Mochaccino.'

Amused, Latte then shook Adaline's hand.

'Ada.'

'All right you two, I'm going to have to break this little team up, I'm afraid. Ada, if you could set up the buffet tables and put napkins and salt and pepper on the long tables, that'll keep you busy right up 'til dinner. Skinny Mochaccino, come with me. You're peeling mushrooms and then you're taking out the trash.'

There were three tours staying at the chateau that night, so by the time Ada had carted out the equivalent amount of glassware and silverware and stacked dinner plates on either side of the bain-maries, her arms were tired. She arranged the salt and pepper shakers in a long curvy line on each table, set out so many napkins she hoped Gateway had a tree plantation somewhere, then returned to the kitchen with time to spare. She wondered who had failed to turn up for kitchen duty from the other groups.

Rory was out lighting the burners under the bain-maries when Latte pointed at the enormous fridge and asked her to pass him a jar of garlic. When she didn't find it on one of the shelves of the door, she bent closer and started turning containers on the main shelves.

'I'm not going to recognise the label,' she called over her shoulder. 'What's the French word for garlic?'

But she never got her answer.

Ada stumbled back. Screaming. She bumped into the wheeled counter behind her then fell to the floor.

There was a head in the fridge. In a jar. Its mouth gaping and its eyes white and horrible.

Then there was laughter.

Rory was back in the kitchen and he was using the doorframe to keep himself on his feet. Latte was laughing too, bent double and clutching his stomach.

'What the hell is that?' Adaline demanded. She'd knocked the bowl of mushrooms over when she'd fallen, they were on the floor and on her lap, and one had found its way into the breast pocket of her shirt. She ignored them and pushed herself to her feet. She crept towards the fridge and peered at the large jar at the back, tucked amongst condiments and ingredients. It was a head, yet just a very clever picture of one; life-sized, curved around the inside of the jar and coloured to appear as though submerged in a kind of juice.

Ada straightened, her narrowed eyes on Rory. 'You tool.'

His laughing intensified.

Adaline charged. Mushrooms squashed underfoot. Rory yelped and dashed away, and she chased him through the dining hall, through the foyer and up the stairs. He ran to his room, clumsily opened the door and barrelled inside, but she threw her weight against the door before he could close it. It flew open and he stumbled back, hooked his foot on the bunk bed ladder and toppled over.

Panting, Adaline stood over him. 'Serves you right!'

When his surprise subsided, he began to laugh again.

Recognising the suitcase leaning against the opposite bed as Rory's, Adaline crossed to it and collapsed onto the mattress. Breathing hard, she stared at the underside of the bed above her, then she began to laugh too. Eventually they both calmed down enough to sit up, but it was a long time before they managed to speak.

'Oh my god,' Rory said, breathless and delighted, 'that was classic. I've never heard someone scream like that.'

'Liar. I bet you make people scream like that all the time.'

'Yeah, but you were screaming mid-air. How's your bum?'

'About as good as yours, I suspect. You tool. And Latte was in on it, I can't believe it! He seemed so harmless.'

'He took some convincing.' Rory got to his feet then pulled Adaline to hers. He hugged her tight then said, 'Thanks for being such a good sport.'

'Yeah, yeah, bite me.'

Rory pointed at the mushroom still in her shirt pocket and started laughing again. Adaline took it out and dropped it in his suitcase.

He opened the door for her and they walked downstairs.

'Everyone's going to laugh at me,' Adaline said, her eyes on the archway leading to the dining hall.

'Nah, I asked Latte to leave it in the fridge and not let on we had anything to do with it. The best part of a practical joke is keeping people guessing.'

'But you came clean to me.'

'I wouldn't have if you hadn't fallen on your arse. I was all set to act concerned but I just couldn't stop myself from laughing, you were hilarious.'

Dinner was served without mushrooms. A lot of people on their table grumbled about it and Rory and Adaline had a hard time keeping their heads down and expressions neutral. When a staff member in the kitchen screamed half an hour into the meal, Rory drank an entire glass of water to keep himself from losing it. After that, rumours flew. Adaline played along, confessing to having been frightened by the head too, but she said it had been there before she'd gone in for kitchen duty, so suspicion turned towards staff. Rory described how gross it was, then someone brought it out and propped it by the water urn so everyone could see for themselves.

Latte kept his word and gave nothing away, and Adaline fancied herself part of a fleeting secret society. Without even trying, Rory gave her exactly what she wanted – distraction, gaiety. A ruthless disregard for consequence.

She looked at his smiling face and craved more.

10 WATER OF LIFE

There was an hour between dinner finishing and the party starting, which gave everyone enough time to glam themselves up and choose what underwear they were going to show off. Claire, Jenny and Beth each wore theirs over their pants – leopard print, hot pink, and frilly – and Rachael, who wanted to wear a skirt, wore a bra over her singlet top. Holly and Adaline wore their underwear like headbands. The girls in relationships complained, saying they hadn't brought their best pieces because they hadn't imagined anyone would see them, and Adaline found herself feeling shy. She, too, hadn't imagined anyone seeing such things but now that they would, she wanted to wear her good ones. Her G-string and half-cup set were electric orange with blue accents, interesting to look at and flattering. Not that the latter mattered so much tonight.

She thought of Rory, reminded herself that it didn't matter what he thought of her underwear, then followed the girls into The Cave, the dark, strobe-lit basement nightclub beneath the chateau. They hadn't been patient enough to arrive fashionably late, but neither had anyone else. It was only nine o'clock and already the line at the bar was six deep and six across. The dance floor was full, the music was loud and there were more than one hundred people crammed into the converted wine cellar.

Adaline danced. She drank. She laughed at people's imaginative interpretations of the theme. Maree was wearing her bra on her head, and being rather busty, the cups were large enough to look like a strange kind of crown. Will was also wearing one of her bras and had stuffed it with napkins. A lot of the guys had managed to convince girls to loan them things, and one guy was wearing something that had a certain BDSM vibe to it. Danya was partying hard. He wore underwear like a mask and drank as enthusiastically as he danced. She remembered he had a day off tomorrow, as did Jack, who was wearing green boxer shorts over regular shorts and fending off the advances of one of the American girls in his group.

It was a half an hour exercise to get a drink at the bar owing to the queues, so everyone was holding two drinks and queuing again before they finished the second. Rory got her one whenever he went up, a favour which she returned. They queued together twice and at one stage thought it would be funny to exchange underwear, so when Adaline tottered upstairs and wandered outside into the starlit night, his boxer shorts were hanging around her neck like an absurd necklace.

The noise from downstairs was softened by distance, but Adaline pitied anyone who was trying to sleep. The whole chateau had transformed into the biggest party Adaline had ever been to.

Shapes on the darkened grass around the pool moved and murmured, bushes rustled and giggled. Latte hurried around the corner, his hand in a guy's from another tour. There were lights on in the rooms upstairs and silhouettes in the windows. Underwear, and the clothes beneath them, had started coming off.

Feeling a little buzzed from the vodka premixes she'd drank, Adaline wandered towards the coaches, thinking to walk past them to the gates and back again, then maybe up to bed. She wasn't all that psyched about dancing for hours on end, she'd never been the type, and she wanted to feel better tomorrow morning than she had this morning. She had no way of telling the time, but she imagined it was getting close to midnight. Early by her travel companions' standards, but a respectable time to turn in for Adaline.

The door of the coach nearest her opened with a hiss, startling her and making her stop. Jenny came down the stairs, smoothing her hair and holding the pink underwear that had once been over her pants. Her steps were overly considered yet unsteady, as were those of the man who followed her. Danya was red in the face and grinning. Neither paid her any attention as they moved inside to return to the party. Adaline stood very still. She wondered how far it had gone between them. Was there a pair of seats she should avoid next time she boarded? She abandoned her idea of walking to the gates and turned back to the open front doors. Bed. Before she saw anything else she couldn't unsee.

Except a man's voice came from the darkness. 'Hey.'

She hesitated, bathed in the butterscotch glow of the light from the foyer. Jack walked out of the shadows and joined her on the steps. 'Having fun?'

She relaxed. 'Yeah. I'm calling it a night, though.'

'Me too.'

'But you have a day off tomorrow,' she said, as if he needed reminding.

He flashed her that unusual close-mouthed smile. 'And I want to enjoy it. Besides, things were getting a little out of hand down there.'

'Oh?'

'Eighteen year olds. On me. Everywhere.' He moved his arms about himself.

'Ah. Well. I can only imagine.'

He followed her across the foyer to the stairs. As they climbed, he said, 'So who's chasing you?'

She laughed. 'No one's chasing me, I was just walking.'

'How about running, tomorrow?'

She paused on the first landing and considered. 'Maybe.'

'Turns out I missed running with you this morning. Maybe we could make a thing of it. I know some great tracks, could show you a few things.'

Adaline considered him. It had been a shame to miss another jog in the Paris dawn and that balancing bird outside the gates when they'd arrived had made her want to fly through the vineyard herself. Dawn here was something she wanted to both see and be a part of. 'That sounds fun,' she said, 'but let's not lock it in. I'm on holidays and you're offering me structure.' She sounded so casual, so unaffected. When had she become such a good actress?

'Okay,' he said, 'I'll be at the gates at six-thirty. If you're there, you're there.'

'Okay.' She imagined herself jogging through the thick twisted vines, cresting hills to heart-stopping views, and felt excited. She'd be there.

Jack looked away, down the corridor that led to her dorm room then back to her face. He didn't appear to see what he was looking for. 'Your mum called again. Twice today.'

Adaline recoiled. She crossed her arms over her chest and dropped her gaze to the floor.

'Not my imagination, then.' His voice was soft now, patient.

'What did you say to her?'

'That I would pass on a message once more, but that I wasn't an answering service.'

Adaline looked up. 'You said that?'

'No. I listened, I wrote down her details. I told her you were fine and that I would let you know she'd called. Again. Adaline, if you don't want to speak to her, I need you to tell her yourself. I don't have the time or the inclination to involve myself in family dramas. I'm dealing with enough.'

'Of course.' Adaline felt like a scolded child. The warmth of her embarrassment blended with the heat of her sudden fury. The woman was a poison. She was in another country and still she managed to get Adaline in trouble, still she managed to isolate her. This moment had nothing to do with Georgia Sharp, and yet she'd infiltrated it. Adaline thought of weeds pushing through hairline cracks in concrete, of trees clinging to rock faces and thriving, and empathised with the concrete and the rocks. No sooner had she thought it, she felt terrible.

Poison or not, weed-like or not, Adaline's mother couldn't help it. Without making excuses for her – because of course there were ways to do things better, to be better – Adaline recognised that Georgia was an ill woman. It was her illness that spoke through her, that moved her fingers across the phone, that pushed her to reach for the daughter who had fled her side. It was hard to blame her and Adaline's resentment was like a cancer – a dark, twisted knot that shouldn't be there but was.

'I'll fix it,' she said to Jack's feet. 'She won't call again.'

She braced herself for Jack's sympathy. Her mind scrabbled for excuses and stories to tell him when he pressed for information.

Jack shifted. 'Good.' He didn't ask. He didn't even seem curious. He truly was too burdened by his own problems and responsibilities to pretend to want to hear about her own.

She looked up.

Footsteps crossing the foyer made them both look down the stairs. Rory was approaching, clearly looking for someone or something. His eyebrows lifted when he saw the pair standing together on the first floor landing.

Jack waved then turned to Adaline and smiled. 'I knew there had to be someone chasing you.' He stepped around her and began walking up to the next floor. 'Goodnight, Adaline.' He pitched his voice further. ''Night, champ.'

Adaline waited for Rory to join her, her orange bra like earmuffs on his head, then walked with him to the corridor where they would part company. Knowing where his room was now, she knew he would turn left and she right.

'You had enough, or something?' he asked, dawdling at their carpeted crossroads.

'It's not really my scene. And I'm feeling a little … weird.'

'Did you have some of that "water of life"?'

'Eau de vie? They said it was a wine extract but it tasted like petrol.'

'Yeah, it's also about seventy-five per cent alcohol. You going to bed?'

She nodded but leaned against the wall by the fire extinguisher. She wanted to tell him about Jenny and Danya but didn't want to be a gossip. 'Are you?'

'I was thinking of short-sheeting a few beds first.' He grinned. 'Imagine climbing in after a long night, drunk off your nuts, and finding you can't straighten your legs.' He touched his fingers to his temple. 'Problem solving skills won't work this early in the morning.'

She smiled and shook her head. 'But they'll all know it was you when you're the only one sleeping properly.'

'Actually, a lot of people have been leaving their doors unlocked because there aren't enough keys to go around.'

'You're trouble. I should stay away from you.'

'Safer to stay close, I imagine. Want to help?'

She pushed off the wall and followed him down the corridor leading to the boys' rooms. 'I'm not being your accomplice.'

'Keep me company, then.'

'I'm pretty sure that still makes me an accomplice.'

He tried the first door, found it locked and walked to the second door. It opened. Suddenly Rory was unsteady and clumsy, and when he sloped into the room and slapped on the light, groaning loudly, Adaline expected people to shout. But no one did.

She peered around the door frame. Rory was standing straight again, no longer feigning drunkenness. He grinned wickedly. 'Empty. Come in and shut the door.'

She did, hovering by the sink as he chose a random bed, stripped it and remade it. She followed him into five rooms, even his own. The bed picked in there was less random and more targeted: Pies was the lucky victim.

Everything was going well until the sixth bedroom.

Adaline was talking quietly about the picnic and hike when they heard someone coming. Rory straightened – finished with the bed – and listened. When the noise stopped outside the door, he urged her over. She went to him without thinking. Someone grappled clumsily with the handle as he pulled her against his chest and spun to push her back against the wall. The door opened at the exact moment that Rory dipped his face down to hers and grabbed her hip with one of his big, trouble-making hands.

Her hands were around his back, clutching his shirt, so Adaline knew whoever had come in would see two people in a seemingly passionate embrace, covering up what they'd really been doing in here. But her body didn't seem to care about the reason, only the reality. His mouth was so close to hers that it was touching the soft flesh between her upper lip and nose. The warmth of his breath was a kind of caress and the scent of him was all-consuming. Her breasts were flattened against his chest and his leg was brushing against her inner thighs. As the guy in the doorway made a startled, awkward sound, Adaline closed her eyes and thought about where Rory's hands were. The one on her lower back lifted from her shirt and his body rocked against her in a way that suggested he was waving the guy away. He moved to the other side of her face, as a kissing couple might do, dragging warm air across her lips and throat.

'Sorry man,' said the intruder. 'I'll c'back.' He stumbled then lurched out to the hallway and slammed the door.

Adaline could feel Rory's heart beating fast, matching the rhythm of her own. They were alone again yet she hadn't let go. And she didn't want to.

Maybe she'd romanticised him. Was it possible that she could capture this moment and kiss him without it leading to strings of other moments that would bind her? Could they just enjoy each other and want, not need?

They stood there, breaths shallow and bodies crushed together. Adaline couldn't decide. Her instincts warned her against toying with him even as her skin felt magnetised.

It was Rory who broke the spell. He kissed the tip of Adaline's nose and drew away. 'Holy crap,' he said, taking a few steps back. 'Sorry about that.'

Adaline pushed off the wall and blinked at him. 'It's okay.'

'I reckon we got away with it, but we should get out of here.'

He hurried her out the room and switched off the light. They moved quickly down the corridor, back to the crossroads. When he smiled at her, two orange half-cups over his ears, she wondered how such a joker could have such a serious effect on her body.

She lifted his boxer shorts from around her neck and handed them back.

He gave her the bra.

Neither spoke for a moment.

'Lucky I didn't go on my own,' he said quietly. 'I shudder to think how I would've got him to leave without you.'

They began laughing again.

11 THIEF

She ran like she had the devil on her heels, and Jack, who was possibly fitter and definitely more familiar with the terrain, struggled to keep up. Adaline's strides were long and her arms pumped powerfully at her sides. Her hair sailed in a wind of her own making. She was looking where she was going more than she was seeing where she was, and for that reason, Jack stopped her.

'That's the way to The Overlook,' he said between deep, desperate breaths. He dropped his palms onto his knees and panted at the ground.

They'd stopped at a discreet fork in the road. The path that she and her tour mates would walk later today was partially concealed by long grasses and the small rock marker that indicated the way was almost lost amongst a profusion of flowering weeds. He pointed it out to her and she nodded, unable to speak as she fought to get her breath back.

Flushed with exertion, her chest heaving and her eyes bright, she looked like sex in running shoes. Jack's eyes lingered on the place where her damp hair clung to her neck. He imagined being the reason for her exhaustion – wet skin against wet skin, and looked away.

'You going on the picnic?' he asked. He put his hands on his hips and began to walk around her, needing to keep his muscles warm and his mind on other things.

'I am,' she said, in a voice so breathy Jack's thoughts immediately returned to sex.

He could guess who would share her picnic basket – the dark haired Australian, the joker – Rory – he had a way of coaxing wide smiles from Adaline and his eyes always followed her. Did Adaline's eyes follow Rory?

'I'm not,' he said, pretending she'd returned the question.

She nodded again.

Jack used his chin to point at the vista. Dawn was minutes away and if they moved now, they'd catch the sunrise from a higher vantage point. The vines were beginning to lighten, as if waking up from the inside, and he wanted to see the appreciation in Adaline's eyes when the gold light seemed to set them on fire.

He began to jog. When he heard her behind him and heard her footfalls become rhythmic, he moved into a run. Sweat was cool on his neck and his shirt was dark with it. The world around him was foreign but familiar. He'd run this road many times and many others around here just as often, but it was something altogether different to share these morning shadows. Adaline followed him as hundreds had done before her – he was a leader in profession and nature – but he got the sense she would leave the moment things no longer suited her. She was not blinkered by his expertise as so many others were. She had come here with ideas and goals and something else he couldn't name that seemed to change the gravity around those who didn't suit her mood.

She appeared to seek nothing more complex than a good time. She hadn't engaged in the coach politics, hadn't made herself an ear or shoulder to those who wished to speak about their problems. Like a compass, Adaline turned from all distractions bar north. Was north a lack of consequence? Was it a reluctance to connect, to share, to be predictable? Jack didn't know, and his inability to pigeonhole her made her fascinating. She appeared highly empathetic, highly in tune with the emotional climate around her, yet there was something about the way people interacted with her that displeased her. What was it?

He'd asked her about her mother twice now and her reaction had been so negative that he wouldn't ask again. This suited him, as he wasn't particularly curious. It wasn't a high priority to learn much more about her family beyond the minimum required to get his job done, so he found himself perplexed. He was both fascinated and wholly incurious about the same person.

That being the case, what did he want to know, if anything?

If he could have her, he realised. If, for the next few highlight-saturated days of her life, she would return his desire.

She wasn't clingy, she seemed to have and be all she fundamentally needed – she wasn't looking to be completed any more than he was. In fact, she appeared to favour fun and freedom over establishing deep connections, romantic or otherwise. Maybe she was perfect – for what he needed, for what he was capable of offering. She wasn't like the others who pawed at him and wanted promises. Maybe they could share something passionate but finite, where his job wasn't endangered and her holiday wasn't monopolised by the building obsession typical of someone looking for an epic holiday romance.

For just a little while, his nights could be shared.

They crested the peak and dropped their pace to a fast walk, then to a slower one until they stopped entirely. She stood beside him dragging air into her lungs, and watched the world change. The vines were in bloom and some were bloated with young grapes. The sun touched them and suddenly the fruit looked like gemstones. Shadows shortened and birds began to sing. The roses at the end of each row became vibrant.

Jack breathed it all in and wondered what might change between this sunrise and the next.

* * *

Adaline thought about Rory in the shower. Their faux kiss had made her heart beat as fast as this morning's run had, which was problematic considering her recent vow to leave him alone. She thought about his breath on her face as she lathered shampoo into her hair, and imagined herself back in his arms as she dried herself.

She'd known intimacy only once before. Months of foreplay with a friend in her social circle. Awkward exchanges of affection as they'd guessed their way forward, then kisses that had both satisfied and starved. He'd been patient and kind and he'd made her laugh – a winning trifecta for her first time. It was likely there would have been many more times, but Ada's mother had spiralled shortly after and there hadn't been room for any other relationships in Adaline's life beyond family. Adaline had become a full-time carer and after a while her friends had stopped being patient. She didn't blame them. Friendship could only be one-sided for so long. She'd enjoyed graduating alongside them and taking on the world for a few months before everything had changed – she'd had a glorious summer. Following that, she'd kept the company of book characters. They'd embraced her in between the grey conversations of depression and taken her away from the house she'd come to loathe.

It had been gun metal grey once, with bright blue accents and a sprawling yard at its feet perfect for a dog and a game of cricket. Now the grey and the blue mirrored the mood inside and the yard kept the world at a distance. There was only the black dog people spoke of – the metaphor – and there was no one to play an innings with anymore.

Her home had become a house the day her father left. He'd reached the end of his rope, he'd said. He'd slipped off the end of it, wished his daughter good luck, and traded Adaline's freedom for his own. Now Adaline was at the end of her rope, standing half a world away trying to decide if she was going to slip off too, or tie a knot in the end and hold on.

Someone knocked on the bathroom door.

'Won't be long,' Adaline called back.

She dressed quickly and dragged her thoughts back to the more recent past, to the moment she'd almost given in to the temptation of proximity. No one had drawn her close for almost a year and she'd forgotten the simple sweetness of it. Intimacy given freely – intoxicating.

Adaline gathered her things and stepped out of the communal bathroom, her hair un-brushed and wet on her neck. In her dorm room she thread it into a loose braid, pushed a light skin of foundation over her face and pulled on her joggers. She would be the last down to breakfast, made late because of her run then the long queue to shower. Considering the hour some of the girls had staggered into their beds she was surprised to be last, but the smell of cooking meat had wafted up the stairs and slipped under their door. She supposed it was a powerful lure.

Scenarios rolled through her mind as she locked the room and walked to the dining hall. Rory greeting her with a loaded plate and a smile wider than a strip of bacon. Rory walking with her to The Overlook, taking her hand when she stumbled then not letting go. Rory pulling her into a doorway and kissing her for real.

What this what she wanted from him, then? Intimacy at every opportunity, demonstrated preference? Surely not when such things meant routines and expectations. So a fling? A passionate, fleeting heat that reminded her what it was to be connected to a person? He would be patient and kind, too, and he would certainly make her laugh, but weren't some things better left unexplored? She'd been so long without intimacy what was the point of reintroducing it now, and for so brief a time? It would leave a long tail, a seemingly endless reel of nostalgia and a feeling of being apart keener than the one she'd learned to live with. She'd be injuring herself for a moment of pleasure, there was no balance in that.

Adaline stepped into the dining hall, loaded up her plate with what scraps were left after a hundred hungry mouths, and found a spare seat beside Jenny. Danya's flushed face came to mind and Adaline forced a corner of toast into her mouth. *That* she would deny knowing about until she was blue in the face. She listened to the exaggerated tales of last night from those seated around her and smiled to herself when a boy she didn't know complained about the housekeeping.

'Made my bed wrong, didn't they?'

Claire waved her fork at Adaline. 'Did you see Zoey last night? All boobs. If she was taller, she would've knocked Jack in the face with them.'

'Zoey's eighteen, isn't she?'

'Yeah, the youngest. Maybe the wildest, too, time'll tell.'

'Anyone else surprise you?' Adaline asked. She glanced at the crispy strips of bacon being devoured further down the table and swallowed a mouthful of spit. It was lucky the sunrise had been spectacular, otherwise Adaline would be indulging some pretty unkind thoughts about Jack right now. Adaline looked back at Claire.

Her eyes were shining with amusement. 'Asking about anyone in particular?' Claire asked.

Adaline dropped her eyes back to her plate. 'No.'

'I didn't see Rory much.' Claire's tone suggested she wished she could have said otherwise, her answer lacked intrigue.

Adaline wondered where he was but knew she couldn't look for him now.

'You know who I didn't see,' Jenny broke in, 'Rach. Doesn't she have a boyfriend?'

'Yeah,' Claire said, 'and she was on the phone with him for ages. Beth said she found her in the room crying 'n shit. The dick's making her feel bad about being here.'

'Dick,' Jenny agreed.

Adaline finished her slice and pushed away from the table.

Claire looked up at her. 'What's the rush?'

'I was thinking I'd ask Jack if any baskets are left over.'

'Picnic baskets?' Claire shrugged her mouth. 'I think they make them to order. You were supposed to put your name down last night.'

Adaline nodded, too late remembering Jack's directions before they'd stepped off the coach. 'I guess I'll scrounge up some more breakfast then, something I can take with me.'

She approached the buffet, her attention on the enormous bowl of apples. Someone bumped hard against her as they hurried past. Two steps later someone else cut her off. Adaline's irritation flared. She turned, brow furrowed and words crowding her tongue – but stopped.

There was a commotion outside the dining hall. Someone was shouting and people were leaving their seats to investigate. Curiosity made her follow.

It took a moment for her to recognise the guy on the stairs. She placed the face but not the name. He was in her tour group, he and his friend kept mostly to themselves. He was gesticulating wildly and appeared to be wearing the same clothes from yesterday. They were rumpled enough that he might have slept in them. His expression was wild and his carrying voice sounded brittle with rage. 'You're not helping!' he said, throwing the accusation down to the man standing a few steps below him.

Jack held up a hand. 'Let's go upstairs and have another look —'

'It's not in there! None of it's in there!' He became aware of his audience. Even from across the room, Adaline saw his eyes flash with hate. 'I'm going to beat the shit out of whoever did this!'

He was a big guy, Adaline didn't doubt his ability to level anyone stupid enough to get in his way, but why the agitation? Why the threats?

Fingers hooked into the inside of her elbow. Rory dropped his mouth to her ear and murmured, 'Time for our picnic, I think.' He squeezed her arm, waited for her nod then led her to the trestle tables beside the grand front doors. Dozens of hardy looking baskets crowded the table tops. Names had been penned onto small tags tied to the handles. Adaline was startled to see her name under Rory's. Without pause, Rory hefted theirs free. Still with a guiding hand on her arm, he led the way out of the chateau into the golden light and mountain air.

'What was —?'

'In a minute,' Rory cut in. His lips were pressed together and his expression was serious. Having been on the receiving end of so many of his smiles before now, it was hard to reconcile this Rory with the one from last night.

They hastened down the steps then crossed the driveway in long strides. His eyes touched on the faces of those lingering by the coaches. He looked over his shoulder. When they passed between the grand front gates he appeared to become easier; his shoulders dropped a fraction and some of the worry left his face.

'Now can you tell me what's going on?' she asked. He'd boosted her heart into a frenzy again but this time it had nothing to do with his proximity.

'Someone was in Anthony's room last night.'

Adaline processed this. 'He's *that* pissed that someone short-sheeted his bed?'

'No. He's *that* pissed because someone stole his passport and cash.'

Adaline made to stop but Rory kept her moving. He glanced over his shoulder again.

'Why are you acting so dodgy?' she demanded. It was impossible to think that he'd had anything to do with the theft, she refused to entertain the idea.

'*Think*, Adaline. The thief wasn't the only one taking advantage of unlocked doors last night.'

'Holy frick.'

This time Rory let her stop. He dropped his hand from her arm, his expression grave. 'Did you tell anyone what we did last night?'

'No, of course not!'

'Are you sure? Did you acknowledge the prank in any way?'

'No!'

Rory pushed his hand across his face and looked away. Adaline replayed every conversation she'd had since leaving Rory in the corridor. She hadn't said a word of it. She'd wanted to – walk into her dorm room and tell the girls she'd almost kissed him, that she'd been brave and wild and reckless, that she'd held in her arms the embodiment of trouble and mischief – but she'd climbed into bed quietly and she'd said very little at breakfast. Her run, she remembered. Not too long ago this path had led her to dawn, had she said anything then? It was unlikely, she'd been too preoccupied. And there was only so much you shared with your tour manager anyway – it was like telling tales to the teacher.

'I didn't say anything,' she said, sounding more certain now. 'Did you?' He held her reputation in his hand the way she did his, she realised.

'Of course not,' he returned.

'Then we're probably okay.' She smiled weakly. 'Right?'

He nodded. 'Probably. I don't think anyone saw us, but let's keep a low profile this morning.'

Adaline's smile slipped. 'The drunk guy. In the last room.'

Rory stiffened, then relaxed. 'He didn't see either of our faces.'

They began walking again, irregular lazy strides towards the peak. Their reassurances had loosened the urgency from their bodies. As birds mapped flight paths overhead and insects whirred and clicked in the long grasses flanking the road, Adaline gathered her courage to address the second surprise of the morning.

'What's with the basket?' she asked. The basket in question was presently swinging back and forth beside Rory's leg. The small names card flapped in the created breeze.

'What about it?'

'We're sharing it. How did that happen?'

'I put our names down last night.' Swing. Swing. He looked over at her.

'What?'

'You didn't ask me.'

'We talked about it yesterday. You don't remember?'

'No.' Maybe they'd talked about it after a few shots of vodka when things had felt shiny and nonsensical, or on a rest stop driving here when she'd been foggy and hungover. Either way, the outcome would have been the same: she wouldn't have committed to it. Her aversion to promises – big or small – guaranteed it.

Rory shrugged. 'Maybe I misunderstood.' He glanced at her again and grinned. 'Or I heard what I wanted to. What, is your name on another basket?'

'No.'

'Good, then you won't starve today.'

'I guess I won't. Thank you.'

She laughed when he attempted a graceful walking bow, arms extended from his sides. She leaned in to his attention. What a treat to be thought of and spoiled, all without an expected exchange. Her gratitude made her thoughts clumsy.

'We turn here,' she said suddenly. They'd reached the fork in the road Jack had pointed out to her. She checked for the rock marker to be sure, saw it and stepped from the main road. She turned back when Rory didn't follow.

'There's no sign,' he said. He frowned at the path then opened the lid of the picnic basket. A moment later he was holding a photocopy of a map. The light through the page showed Adaline a thick orange line, no doubt highlighted by a helpful Gateway crew member.

'It's this way,' she insisted.

Rory moved his face closer to the map. 'I reckon the turn-off's another K or so.'

'I know it's this way.'

Something in her tone made him look up. 'How? Your spidey-senses are tingling?'

Adaline opened her mouth then closed it. How to explain that this was the second time she'd been here this morning without giving away that she welcomed the occasional daybreak with Jack? It wasn't a secret so much as something she didn't want to share, and if Rory's thoughts had been at all similar to hers following their almost kiss, jealousy would surely come into play. She didn't have the tolerance for it, or the wish to explain herself. It was another strike against deepening this relationship; the need to be mindful of her actions, of the company she kept, of the things she said. She had enough of that at home.

'Let's take it in turns navigating,' she said, 'and make this my turn.' She didn't know the way beyond the stone marker, they could make a game of it.

Rory stared at her for so long she became self-conscious. She was just starting to think he was reading her mind when he broke eye contact to look at the map again. 'I suppose it hardly matters,' he said. 'If we keep heading up we'll get there eventually.'

'That's the spirit.' Adaline pivoted on her heel and led the way.

Five hours later they shuffled back past the stone marker, legs aching and stomachs full. The Overlook had been worth the hike for the view alone, and it had been fun playing games when the others had joined them, but now all they could think about was the pool. The picnic basket was empty, Adaline and Rory had talked about everything from superheroes to hypothetical lotto wins, and the thief amongst them was all but forgotten until Adaline returned to her room to change.

Her gaze fell on the orange underwear she and Rory had shared last night, that he'd been wearing so ostentatiously in the room they'd been seen in. She bundled them up and tossed them in the bin.

12 CONNECTION

Had Adaline thought ahead about the many hours she would spend driving between points of interest in Europe, she would have packed more things to read. It didn't matter that she'd failed to plan for this, though, because the coach had come to feel like a mini-world, and its strange population helped to pass the time.

Jack had started the long drive from Bordeaux to Cannes with a grave warning about theft and caring for personal property. He'd warned everyone that the passport and money thief could be on the coach, then he'd elevated the mood with the day song, which some had sang along to and others had tried to muffle. At least half of the coach were nursing hangovers following a second big night in The Cave. An hour out of Toulouse the games had started. Coach speed dating, where the aisle seats had become hot seats, had been Adaline's least favourite. Out of her comfort zone with small talk and forced intimacy, she'd mumbled her way through a dozen awkward exchanges before people had blessedly lost interest, and Rory had got his seat back from her new neighbour.

Two rest stops and a bellyful of roadside nougat later, they were on the last stretch. Rory was slouched so low in his seat that Adaline had to look down to meet his eyes. Being so tall, the cramped seats where making him uncomfortable, and after six hours on the road he was contorting himself in strange ways to make it bearable. Presently, his legs were over Adaline's knees and his feet were hanging in the aisle.

Rory rolled his phone end on end, bumping it against his stomach. Adaline's number was in there now. She wondered what he'd do with it, if anything.

'Maybe you need a careers adviser,' he said. They'd spent the last few kilometres discussing Adaline's lack of plans since she'd graduated high school. Rory found it hard to believe that she hadn't been nursing a burning desire to be something particular once she broke out into the real world.

'Maybe.' She hadn't mentioned her mother and all the obligations associated with her, it was too heavy a conversation for a holiday. This meant Rory was trying to navigate an enormous information gap and didn't even know it. She said, 'Or one of those expos with brightly coloured stalls and what not.'

She twisted some of the hair on his leg into a little scroll and released it. At first it had been strange – the proximity, the touching – they'd both been shy and clumsy. But as the distance travelled had grown, the distance between them had reduced. It had been hours since a part of her body had not been in direct contact with his. It was unsettling, there were times when his arm would graze against the side of her breast or his warm breath would roll along her throat, but it wasn't scary. It was kind of nice. Really nice.

How quickly, how completely, they had slipped into an intimacy unlike any she'd known before.

'Move to Sydney and study medicine,' he said. 'I'll carry your books to class.' His smile was fast and distracting – it took her a moment to understand what she'd heard. She thought of the kids' recreation centre he worked at, acting like a monkey with a bunch of tiny people who no doubt hero-worshipped him, then pictured him in a lecture theatre, serious and well-behaved. The second picture sat askew in her mind, a poor fit compared to the first.

'Do you want to be a doctor?'

'Could you sound more surprised? What, you didn't think I'm smart enough?'

She waved her hand back and forth, as if scrubbing the moment away. She'd never doubted his intelligence, Rory was clearly well-read and clever. In the last few days they'd talked about everything from religion to poverty. Science, literature, comic book heroes and ice cream flavours – they'd touched on a little bit of everything and he'd had a valuable opinion about each. But a doctor? That job was for grown-ups.

'I'm sorry,' she said. 'Of course you're bright enough. It's just such a serious thing to do.'

'Ah. So you don't think I'm *mature* enough?' He crossed his eyes and poked his tongue at her.

She smiled but didn't take the bait. 'What kind of doctor?'

His expression softened. 'A paediatrician.'

'Kids,' she murmured.

'Yeah.'

Something akin to awe blossomed inside her chest. When Adaline spoke again, it was with deep affection. 'That's wonderful. Are you starting in January?'

'Nah, mid-year intake. I start soon after getting home. Sydney Uni. You should see the campus, it's awesome.' He described the blend of old buildings and new, the famous quadrangle that had been in movies and the life he would have being so close to the city, and Adaline listened closely, hearing both the details and the excitement that saturated his every word.

Adaline imagined him walking the streets of Sydney, his course books under his arm, maybe a takeaway cup of coffee in his hand, and the picture felt right now. She wished she could imagine herself somewhere with the same kind of clarity. 'Will you keep living at home?'

He shrugged. 'There's a few guys from school, we're talking about getting a place together. Renting for a while. My parents are worried I've blown all my money on this trip, but I've got some savings stashed away. I've wanted to live in the city for a long time, it was always the plan, you know?'

Adaline didn't know, and she envied him his foresight. Rory had a direction. Maybe even a calling. 'It sounds wonderful,' she said, 'all of it.' She laughed softly. 'I'm a little jealous.'

He held up his phone. 'Want me to see when applications close?'

She laughed again. 'Yeah right. If Sydney Uni accepted my application they wouldn't be the university you think they are. I'm lucky I graduated high school.' She drank from the plastic bottle she'd refilled at the last rest stop and couldn't decide if the bad taste that flooded her mouth was from her drink or her honesty.

Rory frowned. 'I find that hard to believe.'

Adaline shrugged. She didn't feel like qualifying that she'd got good grades – implying she was clever enough for university was counter-productive, it would fuel his questions. 'Have you always wanted to help kids?'

Rory hesitated, then accepted the deflection. 'Yeah. I mean, I don't have a sob story. There wasn't a blinding moment of clarity or anything like that. I've just always known I was heading that way. From cradle to stethoscope to grave.'

'Don't knock blinding moments of clarity, I'm counting on having one of those myself.'

He grinned and nudged her. His long fingers lingered a moment then fell away. 'Being realistic and planning for a miracle?'

'Exactly.'

Rory shifted, attempting to lift some of his weight off Adaline's legs. Blood seemed to surge back to the points where he'd rested, making her skin sing. She watched where they still touched, willing him not to break the connection entirely, and worked to bury the anxiety which was clawing up the walls of her chest. She had time, she reminded herself. She didn't have to have all the answers now and it wasn't helpful to compare her life with his. He'd walked a different path, with different feet and a different destination.

'We're almost there, people,' Jack said into the microphone. 'Ten more minutes and Danya throws the cage door open.'

People cheered. Adaline sighed and dropped her head against the seat. Wordlessly, Rory offered his palm to Chris, who was sitting behind him. Skin slapped against skin.

Adaline had read up on Cannes throughout the day, but despite all the sights her guidebook promised and all the websites that linked it to the best of the silver screen, she was struggling to muster up the energy to be excited. It had been such a long day. Gateway was, she thought with building exhaustion, all about early mornings and late nights. A lot of people had found the stamina to party hard again last night, but Adaline had opted to – needed to – recover and recharge. Those same people would probably do it all again tonight. Their stamina was as admirable as it was crazy.

Rory's eyes were bloodshot. He'd joined the Australians in The Cave last night, perhaps thinking he'd sleep through today, but when Adaline had helped herself to the seat beside him, he'd changed his mind. He hadn't so much as dozed.

Sleep debt, she thought. People were going to get run down then sick. She'd heard about the Contiki Cough, what was the Gateway equivalent?

'All right, people,' Jack said, 'listen up for a second. Dinner's at seven – that's in an hour for those who've lost all sense of time. We'll have bottled water in the food tent, take an extra bottle for brushing your teeth, etcetera. Danya will do a run into town at eight-thirty but then he's done for the night. I'll pass out the address on the ride in, you'll need to catch a cab back. The room sheet's making its way back now. Breakfast is from eight and we leave for Nice at ten. Your stuff needs to be by the coach by nine. This is us.'

All around her people turned in their seats or stretched their necks to see. Rory, wincing, pushed himself up and lowered his legs to the floor. The connection broke.

'There's your site crew, wave 'em in.'

The site crew, despite their enthusiasm, were lucky to get half a dozen half-hearted greetings.

Five minutes later, Adaline was hauling her aching body down the aisle past the little nests people had constructed in their allocated spaces. Blankets, clothes and headphone cords sagged from seats and armrests. Various personal items lay abandoned in the haste to disembark. There were crumbs and spills and mysterious stains – Danya's no doubt already stretched mood was going to snap.

This was the longest driving day. Jack has promised this as they'd all moaned and grizzled at the second rest stop, and promised it again another hour down the road. A blessing, because Adaline's patience had frayed and it would be harder to get on the coach knowing there was worse to come. She wanted a shower, she wanted to stretch, and she wanted to be more than a metre from the nearest person. Rory's company had been wonderful, but it had been so constant. In eight and a half hours, she'd had approximately eleven minutes to herself in two rest stop bathroom stalls. She couldn't remember ever spending so much time with the same person before – except maybe the random guy in the middle aisle seat on the flight over here, but they hadn't talked to one another so it didn't really count.

Others had similarly struggled. Conversations had started and stopped, tailed off awkwardly and become increasingly short-tempered. People had stalked the charging station and bickered over turns. Jack had been complained to, complained about, used as a distraction and ignored – he'd been pushed to his limits, she suspected. She'd been wrong to wonder if he could handle this when she'd first seen him at the pre-departure meeting. He'd taken it all in his stride. But looking at him now, repeating things he'd just explained to the group to those who hadn't listened, he looked ready for a little space, too.

Adaline wondered if he shared a room with Danya, or if he was lucky enough to score a single room.

What she wouldn't give for one of those right now.

She pawed through the luggage Danya was dragging out from the undercarriage, pulled hers free and stepped away from the melee. Rachael and Holly had put her name under theirs, and by the time the room sheet had reached Adaline, the Swedish girl named Lisa had penned her name in the last spot. Smaller rooms this time, which would be nice.

Adaline waited her turn as Jack began handing out keys. When he approached her Adaline put her hand out to accept one, but what he gave her wouldn't open a door.

'Have a phone,' he said, quiet but light. 'Next time it rings – and it rings every hour or so, now – be a pal and say hi to your mum for me.'

Adaline closed her fingers around the device and quickly dropped her hand from sight. Startled, she watched him walk away. He handed a set of keys to the Mexican sisters, then two sets of keys to Lisa, who held them up then led the way.

No one appeared to have noticed the strange exchange.

Rachael paused on the path when a stone caught in the wheel of her suitcase and Adaline stopped to wait for her. She glanced up at Adaline, then back at the people still waiting for their bags. 'Hey, I hope you don't mind Hols and me stealing you for our room.'

'No, of course not.' She watched Rachael tug the stone free, and thought a change might be nice. She liked Claire, Jenny and Beth, but Rachael and Holly – they were less combative.

'Thanks,' Rachael said, straightening. 'I think the other girls got Lois.'

'Lois is the blonde?' The Nordic blonde bombshell from Texas with a mouth on her that never stopped. She lived in push-up bras and tight T-shirts, painted her lips a dozen times a day, and had the biggest suitcase on tour – which didn't have wheels and she was unable to carry.

'Barbie, yeah.' Rachael sounded pleased to have dodged that particular room arrangement. 'So are you and Rory engaged yet, or what?' Adaline narrowed her eyes and Rachael laughed. 'The two of you are becoming a bit of a two-for-one deal. You're sweet together.' She hauled her suitcase up the steps leading to their room. 'Makes me miss my boyfriend.'

Adaline followed, at a loss for words. There was little point denying her chemistry with Rory, but nevertheless it made her nervous to think people were pairing them up. Was Rory also being teased and encouraged by his friends? What did he make of it all and what did it mean for what happened next? Whatever his interpretation and whatever he wished for, Adaline needed to be sure of her position first and she was running out of time to make up her mind. She'd swung between wanting more and this being enough too often and for too many days.

What if he made a move? She'd have no answer for him. Or worse yet, she'd be impulsive – and who could guess what decision she'd make at the time. The yes or the no hardly mattered, it was that she wouldn't be able to take it back.

Rachael's laugh cleared her mind. 'You look like I just asked you to tell me the entire square root of pi.'

Adaline decided to change the subject. 'He's unhappy? Your boyfriend.'

Rachael grimaced. 'He hates that I'm here.'

'Without him?'

'At all. He's small town and he's worried the bright lights of the world are going to lure me away.'

'Will they?'

Rachael took a moment to answer. She gave too much focus to pulling her suitcase across the room and parking it at the foot of her bed. 'I don't know. I don't think so. I'm doing this now before it's too late, I don't know why he doesn't understand that.' She fidgeted with the zip, gave up when it stuck, then pushed her hands through her hair.

Above her, Holly huffed from the top bunk.

'Would you like top or bottom?' said another voice.

Adaline turned. Lisa stood by the other beds, her delicate hand on the ladder. She looked like one of the women who waved at prizes on television game shows.

'I don't care,' Adaline said. 'Whichever you don't want.'

'I would like the bottom.'

'It's all yours.' Adaline parked her suitcase out of the way, withdrew her phone from her daypack and hoisted herself up to her new bed.

'Why do you look like that,' Rachael said to Lisa, 'and I look like this? We've had the same crap day.'

There was free Wi-Fi in the room, so Adaline checked her emails and accepted the half a dozen friend requests on her Facebook profile. She browsed through the photos she'd been tagged in, hissed at the unflattering ones of her wearing boxer shorts around her neck, then saved a copy of a nice picture of her and Rory that she hadn't known had been taken. They were sitting on the hillside of The Outlook, hips touching, backs to the camera. They were looking in the same direction, the only two in the picture. It was like they'd been there alone together, in their own little world.

In many ways, they had been.

Adaline hovered over Daniel's friend request, unsure, then exited the application without accepting it. She wrote a quick email to her dad, assuring him she was alive and happy, then went back into Facebook and stalked Rory's profile.

Dinner was a bland but filling selection of vegetables, chicken and bread. Beth was on kitchen duty with the girl Rachael had called Barbie and both of them looked dead on their feet. Looking around the equally bland dining hall, Adaline realised her tour mates had used the time between disembarking and eating to get ready for the night ahead. The girls were in colourful dresses with flat-ironed hair and complicated up-dos. Some boys had shaved, almost all of them were in collared shirts. And there was Adaline, still in the clothes she'd been wearing on the coach, hair falling over one shoulder in a frayed plait and shoulders rounded with fatigue. She was run down. Her stomach felt strange and she'd lost her appetite somewhere between here and Toulouse. Another night drinking … just the thought of it was exhausting.

Adaline flattened her mashed potato with the side of her knife and wondered how she could make her excuses without causing a fuss. Her little group was so tireless and she was sure Rory would want to spend more time with her, he wouldn't be easy to shake.

That sounded unkind.

Adaline closed her eyes and concentrated on her breathing. The room felt like it was rolling.

She didn't want to *shake* Rory. In fact, if Rory was content to share a couple of lounge chairs and a comfortable silence, she'd cheerfully greet dawn by his side. But he wanted to see Cannes. He probably wanted to dance and move from group to group, a bright nebulous of energy and charisma. Even now he was holding court two tables over, stringing his audience along towards a punchline. Adaline had a hard enough time keeping up on her best day.

'Adaline.'

Adaline blinked and Maree came into focus. Then Will did, then Jenny and Claire. All of them were staring at her.

'What?' She twisted her fingers around her hair, as if to tidy it. Everyone was dressed so nice.

Maree exchanged a look with Will. She looked the nicest of them all in electric blue and chunky gold costume jewellery – as if ready for a photo shoot, just like she had in Paris. She looked back at Adaline. 'Your phone's ringing.'

Adaline blinked. Her phone was in her satchel in her room.

She started, realising her mistake. Jack. His slim smart phone was in her pocket, and Smashing Pumpkins was singing about today.

Adaline hastened to her feet. Her cutlery clattered to the tabletop but she barely registered the noise. Her fingers were clawing at her pocket, dragging the device free. The screen showed an international number, one she recognised. She turned, her eyes touching on dozens of faces before she found her tour manager's. He was sitting at a corner table with Danya and the site crew who'd waved their coach in. There was a forkful of chicken halfway to his mouth. Their eyes met. With his free hand Jack extended his thumb and littlest finger, imitating a phone. He lifted it to the side of his face and she looked away.

She'd imagined a hundred ways this conversation could go, but in none of those scenarios was she standing in the middle of a dining hall. Adaline pushed her chair further back from the table and stepped around it. Without meeting anyone else's eyes, she hurried out the side door into the warm night.

Insects whirred and a car rumbled down the nearby road. The Smashing Pumpkins were singing about tearing their eyes out now.

She connected the call.

13 BED BUDDIES

'Adaline?' It was Georgia Sharp, across the world and yet for all the difference it made, at Adaline's side. The slap was almost tangible.

'Mum …' Words failed her.

But they didn't fail her mother. 'I've been calling and calling. Do you have any idea what you've put me through these last few days? I couldn't reach you, I've been a wreck. You couldn't find five minutes to call me, to check in?'

Nothing, Adaline thought, about Adaline. No questions about the world she was seeing, about how she might be feeling being away from home for the first time. No remark about the biggest adventure of her life to date. There was only Georgia. Georgia and the things she saw, the things she felt.

'I've been sick, baby – it's been bad.'

Adaline flinched away from the belittling endearment. More often than not it was Adaline keeping their little family afloat; paying bills with government assistance money and a percentage of her dad's fortnightly pay, drafting cover letters to attach to her mother's resume in the times she felt excited to work. Adaline was the full-time carer, not Georgia, the parent. The 'baby' nickname had always set Adaline's teeth on edge, and some days she suspected her mother knew that. It was a passive aggressive way of reducing Adaline's importance and diminishing her efforts. It was unkindness masked in affection.

'Those breathing exercises aren't working and the neighbour's gone mad – he's shaping those god damn hedges again. All day with the chainsaw, with the shaping, with the bloody circles and squares and I can't sleep. I need you here, don't you understand? I've been in the same bad mood since you left me, I can't shake it.'

Adaline closed her eyes and pressed her palm against her stomach. She felt unsteady and disorientated. Shock? Anxiety?

The noise from within the dining hall seemed to pitch. Adaline turned. People were standing, gathering their plates and crossing to scrape the scraps into the large bins by the kitchen doors. One of the doors opened and the first of her group stepped into the night.

Adaline moved out of sight, down an unlit path that felt as claustrophobic as the conversation she was having.

She didn't want to be seen or worried about, she just wanted to be invisible, un-trackable. How far did she have to run until no one could pursue her … until her legs gave out? Or her heart?

The one-sided tirade continued. 'You didn't leave me any passwords. There's mail coming in and it's asking for things. Money for things I don't think we have. I've stopped opening them, they confuse me. It's all too much. The phone keeps ringing but it's never you. It's people looking for you. They're following up on things you said you'd do. But you haven't done anything because you're god knows where and you don't *give a shit* anymore.'

Georgia burst into tears. Ugly, wailing sobs of frustration and betrayal. She cursed Adaline between breaths, complained, and seemed wholly unaware that her daughter hadn't spoken for most of the time the call had been connected.

'You're just like your father,' she spat – her penultimate insult – then she ran out of steam and became quiet.

Adaline heard the coach engine rumble. Everyone was leaving. There hadn't been a single person in that dining hall who'd been dressed for a night in. Adaline was by every definition, alone.

Her stomach pitched, then settled. Pitched, then settled.

She squared her shoulders. 'You're lucky that's not true.' If Adaline was just like her father, this conversation wouldn't be happening. 'Are you taking your medication?'

'When I remember.' Her mother's voice had become sulky, like that of a scolded child's.

'I put reminders in your phone, an alarm should —'

'They were waking me up. I turned them off.'

She was sleeping during the day again, Adaline realised. There were no alarms at night, that excuse wasn't applicable.

'Turn them back on and if they wake you up again, scream and shout and whatever, but get up and take your pill at the same time. Then you can go back to sleep.' She paused. 'Turn them back on,' she repeated.

'You say that like it's easy. You have no idea.'

Adaline despised the flippancy of that remark. Of course Adaline had an idea, Georgia wasn't the only one living this nightmare. Her mouth felt strange. She swallowed and tried to level out her temper.

'You can't call this number again.'

'I need to talk to you.' Georgia's voice went high with panic. 'This is the only way to reach you. You calm me down, you know you do. If that man is giving you any problems —'

'That man is my tour manager and this is his phone.'

'I don't care. I need —'

'Mum.' Adaline drew a deep, unsteady breath. 'You can't call this number again. And I don't mean you shouldn't, I mean you will not be able to.' She stressed these last words. 'I'm going to block your number on this device. You're harassing him and it's got to stop.'

Georgia started to scream.

Adaline pressed her eyes shut and moved the phone away from her ear. She swayed. 'If you need to contact me, email —'

The screaming became unbearable.

Adaline ended the call. She buried the phone deep in her pocket and opened her eyes. She'd ask Jack how to block certain numbers on his model. She'd apologise.

Her mouth filled with spit. Then she vomited.

* * *

The next time Adaline opened her eyes, she saw the ceiling of her room; pale grey with a network of hairline cracks and signs of damp in the far corner. It was strange that it was so far away. Stranger still that it was lit by the weak light of dawn. Hadn't she closed her eyes in the dark? Outside?

She made to roll over but a dull ache behind her eyes made her pause. She was stiff in strange places and her stomach felt like the inside of a drum. She was starving. When had she last eaten? The dining hall eased to the front of her mind. The mashed potato, the chunky gold costume jewellery. Everyone staring as she hurried outside with a ringing phone that didn't belong to her.

Her mother.

Horror replaced discomfort. Oh god, her mother. She'd called, she'd hijacked. She'd thrown a heap of guilt over Adaline's head and had a tantrum when the conversation hadn't gone her way. Her shrill screams had reached down to the marrow of Adaline's bones. Then Adaline had been sick …

She rubbed her eyes and frowned. Her gaze dropped from the ceiling to the far wall, and something niggled in the far corner of her mind. Something wasn't right. Something was different. She wasn't on her top bunk for starters.

Ignoring the bursts of pain that shot through her mid-section, Adaline pushed herself up on the mattress.

She wasn't even in her room. And there were feet at the end of the double bed. Feet connected to long, hairy legs. Adaline's pulse skipped. She turned quickly, and realised with a start that she was sharing a room – and a mattress – with her tour manager.

Jack wasn't wearing a shirt. Even in sleep, his back and shoulders looked strong, and they were made all the more alluring by the colour on his left shoulder blade. The silhouettes of five red bats, wings outstretched, facing each other in a circle. He had stripped down to his boxer shorts and slept with his knees bent.

There was a bobby pin on what had come to be her pillow. Jack's phone was on the bedside table and none of this was making any sense. She still wore the now grimy clothes she'd worn yesterday but her joggers were by the door. She moved again, this time to collect her shoes – and hopefully her senses – and Jack stirred.

He lifted his head a fraction and looked over his shoulder. 'What's wrong? Are you going to be sick again?'

'What? No!' Adaline stood and turned. 'What the hell is going on?'

Jack pushed himself up further. 'You were sick and you didn't have a key on you. I brought you back here so you could sleep it off.'

'The owners would've had a spare key!'

Jack swung his feet to the floor and rubbed his eyes. His back to her, he shrugged. 'I didn't think of that.'

'Oh my god.' Adaline pushed her palm against her cheek and turned on the spot. 'Oh my god, I spent the night here. The girls are going to be wondering where the hell I am. When they find out they're going to think we slept together. They're going to tell people.'

They're going to tell Rory.

Abruptly, the nausea returned. Adaline clutched her stomach and doubled over.

Jack rounded the bed to stand at her side. He touched her back lightly, as if meaning to support her. 'Do you need the bathroom?'

Adaline considered this, then shook her head. Very slowly, she straightened. When she turned, Jack wasn't there. A soft click behind her told her where he'd gone. The shower fan whirred to life – it was connected to the light switch just like in her room. She blinked hard then shuffled over to the bedside table. She touched the home key of Jack's phone and the screen lit up. It was still early, just on six. No one would be up. If she could just get back into her room, maybe no one would know.

She heard the toilet flush and turned. When Jack stepped out of the bathroom looking more awake than he had a moment ago, she hesitated. She hadn't handled this well. Never mind that all she wanted to do was run back to her room, she owed him her gratitude and an apology. He'd probably hated bringing her back here to one of the few places he got some privacy. He'd let her into his space, his bed, and she'd yelled at him for it.

'I'm sorry for shouting at you,' she said. He glanced at her, crossed the room and tugged a shirt free from the large backpack leaning against the wall. She watched him pull it on. The curtains fell on his toned chest and stomach, and the bats returned to the dark. 'I'm … I was disorientated.' She gestured vaguely at the bed. 'Earlier.'

'It was lucky that I found you,' he said. He lifted his pants from the floor and stepped into them. 'Lucky also that your mother kept calling – I followed my ring tone and found you half in a garden in the dark.'

Adaline flinched.

'I'm guessing you drank the water.'

'The water?'

'The tap water. I warned everyone each time the coach stopped.'

Adaline remembered re-using her plastic bottle from yesterday, re-filling it at the chateau, then again at the rest stops on the way. She'd become thirstier throughout the day and increasingly fatigued and queasy. She'd blamed the hours on the road, the stresses back home – everything but failing to listen to simple directions. She nodded.

Jack stepped around her to get his phone. He checked the screen then pocketed it. 'You'll be thirsty. You're probably a little dehydrated, which is ironic, I know. Grab some of the bottles from the dining hall on your way back to your room.'

'Thank you.' She almost choked on the words considering how much trouble this had likely caused, but they needed to be said. 'For not leaving me and … and for bringing me here.'

Jack shrugged. 'Sure. You snore, but —' He laughed when she moved to swat him. 'Hey!'

'I do not snore!'

She was struck by the curious sensation of something new, but Jack spoke again before she could interpret it.

'Do I want to know how things went with your mum?'

Adaline pushed her hair back from her face. 'I told her to stop calling you.'

He shrugged his mouth. 'Was that before or after the eleven missed calls?'

Adaline's lips parted. 'You're not serious.' But she knew he was. Telling her mum to stop calling had been pointless; Georgia did what she wanted and when, she always had. She didn't care who she inconvenienced, who she hurt or stepped on to reach what comforted or pleased her. In Adaline's absence, Georgia had convinced herself she couldn't be happy without her, that her daughter calmed her down and made the world a little easier to bear. It was a role Adaline didn't deserve; at home she'd been the voice of reason, but Georgia had only listened when it suited her. Adaline was mostly the pill fetcher and verbal punching bag.

'I'm sorry about that,' she said. 'I may have made it worse. Can you block numbers on your phone?'

Jack opened the bedside table drawer and removed a silver-faced watch with a brown leather strap. He fastened it around his wrist as he considered his answer. 'I can. Are you sure that's what you want me to do?'

Adaline nodded. 'I'll call her on my phone if I need to. You have her number if for any reason you need to contact her.' She paused, found her resolve and continued. 'She has no reason to be contacting me. Block her.'

It was a sharp twist, the betrayal. It started low in her stomach then moved higher, behind her ribcage. For all her flaws and manipulations, Georgia was her mother and Adaline was turning from her. Perhaps she *was* becoming more like her father. Perhaps Georgia was forcing her to be.

Something appeared to have occurred to Jack – he'd become very still. He half turned to her, turned away then turned back. 'I should have asked ... do you want to go running? There's time if we keep it under half an hour.' Adaline's hesitation must have appeared clear on her face, because he hastened to add, 'I can meet you down the road.'

'No, it's — I'm still a bit sensitive.' Her hand fluttered over her stomach then dropped to her side. 'I think I'll sit out on anything too strenuous today.'

His expression cleared and he nodded.

She was halfway to the door when she realised what had felt new. It had been the first time she'd made Jack laugh. She turned back, intending to remark on it, but the words toppled from her mind when she almost collided with his chest. She stumbled back, surprised.

'Sorry,' he said, his hands coming up to steady her. They lingered on her elbows then dropped away. Adaline's heart tripped into a jog. He said, 'I was just walking you to the door.'

The warmth of his body stroked against her skin. She thought of the distance between them, then glanced at the bed and wondered if there had been less. Had she curled into him in the night? Had his arms come around her? Had the mouth so near to her now hovered over her own in the dark, or grazed the curve of her neck? As far as she knew, she'd slept soundly, but she couldn't account for what she might have done unconsciously. Had she even been aware of Jack beside her, dressed in nothing more than boxer shorts? How aware of her had he been? As aware as he was now?

Jack followed her gaze to the bed, then turned back to search her face. 'Adaline —'

'Thank you again,' she interrupted. She had the wild notion that she didn't want him to finish that sentence. 'For what you did. For helping me. If anyone finds out, I hope you don't get in trouble.' As much as she hoped both of them didn't get a reputation.

He moved a fraction closer and tried again. 'It was a pleasant surprise, if that makes any sense.' He touched the back of one of her hands. 'I'm glad it was you.'

'That ...'

He laughed. He stepped away and scrubbed his face with his hands. 'Sounds ridiculous, I know.'

She covered the skin he'd touched with her other hand. 'Jack, I'm not ...' She floundered.

But she seemed to have said enough. Jack's eyes lit up with sudden confidence. 'Looking for anything serious, I know. I can see that about you. You don't want to be tied down or paired up. You want to do what you want when you want to – I'm the same.'

Adaline pushed harder against her skin, dragging it beneath her palm. 'I'm not sure what you're saying.' Although she thought she was. She was quite sure Jack was hedging to be friends with benefits, that he was offering a low-maintenance holiday fling that would end without the drama she was – to Jack, at least – so transparently avoiding. An altogether different kind of exercise to the one they already shared.

She'd thought about it. It had been impossible not to when he'd been striding ahead of her, sweat making his skin shine and the run making his muscles bunch. She'd followed his shoulders as much as she'd followed the path, and he'd crept into her thoughts on the odd occasion wearing about as much as she'd seen this morning, but they'd just been thoughts. Thoughts that had had to make room for other thoughts – ones about Rory. Those were more insistent, more daring – those thoughts were almost plans.

'I'm saying,' Jack said, glancing at her hands as if he would take them were she not holding herself, 'that there's something between us and it could be more. More, but not too much.'

Adaline released her hands to make air quotes. 'So I'd be "special" but not "important".' She straightened all her fingers, a double stop which halted his wide-eyed approach. She ducked to grab her shoes from by the door, then wrenched the door open without waiting to put them on. On the threshold she turned. With a markedly different tone, she said, 'I'm not mad. I'll probably be flattered in a few hours, but right now it all sounds a bit cheap.'

The small stones bit at her feet as she hurried down the path between the cabins. She didn't look back and she didn't pause to put on her joggers until she was out of Jack's sight. There were no lights on in the windows of the cabins around her, and someone's snores were carrying through an open window to her left. There was a good chance no one had seen her speaking with him, or fleeing so dramatically from his side, and if she was clever enough, there might be a way to get back into her room without needing to explain herself too much.

She couldn't make sense of what she'd said to Jack. The indignation hadn't felt real and she'd taken no insult from his offer. There'd been only panic. Instead of saying no, she'd feigned hurt feelings. That would come back to bite her later, because it meant the conversation probably wasn't over. He'd want to apologise at the very least, which would be awkward as hell.

She hurried through the breaking dawn.

When she reached her door, she knocked softly. She made no attempt to improve her appearance, but she began to labour her breathing. When Lisa opened the door in her pyjamas, Adaline had worked it up to a pant. 'Hey,' she said. She wiped her brow. 'I forgot to take a key with me. Sorry.'

Lisa rubbed her eyes and stretched her face. She peered at her roommate through the fog of recent sleep. 'You were … jogging?'

Adaline nodded, her chest fast rising and falling. She stepped inside when Lisa moved aside. 'Sorry,' she said again. 'Go back to sleep, there's a few hours before breakfast. I'm going to have a shower.'

When Lisa was back in her bed, Adaline mussed up the sheets she hadn't slept on. She grabbed her towel hanging between the rails of the bunk beds and slipped quietly into the adjoining room.

She turned on the shower and the crashing water sounded like the raging static in her mind. Wide-eyed and confused, Adaline stripped out of the clothes too many people had seen her in for too long.

She thought of Jack lying on his side in bed, his back moving as he breathed through a dream; of Rory's legs on her own and his lips on her forehead. She thought of Paris and Rome and Verona and Athens. Her mother. Her father. All the things she was running from and all the things that had pursued her, and she wondered how anyone could look at her and want to be a part of that – if even for a short moment in time.

14 MESSAGE RECEIVED

For many months now, the clock in the hallway had been one of Adaline's most constant critics. Georgia moved in and out of her moods and always within varying degrees, but the watercolour clock her mother and father had bought on their honeymoon was perpetual. In ceaseless countdown.

Adaline was always running out of time. And somehow apart from it.

There was never enough of it of a morning, before she opened her door and the storm broke, or enough of it when she wanted to get away. Because her mother saw time differently. It was swollen in her mind, suffocating and aggressive. It overwhelmed her, and only Adaline could smooth the way forward.

A two hour reprieve with friends for Adaline was, for Georgia, a great stretch of time alone. She was reminding Adaline of this as she shadowed her around the house, wringing her hands in her shirt, shamelessly begging Adaline to cancel her plans.

Adaline hurried into the bathroom and slammed the door behind her. She'd broken the lock last week, sabotaged it against Georgia locking her out again and threatening all kinds of things through the door, so today she had to hold the door closed as Georgia pushed on it from the other side.

Georgia's words became wails. She slumped onto the carpet and began to cry. Desperate, wracking sobs that wormed into Adaline's stomach and made her feel sick.

Adaline pressed her back against the door and slid down to the cold tiles. Her knees against her chest, she pulled her phone from her pocket and held it, deciding. She closed her eyes and concentrated on her breathing. It took a moment to steady herself.

Georgia, on the other hand, seemed to gain momentum.

Adaline thought of the watercolour clock, of how nice it would be to not see two hours elapse on its pretty face, then sighed and opened the messages screen on her phone.

Below half a dozen exclamation marks and heart emoticons sent from her closest friend – who hadn't seen her in six weeks – Adaline undid all her hard work from the night before.

I'm so sorry, she wrote, *I know I promised I wouldn't cancel, but I can't make it. Things are really bad today. Can we reschedule?*

It felt like throwing a match on a tinder bridge.

She never received a reply.

15 KNOW WHERE YOUR TOWEL IS

It was a cloudless, warm day when the Gateway coach pulled back on the road and left Cannes in its wake. Nice was only a short drive, so Rory hadn't dressed in his usual travelling clothes. This time he was in board shorts and a T-shirt and he was thinking about the beach. The day song played first then Will's playlist carried them through to the outskirts of town.

They drove alongside the cerulean water and the glittering boats moored in the harbour, past gelato bars and restaurants overlooking the Mediterranean Sea. Rory's nose touched the window.

Rocks.

He sat back, aghast. Rocks where in Australia there would be kilometres of sand. Hotels had privatised parts of the coast for guests. There were deck chairs, umbrellas, and rolls of what looked like carpet to protect bare feet from the hot, slipping stones. People baked in the sun; some topless, others so brown Rory thought of his dad's favourite pair of leather boots. No one swam – there were signs beside each beach access point in the sea wall warning of jellyfish. Rory looked at his board shorts with disappointment.

Danya turned the coach away from the coast and navigated through a twisting, scenic road that climbed high over Nice. Rory kept one eye on the vista and another on Chris on the seat beside him. The guy's latest internet find was blowing his mind and he wouldn't shut up about it.

'Dude, a penis necklace. This is awesome.'

Rory lifted a brow. 'It is awesome, but one would wear that.'

They both leaned over the screen of Chris's phone. An international jewellery company was proudly displaying a gallery of the piece on its homepage. In one image, the diamond clad rhodium plated necklace was in profile. Clear as day, the shaft of a penis lay over a set of shiny balls.

'Erectable?' Rory asked, reading the description. 'What the hell does —'

Chris flipped to the second image and Rory forgot how to speak. The shaft was now, as promised, erect. The last image in the gallery was of it hanging around the neck of a model who's face – probably at her request –

was cropped out of the shot. The tiny genitals rest between the swell of her breasts.

'*She'd* wear it!' Chris said, triumphant.

'She's modelling it, she's not someone on the street!' Rory read the price. 'Two hundred and eleven bucks – they're taking the piss!'

He sat back and waited. And waited.

'See what I did there?' he prompted.

Chris blinked. Then he laughed – explosively. He clapped Rory hard on the chest then swivelled in his seat to share his absurd find with the others. Rory listened with half an ear, smiling to himself. Chris repeated Rory's joke – once, twice. People loved it.

It was the first time Rory was pleased to be on the opposite end of the bus to Ada. He was sure word of this would travel to her soon enough, gossip was like air in this group, but maybe it would get there when he wasn't with her. Preferably when he wasn't. Ada was many things and there was a lot he didn't know about her, but Rory was certain that penis humour wasn't a big part of her life. She wasn't a prude, she could have a laugh with Pies which meant she could bring her sense of humour down to the lowest of levels, but she was a lady, too. He liked that about her.

The coach eased to a stop in a carpark big enough to accommodate half a dozen more coaches. The French perfumery that Gateway had a partnership with was world renowned, and there were a lot of girls on board who were desperate to part with their cash today. All around him, the guys looked interested only in so much as they would get to stretch their legs. None of the Australians had girlfriends and they weren't the type to think of their mums. This was a wasted stop for all of them.

Rory looked towards the front of the coach. Ada was standing, waiting her turn to disembark. She looked elegant with her hair up in overlapping braids, but still a little tired. She'd explained she'd been sick when he'd found her at breakfast, and privately, he regretted the lost opportunity. Cannes hadn't been so great that it trumped an evening alone with Adaline, however wretched she'd felt. If he'd known, he'd have stayed.

Chris rose from his seat and stepped into the aisle. Rory followed him and the pair were down the middle stairs and out in the sun before Ada had made it to the front. Rory stepped away from the others, intending to wait for her. Whatever she said about the perfumery, or whatever she said about anything else, would be infinitely more interesting than the guys' complaints.

Ada appeared in the coach doorway and stepped down onto the bitumen. Before she could look around, Jack, who was standing by the door, motioned her aside. Rory slowed his approach. Within hearing distance, he paused.

'How're you feeling now?' Jack asked.

She lifted a bare shoulder then dropped it. 'Mostly better. I'm drinking water like it's going to expire, though.'

'Good. You're probably still a little dehydrated. Keep out of the sun as much as you can at the next stop, it's going to be pretty warm.' Then he lifted her hand and placed something small in the middle of her palm. A pill? Rory wasn't close enough to see. Ada glanced down at it and quickly shoved it in the pocket of her pants. When she looked up, Rory was surprised to see that her expression had hardened. She hadn't liked the exchange.

'I want to apologise,' Jack began, but he got no further than that.

Ada held her hand up. She shook her head then backed away. Jack made to reach for her, but seemed to think better of it.

'Adaline —'

'It's forgotten. Really. This was the only thing?' She pointed to her hip, to her pocket where the small item had disappeared.

Jack nodded, then Ada nodded, then the curious conversation was over. She turned away and strode towards the others, who by now were a good distance across the carpark. Rory glanced at Jack's profile, then hurried after her.

It was an effort not to close the distance between them too quickly. When he was finally just behind her, he called her name and she slowed to wait.

'How're you feeling?' he asked.

She shrugged casually, but he could see her working to clear her expression. 'Better,' she said, 'but I need to get some more water in me. Bottled,' she added. 'My tap days are over.'

'What was Jack apologising for?'

'You heard that?' Ada looked over her shoulder. 'Nothing. A misunderstanding.' She looked up at him and smiled. 'Had you heard of Fragonard before we got here?'

Rory hesitated, wanting to persevere with his questions, but they were almost caught up with the others now. She would be acutely aware of their audience, so he gave in to the subject change. 'No. But if they're as big a deal as Jack let on, then I'm going to be a hero when I take some home for my mum.'

Ada's smile was wide and genuine. 'You would be a hero. What about your sister?'

'Junk?' He couldn't imagine her wearing perfume – wasn't she years too young for that? Wasn't this the kind of thing she'd turn her nose up at? But then again, she had a dressing table in her room cluttered with all sorts of pots and bottles … 'You think?'

Adaline hooked her fingers around his elbow and bumped lightly against his side. 'I do think. But it would be very different to the kind your mum would like. I'll show you.'

An hour later, Rory had a headache. He'd smelled countless concoctions and long ago given up trying to recognise the subtle differences between each. He hadn't had the nose for it, apparently. In the end he'd relied on Adaline;

she'd picked the two little gold bottles that were now wrapped and paid for. He'd need her to remind him who got what before the end of the trip. Permanent marker on the bottom, he was thinking. Just a letter or something so he didn't make Junk smell like some kind of bouquet and his mum smell like she'd rubbed a sugar cube against her neck. The whole experience had been a bit frilly for his taste, but he was looking forward to handing them over and seeing the looks on their faces.

Danya dropped everyone off at the sea wall a short time later. They had two hours to explore but with a sea full of stingers, Rory was at a loss about how to pass the time. He knew very little about Nice, and even less about what he should see in the small window of time he'd been given. As he disembarked, his feet turned almost instinctively in Ada's direction, but two steps towards her a heavy arm dropped on his shoulder and swung him a different way.

'Time to play with the boys,' Pies said. He squeezed. 'Leave her wanting more, my friend. Trust me.'

Why Rory would trust the advice of an overbearing, lewd lad, Rory couldn't guess. What Pies couldn't guess was that his intervention was terribly timed. Ada had instigated almost all of the contact today. She'd reached for him to guide him through aisles, touched his arm when she'd laughed, even ruffled his hair once. She hadn't cringed away from the loose plans he'd suggested as she often had before. In fact, she'd almost made a plan herself. That would have been a first since meeting her. Adaline seemed so reluctant to commit to anything, even something as minor as reminding him to do something.

Something felt different between them. There was a kind of momentum. A greater degree of affection, yes, but there was something else. It was like she was coming to terms with a decision. In all likeliness, a decision about him. He wanted to be there when she made up her mind, not under the baking sun with a group of sweaty guys who were asking locals to point them towards the nearest pub.

Rory shrugged free of Pies's arm and turned back towards the coach, but she was gone. As were all the people she spent the majority of her time with. The crowd of people moving about the mouth of the shopping strip had absorbed her.

'Give her time to miss you,' Pies said, standing at his back. 'It's two hours. You'll both survive it.'

Yes, Rory thought, but a lot could happen in two hours and he'd liked where her mind had been heading. Would he still like it when he saw her again?

* * *

Everyone was wearing their swimming clothes and they were all on the hunt for some cheap beach towels. The clap-clap of flip-flops on the pavement was the sound of summer and the gelato dripping on her hand was sweet and refreshing. Adaline concentrated on the burn of the sun. She thought of Greece. Of the white-washed buildings and the coloured doors. The jewel water and all the things she would do and see. Those islands felt like a mirage sometimes, but places like Nice were a step closer to them.

At her side, Lisa was quiet at last. The blonde Swede had been peppering Adaline with questions about Rory since breakfast and the constant assault on Adaline's private thoughts had been exhausting. For a while, Adaline had suspected that Lisa had guessed more than she'd first let on; that Adaline had not been jogging at all, but rather returning from an overnight stay, perhaps with the boy people had paired her up with in their minds. Then Adaline had wondered if Lisa had come to suspect Jack, because it just hadn't made sense that Adaline would sneak off for a rendezvous with someone sharing a room with three others. But now Adaline was convinced that Lisa suspected neither of these things, she was just living vicariously through Adaline's blossoming romance.

Which wasn't welcome either.

Adaline was oddly proprietary about her Sydney friend. She kept the things they talked about to herself, as if they were secrets shared not just things said in passing or easy conversations. Sharing these exchanges felt like distilling their connection, which she knew was ridiculous. Whatever it was that they had between them wasn't lessened the more people knew about it, but it was extraordinary to be singled-out by such a larger-than-life personality. Rory had the whole tour group eating out of the palm of his hand yet he preferred her. Adaline didn't want that to go away. Talking too much about him might do that. She liked that there were things exclusive to them; the mushroom in her shirt pocket, the short-sheeted beds…

Adaline frowned, remembering Rory's hasty departure from the chateau foyer the following morning. She increased her pace and came level with Claire and Jenny. If there was anyone on tour with a better finger on the pulse than Claire, Adaline had yet to meet them.

'Hey, did that guy ever find his passport? What's he going to do when we cross the border?' They'd be in Monaco tonight and Italy tomorrow.

Claire and Jenny moved apart to allow Adaline to walk between them.

'Anthony?' Claire checked. 'He's just taken off to an embassy to get an emergency passport. Has to catch a train there or something, he might have to stay the night depending on how fast the process is.' She'd styled her short black bob to one side, which gave her a chic punk-rocker look that Adaline could never hope to emulate. On her other side, Jenny had scraped her red streaked hair into a careless knot. She didn't tend to try too hard before the evening.

They walked beneath the shadow of an awning and Jenny lingered at a window display. Adaline and Claire paused to wait for her. They finished their gelatos in silence.

'Does he like gambling?' Adaline asked. She bunched up the paper napkin and lobbed it into the nearby bin. Claire looked puzzled, so she explained. 'I'm just wondering if he'll be disappointed to miss Monte Carlo.' These were not the questions Adaline wanted to be asking but she was coming at it from the side, disguising what she really wanted to know.

Claire's expression cleared. 'Right. I dunno. I don't know him enough to say.' She shrugged. 'He might make it, though. Worst case scenario apparently, he meets us at Venice.'

Adaline nodded. 'Do they know who was in his room?'

Claire stepped closer to the shop window, her attention captured by a small bauble that reflected the sun. 'Nah, his room was unlocked. It could've been anyone.'

'That's a scary thought,' Adaline murmured.

Jenny looked up. 'You know, we left our door open that night.'

'We haven't since!' Claire returned. 'Lucky Rach was in the room most of the night.' She hesitated. 'You know, sort of lucky. Poor Rach.'

Adaline and Jenny agreed and the three kept walking.

Up ahead, Maree, Will, Rachael and Holly had found some beach towels out the front of a tourist shop. Rachael was pawing through the pile with one hand and speaking on the phone. Holly, at her side, looked displeased. Adaline needed no further clue who was on the other end of that phone call. Poor Rachael indeed.

The beach towels were the kind of quality one would expect for ten Euro, but no one minded. Like Adaline, they'd not bothered to pack one. It took up valuable packing space and they hadn't thought they'd need it before Greece.

Adaline moved slowly past the gaudy trinkets. She reached the counter at the same time as Holly. Adaline smiled at her. 'We could hitchhike from here.' She held up her towel. 'Now that we've got the most important thing.' She waited for Holly to understand, but the girl didn't seem to be listening. 'No?' Adaline shrugged and dropped her purchase on the counter.

The saleswoman who reached for it wore so much artificial tan that her pretty green hat made her look like a carrot. She obviously didn't prefer the sun on her doorstep. Adaline tried hard not to stare.

At her side, Holly wasn't concentrating enough to notice. 'The nerve,' she spat.

Adaline raised an eyebrow and glanced over at her.

'He calls and calls. He upsets her. He calls again.' Holly dropped her towel on the counter so hard that were it not material, it might have broken. Her fierce mood was ill-fitting on her tiny frame. 'I swear, it's like he thinks it's a wasted conversation if he doesn't make her cry!'

Maybe it was the pitch of Holly's voice or maybe it was the venom behind the words, but Adaline's mother came to mind. Adaline's stomach contracted unpleasantly. This hostility wasn't welcome, and even though it was only a loyal friend airing her frustration, Adaline's body attempted to reject it. She felt herself close down, close off. Her shoulders came forward and her chin dropped. She handed over a crumpled note, pulled her towel against her chest and stepped away.

'Just think of the phone bill he'll have,' she said. She hoped her voice hadn't betrayed her discomfort. Adaline was not a shoulder to cry on. She was not a sounding board. A bitch buddy. Not here, not on her time. The world and all its issues could find someone else's arms to burden – Adaline's were still throbbing from all the things she'd carried lately.

Adaline stood alone in the sunshine until the others joined her. She walked beside Will, who rarely seemed troubled, and kept a careful distance from Rachael and Holly. She didn't engage Maree much either, whose mood buoyed and soured without apparent cause. At the moment she was jubilant because Will had bought her a pretty yellow glass bottle of perfume, but who could say how she'd feel in a few minutes.

Adaline missed Rory. Absurd, because she'd been with him less than an hour ago, but he was so dependably optimistic and good-natured. He didn't drag her into the mire of his problems. Granted, the growing need between them was concerning. If she was being honest with herself, she craved him. And his cravings for her were both flattering and wanted. The challenge was keeping them at this level.

But surely a catalyst was coming? Maybe Jack would be it. Any more stunts like at the perfumery and people would put the pieces together. She pushed her fingers into the pocket of her shorts and touched the small prongs of her bobby pin. Jack had found it on the pillow she'd slept on and returned it at the first opportunity, god knew why. She was grateful she hadn't had company at the time. What would people think, seeing him offer her such a thing? It hinted at an intimacy they didn't share.

She wouldn't have heard the end of it with Rory. It might have ruined everything.

A halting, rational voice in the back of her mind reminded her that 'everything' encompassed a two week period of her life. Almost seven of those fourteen days were behind her, and the seven days ahead would still be wonderful, with or without her new friend at her side. They'd be markedly quieter and a little lonely – Rory made a lot of noise and took up a lot of space – but they'd still awe. What was a holiday romance compared to Venice, Rome and Athens?

She'd travelled this far for the Bridge of Sighs, the Colosseum and the Mykonos windmills, not for shy smiles and almost kisses. Surely Rory could say the same? What did it matter how they felt about each other – it was fleeting at best compared to the ancient stones of a Roman civilisation. In just over a week they'd board different airplanes and resume their different paths. In years to come they'd remember the warm Mediterranean wind and their first glimpse of the floating city, not the girl with the intimacy issues and the boy with all the punchlines.

Right?

Beside her, Will was wearing his new towel like a cape. He was telling the others a story of a necklace he'd heard about and the absurdity of it was making his voice shake with laughter. Adaline smiled when he looked at her for a response, and her justifications crumbled around her.

She would remember this moment. She'd remember the sun and the sights, but she'd also remember Holly's rage and Will's amusement. The curious tattoo on Jack's shoulder blade and dancing with Rory's underwear around her neck. Maybe those memories would be sharper than those of places. Maybe it all came down to connection and impression.

It was quite possible that the Beaujolais wine region would remain a fond memory more because of the short-sheeting incident and the head in the jar than the glorious views and good wine. Paris was in and of itself wonderful, but she'd shared almost every highlight with someone. There had only been a few occasions when she'd been alone. It was these people who were underlining her experiences on this trip; the things they said, the ways in which they involved her.

Adaline followed the others down the sea wall stairs to the beach. The crystalline water tumbled upon the stone shore with a clack and clatter, so unlike the thick thud of surf and sand back home.

They unpacked their things and settled in the best they could. In the private area to their right, men and women reclined in low seats, protected from such discomfort. Curiously, no one was in the water. Rachael and Will debated the reason for this as Adaline pushed the heel of her hand against her towel, flattening the stones beneath.

These people, she thought, were making all the difference to her experiences. Particularly her favourite person. He was piling highlights upon highlights and although nothing overtly physical had happened between them since the chateau, they were building towards another altogether different kind of highlight. It seemed inevitable. They might have already got there had she not been sick in Cannes.

Did it matter that there was no future? She would miss him either way, with or without the intimacy they were dancing around.

She imagined walking up to him at the coach and throwing her arms around his neck. Thinking of how enthusiastically he'd respond made Adaline's stomach swoop and clench.

It would change a few things. It might mean some expectations, perhaps a certain degree of obligation … could she handle that without going into a tailspin? She'd almost lost it in the shop with Holly and that hadn't even had anything to do with her.

Adaline closed her eyes and concentrated on her breathing. Rory wasn't about to start making demands like her mother. The things he would want from her would feel good, they would be nothing like the things she was needed for at home.

Funnily enough, the same could be said about Jack. He wanted intimacy and familiarity as well.

Adaline opened her eyes. Something needed to be done about both of them.

A group decision had been made whilst she'd been lost in her thoughts. Everyone was on their feet and moving towards the water. Evidently they were all too sweaty to care about the lack of swimmers, and too hot and bothered to wait for Adaline to pull herself together. Will and Rachael were first in, splashing and shouting with relief. The others crashed in seconds later.

Thinking about how to best handle the Jack situation, Adaline hobbled down to the shore. The possibilities were so tangled that she only had eyes for the spot where she would next step.

A clear, gelatine mound made her pause.

Then everyone started screaming.

16 EBB AND FLOW

Adaline screamed. The water closed around her and tossed her like a ball, then the tide retrieved her like a well-trained dog. She angled her mouth towards the cloudless sky, dragged in a desperate breath, then went under again. She wanted to laugh. Scream again. Throw her arms out and let the world have her.

If she filled her lungs and stretched out like a starfish, would the water carry her to the North Atlantic? Would she get there sooner than waiting until next month, for her scheduled, much-anticipated flights? The shark out there couldn't be any worse than the shark waiting for her on the beach.

Adaline righted herself, pushed the water out of her eyes and looked back towards the shore. The shell grit sand had a soft shine under the late autumn sun. It was too cold to be swimming – she was shivering and her jaw ached – but this was nothing to the frost rolling off the lone figure on the beach. Georgia lay on a reclining chair, enormous round sunglasses covering half her face. She could be someone's muse, posed liked that, her pale skin contrasting with her tangerine cable-knit wrap and the vibrant green samphire flats at her back. She was beautiful. Sometimes in the way princesses were, or flowers or vistas. Other times, like today, she was the kind of beautiful that could break a heart.

This was the third day of silence. This beach trip had been a shameless attempt to worm her way back into her mother's graces. She'd hoped the salt winds would scrub away the hurt, but Georgia had bundled herself up, closed herself off, and shut Adaline out.

The way things were going, the pair of them wouldn't speak again until late July, when Adaline was back from the trip Georgia had taken such offense to.

Adaline turned her back and looked out to sea.

Her resolve was strong today. It had wavered yesterday during one of the worst of Georgia's meltdowns, but she'd held out long enough to feel strong again. She needed to be smart about this – play this out carefully. It was still weeks until Adaline would claim some time to herself. Adaline needed a strategy, a long game.

She swam until her bones rattled, then staggered ashore. Her violent shivering was ignored. Adaline could have been a gust of wind for all the attention Georgia afforded her. She grabbed one of the towels, pulled it around herself and dropped into a small ball, making herself a smaller target for the wind. When her towel was soaked through, Adaline shot her hand out for the other one, dry and neatly folded nearby. Her fingers closed around sand.

She lifted her head to look. It wasn't there.

Adaline turned. Georgia had shifted in her seat. Her back was angled strangely, her profile somehow haughty even when still. Between the orange wrap and the white fabric of the chair was a small triangle of blue, just like the blue around Adaline's shoulders.

Adaline didn't say anything. It wasn't worth it.

17 BESTIES

The next leg of the journey was another short drive, and they were back on the coach before Adaline felt she'd given her all to Nice. She'd been a lazy tourist, content to follow her friends from shopfronts to shore. The highlights had been a jellyfish swarm and the clumsy French exchanged between a lifeguard more interested in a sunbaker's bare breasts than Will's inflamed leg. Not something a Lonely Planet guide might have anticipated.

Already she regretted the things she hadn't seen and the opportunities she'd missed.

Gleaming white cruise ships lurched against docks which stretched like veins into the jewelled sea. Narrow roads, chateaus and palms kissed the coast. There was so much more to see than her few hours had allowed. As the stunning views rolled past her window, Adaline wondered if she'd ever return.

The chatter of the people around her was white noise. The animated exchange between the Mexican sisters seated behind her was loud enough to break into her concentration, but it was Lois, the Fort Worth doll at her side, who was the most difficult to ignore. Lois was keen to show off her latest purchases. She held up one item after the next and wouldn't put them away until Adaline had appropriately remarked upon each. It became a kind of game between the girls; Lois waiting for fresh compliments, Adaline trying to think of new ways to say the same thing. This lasted for over half an hour and made the trip drag.

Adaline welcomed Jack's interruption with more interest than most.

'Okay, people, welcome to Monaco, an independent microstate of France. It's the second smallest nation in the world – the first of course being the Holy See that you'll visit in a few days.'

Adaline thought of the Vatican and smiled. She settled deeper into her seat to listen.

'It's said that the average person can walk across the width of this glamorous principality in under an hour. You'll have plenty of time, so if anyone gives that a go I'd love to know about it.

'Monaco is not part of the EU and it has the third most expensive real estate in the world, so I suppose it's helpful that there's no income tax.'

Jack carried on for another ten minutes; he spoke about the late Grace Kelly and her prince, about the world-renowned casinos and the annual Grand Prix motor race. His facts were as dazzling as the view of the Maritime Alps. The sparkling Mediterranean lay beneath glittering boats and cruise ships, all anchored in the picturesque port. Everything was razzle-dazzle, luxurious and soaked with sun. So beautiful and extraordinary, unlike any vista Adaline had seen before.

'I've got a treat for you tonight,' Jack said in closing. 'Only two to a room.'

Lois swivelled in her seat. Her long fingernails dug into the bare flesh of Adaline's leg. 'How exciting!' She leaned close. 'You want to room together?'

Adaline's mouth fell open. She'd been longing for an end to this forced proximity now she was faced with a whole night of it. 'S-sure. Unless someone else puts my name down.'

Thankfully, Beth had.

Lois pouted prettily then wrote her name next to Lisa's. 'Maybe we can ask them to swap?'

'Maybe.' Adaline leaned back so Lois could pass the sheet across the aisle, and thought how to best intercept the Texan's plan.

'So exciting!' She bumped Adaline's shoulder and did a small chair wiggle.

Adaline smiled weakly. She shook her fists in front of her chest in a show of excitement. Lois was an extreme extrovert; boisterous and affectionate, larger than life. To Adaline, she was exhausting. She also touched when she spoke, which made Adaline feel crowded. They'd walked towards the coach with their arms linked, which Adaline hadn't instigated, and now Lois looked like she wanted to hug.

Adaline turned quickly towards the window and remarked on something in the distance. Lois gave it a passing degree of interest then began chattering about what she might wear out tonight. By the time they pulled up at the Gateway village, Adaline was convinced everything Lois owned either sparkled or plunged.

When Adaline followed Lois off the coach, she made eye contact with Jack and blinked significantly. He smiled his closed-lipped smile and made a point of asking Lois how her trip had been.

'Awesome. I got Adaline here all to myself and we talked girl things.' She waved a hand. 'You would have hated it but it was so much fun – we have the same taste in everything!'

Jack glanced at Adaline. 'Is that right?'

Adaline didn't want to be unkind, so she didn't answer. Instead, she smiled and moved to step around him. Her suitcase was on its side by Danya's feet. He was fast burying it with other bags.

Fingers around the inside of her elbow made her turn back.

'Can I speak with you for a moment?' Jack asked. His voice was low, but light.

She glanced at Lois, who had moved past them to pick her way through the bags, then nodded. They stepped away from the front steps.

'We're fine,' she said, wanting to end the conversation before Jack could start it again. 'You can stop this,' she waved her hand between them, 'this checking.'

'I'm glad to hear that,' he said. 'I'm sorry that I misread you —'

'It's fine.'

'— but that's not what this is about.' He hesitated, as if to brace them both for what was to come. 'Your mum's still calling me.'

Adaline glanced over at the group then crossed her arms over her chest. 'I thought you were going to block her.'

'Think how that would look, Adaline. She's one thought away from a formal complaint as it is.'

She was jeopardising his job, she realised. These phone calls were putting him in a no-win situation: ignore them or answer them, either way he wasn't giving Georgia Sharp what she wanted. And with Adaline refusing to take the heat, he was stuck.

She shrugged, feeling sullen and resentful. 'No points to Gateway for giving her your number.'

Jack pushed his thumb and forefinger against the bridge of his nose. He looked tired. 'It's a work number and she feigned an emergency.'

Rather than withdrawing like she'd done before, Adaline leaned in. She pushed her open hand against her chest. 'I have a right to not be in contact with whoever I choose. I know what an "emergency" is for my mother and it's not something I'm willing to turn on my phone for.' She eased back and lowered her voice. It was a struggle to get her temper in check. 'I'm sorry you're in the middle.'

'Just not sorry enough.' Jack's temper was rising, perhaps surpassing her own. He didn't look tired anymore, he looked angry. His eyes were narrowed and his shoulders were back. He'd wanted this to go a different way. He'd probably planned this conversation and imagined himself free of the drama by the end of it.

'No.' Adaline's voice dropped to just above a whisper. 'Not sorry enough.' She swallowed. All the people filing off the coach were no doubt watching the spectacle they were making of themselves, but right now they felt a world away. 'You think you'd give anything for this woman to stop, to leave you alone.' She touched her chest again. 'I did. I gave almost everything I had – thousands of dollars – for just two weeks of peace. So I'm not nearly sorry enough and nothing you can say will make me be.'

The hard lines of Jack's expression smoothed and the combat went out of his posture. He straightened and touched his face again. 'Fine. Christ, fine.'

Suddenly too exhausted to acknowledge this, Adaline turned away.

Again he took her arm. 'That's not all I wanted to say.'

For the briefest moment, she wondered if he'd make another pass at her, but that thought was just an echo of something that would never happen again. That offer seemed like a lifetime ago now that he finally saw the warning sign dangling from her neck. She arched a brow in question.

'Tomorrow morning,' he said, careful to not be overhead, 'I'll be running across the country. Border to border.'

Interest caught, Adaline waited.

'It'll take just over an hour. I'll be leaving at five-thirty from the front gate.' The corner of his mouth turned up. 'If you're there, you're there.'

18 BLUFF

The Monte Carlo Casino was like a dream. Everything was bright with lights or polish, the fabrics were bold and expensive. All around them bets were placed and stakes were raised. Adaline could feel the highs and lows of ebbing fortunes. She sat with the others in a cocktail lounge which boasted furnishings more expensive than what her holiday had cost, and drank slowly from a champagne flute accented with lines of coloured glass. From her seat she could see half a dozen high rollers and hear the click of chips and the snap of cards.

She wasn't a gambler. This environment was alien to her, but she could still appreciate the grandeur. It was a world renowned destination, a mecca for the rich and famous. It made the modest casino in Adelaide seem like a run-down TAB. The French champagne was perfect, it tasted unlike any sparkling Adaline had tried before. She knew as the mouthful of silk flooded her palette that she would never taste its equal again, for it was absurdly expensive. Or so said the men who had paid for two bottles of it. They were determined to charm Claire and Holly, and it seemed only the best would do.

Holly was blushing furiously. Her hair hung between her and the blond man seated to her right, a curtain between his advances. She mumbled and stammered over a lemonade she'd bought herself, Claire's complete opposite, who was responding to the flattery with coy smiles and trilling laughter. As Adaline watched, Claire touched the flute to her lips, drank, then moved the man's gaze to her throat with one trailing finger as she returned the glass to her lap. It was artful. The boy that she liked back home seemed far from her mind. Seated on her other side, Jenny was taking full advantage of the spoils. She topped off her glass and began drinking from it even before she'd settled back in her seat.

They all should have been speaking about the theatre, or fine wine, or whatever it was people spoke about when they were wearing their finest things and guests in a place such as this. Instead, they were all behaving in a manner better suited for a shopping centre food court.

Will was sitting with Rory, and the Canadians Chris and Hamish. It was the closest Adaline and Rory had been to one another since the perfumery. The boys were laughing too loud and knocking their glasses together too hard. Maree, who was sitting closest to Adaline, was arrowing peevish looks at them across the long oblong table and being incredibly difficult to speak to. As was Lisa, who seemed to be avoiding Adaline at the moment. Adaline didn't feel she'd done anything to upset the Swede, but even if she had, she wasn't in the mood to reassure or apologise tonight. She wasn't much in the mood to even be here.

It was glorious and humbling, and she'd never forget the lavish, almost surreal things she'd seen tonight, but she was tired and run down. Lois had talked at her the whole time they'd been in the shared bathrooms. There'd been no escaping her, not even on the coach into town.

This madness could not continue.

Even now, Lois was sitting on the couch beside Adaline, her hip touching Adaline's hip. She was holding court with Daniel and wearing a dress Adaline would have worn as a shirt. The blush pink halter flirted high on her bronzed legs and had drawn almost every eye in the room. Daniel had the best seat in the house and knew it. He was not, however, putting his best foot forward. Right now he was trying to convince Lois that violence didn't always deserve a negative association. War, in his opinion, could be rejuvenating for a country and its people.

Lois glanced back at Adaline, who looked away.

Daniel's words were running together, a mix of passion and liquor. He was gesticulating wildly and leaning far forward in his seat. Lois's back pressed against Adaline's arm.

On the other side of Maree, Rachael was curled around her phone. Her fingers flew over the keypad, paused, then flew again. She didn't seem to be aware that Holly was desperate to be saved, or that Jenny had pinched her champagne from the table between them and drank it.

Beth was off to the side of all of it, her back turned to the group. She was speaking softly into her phone to her sweetheart back home. Daniel was somebody else's problem for the moment, she was off-duty.

Nothing about this group was elegant.

Adaline's eyes met Rory's. She smiled automatically. His returning smile was wider and this brief connection made her wish it were just the two of them here, enjoying a quiet drink and a rich conversation. If not here then at the village, if not at the village, somewhere back home where she felt safe.

Rory's smile softened. He put his glass down. Just as he began to extract himself from his little group, a number of things happened at once.

Lois asked Daniel to speak to someone else. He called her ignorant and swiped a hand between them. A move of dismissal, a sign of aggression – it was hard to tell, because it was interrupted. His hand hit Lois's champagne glass and it flew from her hand. What remained in the glass flew over her shoulder and splashed against Adaline's chin and neck.

'Oh!' she cried.

Everyone stopped talking and stared. Rory, who has half up from his seat, changed direction. He went to Daniel and stood over him until Daniel got unsteadily to his feet.

'Riding to the rescue?' Daniel asked, his tone dripping with disrespect.

'Step back,' Rory demanded.

'It's just champagne,' Adaline said quickly. She squeezed her wet hair and stood.

Chris and Hamish were on their feet now too and Beth was hurrying back to them all, her phone forgotten in her hand.

'He's drunk and aggressive,' Rory said, his eyes not leaving Daniel's face, 'and he should step back before he hurts someone.'

Lois rose and started pressing a napkin to Adaline's collarbone. Adaline waved her away.

Beth put a hand on Daniel's chest in a gesture Adaline imagined she thought would reassure him, but he pushed her away savagely. He put two hands up in surrender and backed away.

'Outnumbered,' he said, sounding wildly amused. 'Brawn over brains, ey boys? Brawn over —' He stumbled backwards down the step that led to the bar foyer.

Again he pushed Beth's reaching hands away. She ducked her head, hesitated, then followed after him when he whirled around and stalked away. Adaline heard Beth call his name, then again, much softer with distance. Adaline felt people's eyes on her. They murmured to each other, offered reassurances to Lois, then slowly returned to their conversations or text messages. Lois turned around.

'I'm sorry, Ada.' Her fingers hovered over Adaline's cheek.

Adaline shrugged it off. 'It's fine. He didn't hurt you?'

'No.'

That one question was all Adaline could spare. She didn't want to be a part of this moment anymore, or so closely associated with someone who might soon need support. She stepped back, flashed Rory another smile, and made an excuse to leave. 'I'm going to clean up.'

As she moved past Rory she touched the side of his hand. 'Thanks for getting rid of him.'

She'd message him from a cab, she thought, when he couldn't stop her. So he wouldn't worry. She no longer wanted to be alone together, she just wanted to be alone.

'Of course,' he said. 'If —'

'I'll talk to you later.' She lifted her hand away from his, which was now seeking some part of her to hold on to. 'I have to clean up.'

'Okay.' The word was saturated with reluctance. He let her go.

She hoped he wouldn't stay there waiting for her. She hadn't made any promises to return, but he wouldn't realise that immediately.

Exhausted and agitated, Adaline walked past the bathrooms, out the front door and down to the street. Valets greeted the drivers of luxury cars. Tourists snapped photos. On the far stairs, someone's arrival had the interest of photographers.

Adaline was in a cab – and back in control – within minutes.

19 PUNCHLINE

'It comes and goes,' Jack said to Adaline's back. 'You're over it at the moment; the group, the individual personalities, the dynamics, the pace. Everyone feels that way on tour at one time or another. Shove fifty-odd people in a small space day in day out, you're going to see the best and worst of each other.'

'I've yet to see the best of Daniel,' she replied. She pushed her hair back from her forehead and her hand came away slick with sweat.

They'd jogged the length of the country and back again. Exhilaration was vibrating through Jack's body like strings on a double bass. This was a first for him. He'd struck out from the Gateway village before with the intent to reach the opposite border, but without someone at his side to challenge him he'd turned back. This had been one of the outstanding items on his bucket list and Adaline was the reason he could now cross it off.

Her temper amused him, it was like watching a small dog protecting its turf – hackles up and bark worse than its bite, but it also gratified him. It had been the key ingredient to Adaline's endurance this morning. Fired up about manners, spilled drinks and overbearing roommates, she'd kept a pace he'd struggled to match.

He'd seen this behaviour before, many times and manifested in many different ways. The tour pace was a shock to the system. Almost everyone drank more than they'd first intended to, almost everyone began to crave their own space and schedule. Even the loudest of the group grew tired and cranky after a week or so on the road.

Jack used the bottom of his shirt to dry his face. He raised his head and opened his eyes, and caught Adaline's gaze on his bare stomach. She blinked and looked away. When she looked back and he raised a brow, defensiveness burst from her like a solar flare.

'What?'

He shrugged and pulled his shirt down.

'*What?* I looked. It doesn't mean anything.' She waited, but he didn't supply the words that she could use to ladder her way off the hook. Adaline pushed her hand over her forehead again and dried it on her pants. She looked more flushed now than she had on the crest of the tallest peak they'd crossed. She arrowed a look at him that made his lips twitch. She said, 'You look at me.'

He smiled. 'Yeah, but it means something when I look at you.'

'Give me a break, not this again.'

'Okay, I'll bite.' He bent at the waist, extended a foot to the side and reached for his shoe. 'How did I get this so wrong?'

Adaline stood still, indecision clear on her face. For a moment he thought she'd leave the way she always did when conversations got heavy, but she surprised him again. She sank into a stretch beside him.

She dropped her head down and her high ponytail fell forward over her face. 'Wrong?' she said to the ground.

'Yeah. You seemed easy enough to work out. Independent, lots going on in your head. You don't want anybody to get too close but you can't help connecting with people.'

Somewhere beyond the first line of cabins a door slammed. His tour group was waking, which meant this moment was ending.

Adaline straightened, met his eyes then sank down to stretch her other leg. 'You're not wrong so far.'

Jack switched legs too. 'I figured with everything going on in your head and going on at home, you'd be up for some fun.' He straightened. 'The kind that started and ended on tour.' He held up his hands before she could restate her protests. 'You're not that kind of girl or whatever, but I'm telling you, you've paired yourself up with a problem.'

Adaline had heard the door too. He could see that half her mind was out of this conversation. She said, 'You're going to start causing me problems?'

'You haven't paired yourself up with me.'

He could imagine the part of herself that was halfway back to her cabin turn on its heel. She touched her face. Her neck. Her collarbone. 'Rory?'

'He's going to make a move. Are you going to shut him down too?'

'I … no.' She looked away. 'I don't think so.'

Jack felt his pride warble. Ego, competitiveness, it was all there, vying for real estate on his tongue. Why the young kid over the older, more worldly man? The punchline over the conversation, the lad over the leader? How was it possible that Jack hadn't come out on top in all of this? He imagined all his questions and complaints filling his mouth like spit. He swallowed. 'He's going to want more than I think you're willing to offer.'

The air around her seemed to push into her skin and fill her up. She grew larger before him. 'I don't have any problems saying no.'

This, he knew. What he didn't know was how she wasn't following this conversation. 'I'm not talking about sex, Adaline.' He dropped a pointed look at her stomach. 'But you sure do seem to have that on your mind a lot.'

The surprise on her face brought forward a smile on his, and with it a surge of pity for all the things that loomed before her. There was no doubt in his mind that Adaline would remember this trip for a lifetime, not just for the sights she saw and the things she touched and tasted, but for the heart she broke. He wondered if it would be in Italy or Greece, and out of sheer practicality, wished it would be the latter. He didn't see his groups much on the islands, so their heartache wouldn't affect him much there.

Even though Jack wanted her and he envied Rory her preference, he found a little room in himself to pity Rory, too. No one wanted to be dumped on holidays. Dumped, passed over, used. It was a bitch to get so close to a woman's heart only to realise you left your bolt cutters at home. Jack had made a similar discovery many years ago, and he was still waiting for this nomadic life to heal him.

He and Adaline parted ways and the day officially began.

On the short walk back to his cabin he was intercepted by four people. Two wanted advice on the amount of money they'd need in Venice and one wanted Jack to ban Daniel from rooming with him 'Ever. Again.' Another wanted to pleasepleaseplease use Jack's power adapter until they were back on the coach.

No one spoke to him directly in the shower block, but there was no way to avoid overhearing the adult details of Anthony's hook-up with Zoey. As always, people had taken full advantage of the double occupancy cabins.

Jack squeezed in a few minutes of paperwork between getting dressed and taking his bag to the coach. He began boasting about his cross-country run the moment Danya joined him at the staff table in the corner of the food tent, but Danya being Danya, he wasn't impressed. He wasn't even interested. Jack stopped himself sharing the one detail that would secure the man's attention and spoke to the site crew instead.

Danya didn't know Jack had made a friend this time, or that Jack had had company most mornings for over a week now. Conversely, Jack knew Danya had slept with Jenny at the chateau and would likely sleep with Rosa in Venice – for a bad-tempered man with a receding hairline and a slight paunch, he did all right for himself – and Jack knew these things with more detail than was necessary. Danya was a sensationalist gossip. Jack didn't want Adaline on Danya's radar at all.

He looked for her in the room, suddenly curious.

He was unsurprised to find her with her regular crowd, wedged between the New Zealand couple who were having problems. From where he sat, she looked like an unwilling buffer between unmet expectations and confusion. He'd be surprised if the pair of them lasted the long haul flight home, but saying that, he'd been wrong before. People were always surprising him. It was probably because they weren't being themselves on tour.

Jack saw versions of people. The parts of themselves they wanted to be or couldn't be at home. The parts of themselves they were saying goodbye to or the parts they were exploring for the first time. It made it hard to predict or understand when people were faking it, or trying a personality on. His Adelaide running partner was case in point. She was acting so unaffected and removed, but one phone call from home could reduce her to her knees. She'd convinced herself that this holiday was a reprieve from a life that she had to return to, and she'd convinced everybody else that she wasn't someone they could turn to or make plans with.

But the last part was a lie. Jack was certain that Adaline was a well of deep feeling and empathy – she was just full to the brim with her mother's issues.

Maybe she could run away like Jack had, and find her answers on the endless road. Maybe she could forget Rory – who at this very moment was watching her over his mug of coffee – forget her mother, and never go home. She was too young to carry so many burdens, and her smile was too pretty to be so infrequent.

She seemed to love the world. It would embrace her and hide her if she wanted it to.

Jack looked at his watch, drained his mug and stood. It was time to get back on the coach. With coffee still singing in his throat, he called an end to breakfast. As chairs scraped back and conversations pitched, he gathered his things and wondered what dramas might unfold in fair Verona.

20 OH, ROMEO

There were songs written about how Adaline was feeling right now. Every cliché she could imagine moved to the front of her mind and widened her smile. She was on cloud nine. She was floating. It was the best day of her life and all the breath had left her body. Within sight of where she stood on Giuseppe Mazzini, just apart from Verona's main shopping street, was Casa di Giulietta.

'This fourteenth century house,' Jack said to the group, 'is linked to Shakespeare's star-crossed lovers because of the similarity between the name of the previous owners of the house – the Cappellos – and Juliet's family, the Capulets.'

Jack was standing on the corner of a step, higher than the tour group. Behind them, other tour leaders walked through the crowds holding things above their heads for their tour groups to follow. Thousands had flocked to the famed location. Just as many had surely bumped against Adaline on their way to get there.

'It is said that travellers who rub the left breast of the bronze statue of Guilietta will be lucky in love, and hordes of tourists visit that courtyard every year. People,' Jack's voice pitched higher as he tried to reign in the group's wandering attention. 'It's illegal to leave love letters in the tunnel – there's a huge fine if you're caught doing it. Don't say I didn't warn you.'

People began to break away, walking towards the very cave he spoke of. Jack threw his voice even further. 'We'll meet back at the bus in two hours. Don't be late!'

A few people – Adaline included – checked their watches and noted the time. Jack stepped down from his makeshift pedestal and began walking towards her. He was intercepted by the three Chinese girls on their tour, and because Adaline didn't want to speak to him at the moment, she made use of the delay. She rallied her friends and as one, they moved towards the narrow cave which led to the infamous courtyard.

She didn't get far into the arched passageway before wonder slowed her steps. Illegal or not, thousands of notes were plastered to the stonework, wedged between cracked mortar or adhered with tape or chewing gum. Thousands of pieces of people's hearts, captured on scraps of paper, exquisite stationary and strips of fabric. Dante loves Clare. Erica hearts Jordan. Yumi and Amit forever. Some declarations had fallen to the cobbled stone path and been trod on, and amongst all the touching sentiments were thousands of pieces of old gum – unsightly relics of those who had defied the law to declare themselves.

Adaline moved closer to the wall and read whatever English words she could easily see. There was so much love in the world, and so much despair. Some letters spoke of pain and loss, others of secret longings and lustful thoughts. All the same, many lovers had passed through here, pilgrims to an old, tragic love story that should have ended differently.

She wondered what she would write were she to contribute to the wall. Once upon a time she might have written her name above Paul's, the sweet boy who'd been her first and only.

The steady tide of tourists bumped her along, then she was standing in the sunlight again within a small courtyard surrounded by high buildings and locked gates. Secured to the ironwork were hundreds of padlocks in every brilliant colour of the rainbow. Vendors were selling them, Adaline realised, a legal, profitable way for lovers to avow themselves within sight of the balcony that had witnessed fated love. Except that the balcony was so high, too high for anyone to scale. A twentieth century addition to a fourteenth century building. A space barely wide enough to contain a single, lovelorn woman, let alone a couple, however closely they clutched one another.

Adaline watched tourists step out onto the balcony and gaze down at the courtyard full of people below, one after another in an endless procession, all posing for photos, and felt so far away from the beautiful words that had romanced her in high school. Shakespeare had not been here. This had not been the place he had seen as he'd penned the infamous scene. And yet there was magic here. There was no denying the energy of the place, nor the giddy delight of those around her. To some, Romeo and Juliet might once have been here. To some they were not the fictional manifestation of a gifted mind, and proximity was enough.

To Adaline, however, this place did not make her feel the way that she'd hoped.

Thinking a little participation would go a long way to helping her absorb the atmosphere, Adaline took her turn posing for a photo with the bronze statue of Guilietta, her left breast flat and shiny after years of attention. Adaline gave it a rub, laughed as she watched Will's exaggerated enthusiasm as he did the same, then bought a green padlock and waited for the right letters to come to mind. It might have been that her gaze happened upon Rory at that moment, or it might have been that he was already on her mind, but it was his initials that she wrote beneath hers on the plastic surface, then enclosed within a small heart.

The snap of padlocks locking around the bars sounded to Adaline's mind like certainty and promise. And the man who's initials she held in the palm of her hand offered her neither.

It suddenly seemed foolish and wrong to anchor their names to this place in such a way. Their names didn't belong together – not the way that lovers' did. They were too new, too fleeting, too … undefined.

She closed her fingers around the green padlock and shut her eyes. When she opened them again, she bought a second padlock – a purple one this time – and she drew another heart on the face of it. Within the shape, she wrote just her name. When she snapped it shut around a length of bar cluttered with locks, she claimed certainty and promise for herself.

The green padlock went into her satchel.

High laughter and excited shouts drew her attention towards the far corner of the courtyard. Rory was the centre of attention again; there was a small circle of their fellow tour mates standing around him, their smiles broad. When the conversations around her quietened, she realised with a start that he was reciting lines from the play.

'— yonder window breaks? It is the east and Juliet is the sun!' He gestured dramatically at the balcony high overhead and smiled when people clapped and cheered. 'Arise, fair sun and kill the envious moon who is already sick and pale with grief that her maid art more fair than she.'

'More!' some women cried.

'That's what I said, "more fair than she"!' They laughed. Rory kept his hand aloft and visibly scrabbled to remember more. 'It's my lady, oh, it's my love! She speaks, yet she says nothing; what of that?' His delivery was equal parts clumsy and charming. And for what he lacked in accuracy, he made up for in enthusiasm. With each recalled line his audience grew, and every word brought him closer to his monologue becoming a dialogue. Who would be his Juliet? Rosa, who stood so close? Perhaps Lisa, who watched from the wings with wide, adoring eyes? Who amongst those around him knew the lines which fast approached?

'See how she leans her cheek upon her hand.' He mimed the action, and then a tourist stepped in Adaline's line of sight and he was lost.

She moved closer, curious. She knew this play, knew how much he was botching the lines but it didn't matter, he was endearing himself to everyone who could hear him. The bard's verses were so apt for this place; they heightened the magic, even if they were spoken by a man in his teens. In fact, that made it more perfect – Romeo having being so young himself.

'Oh that I were a glove upon that hand, that I might touch her cheek!'

No one volunteered the next line, and Rory appeared to have finished. He was laughing and accepting claps on the back and arms squeezes from his delighted fans. But what if she spoke? What would happen if she dared to contribute?

'Aye, me!' she said. Her voice wobbled with nerves.

The people around her turned, all smiles, eyebrows raised. The crowd parted and space connected her with the man who was practically renovating her insides. Would he play along, or would he turn his back, end the moment and make her regret this?

Rory stared at her, his expression tethered. Then his mouth curved so slowly it seemed like a trick of time. 'She speaks.'

Their audience murmured.

'Speak again bright angel.' He stepped towards her, pure energy lighting his eyes now. 'For thou art as glorious as this night, a winged messenger of heaven.'

Her heart stuttered. It was working. Whatever this moment was and whatever it might lead to, it was working. She smiled, shy now, and had the honour of reciting the infamous line. 'Oh Romeo, Romeo! Wherefore art thou Romeo?' She knew the lines which followed, had read them countless times in school, but instinct told her not to recall them. Stopping at the question somehow heightened the drama.

Three strides away from her, Rory stopped. He looked suddenly playful. He lifted his arms, palms up, and spoke to the crowd now. 'Shall I hear more, or shall I speak at this?'

Applause startled her. People whooped and smiled, they bumped against strangers or kissed their partners, and the moment was over. Rory dropped his hands and walked to her, his expression beatific. They stared at one another for a long, loaded moment, then he pulled her into a hug and laughed against her hair.

Adaline closed her eyes and breathed in the familiar scent of him. It didn't matter that they were being jostled by tourists or that she'd just made a spectacle of herself, all that mattered was this moment of connection. She'd never experienced anything like it. It was so tender and intense that it almost toppled the carefully arranged dominoes around her heart.

Discomfort tickled, then scraped, then burned. Guilt filled the spaces between her cells, like insidious gas. She wasn't making this easy for either of them. Giving in to impulses, singling him out – she was leading him on. If she created her own catalyst through absurd displays of affection such as this then a flaky excuse wasn't going to cut it. Was she in or out?

It was unfair to compare his needs to her mother's and wrong to assume his expectations would stifle her. She knew this, but nevertheless, Adaline was afraid. This was not the escape she'd planned on, this was another kind of devastation. Bittersweet and brief, and another assault on her already battered heart. She wasn't supposed to slip out from the long shadows of her family and fall for the first boy who made her smile. That wasn't how this story was supposed to go. She was supposed to be striding through the streets with her head high and full of plans for the new life she would seize once back home. This trip was supposed to be about *future* Adaline, not *now* Adaline.

Only, now Adaline was starving. For affection, for love. For attention and kind words, worldly experiences and selfish pleasures. If now Adaline wasted away what was the point of trying to take care of future Adaline?

She drew away and smiled up at him. As she was about to speak, Jack's clumsy words came to mind; his own graceless way of summarising the very thing Adaline could offer: no strings. With the shoe on the other foot could she think of a better way to say it? Her smile faded and she stepped out of Rory's arms. She didn't want him to feel cheap and temporary, and she didn't want to hear him tell her the very thing she'd told Jack: thanks but no thanks.

So where did they go from here?

The moment lost purchase. They were two people in a crowd again, no longer a world apart from everything but each other.

She pointed vaguely in the direction of the tunnel, certain that by now Rachael would have lost interest and headed towards the shops along the Golden Mile. Holly would be in tow, as might the others. There was safety and anonymity in a crowd, it would go a long way to reducing how exposed she felt right now. 'I'm going to …' Adaline trailed off. She was going to what? Opt out of this turning point for the Castelvecchio? Ditch him for the Via Mazzini?

His smile slipped.

'You can come,' she hastened to reassure him. 'I'd like you to.' Well, didn't that just combat the whole purpose of leaving? She could hardly get over the almost nature of their relationship with him at her side, she needed space to think.

Adaline rubbed the back of her neck. Unsure what to do next, her first step away was both exaggerated and in slow-motion.

'Will thou leave me so unsatisfied?' he said to her back, his voice urgent.

Adaline slowly turned. 'What satisfaction can thou have tonight?' She was smiling, for they were back to quoting the play. Or so she thought, until Rory abandoned the script.

'What's with you? You're like a light switch; off, on, off.' He swallowed hard and glanced around. His words had shied him. She hadn't thought anything could do that. 'I really like you. I think that's obvious. And most of the time I think you like me too, but …' He floundered, unconsciously mimicking her by pushing his hand across the back of his neck. 'You're off again and I don't get it.' He swallowed. 'I don't understand.' He looked so young standing there with his heart in his hand and his unironed 'I've got more issues that Cosmo' T-shirt. His posture had lost all of its assurance and some of the light had gone out of his lovely brown eyes. His vulnerability pained her. She felt it deep in her gut like a mass of pulsing pins and wire.

'I'm sorry,' she said.

'Okay, but that doesn't help me.'

He was right, of course. An apology wasn't an explanation, and Adaline's situation wasn't a national secret. It just wasn't easy to talk about.

He held his hands up to both sides of his head. 'I'm imagining terminal illness, a boyfriend back home. A looming enrolment in a school of chastity and solitude. You can laugh,' which she was, 'but my imagination's in overdrive. Because I figure all of those things are more likely than you being the type to lead a guy on for kicks.'

Adaline flinched. She curled her arms around herself and stared sightlessly at the faces around her. Her body sang with the need to retreat. Claustrophobia, agitation and anxiety clamoured over the top of each other, each taking their turn at the fore. Thousands of dollars and thousands of kilometres and still she found herself within the scrutiny of someone's peaked emotions.

She wanted to make it right. She didn't want to be at odds with the first person she'd connected with since high school and yet her tongue was crowding her mouth and her throat was feeling tight. Adaline pressed her knuckles to her chest. Her heart was compressing strangely. Everything felt a fraction louder than it had a moment ago, then impossibly soft. She could feel a frenetic tick in her neck and a chill where air and sweat mingled along her hairline.

Rory said her name, but it sounded faint. Had he moved away from her? No, he was still there. He was touching her elbow.

He wanted her exposure. He wanted all things laid bare so he could examine them as a buyer might at a street market – that part was too unpolished, that part too costly. He wouldn't buy today, she was too unique to fit in with the rest of his life.

Adaline's mouth filled with spit. The last time it had done that she'd vomited and found herself magically transported to bed. To Jack's bed. Jack didn't want her laid bare. He didn't want or need to see everything she was selling, he just wanted a disposable part. A cheap toy that would amuse him. The rest of her required assembly and careful handling, he wasn't in for that kind of responsibility.

Rory kept saying something. Over and over. Okay, okay, okay. No – *it's* okay. Something was okay. Not her, she wasn't.

His arms came around her then hip to hip they were moving through the tunnel. Someone's laugh was too loud. The person beside them was on mute.

After seemingly endless steps and unsteady breaths, they were beyond the tall, Romanesque heritage buildings, sitting on grass as apart from the world as possible in a tourist destination. In the shadow of a first century amphitheatre, Adaline finished her panic attack. The dozens of arched recesses on the two storey pink and white limestone facade looked like dark eye sockets, and the building seemed to watch and judge. Within its walls countless spectators had witnessed everything from gladiator tournaments to opera. From construction, Adaline realised, to preservation.

'Take your time,' Rory said.

And she did. It took her so long to find the opening words that Rory started to fidget. She watched him fuss with a loose thread on his shorts for so long that the movements lost all meaning, but she couldn't think how to begin. There wasn't a clear point where the story started, Georgia Sharp had always been a woman apart. Clinical descriptors crowded Adaline's mind, words she'd been told by those with a string of letters after their names, words that tried to capture the waking nightmare and define the chaos. Words that fell far short of the reality.

'My father left us just after graduation.' Adaline swallowed. It surprised her that this was her introduction, there seemed to be so many other defining moments. Yet thinking back, hadn't it been the catalyst for everything Adaline was drowning in now?

Rory's bottom lip pushed up. His expressive face almost did her in. Sympathy cards the world over would never come close to the compassion in his eyes.

'Anyway,' she pushed on, 'some days I hate him for it and other days I envy him.' She was confusing Rory now, she could see it, but there wasn't a script she could refer to, her life didn't read like a shopping list: this and this on this aisle, this and that on another. Her life was a mess, a child's scrawl of impulse and colour. She drew a deep, steadying breath, then said the words she'd never uttered beyond the confines of a doctor's consultation room. 'Borderline Personality Disorder. My mother … she has a lot of problems. Emotionally, personally. She's chaotic. Intense. Behaviourally inconsistent and erratic. Depressed. Anxious. Angry.'

Always angry. Driven further into fury because she had difficulty expressing herself. Combined with her low capacity for guilt, her near-constant sense of victimisation and a startling degree of conceit, Georgia Sharp was a potent cocktail of instability and aggression.

'Aggressive,' she murmured, remembering.

Rory reached across and took her hand. The welcome contact made the nerves in her fingers sing, and she imagined her heart lifting its proverbial head, bolstered.

'People with BPD have serious abandonment issues,' she went on, 'and typically come to hate those they love the most. No one can reach their expectations because their expectations are inconsistent and impossible. This … disorder … poisons everything.'

It was time to get to the point, she thought. There was only so much backstory she was willing to give and her mother had already taken up too much time on this holiday.

'When my dad left she needed me around all the time. I've been doing what I can but I'm … tired. I know that sounds selfish.' Adaline waved away Rory's attempt to disagree. 'She relies on me as much as she abuses me. She hates me most days, even more since dad "abandoned" her. Now I'm here on the other side of the world trying to have a break and just be *young* and she's flipping out because I've "abandoned" her too.

'I haven't.' She blinked and looked away. 'I just want some time to myself. I feel like I'm allergic to being needed at this point.' She considered withdrawing her hand, it felt strange to be connected to him when she was explaining why she needed space, but Rory was holding tight, squeezing occasionally when the story she was telling was particularly tough. It was nice. Reassuring. Was there any harm in taking that from him?

'She's a long way away, but she's kind of not. She's sent me over two dozen emails that I'm afraid to open and she's harassing Gateway because I won't answer my phone. It's …' Adaline floundered.

'Distressing,' Rory supplied quietly.

To say the least.

For a moment she didn't know how to continue. This brief recount of the Sharp family drama had left her feeling like the morning after a sleepless night, then she remembered this was all supposed to be about the pair of them and tried to bring herself back on track.

'What I'm trying to say is I'm struggling a bit with … this.' She pointed between them. 'I'm struggling a bit with everyone, actually. I don't know what I expected. I mean, I wanted to have the time of my life on this trip but part of me wanted to be anonymous too, you know? Then I met you and that's the last thing I feel.'

Rory pushed one of his shirt sleeves up. She glimpsed a pronounced tan line before the material dropped back in place. So much sun, she thought, and idle time beneath it. When would life ever be like this again? Was she making the most of it, or worrying herself into missed opportunities and lessened highlights?

'Am I crowding you?' He was trying to make sense of it. Trying to extract the pieces of information that were relevant to his part in her story.

'No!' she said. 'I love having you around. I miss you so quickly.'

His eyes lit up at the same moment that her self-preservation lashed out against the concession. One hand was trying to keep him at a distance as the other pulled him closer. She was being maddeningly inconsistent. When she struggled to think what to say next, she realised she didn't know what the point of all this was. Was she ending this building intimacy, or explaining why they were having such a slow start?

The confusion loosened a tear from her eye. It rolled down her cheek, full of drama and fear. She dropped Rory's hand to cover her face as more tears came. Her words came out on a moan. 'Oh, c'mon!'

Rory laughed. His warm fingers closed loosely around her wrists. Very gently he pulled her hands away. 'I like your face too much to talk to your hands.'

Adaline blinked hard. When she opened her eyes, everything seemed inexplicably different. Red was green, restraint was action and caution was certainty. She wanted him. Hang the consequences, never mind the details, there was only right now and what was about to happen. She was too much in her head, too preoccupied by the past and the future. It was time to live in the now.

She leaned forward. The memory of standing close in the chateau moved through her mind but it was different – her excitement had applied a filter to it; the edges of the picture were blurred and his mouth was sharpened. Warmth was colour and heat was sound. He'd muddled everything up inside of her and things were about to become so much worse. Taste. She'd soon know the taste of him.

Except Rory didn't see her coming. He turned his face away, looking towards something he was about to tell her. He'd said, 'I heard there's a —' before her mouth pressed against his jaw and earlobe.

Adaline lurched away, horrified. Rory turned back, his eyes round. Still holding her wrists, he held her tighter and made a strange sound of delight and surprise. Then he began to laugh. Adaline had never needed space more in her entire life.

'Oh my god!' she wailed. 'Let go of me!'

'It's okay,' he said. His smile was so wide she had the crazy thought that a bird could land in it. Not a sparrow – a pigeon.

'Stop smiling!' she begged. She tried to twist free of his hold. 'Stop laughing at me! Get away from me!'

He let her go then, but only for a moment. Her wrists were free but he'd reached forward and closed his arms around her in a crushing hold that was half embrace and half restraint. 'Ads,' he said into her hair. His voice shook with laughter.

She continued to squirm. Mortification was hot, she thought. It was scalding oil under her skin. This moment was awful and endless and *hot*. 'No!'

'It's okay,' he tried again. He eased back so he could look at her. She glared at him. His impossibly wide smile widened. Did she love those creases in his cheeks or despise them? She didn't know any more. 'It's better than okay,' he said, 'stop being stupid. Were you just trying to —'

'No!'

'Aww.' He pulled her towards him and pressed his lips to her forehead. Her *forehead*.

Adaline's voice was a shriek. 'Oh my *god!*'

'Stop,' Rory begged. His body was shaking. 'Please. That didn't mean anything. I'd kiss you on the mouth but I don't think you realise how much you've been crying.' Her next attempt to escape was a more violent one. 'Stop! We'll try this again when you're not upset!'

Adaline stopped thrashing. She considered her tear-slicked face and conceded he had a point. She was a mess of tears, snot and emotion: not exactly the poster girl for passion.

It sounded like he wanted to kiss her too, but under different circumstances. So as to not take advantage of her vulnerability, probably. Heroes in books and movies did that all the time. She supposed she appreciated it.

That being said, a kiss would've gone a hell of a way towards forgetting all the mess. She paused. Actually, an almost kiss had worked almost as well. Her mum felt very far away right now.

Rory's arms loosened around her and she was free to sit up straighter. 'I may never look you in the eye again,' she warned him. 'I can't believe I missed.'

'I missed too,' he replied. He sounded so damn happy. 'The moment, anyway. When did we start having a moment?'

'Around about when you didn't run screaming for the hills when I told you my problems.'

'Ah. I'll know for next time.'

Adaline stared at the ground between them for a long moment, then lifted her gaze to meet his. The electricity between them was dazzling. The sexual tension, the longing and the intimacy, it was almost tangible. It seemed to thicken the air. She wanted to tell him she wasn't upset now, that they could try again and get it right. She wanted to know what it was like to sink into everything that he would offer her. Surely she would resurface changed.

'What were you saying,' she asked, 'before I so rudely interrupted you?'

They grinned at each other. Rory pointed across the cobblestone piazza. 'There's a tower nearby with a pretty great view. I wouldn't mind grabbing some food and having a look.'

Adaline lifted her chin imperiously. 'Let us not wander yonder, thoust tests my patience with your idling.'

Rory leapt to his feet, bowed and extended a hand to help her up. 'Then we will make haste, my lady!'

It could have been awkward but they quickly found their rhythm again. Exquisite Verona was improved by their almost kiss, and so distracting that Adaline didn't have time to think what this new intimacy between them would mean. By the time they returned to the coach she'd downgraded the urgency of it in her mind, but when she saw Jack and remembered his words of warning this morning, it all came rushing back.

She was playing with fire. She'd done so much that she deserved to get burned, but now was the time to contain.

Adaline eased her hand free from his before they were seen. She smiled at him – a deeper, more engaged smile than ever before – and boarded.

Fire was both devastation and rebirth. If handled carefully, she could manoeuvre them towards the latter.

She chose the seat next to Beth. She didn't trust herself to keep her hands off him otherwise.

21 DELICATES

The Venice stop-over campsite was the best yet, both in size and amenities. Adaline's suitcase barely hit the floor of the stand-alone room she was sharing with Rachael and Holly before she was back outside to explore with Rory. They found each other on the long dirt drive that seemed to divide the park in half – colliding in their haste to reunite – then they ran from highlight to highlight, laughing like children at an amusement park.

A decommissioned double-decker bus was parked near reception. There were people inside it sitting elbow to elbow at narrow computer stations, browsing the web, writing to family or friends, playing games. Such mundane things when Venice was so close. How was it possible that people were just getting on with their lives? If the anticipation within Adaline's bloodstream vibrated any faster she'd create her own frequency.

When Adaline and Rory collided again outside the bar, both choosing to swing around the veranda pole in opposite directions, Rory took her hand to steady her and didn't let it go until they reached the door of the laundry.

There were two rows of washing machines and a line of mounted dryers. Unoccupied seats in the middle of the long room created aisles and the tiles were the kind of clean only achieved by bare minimum effort. Dust bunnies and grit were like little colonies in each corner, but none of that mattered because they were at the feet of miracles.

A washing machine was a rare sight on tour. If people weren't willing to pay hefty laundromat costs they were forced to hand-wash as needed or wait for a stopover such as this. Adaline had waited for the Cannes stopover but she'd been sick and missed her chance. Now she was down to her last outfit. She hadn't imagined she'd change so often – needing to feel refreshed after a day on the road hadn't factored into her packing considerations and she guessed Rory's situation was just as dire, as this was the second day he'd worn his Cosmo shirt.

She wanted to look nice in her photos tomorrow. She wanted to be wearing clothes that wouldn't make her cringe for years to come. Damn it all,

Adaline was within sight of the floating city and she wanted to do a load of washing. She would have never imagined this reality.

Adaline glanced at Rory. He was looking at her out of the corner of his eyes. There was a beat of silence, then they were both scrabbling for the door, shouting and laughing.

They sprinted back to their rooms.

Adaline emptied her suitcase onto her bed, seized every scrap of fabric she could get her hands on, and burst back outside. Rory skidded onto the road seconds after her. They ran. She thought her lungs might burst from laughing, and when she dropped some of what she carried and Rory scooped them up mid-stride like a football player, she laughed harder.

There was no one in the laundry when they burst through the door, which was lucky, because Adaline might have bowled them over. They charged to a machine each, pretending they were competitors, and threw open the lids.

'Some of those are mine!' Adaline said as Rory emptied his armload into the tub.

'So? Are you delicate about your delicates or something?'

Adaline grinned, but she hoped all her underwear was accounted for in her own machine.

They shared the coins in Adaline's pocket, for Rory had forgot to bring money in his haste to get back here, set the wash types then stood back, panting hard. There were laminated signs on the walls telling them not to leave their washing unattended, but they staggered outside and dropped into the wrought iron bench seat in the shaded corner of the adjoining courtyard. The space was long overdue for a weed and the seat faced the rather uninspiring view of the main drive and freight ships in the far distance, but for this moment, Adaline preferred this to any other place.

She and Rory sat hip to hip, empty space on either side of them. They were travel-worn and wired. Rory's breathing was slowing and she found herself matching it. When he looked over at her, she was already smiling when she met his eye.

'We should get money for the dryers.' He tapped an empty pocket on his cargo shorts. 'Unless you're keen on some more running. We could hold everything above our heads and air dry it.'

'I brought enough.'

They slipped into a comfortable silence, arm against arm, thighs touching. She wasn't crying anymore and couldn't imagine doing so again in the near future, so she wondered when they'd try again. When they'd complete that almost kiss. With any luck she wouldn't bungle it a second time, her pride could only take so much. Now didn't seem like the moment despite the privacy and playful mood, so when? Tonight? She'd heard about this place: the bar here was infamous. Would they be fuelled by liquid courage or would it be something infinitely more meaningful tomorrow in romantic Venice?

Laundry and a much anticipated first kiss – if she'd only known a month ago what Venice would entail. She might have left home with more courage. At the very least, she might have found her sense of humour a little earlier. She'd been so serious for so long.

She'd only just wondered what Rory was thinking when he told her. 'I hear the parties here are pretty wild,' he said, looking towards the tables and chairs clustered around a bar recess in the building opposite. It looked pretty modest from where they sat, but Adaline had heard similar rumours. He said, 'Apparently they've got these really potent drinks. Pies told me he missed going to Venice the first time he came on this tour because he was too hung over to make it to the boat.'

'What a waste.'

'You and I think so, but he's not too fussed about the culture here. Listening to him go on about this bar, I wonder if he might miss Venice again.'

'I can't imagine missing Venice.'

'Sure, but that doesn't mean you should miss tonight.'

'I'll come for a bit.'

He leaned back and sighed, sounding relaxed. 'Famous last words?'

She turned to look at him. 'You know what I've heard? There's a website full of boobs —'

'Boobs?'

'— of women who've flashed for a free drink at this place. I'm not kidding.'

'I hope you're not.'

'Attitude Adjusters,' she said. 'It's all over the message boards. "Potent" seems to be an understatement!'

Rory stood and reached back for her. 'Sounds fun.'

Both on their feet now, they stepped out of the shade and walked a lap of the village. People from their coach were beginning to explore. Some were lining up for their turn on one of the computers in the refurbished bus, others were checking out the bar. There was a small group sitting around an enormous blimp-like piece of art by the water, killing time before dinner. No one moved to join them. Everyone they recognised smiled or waved, but it was as if they wore 'do not disturb' signs around their necks. Adaline couldn't decide if this assumed exclusivity concerned her or not, she was in too good a mood to think about it too deeply. However one thing was certain: they were paired up. Just like Jack had said they were.

He found her when she and Rory were dragging their clothes from the dryers. Jack stepped into the laundry looking every bit out of place, the way a teacher did at a student event. He seemed to catalogue everyone in the room, note who on tour had seen him and who Adaline was standing closest to. For this reason she supposed his gaze lingered the longest on Rory.

Rory saw Jack as he was tying a knot in the sleeves of the shirt he had wrapped around his bundle of clothes. His brows lowered. 'Ads, I think you're in trouble.'

Adaline looked up warily. She searched Jack's face for a sign that her mother had called again, but didn't find it. He seemed untroubled, almost genial. She thought back to their last exchange, replayed it quickly in her mind then relaxed. He'd explained the tour circle of life and cautioned her about Rory, nothing too serious. No, she wasn't in trouble, and surely she wasn't on kitchen duty again? She rolled her clothes into a messy scroll and tucked them under her arm. There was no hiding from Jack here, not when he'd have her cornered in three steps … two. One.

'Hi guys,' Jack said. He carried nothing which suggested he was in here to wash or dry. 'How do you like the village?'

'It's okay.' Rory said. Adaline glanced at him, hearing the change in his voice. 'Something wrong, Jack?'

'Not wrong,' Jack replied, his voice remaining light. 'I just need to speak with Adaline. Mind if I steal her away for a moment?' He extended his arm, indicating that Adaline should lead the way out.

'I'll find you later,' she said to Rory, moving to step around him. She paused when he shot a hand out and touched her arm, stopping her.

'Yeah, okay,' he said. 'This is yours.' He pulled a scrap of fabric from the bundle on top of the dryer. It was mint green and trimmed with lace.

Adaline snatched at it. An unpleasant warmth collared her neck and she turned away before either of them could see the blush rise to her cheeks. Rory was good for a laugh, but there wasn't anything funny about being handed her underwear whilst standing between two men who had possibly thought about seeing them under different circumstances.

She strode outside and kept walking. Jack had to hurry to catch up with her and when he did, she didn't slow.

'Can we talk privately?' he asked.

'We are.'

As if on cue, Lois called Adaline's name. She waved from the doorway of a cabin facing the road and Adaline stopped walking, not wanting to draw closer. It hadn't been luck that Adaline had scored a better rooming arrangement this time: she'd sat up the front of the coach and been the first to fill in the room sheet. The pair had had little to do with each other in Verona because Lois had skipped the history in favour of the shops, and Adaline was hoping that trend continued. She gave a small wave back.

Jack looked from Lois to Adaline. 'I was thinking somewhere a little less … on show.'

Adaline tossed her head and turned to him. 'Am I in trouble?' She buried the lace beneath a warm cotton T-shirt then properly gave him her attention.

Jack lowered his voice. 'No, of course not.'

'Okay.' She tried to out-wait him, to get him to tell her whatever it was that was keeping her from Rory, but he said nothing. For whatever reason, he was determined to avoid an audience. Adaline sighed and indicated that he should lead the way. When he moved ahead she glanced over her shoulder. Rory was leaning on the door jam, his expression bemused. He lifted a few fingers and she made a show of shrugging her shoulders.

There were dozens of small, unremarkable white buildings flanking the middle road and hundreds more out of sight. Everything about the place spoke of transience. There was little to distinguish one cabin from another except for the occasional towel drying on a veranda rail or shoes by the door, and for the moment, the number sequencing didn't make sense to her. It was going to be tough, she thought, finding her way back to her room tonight after one or two of those potent drinks.

Jack led her beyond the closest rows to the road, into a small playground with a plastic seahorse on a large rusted coil. He thumbed its ear, lost in thought. Behind him the slippery slide seemed to reflect the heat of the day. It reminded her of the swing-set she'd played on as a child. For half a dozen summers her father had given her a scrap piece of carpet to slide down on to protect her skin from the hot plastic. She'd outgrown the carpet square before she'd outgrown the slide.

The fond memory was unexpected. It unbalanced her.

Jack, unaware of this, unbalanced her further. 'I can't ask you to have dinner with me.'

She blinked. 'What?'

He waved his hand between them, as if scrubbing the air. 'What I mean … I want to ask you to have dinner with me.' He paused. 'But I can't. Crew sits with crew, it's policy. If we mingle too much Gateway gets complaints.'

Adaline didn't know what to say. She wasn't even sure she knew what was happening.

'I have free time tomorrow, though. After I walk the group to St Mark's Square I'm free until three o'clock.' Jack's closed-mouthed smile was tighter than usual. Nerves, she realised.

Adaline shifted uncomfortably. Holding a bundle of clothes felt suddenly foolish, so she deposited them on the seahorse's saddle and brushed herself down. 'Jack …' Her tongue tripped on ill-formed words. 'I'm not free tomorrow. I mean, it's *Venice*. We can run tomorrow morning or … or grab a drink together tonight but tomorrow I'm going to be the biggest tourist you've ever seen.'

'With Rory?'

'What?'

'Will you be with Rory?'

She crossed her arms over herself. 'I dunno. Maybe.'

Her lack of certainty seemed to energise him. 'Then consider this: I'm a tour manager. I've been to Venice so many times that I'm on a first name basis with locals. I know the city's secrets. I've seen them. I know how to skip queues and where to look. I know the bargains and the tourist traps and I can take you to the best gelataria of your life. Spend the day with me.'

Adaline touched her face and looked away. It all sounded so tempting. It was Venice first class. There would be no wasted moments, no disorientation. She'd see more than anyone else on her tour. Presumably much more than Rory because she doubted Jack's invitation extended to them both. So was that the root of her hesitation? Was it that she wouldn't get to be with Rory? Or was it, she thought, imagining herself following Jack over bridges and down narrow streets, looking where he pointed and praising what he thought worth praise, that she didn't want to see Jack's Venice, but her own?

She'd researched the floating city. She carried a Lonely Planet guide in her bag with a Post-it note checklist marking the Venetian section. She'd read fiction inspired by the place and watched movies which featured it. Adaline had probably visited it as many times as Jack had, except only in dreams. She knew how to skip queues too, and wasn't overly fussed about seeking out bargains – she had money set aside to buy some Murano glass earrings, whatever the cost. She wasn't going to waste time comparison shopping. Which meant Jack didn't really have a lot to offer her.

'That all sounds really great,' she said carefully, 'but I'm sorry, I've got my day planned already.' Understanding his change in expression, she added, 'Except who I'm spending the day with. Whoever can keep up, I guess. I have particular things I want to see and not a lot of time. To be honest, it'll probably work out for the best if I'm on my own.'

Jack pushed his hands in his pockets. 'I can keep up.'

Adaline huffed out a breath. She wasn't doing this right. 'You probably could.'

'Then we're on for tomorrow.'

Oh for god's sake, she thought. She felt that familiar resistance within her, that push against expectation and obligation, and tried to think of a way to make tomorrow sound less like a contract and more like a flexible idea. 'Let's see,' she said. Not the most subtle of deflections, but subtlety hadn't worked so far.

Something flashed in Jack's eyes. Irritation? She couldn't guess. He smoothed it over quickly in favour of an expression Adaline could only describe as calculating. She didn't like it, and she'd bet money that she wasn't going to like the next words that were about to come out his mouth.

'Drinks tonight, then. At the very least.'

'Sure.' She waved a hand between them. 'You'll be at the bar, I'll be at the bar.'

'Drinking together.'

Her patience was now as thin as the lace underwear which had so recently embarrassed her. He was deliberately twisting the things she said, and the way he was speaking reminded her of the morning he'd hit on her. 'Sort of,' she replied. 'Jack, I just want to be clear ... I still feel the same way I did in Cannes. I just want to be friends.'

Jack advanced on her then. He put his fingers to his temples and his voice jumped in volume. 'That's just because you're scared. This doesn't have to be a big thing. It doesn't have to interfere with all your plans, it's just a bit of company. A bit of affection. It's a few days, a few nights of fun.' When she blanched, he hastened to keep her engaged in the conversation. 'I'm coming back to Australia next year. I'm starting my own touring company. I've already got the ABN, I've got a business partner and the deposit for a coach. We could do it properly then.'

Adaline retreated a step. Feeling lost, she raised her hands in question. 'What do you mean?'

'We could date. It's not a holiday fling if we're going to date, right?'

'We're not going to date! What the hell is happening?' Adaline fought against the urge to push him in the chest, to get him away from her. Out of her air, out of her space. He was lonely, she realised. It was a quiet understanding, one that built slowly within her as she floundered against Jack's clumsy, contradictory advances. When it got loud enough in her mind that it stopped her saying the unkind things crowding on her tongue, she lowered her hands and softened her voice. 'Stop. Just stop for a second.'

Jack was a nomad. The least changeable thing in his life was a well-travelled backpack and second to that, a tour coach. People came and went, they shared their highlights with him then returned to lives full of growth and constancies, in doing so leaving him behind. Did he often connect with someone? Share his mornings or his sheets, or even conversations which delved below the surface? Or was this the first time in a long time that he had let someone in? Had Adaline shaken him from his relative anonymity, and in doing so, stirred a need he was now struggling to contain? On one hand he was offering her a string of moments, on the other, a relationship. In the same breath he spoke of exploration and settling down. He was as lost as she was, except Adaline was trying to lessen her obligations, not take some on.

'Okay.' She held up her hand to stop his advances. 'Listen, I'm guessing you're asking yourself a lot of questions right now. Maybe you're lonely and maybe you've been on the road too long, but either way I'm not your solution, all right? If you want to screw around, there's going to be plenty of girls willing to take you up on that tonight. If you want to run, no strings attached,' she spread her hands wide, 'I'm in. But that's it.'

Jack's expression was closed. His muscles seemed bunched with unspent energy. This conversation was clearly not going to plan and he was agitated.

'You'd have me throw myself at another girl?'

Adaline flinched, not liking the language. 'Not "throw yourself".' He had a lot to offer. He'd only have to nod at some of the girls on their tour to get their complete attention. Jack didn't give himself enough credit.

'What then?'

He'd misunderstood. He'd heard jealousy in her reply. She realised this too late, when he'd already crossed most of the distance between them. He stepped into her open arms and folded himself around her. So much taller than herself, she felt like a letter in an envelope, completely enclosed. She looked up to protest but her mouth was claimed. His lips were heavy and hungry. The kiss was both urgent and persuasive, full of relief and bursting with impatience.

On his side, anyway.

Adaline brought her hands in to rest on his chest, then she pushed him away with all her might. He didn't move because she overpowered him, she was much too small for that — he moved because she surprised him. He loosened his arms and she elbowed them away with all the violence she could muster.

She wanted to strike him. Bite him. Kick him until he bled. Alarm blossomed into fear, a spiky ball of adrenaline and surprise bouncing around in her gut. She was alone with this man who wasn't taking no for an answer.

'Touch me again and I'll scream,' she said, and she scarcely recognised her own voice. It was cold and quiet. Unnerving and full of a strength the rest of her body didn't feel. It cleared whatever fog was in Jack's brain, because his eyes cleared and his face went slack.

'Scream?' he repeated faintly.

She put her hands up between them. She wouldn't fend him off with those, she had a greater chance using her words. 'Stay away from me. No means *no*, Jack! I am not encouraging you, I don't want this! You're scaring me!'

She was getting through. He was finally hearing her. His eyes were rounded with what looked to be horror, and his open mouth formed a small circle. He was very still. A light breeze moved his hair, ruffling it as fingers might. At his back, dozens of nondescript cabins surrounded them, making her feel like they were on stage. She didn't like the feeling.

'I'm sorry,' he said. It was a whisper, seemingly all he could manage.

She was supposed to say it was okay, that's what came after the apology. She knew that, but she couldn't do it. It felt like excusing everything and she wasn't ready to. Space and time, that's what came next.

'Don't touch me again. Please just go.' She didn't look at him, instead she stared at the ground between them, wishing he wasn't still so close, so tall.

'Adaline, I'm so sorry.'

He stepped away, then approached.

Not approached, she realised. He was passing, stepping around her to return from the direction they'd come. She continued to stare at the ground, her hands still lifted, until she could no longer hear his retreat. Then she began to shake.

Silly, she thought. She'd overreacted. She was overreacting still. He hadn't attacked her, he'd kissed her. It had been unasked for, even discouraged on more than one occasion, but it was Jack. He just liked her. How many kisses were asked for in movies? How many times did someone swoop in for an impulsive pash? The music swelled, the crowd gasped, it was all very romantic wasn't it?

Adaline felt like an idiot.

She touched her fingers to her temples then covered her eyes. Her heartbeat was slowing even as she wondered why it had elevated in the first place. Jack wasn't scary. A little reluctant to take no for an answer and hell bent on talking Adaline around to his point of view, but harmless, right? Trusted with the wellbeing and enjoyment of dozens of tourists on a weekly basis. Relied upon by those out of their depth, their element, their comfort zone. Jack was … probably thinking she was a complete drama queen right about now.

Adaline dropped her hands to her sides and slowly turned on the spot. Far out, what a mess. Tonight's drinks couldn't come fast enough. She picked up her bundle of clothes, hugged them to her chest and turned to follow Jack back to the road. Within two steps she realised she still had company.

A man. Not Jack. Not Rory, either. A blond, medium height. A beer in one hand and a phone in the other. Daniel. Luck was not with her right now. Of all the people to see when her nerves were as raw as a new burn.

He was leaning against a cast iron sculpture of a mermaid. His clothes were creased from hours on the road and his eyes were narrowed. The light appeared to be agitating him. Very slowly, he straightened and approached. His movements were over-considered, he made sure of each step before he committed to another. A human train wreck, she thought. The epitome of excess.

'Interesting,' was all he said.

Adaline didn't know how to respond. She couldn't guess how much he'd seen and what he'd made of it all. He hadn't felt the need to intervene, which was another strike against her – another possible sign of her overreacting. But another part of her wondered if she could trust a character like Daniel to have an appropriate reaction to a person in distress. Who was to say he wouldn't pull up a chair and watch it like sport?

'Daniel,' she began. Then stopped. There wasn't any more she wanted to say to him. All she wanted to do was pass before he got in her way.

He bowed gregariously as she stepped around him, extending his arms from his sides. He didn't appear to have any more words for her.

Adaline ducked her chin down to her bundle of clothes and hurried back to the main road. She was certain there was a short-cut back to her cabin but there was too much sameness. She needed the main road, and from there, the seventh path on the right, past the old bus and the amenities block.

She didn't meet anyone's eye and she ignored someone who called her name. Her anger towards Jack had subsided, now she was just embarrassed, uncomfortable in her own skin.

Time and space.

Under a blanket with her back to the room.

She'd think about Venice, decide if she needed to apologise, then sleep until the world felt different.

22 ATTITUDE ADJUSTER

People had barely started digesting their dinner when they fronted up to the famous bar, ready for a long, messy night. Adaline could still taste the rich pasta sauce from her spaghetti because Rory had dragged her out of the village restaurant before she could wash it down.

'If you're going to drink,' he'd said, 'drink the good stuff.'

The good stuff was the renowned Attitude Adjuster. A telling promise, she thought, as she paid for one at the bar. Others had heard the signature drink was called an Amnesia, but the ingredients were the same and the outcome seemed inevitable. Hundreds of Polaroids and printed photos were affixed to the back wall; an amusing and yet confronting kind of wallpaper featuring smiling strangers, money, drinks and breasts. So many breasts. Judging by the many faces captured and displayed, flashing for free drinks was a popular choice.

Adaline gave the barman a wry smile as he took her money, and she ignored his pointed, 'See you later' when she turned to leave. There was no drink in the world that could adjust her attitude so much that she'd let a stranger put a picture of her boobs on a wall. He would *not* be seeing her later.

Maree, Will, Beth, Claire, Jenny, Rachael, Holly and Rory had claimed a picnic table with bench seats a short distance from the bar. She squeezed between Rachael and Rory and lifted her glass to clink it against the others'. Everyone shouted a different toast then downed their first mouthful. It was a shock of sweet, sour and heat; the generous measures of vodka, gin and white rum tasted like a mouthful of fire, and yet the Bacardi Breezer and grenadine went a long way to making it worth drinking again. Sweet petrol. All around her people were smacking their lips, laughing over their glasses and shaking their heads.

This drink was going to change lives, Adaline knew it. Whose, time would tell.

Three hours later, it was looking likely that no one would be the same after tonight. Jenny was presently the worst of the group, having downed five Attitude Adjusters and started on her sixth. This one, like the first five, had been free. Maree had flashed a barman too, and was still laughing about it. Rachael was working hard to keep a line of people between herself and Danya, who had taken a shine to her early in the night, and Adaline only saw Beth when the American was elbowing through the revellers looking for her brother, who was more often than not at the centre of a scuffle or heated exchange. Lois was presently sitting on the lap of a boy from another tour group and thankfully hadn't wanted to spend much time with Adaline.

Music was playing through giant speaker boxes, people were dancing and sensible conversation had retired. Adaline had been jostled, pinched on the bum, danced with and hit on, and her second Attitude Adjuster was making this afternoon's drama seem very far away. She'd heard a few people talking about Jack. Apparently he was drinking heavily but keeping largely to himself. Adaline hadn't sought him out and she hoped he kept his distance. If they were ever going to talk through what had happened, it would be best done with level heads. She'd avoided Daniel too after he'd slow-clapped her when she'd been dancing with Rory. He'd tried to high-five her when they'd been next to each other in line at the bar and he'd confused a few people with his exaggerated conspiratorial winks.

Back on the dance floor, Adaline hooked her finger through the belt loop on Rory's pants to keep him close. They bumped their glasses together, drank and swayed to the music. She wasn't a good dancer. She could hear the beat and feel the rhythm, but her body couldn't translate it, so she wiggled her hips and bounced her shoulders, and let the chaos around her disguise just how clumsy her moves were. The dance floor was overbright. The spotlights burned her eyes so she kept her face turned from them, and sometimes the music was foreign. Whenever a classic came on everyone broke into song. Adaline laughed until her sides hurt and sang along, and it was always Rory who got the serenades when she knew the words.

All around her people were doing stupid things. Moments ago, Will and one of the marrieds, Sanjeev, had enthralled the masses with a nudie run – people were still laughing about it. But it was Rory who was making her laugh the hardest. And his shirt, '"Of course you can dance", Vodka', was funnier every time she looked at it. She'd thought to mingle, to share herself around the various groups she felt comfortable with, but instead she'd kept close to her favourite person on tour.

He didn't seem to mind. In fact, they only strayed from one another's side when they took turns lining up at the bar.

Another one of those moments came too soon. Rory drew away from her, his fingers trailing along her hip until she was out of reach, then he was stepping backwards into the crowd, waving his empty glass. She shook her head when he pointed at her – wordlessly asking if she wanted another – then she turned away, looking for her friends.

She found the exact opposite within seconds. Daniel, his face slack and his eyes bloodshot, lurched out of the crowd. He grabbed her shoulder to steady himself and the sudden weight and pressure hurt. She pushed him off. He'd clearly had too much to drink. A novelty, Adaline guessed, because of the higher drinking age in the States. It also meant he mightn't have had a lot of practice in this state of mind. Something he demonstrated when he seized her shirt and tried to lift it.

'Flash for free!' he cried.

Adaline acted without thinking. She slapped him hard across the face. A few people around them hissed and laughed, but it stopped being funny when Daniel grabbed Adaline's wrist and twisted it. She yelped in pain and then there were people between them, a wall of bodies pushing them apart. Someone tall grabbed him and steered him away, she saw a flash of Beth's stricken face, then Adaline was surrounded.

She nodded when people asked if she was okay, let strangers check her wrist and smiled when people made jokes, and it was a few moments before she was alone again. She pressed her injury between her breasts and held her cool glass against her smarting skin.

She turned, more anxious than ever to see a familiar face, and found one high above her. Jenny was standing on the picnic table, dancing with abandon. Below her, people cheered. A few guys touched her legs – to steady her or grope her, Adaline couldn't tell, but Jenny either didn't realise or didn't care. Claire watched on from a few meters away, her expression pinched. Beside her, Maree looked equally unhappy. Will's exhibitionism had embarrassed her, she was still flushed in the face.

Adaline needed Rory back. Carefree, wonderful Rory who wouldn't complain or seek her help. He wouldn't lean on her or pressure her, he'd even go away if she asked him to. She turned again, searching for him in the crowd. Something inside her loosened when she spotted him making his way towards her.

'Are you okay?' he asked, shouting to be heard over the din.

She nodded, even though she wasn't. The music had taken on a kind of thickness in her consciousness, so every time she moved she imagined her shoulders and ankles brushing against a curtain. It wasn't an unpleasant thought, but it was a warning that she'd had enough. She opened her arms and folded them around his shoulders when he stepped within reach. They shuffled from side to side, although Adaline was barely aware of the music anymore. Things were beginning to blur. She hadn't drank much from her third glass, but the first two were starting to hit her hard. Hadn't she told herself to take it easy tonight? Tomorrow – today, she thought, guessing it was past midnight now – was important. Venice was important. More important than these drinks and this party, infinitely more important than a hang over.

She pulled away from Rory, startling him. 'I'm done,' she declared. 'I'm going to bed.'

'What? Why?'

She shook her head. Rather than shouting an explanation, she dragged him away from the speakers and the crowd. When they were standing on the main road she ended up shouting anyway – her ears were ringing. 'I need to sleep this off. I didn't mean to be here this long. Venice!' She put her arms above her head, as if she'd just won a race.

The crease between Rory's brows lessened. 'Ah, Venice. All right, I'll walk you back. You're not going to finish that?' He pointed at her glass.

A group of people shouted, their alarm cutting through the music and madness. Adaline and Rory whirled around in time to see Jenny topple off the picnic table. Adaline put her hand to her mouth. A moment later, the group cheered. Adaline saw the top of Jenny's head as she was hauled to her feet.

She passed the drink to Rory, more than finished with its effects. 'No.'

He took it and handed it to the first person he recognised. It was one of the Australians – Scott maybe. Whoever it was, he whooped, sculled it and clapped Rory hard on the back. Then Adaline and Rory were alone again, apart from the chaos and the noise. Rory kept his drink and drank from it occasionally as they walked slowly away from the lights.

She thought to remark on the absence of a noise curfew, but her tongue felt thick. This was probably a campsite for young people, she reasoned. Or at the very least, the young tourists were grouped together on this part of the site. Maybe the families were staying in cabins beyond the reach of all of this, or in motor homes parked far away. They were probably sleeping soundly, blissfully unaware of Attitude Adjusters and amplified alternative rock. Adaline thought all of this, but she didn't feel clever enough to say it.

Change was coming. Maybe it was here. Things couldn't remain as they were with Rory. They'd flirted against the boundaries of their friendship so often that they'd all but erased the tenuous line between them. It was just a matter of time before a tipping point forced them to commit to a direction; forward, into a deeper, frightening intimacy, or backward. A horrible, tumbling, disorientating backward that would take him from her side.

Rory chose the conversation. And it wasn't a light one. 'What did Jack want earlier?'

He wanted to romance me in Venice, she thought, and kiss me. Luckily that answer never made it past her lips. 'My mum's been harassing him.' The truth, although skewed. 'He wants me to deal with her myself.' When she stepped on a small rock and it almost unbalanced her, Rory hooked his arm around hers to help her balance. 'Which I really should,' she said, frowning at the treacherous road.

'Fair enough. He was in a bad way tonight, did you see? Moping around at a table by himself.' Rory glanced over his shoulder and smiled. 'He'll be right now, though, Rosa'll cheer him up.'

'Rosa?'

'Yeah, they went off together. Hands everywhere.' He lifted his own hand to illustrate against an imaginary person at his side.

'Oh, thank god,' Adaline said. Rory looked at her quizzically. 'Um ... things were almost boring there for a second, right?' Did this mean Jack had redirected his interests? Were things about to become so much easier between them? If he really was with Rosa, that meant he'd heard Adaline – heard her and finally listened. She imagined him drawing the other girl close, folding around her as he'd done with Adaline, and felt only relief.

She moved the subject onto safer ground. 'What do you most want to see tomorrow?'

He thought about his answer. 'Your face when you first see Venice.'

Adaline stopped walking. 'What a *line!*'

His laugh sounded shy and uncomfortable, but his body language was self-assured. 'That wasn't a line. You'll know when I'm giving you a line.'

They'd reached the end of the road, somehow passing her footpath without her noticing. In front of them was a dark expanse of beach – dirt and rock where the sand should be. The lights on the cargo ships in the distance looked like harnessed stars, tethered to the sea, and nestled in its lagoon, Venice slept, for now no more than a smudge on the horizon.

'Give me a line,' she said, staring first at the distant city, then at Rory. She hadn't thought to ask such a thing, the words had just suddenly been between them. She eased away from him so she could better see his reaction. The night was casting long shadows across his face, accentuating his cheekbones and the angles of his nose. The shadows highlighted features that the Mediterranean sun did not, and for a moment she was lost in thoughts of comparison and preference. She thought she preferred the light on his face, if only because it better showed the mischief in his eyes.

'Okay,' he said, accepting the challenge. 'Watch your knees, now. They're about to feel very weak.' She laughed as he took a step back from her and opened his arms wide. He bent forward in a slight bow. 'How's this for a line: of everyone I know, you suck the least.' She laughed harder and swatted at him. 'Or this,' he continued, abruptly changing the mood. 'Sometimes when we stand close enough, I feel like I breathe you in. You smell like sunshine. I don't even know how that's possible, but you do. Like warm grass and summer.'

Adaline's smile slipped. He straightened and watched her, all trace of mirth gone.

She took a deep breath. 'That's a long line.'

He chuckled. 'That's it? I say you smell like a star, and you criticise the length of my compliment? You're something else.'

'Yes I am.' She was surprised she could speak around the sudden weight on her chest. It took all of her strength not to confess that he also had a scent; an intoxicating, distracting one that she had come to associate with comfort and home. Not her home. The kind of home people wrote lovely poetry about. He thought she smelled like a star. Like sunshine. Through the haze of fatigue and alcohol, clumsy metaphors came to mind about both. Then there were other sounds – unwelcome sounds – growing louder and more intrusive. She ignored them and stepped closer.

With one hand she took his free hand. She curled her fingers around his and squeezed. With her other she trailed her fingertips over the line of his cheekbone. He went very still. As she moved her fingers down his neck she felt the fast beat of his pulse, and it gave her confidence she needed to move even closer.

'Get a room!' called a voice. The accent was familiar. It was Jonno, stumbling along the road with his arm around Scott, his cabin key in his other hand. He pointed at them and winked gregariously. 'You two. You twoooo.'

Scott attempted to whistle but only managed to spit on himself.

Adaline screwed up her face and laughed. Rory flexed his hand around her fingers and shook his head.

'Classy,' he said.

It was all very amusing until Jonno and Scott broke apart and Adaline saw who was walking behind them. Daniel; looking the worst of the lot of them, leaning bodily on his sister who was struggling under his weight. Beth was clear-eyed but frazzled. She hadn't been drinking, Adaline remembered. She hadn't had the chance because Daniel had been a full-time job tonight. The American's eyes darted down to Adaline's wrist, then she looked at the ground.

Daniel stumbled on a stone, righted himself against Beth, who winced, then drank the last of the drink in his hand. He threw the glass away and it shattered on the road. 'Interesting,' he said. With that one word, Adaline was back in the playground with him, her lips tingling and her heart racing.

She tugged on Rory's hand. 'Let's go.' Rory hesitated. He looked like he wanted to help Beth. Adaline tugged harder. 'Please.'

Jonno had unlocked his cabin door by now. He slapped on the porch light and swung off the doorway. Scott was gone, presumably inside. Had they lucked out and landed Daniel for a roommate? It certainly seemed to be where Beth was leading him.

'So you don't mind sharing, then?' Daniel said to Rory. He pointed towards Adaline but missed by a good forty-five degrees.

Rory pulled her closer to him.

Adaline was too mortified to be offended by the implication that she got around – Daniel was about to ruin everything, she was sure of it. That perfect moment that had teetered on the brink of a first kiss suddenly seemed so long ago. Rory was about to find out in the worst possible way that she'd just had her lips on someone else, albeit unwillingly. Would Daniel say that she'd pushed Jack away? The malice in his eyes suggested he wouldn't. Could Adaline explain that it had all been a misunderstanding without making herself sound like a fool or Jack sound like a villain?

'Rory.' She stepped away from him, hoping he'd follow. But he wasn't paying attention, his eyes were on Daniel and he looked to be deciding if he should be angry on Adaline's behalf.

'Sharing?' he repeated. There was so much strength behind the question. Daniel was a fool, couldn't he hear it?

'He's drunk,' Adaline said. 'Don't listen to him.'

Daniel's loose smile widened. 'Not doesn't mind ... doesn't know.'

'Know what?'

'You're sharing your girl with Jack.'

'Dan!' Beth cried. 'Be quiet! Why would you say that?'

'Because it's true!' he spat, and shoved her away. She stumbled on the uneven ground and fell to one knee. Beth yelped in surprise then hissed in pain. She drew her hand against her chest before she stood, cradling it. Adaline would have helped her, but too much else was happening. Daniel was laughing. Jonno was making high-pitched noises like he was watching a fight and Rory was looking at her, stunned mute.

He wanted her to deny it. She could see it in his eyes that he wanted her to say Daniel was lying, but she couldn't do it. Another lie on top of a lie on top of an omission, when did it end?

She held up her hand and kept her voice low and level. 'Jack kissed me a few hours ago. I didn't kiss him back. I was going to tell you.' She was almost certain she would have, at some point. Probably. 'There's nothing going on.'

'Ah, but that's not true.' Daniel was enjoying himself. He'd almost forgotten he was nearly legless with drink, tearing her to pieces was keeping his mind off it. She stared at him, open-mouthed. What lies were coming next? 'They spend most mornings together.'

Crap, she thought. Not lies. Adaline looked back at Rory. Her hand was still extended between them. His face was ... closed.

'What's that mean?' he asked. When she didn't answer, he asked Daniel the same question.

Daniel was more than happy to elaborate. 'Ask Beth.' He gestured at his sister, who was standing apart from him now, still cradling her hand. He didn't appear to see that he'd hurt her, or maybe he just didn't care.

Everyone looked at Beth.

How had she known? Adaline wondered. Adaline hadn't told anyone, had Jack? It was possible, but being that it was Beth, it was more likely that Adaline had slipped up somewhere. She'd not made a secret of her running, there hadn't been any point because she came back each time dripping with sweat. She'd just never mentioned having company. She'd never even mentioned Jack unless someone brought him up first, so how had Beth made the connection and why hadn't she said anything to Adaline instead of gossiping to her brother?

Beth was in a complete state. Her gaze was jumping from person to person, never resting on one for more than a breath. Step by tiny step she was backing away. Adaline glared at her then looked back at Rory.

'It's just jogging. *We* can jog together if you like.'

Rory shook his head and stepped back. He looked like a different person, like someone who never smiled. She'd done this, she'd led them to this moment and she had no idea how to fix it. She only knew that getting him away from everyone else was the first step.

No, an apology. An apology was the first step.

'I'm sorry. It sounds so sneaky when Daniel says it but it really was just jogging.'

'And kissing.'

'*One* kiss. He got the wrong idea. C'mon, he's hooking up with Rosa, you said it yourself!'

'All that stuff you said about your mum,' he said, making Adaline glance – panicked – at their audience, 'was any of that true? Or were you just keeping me in the wings? In the dark?'

His question winded her. 'It was *all* true. Of course it was true! Don't lash out at me because you're confused.'

'No,' his voice became sharper, 'I'm lashing out at you because you've been lying to me and I'm feeling pretty stupid right now!'

'I haven't —' She cut herself off and scowled at the ground.

'Enjoy Venice,' he said. Behind him, Jonno hissed. 'Enjoy Rome. Enjoy the rest of it.' He raised his hands above his head. 'I'm out. You're not what … you're not who I thought you were.' Without another word, Rory stalked off into the night. Adaline watched him, her mouth agape, until he was swallowed by the darkness.

By the time there was nothing to see, there was a blunt ache in her chest so paralysing she couldn't take a breath deep enough to fill her lungs.

23 BOARDING

Adaline passed the time guessing if people were coming or going. Thousands of people moved about the airport, greeting or farewelling friends and family, embarking on adventures or returning from distant places. Adaline sat alone.

Priority boarding had rolled into economy boarding, and too soon it would be last call. But her feet wouldn't move. Her mind – it needed to move a little less. She was besieged by thoughts. Good ones, bad ones. Paralysing ones.

She stared at the phone cradled between her fingers. She'd waited until the last possible moment, been available until the last possible moment, but Georgia hadn't called.

Now it was Adaline's time.

She turned it off, flipped it over and used her fingernail to drag the SIM card free. She replaced it with an international card, put the phone back together, but left it off.

Adaline stood, checked her ticket one last time, then joined the end of the line at the departure gate.

24 FLOATING

There were a lot of empty seats at breakfast, and even fewer people made it to the ferry in time for the nine-thirty departure. Rory figured those who had come to the first and not the second hadn't managed to keep their cereal down. Most of the Australian guys were missing, as were the youngest American girls. Those who'd been at the bar last night and managed to rouse themselves shared a number of things in common: they looked terrible and they were moving very slowly.

Rory kept his face turned towards the ferry window, away from the group. He was delaying the moment he saw Ada for as long as possible. Hours ago he hadn't wanted to leave her side, now he couldn't imagine being there. She was sitting up the front where the views were most generous and it mightn't have been a coincidence that Jack sat nearby. He was facing the group, looking rumpled and queasy. Rory had heard somewhere that today was mostly a day off for him, all that he was expected to do was lead them to a glass-blowing presentation in the morning then a gondola ride in the afternoon. Between that, his time was his own. Judging by the glassiness of his eyes and his reluctance to speak – he'd skipped his regular spiel in favour of half a dozen clipped responses to direct questions – he'd use that time to sober up in peace.

Unless, of course, he and Ada had plans.

A sickening, compressing knot in his gut made Rory lean forward and wrap his arms around himself. He played the fool willingly, he loved making people laugh, but this ... he'd been played *for* a fool and the difference was breathtaking. At his side, Will made a sound of sympathy.

'This ride's going to do a lot of us in, I reckon,' Will said. He was holding an apple against his forehead like a cold compress. 'It's going to be a tour of Venetian rubbish bins for me, I think.'

Rory glanced at Maree, seated up the front with Ada and Claire, and wondered what she made of that. She'd dressed to impress again, something he'd noticed she did for all the top touristy spots. For photos, probably, ones that didn't include Will vomiting in the background. They weren't the strongest couple; ten years or not they didn't seem to agree on much, but even for them a separate ride into Venice wasn't good. Things looked to be circling the drain.

Rory could relate on some level. Things had been so good with Adaline, getting better by the hour, in fact, but that friendship had soured now. It turned out it hadn't been the friendship he'd imagined it to be. Not one built on honesty, anyway. He regretted accusing her of lying about her mother. Even as he'd said it he'd regretted it – her vulnerability had been real. Confiding in him had cost her. But he'd been so blindsided. So ... jealous.

He'd never imagined in the hours between bed time and breakfast that she'd done anything more than sleep and shower, but she'd had this whole other thing going on. Morning jogging. Stolen kisses. What else? Late night rendezvouses? How humiliating – Rory had been practically throwing himself at her.

Had there really only been one kiss, and had she really not wanted it? What was the truth?

He was going to go mad, thinking like this. As it was he'd barely slept. He had to shake it off. Forget about what he was most looking forward to seeing in Venice and find himself another highlight that had nothing to do with the wonder on her face. Venice would provide. Of course it would provide. He'd suss out St Mark's Square, maybe buy his mum some fancy blown glass or a mask on a stick, and it would be awesome. He'd sing a stupid love song on a gondola, eat enough gelato to cool the heat in his stomach, and there were plenty of people on this ferry to hang out with.

Will dragged the apple down his face and pushed it into his mouth. It took a few seconds for him to find the strength to bite into it, and even then he didn't look like he had the taste for it. Rory looked out the window at the industrial buildings and ships beyond, and considered his other options. The Canadian boys were good value.

The ferry ride took a little over twenty minutes. In that time, Rory watched the city draw closer and listened with half an ear as people around him gossiped about last night's highlights. So many women had flashed the barmen that it was possible the bar hadn't made much profit, and everyone from the group was nursing a dull headache and sporting a couple of new bruises. It pleased him to hear that Daniel hadn't escaped the night unscathed; not only was he still in his cabin sleeping off seven Attitude Adjusters, but someone had punched him in the ribs and rumours were abound that someone had slapped him across the face.

Rory would have happily been responsible for either. To him, Daniel was the compilation of personality rejects. A mixed bag of all the things people tried not to be. He was also the last person Rory had expected to know something about Ada he himself didn't.

The ferry's engine seemed to change gears. They were nearing a dock where Rory presumed they would berth, but were doing so at a glacial pace. Last night before the cocktails had got a foot-hold Ada had regaled him stories about Venice, so he knew there were strict speed limits in the waters surrounding the city in an effort to reduce water structural damage, the city was sinking, after all, but this knowledge did nothing to ease his mounting impatience. He needed fresh air and distractions, he was feeling claustrophobic and agitated. There were gondolas slicing through the water around them, manned by gondoliers in black and white striped shirts and smart black pants. Ancient buildings rose up from the lagoon, their facades as beautiful as a church interior, their legs submerged. Small boats were moored to private docks and thousands of birds winged through the sky, dark marks against a crystalline blue.

Venice would provide, he thought again.

The chatter within the ferry grew louder. People turned or straightened in their seats, their attention caught, and a moment later Jack was standing at the front, a clipboard in his hand. He smiled slightly when a few people noticed his hickey and began whispering. An uncharacteristic burn of dislike lanced through Rory's torso.

'I tripped and fell,' Jack said mildly. A few people laughed, appreciating the oft-used line for such a bruise. '*Buon giorno*. Apologies to those on board who aren't with Gateway, I'll be quick. Those coming on the walking tour need to follow me across the square. Try to stay together, it'll be very crowded. Those going on the gondolas, we'll be meeting beneath the Campanile at three o'clock. It's very easy to get lost so leave plenty of time to get there. I will be handing out maps at the end of the walking tour and we'll be meeting back here at this dock at four o'clock. If you're late, you're going to have to find your own way back, consider yourselves warned.'

Before he could stop himself, Rory glanced at Ada. He doubted she'd mind such a predicament.

The ferry bumped against the dock tyres and people hastily disembarked. As groups separated they shouted vague promises to find each other for lunch, but nobody knew where they were or where to meet, so the plans were brittle at best. Rory didn't follow Jack. Yesterday he might have been interested in the optional glassblowing and lace making demonstrations, but today he didn't want to look at Jack's face any more than he had to. He shot his hand out and plucked Hamish from the throng.

'Venice?' he asked.

Hamish nodded. 'Yeah, cool.'

Chris appeared at Hamish's side and their group was made. A moment later, it expanded. The Swiss girl Ada sometimes hung out with joined them, striking in a pale blue dress. Rory cast around his mind for her name but needn't have bothered. Hamish knew who she was.

'Hello Lisa.' His tone suggested he wished he knew her better. She gave him a friendly smile in reply then turned the full force of her focus to Rory.

'What is first?'

She spoke nice, he thought, delicate and precise. He shrugged. 'Know anything about Venice?'

'A little.'

'So about the same as me. What do you reckon, forward?'

Forward got the consensus. They followed the masses flocking towards the main square. Rory got a glimpse of Ada's brown hair and pale yellow top, then she was swallowed up by the crowd. He couldn't see who she was with, if anyone, and he didn't know where she was going. She surely had a plan: she'd been dreaming of this place for years. Yesterday he'd believed he'd enjoy the spoils of that.

The warbles of pigeons and the chatter of people made his first in-person impression of Venice a noisy one. Behind him, gondolas and boats nudged against the docks. Beyond the Piazzetta the Piazza San Marco, the social, political and religious centre of Venice, was a wide public space surrounded by gorgeous arched white buildings. St Mark's Basilica loomed over the square, a ninth century guardian crowned with four life-sized horses. There seemed to be more pigeons than people. Every so often birds would pitch into the air like a breaking wave, dodging bodies and delighting children. He gazed up at the striking bell tower, then beyond it to the pyramidal spire where an angel oversaw it all. Flags snapped against three flag poles in front of the church. It was so surreal to be standing here, seeing this place without the barrier of a page or screen.

They walked to the Bridge of Sighs first, through narrow alleyways and alongside canals where clothes flapped and snapped on washing lines strung between buildings. They passed doors half-submerged in water and explored souvenirs shops full of intricate masks, striking stationery and colourful glass jewellery. Rory ate *fior di latte* ice cream in the shade of a sunlit *campi*, posed for photos and tried to keep his mind on the here and now. Lisa rarely strayed from his side. When she'd clasped his arm when she'd seen something particularly beautiful Rory had imagined a different wonderstruck face. When he'd noticed ice cream on her chin he'd not mentioned it. Hamish had, although he hadn't got the response he'd have liked.

Rory was restless. Surrounded by history and charm yet somehow almost unmoved.

Venice hadn't held a medal place on his itinerary, but all the same it should have resonated with him more. His mind was supposed to be preoccupied by language, culture and time, not by a girl. Infatuation, jealousy and impatience, it was the stuff of Shakespearean plays. Brought on by a misunderstanding, he thought, a favoured plot device of the bard's. Had Adaline and Jack been a misunderstanding?

It pained him to think it, but in some ways Rory understood why Adaline might prefer Jack to himself. Jack was worldly, older, a leader as opposed to the centre of attention. He was outgoing and broody, the girls on the coach appeared to love that double act. But more than any of that, he was temporary. There was no risk of him intruding on her life back home, unlike Rory who didn't recognise the barrier of state lines and vast country. The distance wasn't ideal, but it was in no way enough of a reason to not try.

Rory frowned. Meaning what – he wasn't through, he wasn't out? If the physical distance could be surmounted, could this gap in understanding?

He remembered Daniel's words as he followed the others across the stone arch Rialto Bridge. The Grand Canal tumbled underfoot, full of secrets and padlock keys. Private boats, water buses, water taxis and gondolas navigated around each other, ferrying people beneath the famous bridge. Tourists waved to tourists. Cameras clicked. Music drifted out of a nearby restaurant, foreign and romantic.

Daniel had claimed Rory had been sharing Ada with Jack, and Rory – without considering the source – had made Ada defend herself. With all that had happened between them, he should have been on her side. A heat that had nothing to do with the sun collared his neck. They weren't dating. She hadn't cheated. She was in no way his to possess. Other men were free to desire her as he did and last night through his haze of jealousy he'd lost sight of what was important: she'd chosen him. Jack may have kissed her yesterday, but she'd spent all of her time following that with Rory. Her actions spoke louder than anything overseen, particularly by a drunk, malicious git.

Ada has chosen Rory, and Rory had chosen Daniel. What a mess.

He'd make it right. Before the end of the day they'd be fine again and she'd have told him everything he'd missed in this incredible place, everything she'd seen and how it had all made her feel.

Re-energised, Rory led Hamish, Chris and Lisa to a restaurant overlooking the ancient waterway. They drank overpriced water and ate pizza so laden with cheese that ropes of it dropped to the table when they pulled the slices apart. He enjoyed their company; they laughed at his jokes and had clever observations about the world around them, but he wasn't able to give them his whole self. A large part of him was waiting now, counting down to a reunion that would put the electricity back in his blood.

When their bellies were full they crossed the Accademia Bridge into the Dorsoduro district. There wasn't time to put their phones or cameras away between sights, so they carried them at the ready for the entire length of the Zattere waterfront promenade. Fine restaurants, notable buildings and monuments lined the lesser populated walkway, and whenever they spotted a church which would admit them, they ducked inside to appreciate the grand ceiling frescoes. Rory bought a carnival mask for his mum, they turned a couple more corners, then they were almost back where they had started from.

Rory's excitement had transformed into nerves. It felt like birds were landing on his stomach, picking at the spiders that skittered and scraped against his insides. It was almost time to meet for the gondola ride which meant it was very likely that Ada was nearby. Would there be time to apologise before the excursion? Could they forgive and forget in time to ride together? He wanted her at his side in any and every way that he could have her – for the rest of this day, this holiday, throughout the years of medical school.

There were still thousands of people around when they stepped through an arch of the grand building opposite St Mark's Basilica. Pigeons cast fast-moving shadows and tourists moved between the various vantage spots. The late afternoon sun filled the square with gold.

'I hope we get the back seat,' Lisa said, speaking of the many ornate throne-like seats closest to the gondolier's feet that they'd seen today. They were outlandish. Intimate. Something to share with someone you wanted your arms around.

Rory couldn't think of a diplomatic reply so he didn't answer.

'Where are we meeting?' Chris asked.

Hamish cast an unhappy look at Lisa then pulled a printed map from his back pocket. There had been copies of them in every cabin. The green cross was the meeting point for the second optional excursion. Hamish held it up, orientated himself then pointed towards the bell tower. 'Under that, I think.'

Rory was the first to step forward. His abrupt departure from Lisa's side must have wounded her because she didn't try to catch up with him. He strode across the square searching for the pale yellow of a familiar T-shirt. He dodged children, ducked beneath selfie-sticks and stepped between groups.

The closer he got to the looming brick shaft the more faces he recognised. Two of the marrieds, Sanjeev and Niki, were taking in the atmosphere, their arms around each other.

Jenny had evidently caught a later ferry, although from the look on her face Rory guessed that she regretted it. Claire was with her, waving her arms about, expression pinched. A run-on argument from the previous night's adventures, maybe. Claire could probably empathise with Beth in the sense that both girls were caring for their travelling companions more than was fair.

Past them, the Chinese girls were sitting on the ground showing each other their pictures. There were other faces he recognised but ones he didn't have names for. There were too many sub-groups within sub-groups to know everyone. There were some people on tour that he hadn't even spoken to yet.

The face he was looking for was not amongst the others.

Her name was like a drum beat in his consciousness.

Someone clapped him on the back. Rory smiled in answer without registering who smiled back at him. A woman to his right laughed uproariously. Inexplicably, the sound agitated him.

The crowd shifted then and Jack's face appeared between strangers. He was approaching from the direction of the nearest restaurant. A shock of feeling made Rory's nerves sing.

There was no one at Jack's side.

It wasn't until the weight lifted that Rory realised he'd been carrying it. He'd imagined all kinds of scenarios; Jack and Ada walking arm in arm through the narrow, twisting streets of the city, Jack and Ada getting a couple caricature. Jack being worldly and charismatic, and Rory being forgotten.

Across the square their eyes met.

A curious kind of energy shot out from Rory's heart and made his fingers tingle. He felt combative, territorial … primal. If Jack had kissed Adaline against her will, Rory wanted to hurt him. If he'd kissed her and she'd liked it… well, Rory felt about the same. He wanted to charge his shoulder into Jack's stomach, lift him off the ground and let him fall on his back. He wanted to punch the mouth that had tasted her. And because he'd never been a violent person, Rory turned away.

Jack passed within arm's reach of him, his head down and shoulders up. He looked better than he had this morning, although his mood appeared about the same. Rory watched him pass then continued to search for Ada.

Minutes passed.

At three o'clock Jack called the group together. He did a quick head-count, stalled, then at three minutes past held his arm above his head and led the group away from the bell tower.

Rory watched them go. His chest felt tight. It wasn't like Ada to miss something so important. She planned her days around highlights and there was surely very little that topped a gondola ride? Had last night changed her plans? Was she avoiding Rory, steering clear of Jack, or simply keeping her distance from the gossip? People had heard about what had happened. They'd been talking about it at breakfast. Rory had been on the receiving end of endless sympathetic looks today but he hadn't let it get him down. He'd been able to ignore it, for the most part.

Was Ada struggling to do the same?

Rory checked his watch. He could still see half a dozen of his tour mates winding through the crowd, but within moments they'd be gone. He didn't know where to meet them, he couldn't wait here any longer.

After one last desperate scan of the crowd, Rory turned to follow.

'Rooooooooooreeeeeeeeeee!'

He didn't immediately respond – the sound was more battle-cry than name – but then he was called again, and the voice was familiar.

'Rory!'

He turned just as the world collided with him. The breath that rushed from his lungs was obstructed. A mouth pressed down onto his at the same moment that a pair of arms and legs crashed against his torso and held on. His arms closed around the body instinctively and a second later his brain caught up. Ada. In his arms. Wrapped around him. Pressing her lips to his, kissing him like he'd returned from war. In that instant he couldn't have said where he was standing, what he'd done that day, anything before the second her mouth had found his. The kiss was long. It changed from forceful and desperate to languorous and soft, and when they parted at last, Rory's concept of time was so skewed that years could have passed, or mere seconds.

They stared at one another, breathing hard, then she pulled him close again. 'I'm sorry,' she said against his mouth. 'I'm sorry you found out that way. That it happened at all. I promise there's nothing going on with him.' She kissed him hard and quick. He lurched forward when she pulled away, drunk on her affection. 'There's just you.'

He didn't know where to put his hands that would satisfy him for longer than a moment; the back of her neck, the sides of her face, her hips, her arms … he wanted to be everywhere at once. 'I'm sorry,' he returned. 'I can't believe I listened to *Daniel*. I'm an idiot.'

She shook her head and laughed. 'I'm an idiot, too. You're all I could think about today, I kept hoping I'd see you around every corner and then I realised I was late and that I was going to miss the gondolas,' she was rambling, her words running together, 'and I kept thinking I couldn't bear it if you were in a different one to me but why would you want to be in one with me and all I've wanted to do since last night is *fix this*.'

He silenced her with another kiss. A tender one in which he poured all of his understanding and empathy. 'It's fixed.' It was better than it ever had been, he thought. 'Except now we probably have missed the gondolas.'

They pulled apart and looked towards the place he'd last seen someone familiar, but the crowd had swallowed the way. Rory braced for her disappointment. The girl who didn't like to miss a thing had traded one experience for another and he wasn't altogether sure she'd feel a first kiss trumped a gondola ride.

She lifted her chin and pushed her shoulders back. 'You know what? That's fine.' She grinned at his incredulity. 'Really. We've got money and time, we can find our own gondola.' She took his hand. 'And we don't have to be back here by four o'clock either.'

Together they did Venice again, but at her side it felt like the first time.

25 UNBURDEN

It was dark by the time Adaline and Rory returned to the village. Their stomachs were full of pasta and gelato, their wallets were significantly lighter, and even after hours together – always touching – she hadn't got her fill of him. There were people at the bar again, others she saw still in the dining hall, lingering over their plates and conversations. Many of the cabin lights were on.

Everything looked as it had last night, except the world around her was quieter now and the world within her was full of song.

This was a day to do over again. Over and over again. It had been almost perfect.

She'd dragged her feet on the ancient footpaths as they'd returned to the docks. It had felt too soon to leave, but she couldn't imagine how many weeks or years it would take to satisfy her. A dozen lifetimes, perhaps. She'd been the last to board and as the ferry had pulled away she'd felt a subtle pull and snap within herself. Venice had taken a part of her, she hadn't left whole. But it had given her something else, something to ease the pain of separation: it had given her Rory. She would forever be in its debt for that.

She loved the way he held her hand. The way he interrupted her with a kiss when her mouth fascinated him to the point of helpless action. Their conversations had been deeper since the Piazza, almost dream-like as they'd talked about a life beyond tour. It was a life she couldn't have, full of partial absences and long-distance connections, but nevertheless it had been a feast for her soul. She hadn't realised the depth of her starvation until now.

Whenever she thought of home, of introducing the full colour spectrum that was Rory into her grey life, her body recoiled as if struck by something unseen. Conversely, the thought of going to him brought an onslaught of imagined noise; wails and admonishments, guilt-trips and the incessant ping of her phone. Adelaide or Sydney, her mother would ensure they'd never have peace.

Adaline had warned him of this but he'd continued to dream, so she'd shelved her realities and dreamed with him. It had been wonderful. Gravity seemed to have lessened over the course of the last few hours, she no longer felt pushed onto the earth but placed. Rory had given her a high definition moment in the highlight reel of her life. Years from now, maybe packed tight on a commuter train with strangers pressed uncomfortably against her, she would remember this day and smile. Even just weeks from now in the jail that was her house, Adaline would think of the boy in Venice and feel free.

She squeezed his hand and he leaned into her arm.

His face was different. Less affected by time, youth layered upon youth. His eyes were brighter and his cheeks full of lines as the width of his smile rivalled those of the playful marionettes sold back on the island.

They were as happy as each other. For now, obligation was a different season. She'd feel it in time, but she didn't have to worry about it now. This was the summer of their relationship. So long as these dream-like conversations didn't become plans, they would never see the winter.

'I'll come around later?' he asked, bringing his face close to hers. They'd tossed around the idea of a walk beneath the stars, getting one last glimpse of the evocative city before they departed for Florence in the morning.

She hesitated. The urge to push back against even small commitments such as this was still there, but it was lethargic somehow, like the slow winding down of a clock. Comfort, contentment – they were broken teeth in her cogwheels.

She nodded.

They held hands as he stepped away, then fingers, then fingertips. When the contact broke Adaline was struck by a feeling of strangeness. Which was curious. Shouldn't she be used to what she'd always known – distance, space, a lack of affection – not so wholly accustomed to being linked to him as she had been today? Her mind reeled as her heart pouted.

His smile was wistful as he turned away. She watched him a moment, then walked in the opposite direction.

She was the first back to the cabin she was sharing with Rachael and Holly. She imagined the pair of them were at the bar again so she took her time repacking her suitcase, neatening her clothes, wrapping her new Venetian trinkets and preparing her clothes for tomorrow. With every rolled T-shirt and bundled pair of socks she felt more in control. She pushed her state of mind into the things beneath her fingers and straightened, aligned, compartmentalised. In the back of her mind she heard the conversations of gondoliers and the soft bumps of the glossy black watercraft negotiating the narrow waterways. Rory's whispers were like a breeze through her thoughts. He'd spoken so softly, as if the beauties of the water city had been slumbering. Venice would forevermore have this soundtrack to her.

Adaline gathered her toiletries bag and towel into her arms and turned towards the door. As if anticipating her, it sounded a knock.

The answer in her stomach was both pinch and twist. She'd hoped for a long shower before he'd come to her room, an indulgence because of the tour pace. She'd imagined her nerves sliding down the drain with the soap and her muscles relaxing beneath the heat, but now it would all have to wait until morning for she didn't imagine they'd return until late. She wouldn't turn him away sooner, either. Not for a shower. Not even for sleep. Anticipation bloomed and cast her regret in shade.

Fear and desire slammed into Adaline's body, any faster and they would have winded her. What had she been thinking letting him meet her here? Would he want to come inside? What then? Did she want him to come inside? It felt like she'd swallowed a mouthful of insects. Nerves and excitement whirred and pitched.

She closed her eyes a moment and linked her concentration to her slow breath. Feeling marginally better, she opened the door. And blinked. It was not Rory on her doorstep.

'Maree.'

Maree nodded, confirming her own name. She pushed her hands into the pockets of her lovely A-line dress and offered a tremulous smile. Murano glass winked prettily in her ear lobes. Adaline had been with her when she'd bought them, Maree had been inexplicably sad at the time. She looked stunning standing beneath the small spotlight of Adaline's cabin light. Her hair was artfully arranged high on her head, her dress was leagues ahead of the things anyone else wore on tour and the thin belt that drew the eye to her hourglass shape was an exact match to the plum coloured pumps tied to her feet with black ribbon.

Adaline knew instinctively what the other girl had come here for. She wasn't looking for someone else any more than she was about to ask Adaline to come outside and drink with her. She'd come for Adaline particularly and she wanted to talk. The ugly, self-serving part of Adaline snarled at the intrusion. She'd been so careful to avoid the cause behind Maree's ever-changing moods – if she let her in that barrier would crumple. Maree wanted a confidant. Adaline hadn't thrown her hat in the ring for that job yet here they were.

Her fingers flexed on the door. They itched to close it, the polite apology was already balanced on her tongue. Instead she stepped aside.

Maree smiled briefly, ducked her head and moved around her. She turned a slow circle, considering the room, then sat on the edge of Holly's bed. Adaline had the curious sense of being on the clock. Maree wanted to get started.

Adaline took a deep breath then dumped her things onto her bed. She dropped down beside them and pulled her legs up beneath her. 'What's up?' she asked.

Maree touched her throat and looked away. 'I'm sorry for coming here. I

... I'm just sorry.' When Adaline said nothing, Maree hurried to fill the silence. 'I know you don't like getting too close to people – you don't want their worries. You know, except Rory. And I kept telling myself not to come but ... you're so kind. I thought you might listen. I thought you might ... help.'

Adaline's girl apart gig hadn't gone as unnoticed as she'd thought. It also hadn't dissuaded anyone particularly well. Forever the carer, forever the helper – it was like people could smell it on her. With a sigh, Adaline gave into it. 'Did you have a good day?'

'We're in Venice, aren't we? What a silly question!' But Maree's smile was nothing like it should be. She lifted her chin and shrugged a shoulder. 'It was romantic. Beautiful. Old but somehow timeless. And, let's see ... I'm hung over because I tried to drown my nerves last night. Will managed to look at the same things I did yet had no idea where I'm coming from. And sometimes ... sometimes I look at you and Rory and think the two of you are closer to getting married than me and Will are.'

Adaline thought hard about what issue to respond to first. 'You're right,' she said at last. 'It is somehow timeless.'

Maree laughed, caught off guard.

'I'm kidding,' Adaline continued. 'What happened?' Venice – or Will, more like – had not delivered, that much was clear. Adaline suspected Maree had counted down to this part of the trip the same way Adaline was counting down to Greece. Now it had come and gone and left her wanting.

Maree laughed scornfully. 'More like what didn't happen.'

Adaline put her elbows on her legs and leaned forward. 'He didn't propose.' All the over-the-top fashion choices, all the initial exhilaration and gradual disappointment, it all suddenly made sense. Maree had been waiting for that all-important question.

Maree closed her eyes. 'Will, he's ... I'm driving myself crazy. I don't know if I'm ruining this trip for myself or if he's ruining it. I keep thinking there's no better time – we're in Europe, ask me.' She opened her eyes and stared at Adaline. 'But then I think, what if it doesn't matter where we are? What if he never asks?'

'You could ask him. Not propose,' Adaline hastened to add when Maree's expression twisted. 'Ask him if that's where he feels the two of you are going.'

'We talk about our future all the time.'

'You talk about when you're married?'

Maree looked away. 'We have sometimes. Most of the times it's implied, I guess.'

Adaline had no response. She couldn't guess what her role was here. When Maree asked for help did she mean advice? Or was she seeking a sounding board, someone she could speak to without criticism or commentary? For something to do she stretched her legs out in front of her.

Her nerves tingled as blood rushed back to her toes.

Maree appeared uncomfortable with the silence. 'What are you thinking?'

Where Adaline had once seen thin circles of brown in Maree's eyes, there seemed only desperation now. She wore her misery on her mouth, which sagged under the weight of it. Adaline thought of Florence, Rome and the Greek islands, and wondered how much worse Maree would look if those highlights were to host disappointment too. No one should be this unhappy on a holiday through Europe. No one should be this unhappy at all.

She cleared her throat and dropped her gaze to the bedspread. 'I was wondering how long you were willing to wait.'

This was met with one of the longest stretches of silence Adaline had experienced on tour.

She didn't mean to cause trouble, she certainly wasn't suggesting Maree do anything rash, but Adaline couldn't understand why the girl allowed herself to be so uncertain. It was one thing to be unsure about your future because you didn't have the answers, but it was another to not be willing to ask the right questions. Adaline was no relationship expert, having enjoyed so few intimacies herself, but she hoped she'd never allow herself to be a prisoner of her own fear. Thoughts of her mother came into focus then crystallised, but Adaline decided it wasn't the same.

Adaline was just considering whether she ought to apologise when Maree found her voice again.

'I'm not sure anymore.'

Adaline nodded slowly. She didn't still know what to say. Maree clearly had some deep thinking ahead of her and Adaline sympathised, but she hoped Maree wouldn't do that here. Adaline didn't want a front row seat to someone else's relationship drama. She was flat out avoiding her own.

It was good luck then that at that moment there was another knock on the door. Rory was here to save her. Adaline leapt up from the bed and practically fell on the handle. She swung the door wide and her ready smile dropped.

Claire stalked inside, her expression a storm. Her shoulders were pulled so far forward that there were two sharp hollows above her collarbone. She went straight to the spot Adaline had just risen from and dropped on to it. Her typically neat bob was unkempt. Adaline opened her mouth then closed it.

Maree was the first to recover. 'Rough night?'

Claire sniffed viciously. She pulled her knees up to her chest, wrapped her arms around them and glared into the middle distance.

Maree made herself more comfortable. 'Still moving in with Jenny?'

'Not on her life,' Claire said, a dramatic pause between each word.

Adaline sighed and closed the door. She sat on Rachael's bed.

'She's drunk again!' Claire exploded, throwing her arm out to gesture beyond the walls of the room. Adaline supposed she was pointing towards the bar. 'We just moved from rubbish bin to bloody rubbish bin in Venice but never mind that, let's do it all again! Screw tomorrow, too!'

Despite her mood, Claire was clear-eyed and sober. Adaline guessed that it hadn't been a group need for vomit stops today. Claire had been fine and Jenny had been a mess. Adaline pitied her. Nevertheless, Adaline wasn't entirely sure why Claire was here letting off steam, and not in her own room or raging at someone else. Had she known Maree was here?

'I'm sick of looking after her,' Claire went on. She raked her fingers through her hair then hooked them together behind her neck. She looked crazed. She bounced her feet on the mattress. It rocked her entire body and made her little chandelier earrings quiver. 'I'm sick of being the responsible one. This is my holiday too! I have problems too but *I'm* not getting wasted and putting it all on her!' She slapped her hands down onto the mattress and shot her feet down to the floor. 'I didn't sign up for this!'

Adaline stared at her hands and waited for the next knock on the door. What the hell was taking Rory so long?

'Well, it's good to know this stuff now,' Maree said, finding the positive. 'Early. Before you sign a lease together.' Her smile slipped. 'And make too many big decisions. And, you know, adopt a cat or something.'

Claire raised an eyebrow. 'You and Will breaking up?'

This knocked Adaline out of her reverie. 'Claire!'

'What? It kind of sounded like she wasn't talking about me and Jen, that's all.' When neither girl responded, Claire shrugged. 'Okay, whatever. So listen …' Her tone changed and her posture relaxed. The moment had come and gone, steamrolled by the next. 'Zoey's trying to claim responsibility for the hickey on Jack's neck, but he didn't show her the slightest bit of interest at the bar tonight so no one believes her.' She looked at Adaline closely. 'People think you did it.'

Adaline made a very unladylike sound of amusement and tossed her head. 'No way. Not me.'

'I said that, but Daniel's telling everyone you made out, so …'

'Daniel's a moron.' Adaline shook her head. 'Of course he'd be the one to see us.'

Claire's eyes lit up. 'So it's true!'

'No,' Adaline said, 'we didn't make out. Jack kissed me and I pushed him away. There was no …' Adaline searched for the word, wanting to be clear about her position without making Jack the bad guy. 'Mutuality,' she said at last. 'He got his signals crossed. I wasn't into it.'

'Of course you weren't,' Maree said. 'You're into Rory.'

Claire was like a kitten, enraptured by movement, distracted by change. Her eyes shone with new interest. 'Yeah, what's the go there?'

Adaline imagined a butterfly net crashing down on any of her words bold enough to have wings. Claire was sweet and effusive, but not discreet. The feelings tumbling through Adaline's body and her memories of today were private. They were not gossip fodder nor open for any interpretation beyond her own. She shrugged.

'Oh c'mon,' Claire wheedled. She leaned towards Adaline, let herself overbalance and dropped onto the mattress. She propped herself up with her elbows. 'Remind me there's love in the world.'

Adaline was unmoved. 'Claire, there's love in the world.'

Claire made a face and rolled onto her back. Clearly deciding Adaline was too much effort, she moved the conversation on. Letecia had kissed Pies last night, then the pair had been conspicuously absent for a good hour shortly after. Beth and Daniel had argued again. Jenny had slapped Danya. It had seemed unprovoked but Claire supposed it could have been because he'd been coming on too strong with Rachael, who'd spent half the night dodging him and half the night on the phone. Claire said all of this to the ceiling, her fingers on her stomach and her black bob fanning around her on the mattress.

Adaline wondered about the boy Claire had spoken of at the Chateau. Claire hadn't mentioned him since. Had she lost interest? Had the bright lights of the world and the charming smiles of exotic strangers turned her head? Perhaps the distance – even over so short a time – had proved too much. Proximity was so important for some.

It was a luxury Adaline and Rory weren't going to enjoy for much longer.

After Greece, who could say when they'd next see each other again, if ever? How long could she expect the phone calls and texts to last with so many kilometres between them? The rational part of herself didn't want to expect anything from him, and in her absence of expectation there would be no disappointment. But the hopeful romantic in her wished for a miracle, something that closed the gap between them and gave them a thousand reasons to believe in a shared future.

Miracle or not, the Athens airport was going to host her divided heart.

The door opened again, this time with a key. Rachael and Holly stepped in and with widened eyes took in the girls on all the beds.

'So this is where the good time is,' Rachael said, dropping beside Adaline and making her bounce. Holly sat beside Maree. Claire was on Adaline's bed, sprawled out, leaving little space for anyone to join her. With the five of them together, the room seemed too small, too intimate.

Could Adaline just leave? Make her excuses and rescue herself? She'd find Rory easily enough: she'd follow the noise. Maybe he was in a similar situation. Maybe he needed rescuing from tour mates. She tried to picture a bunch of guys crowded together sharing problems and gossip, but couldn't quite see it in her mind.

'Jenny got her boobs out again,' Rachael told Claire. Claire sniffed at the ceiling. 'There aren't many people at the bar, just the die hards. Everyone else must be having little cabin parties too.'

'No party here,' Adaline said.

'Well not yet,' Rachael replied. 'But we're here now. Anyone got any booze? Disco balls?'

Claire sat up. 'Only scandals.'

'Ooh, brilliant.' Rachael made a show of settling herself in. Opposite her, Holly smiled and began to pull the pins out of her hair. 'What's new in the world?'

'Maree and Will are heading for Splitsville and Ada pashed our sexy tour manager.'

'What and *what?*' Rachael cried. Holly's fingers stilled. Her lips parted in a soundless exclamation of surprise, then she began to cough. Hard. She bent over, closing in on herself. Maree thumped her on the back then waved a hand, as if scrubbing the air. 'That's not … Claire for god's sake, stop being such a gossip. Or at least give context.' She looked between the newcomers. 'Will and I are just having a fight.'

'And I *got* kissed,' Adaline added. 'It's an important distinction.'

'Did you kiss back?' Holly asked, straightening. Her eyes were shining and her face was a little flushed. The question was as polite as she could make it, despite her obvious curiosity.

'No. I didn't want him to kiss me. I still don't.'

'What did Rory say about it?'

'He freaked out,' she allowed, 'but we're fine now.'

Claire shifted again. Her smile was full of bargain. 'Okay, you're all caught up.' She held her palms out to Rachael and Holly as if expecting payment. 'Now you have to contribute to the pool.'

Rachael took a deep breath. 'Okay, so Zoey's trying to claim Jack —'

'Heard it' Claire made a rolling motion with her hand.

Rachael was not discouraged. 'Lois skipped out on her room charge at the last place. Apparently she rang home for over an hour then was first on the coach in the morning. The manager threatened to get us stopped at the border if she doesn't pay up before we fly out to Athens.'

The other girls laughed, but Adaline was dismayed. 'How can you possibly know that?' She didn't mean to sound doubtful, she didn't even mean to have the edge of a scolding in her voice, but surely the manager had spoken with Jack, not Lois. Had Jack been so indiscreet as to gossip about something as serious as attempted theft?

Rachael glanced around the room before looking back at Adaline. 'Lois told everyone who'd listen just before we left the bar. Apparently she's really homesick. She hasn't really connected with anyone on tour.'

Adaline dropped her gaze to her knees. She remembered Lois's overwhelming efforts to form a bond between them. Her insistence that they were similar, her constant touching. Adaline had felt like she'd been drowning in the girl's attention, but hadn't until now wondered if Lois had been drowning too.

This trip had made Adaline feel a lot of things, but not isolated and never lonely. She'd been lucky to catch and hold a person like Rory's attention, and had slipped almost effortlessly into a sizable group of people she now considered friends. She remembered her first night, shaking with adrenalin, curled up alone in a hotel room many storeys above strangers taking those tentative first steps towards friendship, and knew her trip as a solo traveller could have gone very differently.

Where was Lois now? Who was she rooming with? Was she having money trouble? Surely desperation had carried her onto that coach and away from that bill. She couldn't possibly have imagined she'd get away with it. Had she been trying to buy herself more time to get some funds together for the unexpected expense?

'Please don't rescue her.' Claire's voice was flat.

Adaline blinked and started. She stared at the girl.

'I mean it. I'm sure she's really nice and all, but between her and Jenny I think I'd start pulling my hair out.' She paused and leaned forward onto her elbows. 'Think of my hair.'

Holly leaned forward. 'Maybe you could rescue me instead?'

'You?' Adaline drew a blank. 'Why?'

'I have to meet Pete's parents in a few days!'

Rachael was the first to react. 'One step at a time, Hols, you need to meet *him* first! I'm sure everything will go great, but if he turns out to be a balding, paunchy forty year-old, I'm going to call the police and tell them he stole my wallet.'

Holly opened her mouth in surprise. Then she laughed. 'He won't be *any* of those things, I've chatted with him on Skype – I'd've noticed!'

Rachael blew Holly a kiss and Adaline smiled. Rachael's affections were both inconstant, and perfectly timed. She could seem unsympathetic and sarcastic, but when it really mattered, she was all heart and reassurance. A firecracker in control of itself. It was a shame she didn't allow herself to go off when her boyfriend called

As if reading Adaline's mind, Rachael offered herself up next.

'If you're going to rescue anyone, rescue me.' She lifted her phone from a discreet pocket in her skirt and shook it between her fingers. As her audience looked sympathetic, she said, 'You'd think setting an alarm to be my boyfriend's first birthday phone call would win me some girlfriend points, but I just got a sulky guilt trip for my trouble.' Her tone was light, but there was pain in her eyes.

Maree shook her head. 'You're a funny one to work out. You're so tough, but the moment Sean rings you fall to pieces. What's happening there?'

Rachael threw her hands up. 'That's what's doing my head in. That's what's waiting for me at home: a soon-to-be fiancé frightened of the world! Assuming I get the money together to travel again, who's to say he'll put up with me taking off again?'

'Put up with…' Adaline echoed.

Rachael waved her hand impatiently. 'You know what I mean. He can't tell me what I can and can't do, but I may not have the strength to put our relationship through this strain again. I'm scared I'll stay in that hick, nothing town because it's easier than travelling again.' She paused. 'And I love travelling.'

'Is it a deal breaker?' Adaline asked. She caught Holly's dark expression but didn't draw attention to it.

Rachael put her face in her hands. She spoke into them, muffling her words. 'No. I love him more than anything. He's a pain in the arse but I'm still going home to him, and I miss him. I just wish loving him didn't equal so small a life, you know?'

Adaline did know. She felt the same way about loving her mother.

Everything inside Adaline was screaming for Rachael to run. 'Are you … hoping he'll change?'

Rachael turned her phone over and over between her hands. 'Maybe a little bit.'

Empathy pulsed so strong through Adaline's system it felt like a second heartbeat. 'You can't count on that,' she said quietly.

Rachael looked at her, and their gazes held. 'I know,' she answered, equally quiet.

Adaline looked away. Another cry for help, she thought. Another distress call, however lightly spoken. She waited for the withdrawal inside herself that was sure to come, but after a moment, she looked back.

There was nothing.

No resentment, no building panic … only sympathy.

And an idea.

Emboldened by Rachael's permission, she got to her feet. All eyes lifted to her as she crossed the room. She put her hand out, palm up. Rachael looked at it, confused, until Adaline took the phone from her. Then she looked stricken.

Adaline said, 'Consider yourself rescued.'

Rachael's protestations were drowned out by cheers.

'You get a thousand friend points from me,' Adaline continued, 'and a break. His calls will just have to go through to voicemail until this time tomorrow. He'll survive it.' She held up her other hand when Rachael began to rise. Rachael paused. 'Give yourself permission to be unavailable. It's not selfish. It's healthy. I promise you, you'll be counting down to speak to him again by the time I give this back.' Or not, she thought. But that was another

161

bridge to cross at another time. 'When was the last time you were excited about that?'

Rachael's expression was a curious blend of misery and gratitude. 'Days. It's been days,' she confessed, 'since I was happy to see his name on that screen.'

'No Facebook either,' Maree chimed in. 'Just be off the grid for a while.'

Holly and Claire weighed in with nods.

Rachael dropped back onto the bed. She sighed. After a long moment of consideration, she nodded too. 'Can I just say … I'm sorry in advance for whatever I say over the next twenty-four hours.'

Adaline smiled. She pushed the phone into the back pocket of her jeans. 'Apology accepted in advance.'

Claire cupped her hands around her mouth and made a trumpeting sound. 'Ada to the rescue!'

Adaline turned a slow circle as the girls all began to trumpet and laugh. Warmth flooded through her body, making the room feel too warm. She crossed her arms around herself and grinned. Yes, she had a saving people thing. Yes, sometimes she was too busy holding other mouths above the water to stop herself from drowning, but right now, that fear was a distant, insubstantial thing. These girls' ridiculous, tuneless noises were as sweet as applause. Off-key thanks of the likes she'd never received from the biggest damsel in distress she knew.

Holly lifted her hand above her head. She wriggled her fingers. 'Me next!'

The energy in the room seemed to build. Each girl tried to speak louder than the next to get their question heard. There was laughter, joy. It's like they were all drunk on confessions. Amongst it all, Adaline heard a knock at the door. She opened it, a broad smile making her unusually aware of her cheeks.

Rory was on the path outside, arrived at last. His eyes widened as he took in the full room. Laughter seemed to nudge past her and roll out the door, a thick, shining thing full of colour. His mouth opened then closed. The laughter switched to teasing whoops and whistles when the girls realised who had joined them. Some called him inside, others begged Adaline to shut the door. It may have been a trick of the soft light and shadows, but Adaline thought she saw his face flush.

Grinning, she stepped down to be level with him on the path. He was so handsome, she thought. His face looked soft, smoothed out by fatigue and comfort, and his hair was flat on one side. Something warm and light did a funny little dance in her chest.

'It's a party,' he said.

'Of course, Rachael and Holly are here.'

Peals of laughter from inside. Smiling broadly, she pulled the door closed behind her. The laughter warped into wails and complaints, then became laughter again. When it was just the two of them, she put her arms around him and hugged him tight. His arms came immediately around her. As she moved back he looked delighted.

'Sorry,' she said. 'I've had a few drop-ins.'

He had such a rich laugh, she thought. It made her think of the crackle of a newspaper and a fast beating heart. The constant need to be with Rory, speak with him, somehow bring her body in contact with his, was intensifying every day. Even so, she hoped he wouldn't draw her away. Something was happening inside that cabin, *continuing* inside without her, and she wanted to be part of it. A memory was in the making, the kind that would always come forward when she recalled this trip. That would fill her with worth and comfort, and remind her that need could bring people together.

'Raincheck?' she ventured. There was a small hitch in her voice. She hoped he hadn't heard it. They'd made plans, she knew. But life had happened. Would he understand that?

Before anxiety could find a foot-hold within her, Rory released her of any sense of obligation. 'Of course. Raincheck. Tomorrow. Next week.' His eyes flashed with humour. 'October. I'm flexible.'

The little dance in her chest became a tumble.

He became abruptly serious. 'But I'm hoping tomorrow.' He paused, then the larrikin was back. 'And next week. And October.'

A small voice in the back of her mind suggested that he'd passed. It hadn't been a test, but it had been a kind of turning point. But was is towards or away from something? It unsettled her that she was as grateful as she was disconcerted. Did she want him to make things easier for them, or had she already decided they wouldn't make it?

Rory took her hand, pulled her close and brushed his lips over hers. It was a slow, sinking sort of kiss, one that got deeper and deeper. She wondered what the bottom was like and bet it was glorious. Or maybe there wasn't a bottom at all, maybe it was all endless depths and boundless wants to be with him.

He pulled away, leaned forward to kiss her forehead, then he left, giving up his moment for her to join another. She watched him go, feeling that curious rubber band connection between them.

When she went inside she didn't think of rescues again, she thought only of the space electronic disco optional excursion in Florence and the Colosseum tour in Rome. She worried with the others about finding a vantage point amongst the crowds during the Santorini sunset, and she was the loudest amongst them to enthuse about hiring a car on Mykonos so they could get around easily.

Adaline, was, by nature, a planner. She'd researched this trip more than she'd ever admit; the places, the optional extras, what previous travellers had liked and disliked about the tour. She'd packed according to weather patterns, bought and read guidebooks on places and customs. Her prep-work would make a scout proud. Yet something she hadn't factored into her plans were people.

It had never occurred to her that Verona on her own would prove anti-climactic, or that she would meet a guy who she just had to share Venice with. No guidebooks or internet searches had hinted at that conundrum. And although the Gateway social media pages and message boards were full of travellers claiming to have made lifelong friends, she hadn't imagined it would happen to her.

Tonight, everything felt different.

Her heart was open.

To new experiences, to change, to these girls.

To love.

She couldn't imagine anything could knock her down from this incredible high.

26 EGO

It was the coolest morning of tour so far. Adaline was anxious to start running to get her body warm. She was waiting on the main road near the internet bus where she could see down four of the larger roads. As yet, Jack hadn't appeared on any of them. She'd done her stretches twice over by now and was running out of patience.

Had he been at the bar last night with the others? Rachael and Holly hadn't mentioned him. Had he met up with the girl he'd spent the first night here with? Had it been Rosa? Adaline could remember. She had no way of knowing what state Jack was in and if he was likely to drag himself from bed. Nevertheless, she gave him a few more minutes.

She was holding her shoe against her backside and stretching her quads for the third time when she spotted movement halfway down the left road. She dropped her foot and waited. Tall like Jack, a dark mop of hair like Jack's. The small flame low in her belly grew into a fire.

Confrontations, she thought. Gross.

Yesterday she would have been content to ignore the problem, perhaps even for the rest of the trip, but last night when she'd been surrounded by her friends and all their various wants and needs, she'd changed her mind. She'd never intended to punish Jack for kissing her, just give him a hell of a lot of space. But now she understood there was kindness in facing this with him, talking to him about it and letting the moment pass.

The figure turned towards her and began a slow jog along the bitumen. When the dark head came up and she saw the pale colour of his face, his steps faltered. She waited, patient, as he worried and wondered. Eventually he resumed his approach.

When he moved up alongside her, his face was flushed. Not with exertion, she supposed.

'Hi,' she ventured.

He was quiet a moment. There was tumult behind his eyes. He ducked his head. 'Hi.'

ONE FOR THE ROAD

'We owe each other an apology.'

Jack's head snapped up and there was suddenly more in his eyes, emotions that she couldn't place. 'We — What? You do *not* owe me an apology. I …' Colour bloomed in his cheeks and down the length of his throat. It made him look like he was choking. 'I forced myself on you and you stopped me. I'm the only one at fault here.'

A sickly, crawling feeling of unease rolled through Adaline's body at the memory. Forced was such a violent word, she thought. Her remembered feeling of being dramatic made her want to reassure him that hadn't been the case, but her fear was proving hard to forget. Dramatic or not, the way he'd behaved with her had sped her heart in the worst possible way. So she didn't reassure him, or contradict his choice of word. She let it hang there between them a moment, and in those seconds the chill in the air was forgotten.

Jack pushed his hand across his mouth and dragged in an unsteady breath. 'I'm so sorry. In my head, you were just being cautious. Waiting for that … that catalyst that would change our relationship. I was trying to convince you, but I was so sure you were already thinking the things I was offering.' He turned on his heel, a quick agitated circle that seemed to expend some excess energy. Hands out, imploring, he said, 'I'm not trying to justify myself.' She raised an eyebrow and Jack's hands fell to his sides. 'Oh god, I am, aren't I?'

He stepped forward and adrenalin surged down Adaline's legs. She'd stepped back before she'd consciously decided to do so. It surprised them both, Jack enough that he didn't try to move closer again.

'I'm sorry,' he said. This time she supposed it was for the sudden approach. 'I'm so sorry, Adaline. None of my excuses or justifications matter, I shouldn't have done what I did, period. I'm sorry I cornered you and frightened you. I'm sorry for everything you felt and for how I've handled things.'

He must have registered her flicker of confusion, because then he said, 'I should have been the one to find you to make this right. Not you.' He swallowed and looked at the ground. 'But I was a coward.'

'And busy,' she said. She didn't mean it as a jibe, only as a way of moving the conversation forward.

Jack blanched. 'That was pride. I fell into the arms of the first woman who wanted me.'

Adaline wanted to ask who, but didn't. Her only reason for knowing the woman's name would be for gossip. She didn't need it. Trying to be good natured about this whole thing, she hitched a smile on her face. 'I hope your ego's back on track, then.'

He flinched. 'Ouch.'

Adaline shot out a hand between them. 'I'm so sorry, that came out so wrong. I only meant to say …' She floundered. 'I don't know what I meant to say.' She dropped her hand to her side. 'Can we just agree that it was a

166

mistake, that it won't happen again and run it off?'

Jack pulled his shoulders back and nodded. 'Yeah, sounds good.' He nodded over her shoulder. 'I run along the road when I'm here. I like seeing the boats on the canal.'

Adaline turned to look where he'd indicated. It was too early for any consistent traffic and all the boat owners would surely be at home or deep asleep within their vessels. She turned back and pointed down the middle right of the four roads. 'I was actually hoping to make a route through here. I still can't get my head around the scale of the place.'

Jack nodded. He shook his shoulders and arms, changed his breathing, then set off down the road she'd chosen. If he'd guessed she wanted to be near people, he hadn't let on. If he knew she had a letter on her pillow telling the Rachael and Holly what she was doing and with who, he'd be mortified. But that's the way things were now, and no amount of apologies could change that. Adaline was willing to move on, but her road forward would be a careful one.

Half an hour later Adaline slowed to a stop, hands on hips and breaths coming greedy and fast. Jack paced, keeping his muscles warm, and for a while, neither of them spoke.

It was Jack who got his breath back first. 'You know much about Florence?'

Adaline did; she'd spent hours researching it and even longer imagining herself there. She knew it was just over four hours from here. That it was considered the birth-place of the Renaissance and was famous for fashion, history and jewellery. She'd collected images of the beautiful city from the internet, read a book simply because it had been set there, and based on a number of reviews and the website gallery images, suspected she knew where she would eat the first day. She shrugged and wiped the sweat from her brow.

'A few things,' she said, dropping her hands to her side and turning to look in the direction they'd come from.

She was just thinking that she needed to better indulge this conversation – this safe, platonic, easy conversation – when he swung it in a different direction.

'What did you do in Venice?'

She told him, and what she said seemed to confirm something for him.

'You've got a knack for finding the hidden gems,' he said when she'd finished talking. 'Rory was lucky to spend his day with someone who knew how to jump the queues and see the lesser known spots.'

She didn't correct him, didn't mention that she and Rory had been at odds until the middle of the afternoon, and if the thought of the two of them exploring the old city bothered Jack, his tone didn't convey it and the obvious tells weren't there.

'I should let you lead the city tour in Rome.' His smile told her he was joking. 'And I think you know more about Florence than you're letting on. Maybe as much as a person can know without having been there.'

Adaline dropped into a deep stretch. 'I like to be prepared.'

'I'm starting to realise that.'

This time Adaline did catch something in his tone: an obvious double meaning which alluded to their unplanned kiss and her less-than-favourable reaction.

A bead of sweat travelled the line of her collarbone then slid beneath her shirt. She pushed her forearm along her damp hairline. This conversation hadn't gone off track yet, but it was angling in the wrong direction.

Time to reign it back in to safer ground.

'Tell me about the space electronic disco.'

27 BOTH

The Florentine Gateway village brought to mind all the movies Adaline had seen about American summer camps. The coach pulled up alongside a large pool surrounded by cushioned lounge chairs. Long rows of trees flanked packed dirt paths leading in a dozen directions and the wooden cabins with small patio decks made her think of fairy tales and breadcrumbs. Site reps bounced up and down in their pale yellow uniforms. Sunbathing guests looked up from their books with interest. Before he released them, Jack reminded them all of the quick turn-around. There were still hours left in the day so they were heading out again. Everyone was instructed to unload ('Eva-ree leetle thing off tha coach!'), freshen up and re-board within half an hour.

With a quick smile at Rory, who'd been her neighbour these past four hours, Adaline followed Lois off the bus, grabbed her suitcase and followed Holly, Rachael, Claire, Jenny and Beth to room 201.

The breakneck pace of the tour was beginning to affect people and a rattling cough was moving through the group. Holly had it the worst of their little circle and she was considerate about it in all the ways she could be, but there were others, like Daniel, who rarely troubled themselves to so much as put their hands over their mouths.

Adaline often found herself looking at Beth, wondering if there was a limit to her patience and just how bad her brother would have to be for her temper to break. Beth hadn't commented about the bruise circling Adaline's wrist. Adaline didn't know what she expected the girl could say, short of apologising for her brother, but Adaline wasn't feeling any forgiveness towards Daniel anyway, so it didn't matter. Alcohol-fuelled idiocy or not, the man was best avoided. And because no one would sit with him on the coach, which left Beth to do it, Adaline was avoiding her too, by default.

Adaline wasn't the first to ease back from Beth due to the company she kept. There were others, like Maree, who tolerated Daniel's egocentricity and ignorance for the sake of spending time with Beth, but Adaline couldn't do it. His personality was such a clash with hers that it made her feel violent and defensive.

If he touched her again she'd do more than slap him.

The cabin made them all squeal and clasp onto one another. There was a large kitchen and meals area flanked by two bedrooms which each slept three. Adaline couldn't touch the opposite walls of the bathroom at the same time and there were chairs crushed outside on the little covered porch. Space. A luxury they'd all quite forgotten. Despite joking that they might never leave, they were back on the coach within twenty minutes, dressed in fresh clothes and sensible walking shoes.

Adaline was pushing a skin of sunscreen up the length of her arms when Zoey's face appeared over the back of the seat in front of her. Lisa, who was sitting across the aisle from Adaline, accepted the bottle when Adaline passed it to her and used a small amount on her chest and neck.

'What's up, Zo?' Adaline asked, taking the bottle back to apply some to her face.

'How are you?'

Yeah, right, Adaline thought, what do you want? The girl hadn't spared more than a dozen words to Adaline so far, there was a curious animosity between them that Adaline couldn't understand and didn't have the interest to explore. 'I'm good,' she said through her moving hands.

'Good.' The American girl shifted, glancing momentarily down at the person who sat beside her – doubtlessly her one of her travelling companions – then seemed to rally her courage. She straightened her spine, lifted her chin and said, 'You don't want Jack?'

Adaline's fingers stilled on her face. 'Excuse me?'

'The two of you are just friends now? You're with Rory?'

Adaline forced herself to unfreeze. She rubbed the bridge of her nose. 'Yes, we're friends. We've always just been friends.' She pretended not to have heard Zoey's second question.

'Uh huh.' Zoey glanced towards the front of the coach where Jack was greeting people as they boarded. 'So you and I won't have a problem?'

Adaline's fingers were covering half her face now, a flesh and bone shield against Zoey's intrusiveness. 'That depends.'

'You can't have both.'

'I don't want both.'

'Then we're good.' Zoey smiled broadly, the way a cat might do upon getting an unfortunate canary, and dropped out of sight.

Adaline shook her head and put her sunscreen away. As she'd predicted, Jack had his pick of women on his tour. With his hopes for Adaline firmly set aside, he had the opportunity to be very busy for the last leg of their trip. She glanced over at Lisa and smiled. Lisa smiled faintly in return then turned to look out the window. Behind her, Holly coughed and apologised. A few seats ahead, the three Chinese girls were playing a fast-talking game that made them giggle every few seconds. It was the loudest they'd been all tour, and thinking on it now, she'd never seen them in any company but their own. The tallest one who was sharing a seat with Pia had her back to her, and was facing her friends across the aisle.

There were so many people on this coach whose names Adaline couldn't remember, people she hadn't spoken to or had cause to spend much time with. Almost fifty people, all united in a dream to see Europe this way, on this tour and at this time, who could part as either strangers or best friends. Or enemies, Adaline thought, her eyes touching on the back of Daniel's head. Whilst it was possible to spend a little time with everyone – Jack was paid for such a challenge – Adaline believed there was more quality in sticking to her small circle. Since last night, she felt some of them had grown closer still. They'd stood at her proverbial gates, banged on the locks and chains, and refused to be dissuaded. Now they were through, in, and she felt fuller for it.

Tour life was a micro-world, just like Jack had said. It seemed to skew everything, too. Small disagreements became infinitely more dramatic, friendships were accelerated and constancy became an infrequent luxury. Danya had been right when he'd lectured them whilst driving out of London, this coach had become their home. The only thing that never changed. The people were the same, but the relationships shifted every day, exacerbated by heightened emotions and travel-fatigue.

The ever-changing dynamics were fascinating to her.

Rory boarded then. He ignored Jack's greeting and moved up the aisle to claim his seat at Adaline's side. No one presumed to sit with either of them now, they seemed to be wearing big reserved signs around their necks since they'd paired up in Venice. It was ninety-five per cent nice, and five per cent a bit of a shame. Lisa was in that five percent. The Swede had withdrawn from her considerably since France, no doubt because Lisa had harboured her own hopes for the man about to sit between them. That was a friendship that had ended seemingly moments after it had begun.

'Nice shirt,' Adaline said as he dropped down beside her.

Rory glanced down at the picture of a stick man on fire and the words 'Tried it at home', and grinned. 'One of my more respectful ones, considering all the churches I'll be seeing today.'

Adaline nodded sagely, although she wanted to laugh. She'd seen some of his more colourful options when he'd shaken them out after pulling them from the dryer, and was inclined to agree that this was one of his more demure choices.

The Gateway village was close to the city, so the drive to Florence was short. When they pulled over and people began gathering their things and standing in the aisles, Adaline's heart began beating that unique rhythm of a new adventure. History and exploration beckoned, they blew in on the wind that rolled through the front door. Flavour, she thought, and heat. She could smell the sun on the bricks and hear the melody of foreign tongues.

It took an age to disembark.

Danya had dropped everyone off next to the Arno River. Jack put his hand in the air, called, 'Gateway!' then led the way into a small square surrounded by multi-storey, multi-purpose buildings. Through a narrow stone archway there was a spacious leather workshop, and once assembled between the various old fashioned press machines and cutting and pressing tables, the group watched a leather box making demonstration and listened with half an ear to the sales pitch that followed.

A number of people were interested in purchasing one of the famed Florentine boxes until they heard the three-hundred Euro price tag. Despite slavering over the handsome leather journals, albums, and writing instruments, no one bought anything.

Wrong crowd, Adaline thought. If anyone here had that kind of cash to throw around, they'd be on a fancier tour. Gateway was a lower cost option for those who wanted to see as much of Europe as possible on little more than a backpacker's budget. Jack needed to re-evaluate Gateway's relationship with that proprietor or he'd never score a kick-back in Florence. She wondered if she should say something to him, if he'd understand she was trying to help. She glanced over at him then looked away, smiling. Zoey was walking so close to him she was almost underfoot, lost in denim blue eyes.

Under Italian law Jack couldn't guide his group through the city, so he led them to the Piazza della Signoria, a L-shaped square in front of the Romanesque fortress-palace Palazzo Vecchio; there they met up with a stout, heavily-accented local tour guide with a pinched expression and a shin-length olive green dress.

A resident of Florence for fifty-eight years, Maura was a wealth of information and to Adaline's delight, she encouraged questions. She led the group to the replica of Michelangelo's David and explained the significance of the statue's disproportionate hands, then she showed them the statue of Perseus holding the head of Medusa. Adaline took photos of the self-portrait the artist had concealed in the back of Perseus's head as Maura explained the popularity of Pinocchio in the town woodcraft and tourist shops. The author of the classic tale, Carlo Collodi, was born and grew up in Florence, something Maura announced with obvious pride.

Next on the tour was the exterior of one of the oldest and most famous art museums in the western world, the Uffizi Gallery. The narrow lane between two wings of the museum, the *cortile*, was lined with columns and sculptures of famous artists like Leonardo da Vinci.

Rory had remained by her side since they'd stepped off the coach, and glancing at him now, she felt a swell of appreciation. He was giving her space to breathe, the quiet to absorb this new world, and the comfort of his company. He might have had a better time at the back of the group, jostling for space amongst the Australians and joining them in their lewd pictures and jokes, but here he was, within arm's length of the tour leader, and a breath away from her. She reached for his hand.

She couldn't have said what made her do it, but the moment their skin touched and his fingers curled around hers, she didn't care. The connection became an anchor, one she wanted, one she felt from her middle. She moved closer and leaned into him, and suddenly Florence looked brighter. Softer around the edges, as if a filter had been applied. She heard the bustle of people and the clamour of the square, but also the much quieter sound of his breath. She filled her lungs, then sighed on a smile.

'This time of year,' Maura called back to the group, 'the line to get into the museum can take five hours.' She waved a hand, signalling them forward. 'It 'tis worth it, but.' The bracelets around her wrist jangled, reminding Adaline that this city was famous for gold jewellery.

There was a souvenir in Adaline's near future. She'd been budgeting for this.

It was convenient then, that the Ponte Vecchio was the next stop on their walking tour. The Medieval stone bridge was cluttered with shops full to bursting with glittering wares and exquisite marbled papers. The Duomo was the last stop on the walking tour, but because Adaline planned to visit it properly tomorrow, she stayed behind with Rory and a few women to browse and purchase wearable reminders of their visit to Florence. Rory bought something small for his mother and Junk, and Adaline finally learned that his sister's name was Clary. The nickname had come about from the never ending clutter that surrounded her, and, Rory claimed, was drawn to her.

He held up the small charm and it winked in the light. 'She'll probably lose this within the week, then find it again when she moves out.'

It was easy to find the group when they were done. The Duomo could be seen from almost everywhere and the grid pattern of the streets allowed for comfortable navigation. Postcard stands, alfresco ristorantes and *caffetterias* cluttered the footpaths on the way. Green crosses were becoming familiar to her, and she was prone to noticing them because of Rory's interest. They were pharmacies – *farmacias* – and chemists. Rory lingered at windows to shops such as these, intrigued by the international branding, packaging and advertising campaigns of medicines he would one day know much more about. His interest in something separate from her made her feel inexplicably closer to him.

As they made their way through side streets and piazzas, pointing and taking pictures, Adaline and Rory's hands found each other's time and again.

On the coach ride back to the village Jack spoke through the microphone the whole time, outlining the optional activities. People listened, coughed, and readied themselves for another big night. They were free to eat dinner when and where they liked. Jack made a few suggestions, then recommended that those who wanted to kick on make their way to the Red Garter Bar.

A short time later, it was an enormous relief to strip off her sweat stained clothes and shower. Adaline stayed beneath the cool stream for as long as she dared, knowing that there were others waiting for their turn, then bound her hair in a towel, dried off and dressed.

The blue and white contrast panelled dress that she'd bought especially for this trip earned her whistles and compliments when she stepped out of the bathroom. She wondered if this had been the kind of purchase her father had had in mind when he'd given her spending money. Adaline felt a rush of warmth under her skin and laughed. She turned on the spot, her smile wide, then dropped into a dainty curtsy. Her friends applauded.

She brought her toiletries bag out of the bathroom and set herself up at the U-shaped booth beside the small kitchen. As she applied her make-up and styled her hair in a complex overlap of braids, she listened to Rachael murmuring reassurances to her boyfriend – their reunion had been bittersweet, of course – and Claire imploring Jenny to take it easy tonight.

'You don't have to get plastered to have a good time,' Claire was saying.

'Wow, thanks mum.' Jenny tossed her long hair over her shoulder and walked out of the room, into the bedroom she was sharing with Claire and Beth. Claire followed her, her shoulders drawn back, and the squabbling continued in there.

Beth, sitting opposite Adaline in the booth, sighed. She was writing a postcard, her letters tall and loopy, but Adaline could guess she was wondering how much sleep she would get when her roommates were at odds.

Neither girl had much to say to the other, so there was only Rachael on the phone and Holly in the other bedroom, coughing away, sounding anything but healthy for her looming date in Rome. Beth finished her postcard in silence then stepped into the bathroom for a shower. Adaline watched her go, her mascara wand lifted to her lashes.

It was over an hour before everyone was ready. Adaline passed the time checking her emails and liking her tour mates' statuses and photos. She almost wrote an email to her mother, but she didn't want to interrupt the long stretch of silence that she'd enjoyed over the last few days. She did not poke the beast. It occurred to her to venture outside and explore the site, but she didn't feel motivated enough. There was sure to be a lot of walking tonight and plenty of time in the morning to see what needed seeing.

At last, the final shoe was stepped into and the final purse fastened. The six of them strode outside, hair and fabric rolling in the breeze, and prepared to give Florence their all.

28 ADRENALINE

Keen for some familiar food, Adaline, Rory, Will, Maree, Rachael, Holly and Claire ate in the Red Garter steakhouse. Jenny came in later with Beth and Daniel after scouting the piazza for more local fare, but they sat at a different table. This was not commented upon, although Claire's neck flushed red with unspoken feeling.

Next door, the Red Garter bar was everything Jack had hinted at and more. Adaline only had to walk into the place to love it, and to order a two litre mojito pitcher to declare it unforgettable.

Far from the traditional Florentine venue Adaline had expected, it claimed to be Italy's oldest American bar. Long wood tables and bench seats filled the spaces between pillars, the high domed ceilings added architectural interest, and a mezzanine level with a wrought iron balustrade gave patrons an unimpeded view of the raised stage. It reminded Adaline of an old-time saloon, although the live band performing with modern amplifiers and skinny jeans created a fun juxtaposition.

The bar served three and a half litre beer towers, frozen cocktails and two litre special pitchers. Adaline went halves with Rory on a pitcher, and the two of them were lucky enough to secure a bench seat in the back corner to share with Maree and Will. A glance around and Adaline realised they were not the first here; the bar seemed full of people from the tour who'd skipped dinner in favour of hitting the turps.

The music was loud, the patrons were wild and rumour had it, the band would soon finish their set and open the floor to karaoke. Adaline shook her head every time someone suggested she pick a song, and was the loudest supporter whenever someone declared they'd try it.

From where she sat, she had a clear line of sight to most parts of the bar, and what she saw was better than television. She started guessing who would hook up with whom; interpreting lingering gazes and frequent proximity, counting down until everyone had a belly full of alcohol and the courage that came from it.

Letecia and Hamish were bumping bodies on the dance floor, drinking deeply from a pitcher they appeared to be sharing. Instead of straws, they drank from it directly, and laughed when it spilled on themselves or missed their mouths. Nearby, Zoey had already secured the undivided attention of a handsome local. They had their hands all over each other and Jack seemed all but forgotten.

The night would not be a conversational one – the music was too loud and interruptions were constant. People joined them, left. Tagged them on Facebook, took photos Adaline would have preferred they didn't. Then karaoke began at the same time peer pressure kicked in.

Maree dragged Claire up to sing Shania Twain's *Man, I Feel Like a Woman*, which was amusing because Maree sang like a theatre star and Claire accidentally spat on the microphone. Daniel – who'd been in the company of a beer tower and a pitcher he hadn't shared – wailed a poor imitation of Nelly's *Hot in Herre* whilst tugging on his clothes and leering down at women who grimaced up at him. Pies led his group in a blokey rendition of John Farnham's *You're the Voice*, a surprising choice but well-executed one, and word got back to Adaline that Rachael was trying to talk Holly into a *Grease mega mix* duet. Rachael was volunteering to be Danny.

Hours later and despite her many protests, Adaline found herself sharing the stage with one of the tour's biggest personalities. Looking quite respectable in a white collared shirt with a green collar, Rory handed her a microphone and smiled over his own. Lights flashed over his face and danced on his shirtfront. Beneath them, people cheered their anticipation.

The tour's day song started and the crowd went wild. Those at tables stumbled to stand on their seats and the rest on the dance floor elbowed their way to the front. Within two verses, there was a mini mosh-pit.

Lady Gaga would have hated to hear her song sung the way Adaline sang it; Adaline tripped over the words and laughed through the best bits, because even with a microphone, she couldn't compete with the roar from the dance floor. Everyone attempted to sing along. She deliberately warbled the final note, which made Rory break off too early and laugh, and their applause was unquestionably the longest and the loudest. She got claps on the back for almost half an hour.

Hours later, their night ended abruptly when Jenny passed out in a bathroom stall. Claire revived her, but the bar manager wanted Jenny gone.

Those who were ready to leave were happy for the excuse to follow the pair onto the street.

Not for the first time in Adaline's life, she vowed never to drink again. She needed to think – clearly – and she needed to find her way back to bed. The lights of the city, not so long ago incandescent and flattering on street corners and between architraves, were now too-bright smudges which dipped and mingled. She turned her eyes from them and focused on the rolling footpath.

Beside her, Maree walked with her hands up, warding off invisible assailants. On Maree's other side, Will was grabbing light poles, launching himself into the air and for a few seconds each time, holding his body adjacent to them. Adaline was sure he'd had as much, if not more to drink than herself, so it was a wonder that he had the strength to walk, let alone show off. Maree whooped and kissed him every time he fell back to the ground. Their tiff had been shelved for the time being.

The same could not be said for Jenny and Claire. They were arguing again, and about the same thing they'd been arguing about for days: Jenny's drinking.

Personally, Adaline didn't mind that Jenny had got them kicked out. Maree and Will had been acting like there was no end to the night and trying to keep up with Rory's ceaseless energy had been exhausting. Holly and Rachael had gone back to the village hours ago because Holly hadn't been feeling well, and part of Adaline wished she'd gone with them. Now she was too tired, too wired. It was getting close to one o'clock, but despite the hour the city was wide awake. Motorcyclists and motorists eased around pedestrians drunkenly veering off the footpaths. Bars, clubs and late-night restaurants spilled light onto the streets, and high above them, the stars winked like Florentine jewellery.

They walked slowly, Maree with her arm up to flag down any passing cabs. Will's grip slipped on a pole and he tumbled to the ground. He was on his feet again immediately, but the blood on his knees and palms secured him a place in the first cab that pulled over.

As he and Maree clambered inside, Will very gingerly, Rory tried to offer the other two seats to Claire and Jenny, but their row had worsened and neither appeared to hear him.

Maree leaned out of the cab. 'Rory, could you come with us? Could you help Will back to our room?'

Rory peered into the dark cab and nodded. He stepped aside and gestured inside. 'Hop in,' he said to Adaline. 'I'll take the front.'

Adaline hesitated. She looked over at her squabbling friends. 'You go ahead,' she said, turning back. 'I'll wait for them to sort themselves out. I have the address, I'll get them back.'

Rory straightened and moved to close the cab door. 'I'll stay with you.'

Adaline stopped him. 'It's okay, Will needs you.' She rose onto her toes and brushed her lips against his. 'I'll be minutes behind you,' she murmured against his mouth. 'Don't you dare go to bed.' She hadn't kissed him nearly enough tonight and there was something magical about the wood cabins and closely lined trees that made her want him to walk her to her door.

His reluctance was obvious.

When the cab carrying half her friends pulled back into traffic, Adaline rallied her concentration to signal down another. Claire and Jenny weren't going to do it.

'Cross the street,' she called back to them. 'They're all coming from that way.'

Whether they agreed with her logic or not, they followed her off the footpath. A car horn made her jump, but someone was just hurrying them along. Lights were everywhere; white, red, bright and dull. She wasn't walking as steadily as she would have liked for someone suddenly responsible for getting this little group home, but she didn't fancy waiting to sober up – not when Claire and Jenny were shouting now.

'It is my problem,' Claire was saying, "cause people come find me when you're embarrassing yourself!'

'I'm not your responsibility!' Jenny snarled. She tossed her hair angrily and tried to catch up to Adaline, but Claire caught her by the elbow.

'You're the only one who thinks that! And you really think I could just leave you when I find you passed out or in trouble? Why do you have to drink so much? Why does it have to be a binge?'

'Shove off, Claire!' Jenny pulled her arm free and used the other to push Claire away.

Claire lost her balance. She slipped out of her heel and tumbled backwards into the lane of traffic they had just crossed.

Two enormous circles of light seemed to swallow her.

Someone screamed. Brakes and tires screeched, then there was the sickening crunch of bones against metal, then bones against bitumen.

The world was in a vacuum – for a moment there was no sound.

It only came back when Adaline started to run. Then sound was everywhere – people shouting, car horns blaring. People in the distance laughing and chatting, oblivious that the world had just tilted.

She was vaguely aware of knocking against Jenny's side, but then she was beside Claire, down on the road, eyes weeping because she was so close to one of the headlights.

'D,' she said to herself. 'Shit. Shit.' She looked around her. The traffic had stopped. They were no longer in immediate danger. 'R for respiratory – no, response. Response. Claire?'

Claire's eyes were closed. She was propped precariously on her left side, facing away from the car. There was blood everywhere and her body looked strange: crumpled and in odd angles.

'Oh, god. Claire?'

'Claire!' Jenny dropped down beside Adaline. At first, Adaline thought she would grab her and wondered what she might do to stop her, but Jenny seemed afraid to touch her best friend. That, or she knew better. 'Claire!' she screeched. 'Holy shit, can you hear me? Say something! Open your eyes!'

Adaline relinquished the role of response to Jenny, and tried to remember the next step in the school first aid course she'd attended over two years ago. 'A,' she recalled. 'A for airway. Jenny, get out of my way.'

Jenny mightn't have done it, except hands appeared under her arms and lifted her away. There were people around them. One of them was the driver, Adaline was distantly aware of him saying she'd come out of nowhere, that he hadn't had time to stop, and they were all watching Adaline, letting her take the lead.

Oh god, she'd had so much to drink. Somebody else needed to do this.

But even as she thought that, she dragged her knees across the bitumen to bring herself closer to Claire's head.

Airway. Was Claire breathing? No, that was the next step. Airway: check that her mouth was clear, her tongue could have fallen back, she could have bitten it.

Christ, did she put her in the recovery position now, or after she'd checked for breathing?

Adaline leaned over Claire's chest. Blood shone like liquid garnet and soaked the shirt Claire had been so proud of mere hours ago.

'Has someone called an ambulance?' Adaline didn't look around, didn't wait for a response. She pushed her fingers between Claire's lips, eased them gently apart and checked inside for anything that might be blocking her throat.

Behind her, Jenny was losing it. She was screaming for an ambulance, over and over again.

'Take her over there,' said a stranger's voice, 'and turn your headlights off, you're blinding her. *Ora, sbrigati.*'

So many hers, Adaline thought. Was the first Jenny, and the second Adaline?

When the brilliant lights snapped off, Adaline got her answer.

Her eyes struggled to adjust, there was remembered light swimming across the awful sight below her, and tears fell down her cheeks, both from strain and grief.

Breathing. Was Claire breathing? Adaline shifted her position again, lowering her cheek to Claire's open mouth, keeping her eyes on Claire's chest, desperately hoping to see it rise and fall. It did. Adaline gasped in a breath – she'd held her own as she'd waited for Claire's – and straightened.

'She's breathing,' she said, to no one and everyone. She had to think, had to start at the beginning. 'D, R, A, B… C. Compression. No, no, circulation.'

A ghost hand appeared at Claire's neck. Two strange fingers searched for a pulse. Adaline watched, both numb and energised. Her own pulse was racing.

'Okay,' said a voice above her. The voice of the man attached to the hand. Heavily accented, very firm. Telling her, she knew, because somehow she was in charge.

It was time to stop the blood. To immobilise – or could that wait for the ambulance?

Adaline's body was a riot of questions, nausea and adrenaline. She'd hurt herself, but the pain was so far away she couldn't tell how, or even where. Somewhere throbbed.

'I need bandages,' she said, looking over Claire's mangled skin.

'Here.' A woman this time, breathing fast as if she'd been running. She dropped down beside Adaline and offered her a compact kit, something similar to the first aid car kits used in Australia. Adaline took it from her.

Somewhere in the dark recesses of her mind, she registered that the woman was kneeling in blood.

That Adaline was kneeling in blood.

Panic was a thousand balls of glass pushing through her veins, cutting her apart, opening her up. Her stomach rolled – first left, then right. Stirring her dinner and the many drinks she'd washed it down with.

She was unzipping the kit, fumbling with the case, when it occurred to her she hadn't thanked the woman.

'Thank you,' she said, glancing up then returning to her task.

'You said that already,' said the woman. She touched Adaline's arm in a global gesture of comfort, then held both hands out, palms up.

Adaline hesitated, then thrust a plastic wrapped gauze roll into the woman's right hand.

'Shit, recovery position.' Adaline dropped the kit onto the road and turned back to Claire.

Her friend was already half way there, so Adaline needed only to straighten her left arm and draw her right leg across her left one, propping her up. She did this very gently, as Claire's leg was raw skin and misshapen bone. She thought for a moment if she should have rolled her onto her other side to spare her leg, but Adaline didn't want to move her any more than was absolutely necessary.

Spinal injuries … please, no.

Beside Adaline, the woman had taken the plastic off the gauze and was wrapping the material around Claire's right ankle. She'd used Claire's inflexible clutch purse as a splint, the closest appropriate thing on hand.

Another man had joined them and was wrapping her knee with a second bandage. Her spoke rapid Italian to the woman at Adaline's side, who spoke just as rapidly back. Between them, the gauze on Claire's knee changed from white to red. Blood pooled on the road.

Adaline refocused on Claire's airways, repositioning Claire's head on her arm and nudging her mouth wide to keep the passage clear.

She dragged the first aid kit towards herself, thinking of triage, thinking of what came next and what was most important. And until she heard the whine and wail of sirens, all she thought about was blood, and how to stop it.

When hands touched her, curled around her and tried to pull her away, Adaline's first instinct was to pull her arm free and shove – but that's what had caused all this. She forced herself not to react so violently.

'*Va bene, io sono qui per aiutare. Fammi vedere la sua.*' The paramedic had a kind face, and although his words were meaningless, his tone went a way towards calming her.

'*Inglese,*' said the woman beside Adaline. She pushed herself to her feet and a second paramedic took her place.

The paramedic beside Adaline spoke again, but this time Adaline could make sense of it. 'Hello, I will help. Please step back.'

Adaline welcomed relinquishing the front seat, and moved quickly.

She wasn't standing for more than a second before someone was touching her again. This time, it was the guiding hands of a police officer. He steered her away from Claire, over to the footpath where a second officer was trying to make sense of Jenny's garbled explanations and pleas for reassurance.

Adaline sat, although she dropped so hard, it was more like a fall.

The officer crouched beside her. '*Inglese?*'

She nodded.

'You're hurt.'

'No,' she said.

His eyes dropped to her knees. When she followed his gaze, she was surprised to see that she'd torn them up on the bitumen as she'd moved up and down the length of her friend's broken body. There were small stones in the scrapes, stolen from the road which looked set to steal from them.

The police officer said, 'What happened?'

What a loaded question. They'd drank too much. Adaline had insisted they cross the road. Jenny had pushed Claire and Claire had fallen. The car hadn't stopped, hadn't been able to. All of this she knew, but what *had* happened? What would?

Jenny answered his question, fast and full of emotion. Adaline was only half listening, everything was slowing down. She kept seeing the accident happen, again and again, like a movie stuck in a loop. Why was the officer blinking so slowly?

'Now you,' he said, smiling kindly at Adaline. He glanced at the officer beside him, who worked to hold Jenny's attention. Jenny burst into frightened tears.

'We were crossing the road.' Jenny had already confessed to pushing Claire, there wasn't really any need to disguise that fact, but Adaline found she couldn't repeat it. 'I said we should cross the road. It wasn't the driver's fault – she fell into the lane we'd already crossed.'

'Who is she? She is your friend – what's her name?'

'Claire.'

'Claire what?'

Adaline didn't know. There were so many names to learn on tour – forty-eight first names and she hadn't even managed that. Last names … she had no idea. Hadn't she seen it on Facebook? Trying to remember felt like grasping at fog. 'Jenny's Claire's best friend.'

Jenny's sobs worsened.

Adaline answered a few more questions, all the while pushing hard against the advancing black. When she couldn't hear over the roar of noise in her ears, or see past her own tears, Adaline grasped the officer's wrist and asked a question of her own.

'Do you need anything more from me?'

'Not right now, Miss.'

And then nothingness was a thing. It smothered her and dragged her down, into the black where there was fear and peace, into the roar of blood, and whatever else was waiting in the dark to claim her.

29 AFTER

When Jack's dream became a musical, he opened his eyes. Disorientated and exhausted, he shot his hand out over the bedside table and slapped his palm down on his ringing phone. With great effort, he lifted it and moved it to his ear.

'Okay,' he said stupidly.

'Jack? It's Nathan from Gateway.'

Christ. Jack rolled up into a half sitting position and rubbed his eyes with his free hand. Nathan from Gateway meant another desperate sob story from Adaline's mother. He needed to record himself; a placating comment here, an understand murmur there. It would save everyone a lot of time. She didn't listen to any of it anyway. As far as Georgia Sharp was concerned, Jack was a talking, hated wall between her and her daughter.

It'd been a nice few days, too. It was a shame to ruin what he'd come to think of a streak. A holiday within a holiday. When was the last time she'd called, was it Verona? He'd been trying to catch up on some paperwork in the sun. She'd called him a bunch of names, threatened to get him sacked then cried until his coffee had gone cold. She'd abruptly hung up and he'd hoped that would be the last of it.

'Put her on,' he grumbled. He wasn't going to bother with a new excuse. He was just going to tell her Adaline didn't want to talk to her. It was hardly going to worsen Georgia's already low opinion of him.

'Jack, focus. There's been an accident.'

All of the muscles in Jack's sagging body seemed to inflate in an instant. He was sitting up straight, his eyes wide, before he'd fully registered that Georgia wasn't on the other end of the line. An accident, he thought, his mind racing. Who'd come back with him, who'd stayed out? 'Tell me,' he said, his voice sharp.

'Three girls.' Nathan's voice changed as he checked his facts. 'Claire Edwards, Jenny Mortimer and Adaline Sharp. They've been taken to hospital by ambulance. Claire was hit by a car and the other girls are being treated for shock and abrasions.'

Jack swore. He leapt from bed, suddenly wide awake and strategising. 'Text me the address. I'll call you back when I know more.' He hung up and dressed quickly. Claire and Jenny, he thought, and Adaline. Never mind their history, never mind that she didn't return his feelings, right now her name was a bell toll in his mind and there was too much world between them.

* * *

Adaline may have fallen into the dark, but she woke in the light. Bright, artificial light, surrounded by white walls, linoleum floors and stiff sheets. It took a moment for her to remember, then she wished she could forget.

Claire.

Adaline was at the hospital. She'd fainted, been treated for shock, and then been helped into the back of a police car with Jenny. She hadn't said a word, not of comfort, not of blame – she hadn't had the energy for Jenny's breakdown. The girls hadn't spoken all the way here, and now they were sitting together in the waiting room waiting for news that seemed like it would never come.

Whilst they sat here, covered in Claire's blood and stunned into silence, the rest of their friends slept or waited. Perhaps worried. It was a little past two-thirty in the morning and Adaline was both awake, and tired to the point of feeling ill. Or maybe that was all the mojitos. She thought of Rory looking for a cab that wasn't coming and hoped he'd thought to check his messages on Facebook. It was the only way Adaline could reach him and now, at the request of staff, her phone was off, which meant he couldn't reach her.

It was funny to think that one moment she'd been concentrating so hard on putting one foot in front of the other, and the next she'd been responsible for ensuring someone's airways were clear. As her heartbeat had accelerated, so had her sobriety.

The waiting room of the Saint Maria Nuova hospital looked much like its Australian counterparts; lined with uncomfortable seats, papered with fact sheets and posters, albeit mostly in Italian. There was a potted plant in the corner. The fluorescent lights made it hard to tell if it was fake or not.

The double glass doors rolled open and a tall man in jeans and a creased Gateway T-shirt hurried inside. Jack must have gone back to the campsite. He must have been in bed when he'd got the call. Seeing him dressed this way was another reminder of how serious this once-silly night had become. He saw them and shock stilled him. They were a sight, she knew. They looked like horror movie survivors and Adaline had squares of gauze taped to her knees. Jenny … well, Jenny looked like she'd never sleep again. It hurt to look at her agonised face – it did twisting, contracting things to Adaline's heart.

'Adaline, Jenny,' he said, hurrying over. He dropped to his haunches in front of them and moved to put a hand on each of their knees. Adaline stopped him and offered her hand instead. 'How are you holding up?' he said.

It was an interesting first question. Not *are you okay*, because there were a number of answers for that. Not *what happened*, because he already knew as much as he needed to right now.

'I don't know,' Jenny said. Which was what Adaline was going to say.

Jack looked at her and she swallowed. 'I don't want to be here anymore.' Her voice sounded small and brittle.

'Okay. I've spoken with the police and they said you don't need to stay, they have all your details. I'm going to speak with a few people here about Claire, and then we'll go back to the village.'

'I'm staying.' Jenny's voice cracked. She stared at the opposite wall, glassy-eyed and expressionless, looking to Adaline's eyes like one of the statues she'd seen in the Piazza della Signoria today, gazing out at the middle-distance.

Jack didn't argue. He squeezed Jenny's knee then crossed the room to speak with the woman sitting at reception.

Adaline began to slowly gather her things, and she held them to her chest for the entire time it took Jack to get his update, leave his details and explain that he would be leaving for Rome tomorrow. Ordinarily, that would have sent a jolt of excitement through Adaline's body, but there wasn't any room for another emotion, not when there were so many emotions squabbling inside her now.

Jack looked grim when he returned. This time he sat on the edge of the seat beside Adaline, his body turned so he could speak as intimately as the room would allow. Before he spoke the first word, all the colour seemed to fade from Jenny's face. 'They'll only tell me that Claire is unconscious.'

Jenny turned away and began to cry.

Jack changed seats to sit beside her. 'Jenny, I know there's a lot going on right now, but I need you to think about something for a second. Are you listening?' He spoke kindly, and he waited for the worst of her sobs to subside before continuing. 'If you want to stay on the tour, I will make sure you're kept constantly updated on Claire's condition. But,' he held his hand up, because Jenny was now looking at him in horror, 'if you want to stay, I need to know now so I can arrange everything for you.'

'I'm staying.'

He nodded, clearly having expected the answer. 'Do you have travel insurance? Good, okay. I'm going to make a few calls, we'll sort out a place for you to stay from tomorrow night, somewhere close to the hospital. But for now, I want you to come back to the village.' He held up a hand again, stopping her protests. 'There's nothing you can do here. Claire won't be up for seeing anyone for another few hours. I'll come back with you then, what do you say?'

Adaline got to her feet and walked away without hearing Jenny's reply. It must have been a stubborn one, because neither stood and Jack started speaking again.

Whatever Jenny decided, Adaline was leaving this hospital. She needed to sleep, it would be the easiest way to put more time between her and the accident. Assuming of course, that she didn't see bright orbs, broken bones and blood when she closed her eyes. But a small part of her didn't want to return to the village – to the concern and the questions. She didn't want to relive it again. Talking to the police had been awful enough. And yet there were almost fifty people who would feel a connection to this night, to Claire, Jenny and Adaline, who would want more details than the average passer-by.

Jack could do it, she thought. Jack should do it. Not her. Not Jenny. All Adaline wanted was to be left alone, to sleep dreamlessly. Surely no one would deny her that?

It seemed like an age before Jack was able to convince Jenny to return to the village, and he had to support her as they walked outside. After everything that had happened tonight, Jenny was still drunk. Although Adaline suspected that fact was reversed in Jenny's mind: Jenny was drunk, which was why everything had happened tonight.

The blame game took no prisoners.

Jack sat in the front passenger seat on the cab ride back. He turned around to check on them often, but Jenny never looked anywhere but her lap, and Adaline found no comfort in his eyes and so faced the window. She thought about Rory and wondered if he could have made her feel better about this, if there were any words in this world that could. He would find out with everyone else tomorrow, probably at breakfast, and maybe he'd want to talk to her, maybe not.

Not for the first time, Adaline wished she was with Rory instead of Jack.

Adaline thought about Claire's parents for the rest of the trip, who had doubtlessly been called by now. How awful to receive terrible news from the other side of the world, to be rendered useless by distance. She wondered if Claire's parents had the capability to get here.

Poor Claire. When she woke, she'd be in a world of pain in a foreign country, with only Jenny at her bedside. One of the two people who'd put her between those crisp white sheets in the first place.

Gravel crunched underfoot as they walked along the path between the cabins. There were no lights on in any of the rooms they passed. It had to be close to three-thirty now, and everyone was either asleep or passed out. Everyone except Jack, Jenny and Adaline, three shadows on the path, stooped forward, shoulders slumped, burdened by bad news.

When Jenny knocked on their cabin door, lights came on almost immediately. Holly reached the door first, and a butterscotch glow burned behind her, almost casting her in silhouette. Before anyone could speak, Rachael and Beth appeared. They looked as dishevelled as Adaline felt, but their urgent expressions made her inexplicably cross.

She hadn't wanted this – hadn't wanted everyone to be waiting like this.

Holly put her hand to her mouth, registering the blood and the bandages and the all too horrible absence of Claire. 'Oh no,' she murmured. Not the wild night they'd probably imagined the three of them having, not the reunion they'd expected. Adaline dropped her gaze to the ground and wished she or Jenny had had a key, that they could have slipped quietly inside, if Jenny would have allowed it.

Jenny stepped inside and into the arms of the three women waiting for them.

'Adaline,' Jack said, 'hang back a second.' He motioned her towards him. With a sluggish burst of effort she dragged her feet away from the door, and beyond that the bed that lured her like a siren song.

'The police officers told me what you did,' he said, keeping his voice low. 'Witnesses said you were amazing.'

'I'm tired,' Adaline murmured.

Jack's expression changed – just by a degree. 'Okay. You're still in a bit of shock. But I just wanted to say that … I don't know, well done.'

Well done for not standing by as your friend bled out, Adaline thought. Well done for looking after her just minutes after luring her onto the road. She nodded. 'Okay. Thanks for coming to get us.' She turned back to the cabin, saw the mess of arms around Jenny and turned back. 'Can you please … keep everyone away from me?'

He nodded. 'Does that include me?'

It did. 'Just for a little while.'

'Okay. And Rory?'

She hesitated. 'I don't know.'

When she was within a meter of everyone's reaching arms, Jack called to them. 'Ladies, can I speak with you three for a minute? Jenny, Adaline, sleep well. I'll speak to you both a bit later.'

Instead of claustrophobic hugs and grasping, clutching hands, Adaline got three, quick arm squeezes and then the doorway was clear.

She thought about climbing into bed as she was, but then remembered the blood. With the last scrap of energy in her body, Adaline changed into her sleep clothes and dropped her dress into the bin. She never wanted to see it again.

30 NEEDED

Adaline slept fitfully. The lights were brighter in her nightmares than they were in the room she shared with Jenny, but the nightmares were quieter. Jenny cried a lot. She staggered out to the bathroom half a dozen times, and finally woke someone with her noise who must have got up and looked after her. Much later she staggered in and pulled on a change of clothes. She reached up to Adaline's top bunk and shook Adaline's arm.

'I'm going to see Claire,' she said, her voice thick. 'Are you coming?'

Adaline pretended to be asleep. Jenny tried again, then once more, then gave up. As she left the room there was a curious exchange of lowered voices. Adaline wondered if they were judging her. If they knew that she didn't want to go back to the hospital, that the thought of seeing Claire again made her feel sick and furious.

Too much. It was all too much.

She heard the soft rustle of fabric and realised Jenny hadn't left the room after all. Sulking, she thought, or like Adaline, hiding. Adaline kept still, even as the soft squeak of rubber on metal meant Jenny was climbing her bunk ladder. Another squeak, then another, then the mattress was sagging under new weight and it was all Adaline could do to not push herself up and scream in the girl's face.

Then the scent of country air rolled over her and everything changed. *Not* Jenny. Not Jenny here to drag her to the hospital, but Rory here to fix everything.

She wanted to see him more than she'd ever wanted to see a person, but she didn't want to talk to him. She didn't want to say a single word, kind or otherwise, because there were no words for what she'd seen and how it had made her feel. Every word felt woefully inadequate.

He climbed awkwardly over her, careful to give her knees a wide berth, which told her he'd been briefed. He lay beside her and seemed unsurprised to find her eyes open. He didn't greet her, didn't explain his arrival. He didn't say anything at all. And minutes later, when her startled heart had slowed, she settled into the unexpected companionable silence and nuzzled closer. He put his arm around her and the world was kept at bay.

Gratitude overcame her. She couldn't think of anything beyond his proximity to her. She moved her hand above the sheets, felt him shift, then his hand was around hers, exactly as she'd wanted it to be. She tried to push the heat of her heart down the length of her arm, because if he could feel it, he might understand. She tried to give him her hurt, her gratitude and her need, and fought to keep her eyes dry and clear.

Sleep kept dragging her under, strong, dark fingers that let her surface only for a few disorientating seconds at a time. Each time he was there. Sometimes watching her, other times dozing. She liked when he was sleeping the best. His vulnerability lessened hers somehow. Vulnerability shared was vulnerability halved, she thought.

When she finally got up, it was almost midday and the bloodied dress she'd thrown in the bin last night was gone. She was grateful to whoever had done that, and sorry because it would have been a distressing task. There was only one unread text message on her phone. Jack had done a brilliant job of keeping everyone away from her, but it was unsurprising to see that Maree had ignored this and reached out to her anyway. She had vague memories of someone knocking on the door and wondered if that had been Maree, then she wondered how long ago Jenny had left for the hospital and how Claire was now.

Her heart squeezed as if trapped between two hands determined to touch. She had to get out.

Adaline lurched towards the bathroom and slammed the door. If Rory had been sleeping, she doubted he was now.

Old blood ran off her in the shower, circled the drain and was carried away. Adaline stumbled out of the shower to vomit in the toilet, then stepped beneath the spray again and tried to feel clean. But the grime seemed to be inside her. She didn't cry, but she hardly breathed either. Just short, ragged gasps that made her feel breathless and faint.

Rory was waiting in the small kitchen when she came out and he offered her a wordless smile. She dropped her head and shuffled into the bedroom to drag on some clothes for the day. When she came back, she realised Rory hadn't been as idle as she'd first thought. There were gauze squares and bandages on the dining table. Butterfly clips, sterile wipes and scissors. All waiting for her, all needed after she'd ruined her dressings in the shower.

She sat at the end of the U-bend bench and watched as he got to work. His fingers were careful, painstakingly slow as he rolled her pants legs up over her raw knees. She hissed in a breath each time he touched the sterile wipes to her broken skin, but found comfort in the rise and fall of his voice as he hummed the first verse and chorus of *Bittersweet Symphony*.

It had been such a long time since there had been words between them, she felt a curious pressure to break the silence with something worthy. A confession? A detailed recount? Some kind of proclamation about what it meant to her that he was here? The day trip into town would have left long ago, he'd given up another day in Florence to comfort her.

'You're good at that,' she murmured. 'The kids are going to be lucky to have you.'

He smiled as he secured the bandage over her left knee.

I'm lucky to have you, she thought. The words had weight within her, flavour even, but she wasn't brave enough to speak them.

He rolled her pants legs back into place and stood. She watched him gather the torn plastic and used sterile strips, watched him put them in the kitchen bin then bundle the rest of his first aid supplies together. Here was the serious Rory, the one who would one day have letters afters his name and lives in his hands. She was glad she'd got to see it. Something nice to come out of this whole nightmare. It was ironic, really. She'd been so determined to keep his needs and problems at bay, yet here he was tending to hers without even a whisper of complaint. And it felt … nice. To be the patient, the centre of someone's attention. Oddly enough, it felt nice to be vulnerable.

There wasn't room for such a thing with her mother; vulnerability with Georgia meant opening herself up to ridicule and manipulation.

If this trip had taught Adaline anything so far, it was that she needed to have a heart to heart with her mother when she got back. They needed to agree on boundaries and responsibilities. Georgia needed to understand the impact her illness was having on Adaline, emotionally and psychologically. Adaline didn't want to become a cliché, she had no intention of blaming her parents for everything that had gone wrong in her life, but she needed to empower herself. If she was unhappy being a primary caregiver for her mother she needed to change her thinking and her behaviour. She needed to stop enabling her mother's inconsistent dependency and give Georgia the tools to better help herself.

'Next on the agenda,' Rory said, lifting a tube of sunscreen she supposed he'd brought from his bag, 'a distraction. After that, if you feel like eating we'll eat.'

Adaline smiled. She took another drag of country air and held it in her lungs. 'Thank you,' she said on a long exhale. She waved her hand vaguely. 'For everything you're doing. And everything you're not doing so you can do this.' She made a face. 'You know what I mean.'

He grinned. 'Strangely enough, I do. And no problem. Here.'

He stepped closer, squeezed a worm-sized amount of sunscreen onto his palm and reached around her to press his hand flat against her back. She felt the difference between his warm skin and the cool lotion, then the flush of heat when he moved to stand behind her and began rubbing it in with firm, lingering strokes. He kissed the nape of her neck as he applied more.

Adaline closed her eyes. In the darkness there was little more in the world beyond the different pressures of his lips and hands. When he eased her shirt and bra straps aside she wondered if she was bold enough, opportunistic enough to take advantage of the empty cabin, but in the end she took too long to decide.

He reversed their positions and she felt the mood change. Standing behind him now, the tube of sunscreen in her hands and the lotion on his neck, she could sense his anticipation for the activities ahead. If he had noted their unexpected privacy and wondered how far things might go, he kept it to himself. It probably hadn't occurred to him that she'd find room to feel desire amongst all the shock.

'We have to take a taxi,' he said, turning and taking the sunscreen back from her. 'Can I leave this on your bed? I'll get it later. And you'll need something to cover your shoulders.' He looked at her exposed shoulders and neck, her skin gleaming now, and shook his head. 'I feel like a saint saying that.'

Her phone chirped when she was pulling a cotton collared shirt from her suitcase. It was connected to the site Wi-Fi, she realised, and a quick glance at her home scream told her Facebook was in meltdown. She hesitated, her fingers hovering over the icon. It could only be the accident and all these notifications meant she was tagged in something unknown.

Adaline tapped the screen and the application opened. Small red balloons over everything confirmed what she'd suspected, but the post originator surprised her. 'Claire,' she said. Her other hand flew to her chest.

'What?' Rory asked, coming into the room. All the extra bandages and first aid supplies were in a plastic bag hanging from his wrist.

'Claire's posted a picture on Facebook,' Adaline said, 'and she's tagged me in it.' She lowered her phone so that Rory could stand beside her and see it too. Claire was in a bed looking very tired and pale, but smiling. She'd checked in at the hospital and the status below the picture read:

Broken bones bruises & a hell of a lot less skin. Im fine & Im lucky - **Adaline Sharp** *was with me & a total hero. Lucky to hav met u, grl. Thx evry1 4 the msgs, Ill be comin home in abt a week. PS send me stuff 2 read, almost evrythn here is in Italian!*

Nothing about Jenny, who was doubtlessly at her side. Nothing about Adaline being the reason the girls had crossed the street. The post had almost a hundred various reactions and over sixty comments that Adaline didn't bother to read.

'Facebook should give you a medal profile picture,' Rory said, his voice light but tinged with pride. He put his arm around her and nuzzled his nose into her neck. 'Very cool under fire, I heard.'

They were talking about it, she thought with disappointment. Their lovely silence this morning had made the whole mess seem so far away, but by checking her phone she'd brought it into the room with them and onto the tips of their tongues.

'They shouldn't,' she murmured. She touched the Facebook message icon. There were a few from the girls she spent the most time with and to her surprise, there was one from Jack.

Hope you're okay. Claire is awake and asking for you, what should I tell her?

Adaline exited the application and left her phone on the kitchen bench. She didn't know what Jack could tell Claire. She didn't know if she wanted to go to the hospital and face this, or turn from it. This was all hitting a little too close to home. Of course, Georgia wouldn't have spared a thought on thanks or praise, but once again Adaline was at the centre of it all. Speaking to doctors, being responsible for passing on information and tending to a patient. The responsible one, the courageous one. How many times had doctors praised her for the things she took on, for the things she carried? Over the years the compliments had come to mean something else to her. They'd become reminders. *It's incredible what you're doing for your mum, Adaline,* she remembered. *Keep it up, you have to be strong for her.* Or the less confronting but equally binding, *You're a rock, Adaline. She's lucky to have you.*

Where were the others questions? The questions about Adaline, about the rock and whether or not it was crumbling, about her strength and whether or not it was faltering?

Was it only two nights ago that she'd rejoiced in her deepening connections with the women on tour with her? When had she lost sight of her goal? This tour was supposed to be a reprieve. An escape from a life of responsibility. Connection meant obligation, she thought, turning from Rory and shrugging into her shirt. She'd forgotten. She'd let her guard down. Now because she'd allowed herself to connect with Claire, she was – to a degree – responsible for her. For her being on that road, even for her happiness. Claire was expecting, hoping for her to visit, and she was justified in that expectation and hope. As justified as Georgia was in hoping for a phone call. Adaline had switched one relationship for another. For almost ten others.

'Hey,' Rory said, his voice soft behind her.

She pressed her eyes shut a moment then turned, a smile on her face.

'You don't *have* to do anything right now. You don't even have to come with me. If you need to be alone, I'll go sit outside on the step.'

Adaline laughed, surprised. 'That makes you sound like a dog.'

He grinned. 'Give me a bowl of water and something to chew on and I'll be set.' He moved closer, took her hands and became serious. 'I'm here to do whatever you want and give you whatever you need.' He swallowed. 'I know you're freaking out right now, but … please don't send me away.'

She freed one of her hands to touch his face.

'I'll feel it with you,' he continued, urgency creeping into his voice, 'or I'll help you feel different.'

His lovely words made her inexplicably sad. She thought of how much time they had left, of how determinedly he'd secured a place at her side. There was a want within Adaline that she had never known before. The throbbing ache in her heart was so loud it could be mistaken for footsteps. Why couldn't she have met Rory on an Adelaide street? Why couldn't she too have been destined for Sydney University, or in some way entwined with the life he was going home to?

The cost being, of course, that she never would have met him here.

She thought over the impact he'd had on her trip. It had been profound. Whenever she thought of France or Italy, of practical jokes or even escargot, she'd think of him. If meeting him at home meant losing this Rory, the price was too high.

He was the exception, she realised. A man apart from the things that bound her and weighed her down. By his side, within his heart, she had never felt more free. She needed that today. She would take as much of his levity as he was willing to give, and she would give whatever she could – everything she could – in return. She hooked her hand around the back of his neck and pulled him close.

'You and me for as long as possible, okay?'

He kissed her in answer. One moment she was upright, her arms loose around his neck, the next he was dipping her like a heroine in a classic movie and she was clinging to him. Her laughter was as cleansing as the sterile strips. Rory kissed along the line of her throat, squeezed their torsos together in a sideways embrace, then righted her.

'So what's your grand plan?' she asked through a smile that might have shown all her teeth. Whatever it was, she hoped there was time for the Duomo, too. She wouldn't be seeing it in the state of mind she'd expected to when she'd been back home dreaming of the day, but all things considered, it was better than not seeing it at all.

'The Duomo first,' Rory said, becoming all business, 'of course. Then a surprise.'

Adaline closed the cabin door on the sound of her beeping phone. The world and all its wants was going to have to wait.

31 CAT AND MOUSE

Almost two hours later when Adaline and Rory stepped back out into the Piazza Duomo, the cathedral towering over them, the radiant heat from the concrete paths and marble facade was rippling the air. People huddled in shade beneath awnings and arches, fanning themselves with everything from maps to hats. Sweat glistened on brows and windows high above the street were closed against warm air which offered no relief.

Adaline didn't know when they were expected back at the village, she hadn't heard Jack's usual breakfast speech, and the heat combined with her mental fatigue meant she wasn't fussed about seeing the many other Florentine things she'd hoped to before today. If Rory led her to a cool courtyard somewhere, or found her a shaded bench seat, she'd be happy. It didn't matter what she saw now because Florence was, and always would be, that accident now. Maybe in time she'd remember admiring the dome's frescoes without thinking of the bandages encircling her knees. Hopefully she'd forgive herself for being too tired to do much during this perhaps once in a lifetime opportunity. Despite all her plans, her research and her curiosities, today she was willing to be led.

They turned in the direction of the river and walked alongside the beautiful pink, white and blue mosaic tiles covering the cathedral exterior, past tourists trying to look everywhere at once, past a queue that was forming now that the lunch hour had passed. She glanced over her shoulder at the remarkable dome and the opulent design, then she walked on, knowing as she did that she would never remember it quite right. The Santa Maria del Fiore's beauty would pale in her memory, and the photos they'd taken would never do it justice. The same could be said about everything she'd seen since starting this trip.

Whenever they had the choice, they opted for the narrow, less busy streets over the wider ones, and for this reason they saw a quieter Florence than other tourists might.

Rory left her outside a small supermarket, and minutes later, was buying two buckets from a cashier. He angled them towards the woman, asked a question that made her smile, then followed her away from the register. Through the front window, Adaline watched them walk down a grocery aisle and disappear through a back door. She frowned and turned back to the street.

They'd found their way to the Piazza della Republica, Florence's city square, and it was easy to wait for Rory to return when there was so much around her to see. Long buildings bordered the square on three sides. On the fourth were two porticos connected by an arch with reminded Adaline of the Arc de Triomphe. Large concrete balls kept cars out of the square and a merry-go-round filled the air with plinking music and children's laughter. People sat on the steps at the base of a column monument, and cafes were busy with drinking and dining guests.

Adaline turned when the shop bell tinkled, and there was Rory, walking through the doorway with a bucket in each hand full of colourful round rubber shapes. Water balloons. No doubt brought from home and filled in a sink customers wouldn't typically see. He was enterprising, she thought, and the best kind of trouble.

'One each,' he said, handing her a bucket. 'The piazza as the boundary.'

The bucket was heavy, and yet the levity it promised made it almost weightless. Water games on a scorching day in Florence, was there anything that could rival that?

Adaline grinned and lifted the top-most balloon from the pile.

Rather than retreating, Rory stepped closer. Too close to throw at, but not close enough for the parts of her that reached for him. She angled her face up, ready for the kiss, for the connection that she craved. He set his bucket down and rest his hand on the small valley between her shoulder and collarbone. His thumb eased her shirt aside and Adaline's heart beat faster. He looked at her as if there were no one and nothing else in this crazy, beautiful, heartbreaking world, then his smile changed. There wasn't time to react. The hand she hadn't been paying attention to buried a small balloon between her skin and the shirt he had lifted away. He pushed it, and it exploded. Tepid water saturated her shirt and bra and rolled down her ribs and stomach.

She gasped and swung at him but he'd already retreated, holding his bucket aloft and dancing out of reach like a wicked faery. His laugh was maniacal.

'You didn't say go!' she cried. 'You're supposed to say go!'

'Right,' he said, 'because every war in history started when two parties agreed to fight at exactly the same time.' He had a second balloon in his hand and he wore trouble like a mask. 'Don't be a sook, Ads —'

'I'm not being a sook!'

'— and recognise my superior skills of deception!' He thrust his hand into the air, then spluttered a curse when plastic flexed and snapped around his nose, then exploded.

Adaline reached for a second balloon and pitched it at his groin as he dried his face on the sleeve of his shirt. He made a startled, wounded sound, then pitched his balloon at her but missed. It burst on the footpath behind her, making tourists scatter.

'You should have told me you didn't have any change for the toilet,' she teased.

Then wisely, she ran.

She heard a few balloons burst near the bottom of the bucket, and forced herself to slow. She held it away from her body and laughed. A narrow path between the alfresco seating and shop fronts concealed her from the man who pursued her.

She heard Rory pass, distinguishable by the sloshing sound in his bucket. She stepped out to follow him. However tempting a sharp shot to the back was, she couldn't be sure she wouldn't hit a passer-by, so she stowed her balloon and waited for a better opportunity. She followed him through the square, ducked behind the merry-go-round when he checked over his shoulder, and buried a balloon between his shoulder blades when there was a gap in the crowd.

His shout of frustration made every tense second worth it.

He whirled around, she squealed, and he pursued her past painted horses and cushioned thrones. People leapt aside, others picked a side and cheered for their team. Adaline executed a surprisingly complex mid-run three-sixty turn, but her balloon sailed over his shoulder and burst apart on a teenager's thigh.

Adaline turned back, shouted an apology in English then in Italian, and got her face wet for her trouble.

Rory laughed, delighted. Another balloon burst open on the flagstones beside her and wet her ankle, then Adaline lost him in the crowd.

Their cat and mouse game lasted about fifteen minutes, the role of cat changing regularly. Adaline had to stop often to pant in the shade, and she started to wise up to Rory's methods in time to avoid a few tricky shots.

She'd used half her arsenal, and hadn't seen Rory for a while now. Those on the block who knew their game were good sporting enough not to give their hiding spots away, so Adaline didn't look to the public for knowing smiles or subtle hints. She was beneath the arch, her back against the stone wall. It was an excellent spot to get her breath back, but her line of sight was heavily impeded by columns and free-standing shops.

It was nice in the shade. Nice enough to consider waiting here until Rory found her.

When three small kids hurried towards her, smiling broadly with their hands behind their backs, she didn't think anything of it, she assumed they would pass. But their smiling faces came closer, and Adaline realised too late that they were armed.

Pink, yellow and green flew towards her – breast, shoulder, stomach. Yellow again, in the knee this time, then two blues to the chest.

The children screeched and laughed, then ran, clutching onto one another.

Adaline looked down. Her clothes were plastered to her skin, and as the water ran down her body, soaking whatever fabric had so far survived, she thought of Claire. Of the way her pretty top had flattened against her breasts and stomach; the way blood had dripped from her elbows and fingers, and filled the shoe she hadn't lost. Points of impact from the balloons reminded Adaline of points of impact from the road. Of everything changing so fast, and forever. Laughing one moment and trying to breathe through the next.

She slumped against the wall and slid down to the stones.

Seconds later, a shadow fell over her. And it laughed.

'You should see your —' There was a clatter of plastic on stone, then Rory was squatting beside her. 'Ads? Shit, did they hurt you? I told them not to aim for your knees.'

She blinked away the memory of last night and looked up at him. 'I need to go to the hospital. I need to see Claire.'

Rory donated their buckets of water balloons to a bunch of kids on the way to find a taxi, and the sun was so brutal, they were dry by the time they were on the road.

32 BLAME

Adaline stared at Claire's hand, at the drip which protruded from it, and struggled to think of anything else to say. They'd exhausted thanks and apologies, had spoken briefly of what Adaline had done before coming here, and were presently in their longest silence yet. Claire stared at the sheet covering her lap. Adaline could see where someone, no doubt Jenny, had tried to brush Claire's hair around the tubes. All the blood had been washed out, but there was a small spot on the bottom right of the pillow that Adaline's eyes kept returning to.

Rory hadn't come in. He'd reminded her that Claire hadn't asked to see him and was waiting outside in the corridor. Jenny didn't know Adaline was here, she was asleep in one of the chairs, her chin on her chest, and Jack had stepped out when she'd arrived. It was a little amusing to think of him and Rory alone together, but she supposed a hospital was the best spot for it.

'Jack told me you got hurt,' Claire said.

'It's nothing.' Compared to Claire's broken shoulder, arm, wrist and ankle, it wasn't worth mentioning. It certainly didn't deserve Claire's sympathy. 'When do you think you'll get out of here?'

'Dunno. They're still checking how bad everything is. They reckon I might've knocked my hip about, which feels likely. And they're doing all these tests on my head.'

They looked at each other, then away again. This was the end of the road for Claire. The end of the tour, the end of the holiday. Adaline had known this last night, but it pained her to hear it confirmed.

'And Jenny?' Adaline asked.

'She's staying.' Claire looked at her sleeping friend and pressed her lips together. 'As she should.'

'You blame her?'

Claire sighed and looked back at her lap. 'I dunno. I know it was an accident. It's not like my best friend threw me in front of a car on purpose, and I know I should let her off the hook.' She paused. 'But she wants that too much. If she didn't want me to forgive her so bad, I would have done it already.'

Adaline didn't comment.

Claire shifted, winced. 'When do you leave tomorrow?'

'Seven-thirty, I think, I can't remember. I'm sure everyone wants to see you before then.' She was speaking about their group and not the coach-load of people who claimed no friendship with her, but this didn't need to be said, Claire understood.

She nodded. 'I'll ask Jack to open the floodgates. Our first tour goodbye.'

Adaline swallowed. 'The rest of the tour is crap, anyway.'

Claire laughed gingerly. 'Thanks for saying that. Listen, can you do me a favour – take a picture?'

Adaline nodded. She reached for the phone on Claire's bedside table and centred Claire in the shot. The mouth of the Claire on the screen moved. 'I want you in it.'

Adaline looked over the screen at the broken girl in the bed, then moved over to her despite how desperately she wanted to say no. She flipped the camera so she could see their faces, copied Claire's middle-range smile, captured the moment, then put the phone back on the table.

'Good luck,' she said, 'with everything. For what it's worth, I wish this wasn't where we were saying goodbye.'

'Thanks, Ada.'

Adaline turned for the doorway. Claire called to her before she reached it.

She said, 'Because I'm not going to see how the story turns out, can you give me a spoiler?'

Adaline's brows drew together. 'What do you mean?'

'Is this just the beginning or just a moment in time?'

Adaline's brows came together. 'We'll always be friends, Claire. There's Facebook and email, and I've never been to New Zealand, so you never know.'

Claire's bruised face relaxed into a soft smile. 'That's really nice to know, but I meant you and Rory. Are you ditching him at the airport or giving long distance a go?'

Adaline crossed her arms and looked down to her shoes. There were faint water marks over the toes from her recent battle – already one of her most prized memories of this trip. She thought of the man in the corridor waiting for her, of the weeks and months he'd wait if she asked him to. Adaline didn't question her own patience; waiting for Rory would be the loveliest, brightest part of her days back in Adelaide. Knowing someone was out there who wanted and appreciated her would get her through all manner of less pleasant moments with her mother. Her main concern was when it all came to an end. Surely an attempt at long distance was just forestalling the inevitable? They were both young with a lifetime of choices ahead of them. Dating across state lines was ignoring the shelf life of their relationship. It would hold them back. Rory, she amended. It would only hold Rory back.

Wouldn't it be better for their promises to end on tour? For Adaline to return home heartbroken but at least distracted by everything else she now carried in her heart and mind? If Rory ended things on a Tuesday in November or something equally inconsequential, what would Adaline surround herself with to get her through? At least if it happened now she wouldn't have to cast her mind far for memories which still moved her. She'd think of the Mediterranean Ocean she'd so recently floated upon, or remember the warmth of the sun in Italy – things that time hadn't yet blurred at the edges.

It frightened her to think of how little she had back home. How small her life had become. If she brought something as large as her feelings for Rory into it and her world stretched to accommodate it, what would her life look like if she then took it out? Stretched, misshapen. It would never fit right again.

'I'm guessing you haven't decided.'

Claire's voice brought the room back into focus. The beeping machines, the soft conversations of guests surrounding adjoining beds, the bustle of staff outside. Claire's expression was pinched. There was pain amongst her curiosity, Adaline could see the shine of it in her eyes.

'No,' she replied, 'I haven't decided.'

'Seems like a no-brainer to me, but you must have your reasons.'

'A thousand for and a thousand against.'

Claire nodded. 'Good luck with that. I'll stay tuned.' She glanced down at the white sheet that concealed her mangled ankle. 'From here.'

Adaline mustered a weak smile. 'Bye Claire.'

'Bye Ada.'

She left.

The first thing she saw beyond the room was Rory sitting in a visitor chair. He was slumped forward, elbows on his knees, reading a brochure. His chaos of hair lay in every direction and there was a scrap of red balloon sticking out of the top-most fold of his rolled up sleeve. He looked like a kid in this serious setting, a lifetime away from the man who would stride similar hallways as a doctor. She slowed and stopped. For a moment, she just took him in. She wanted that future for him. More than that, she believed he would be the kind of doctor that made people like Claire feel seen and vital. In Rory's world, everyone was invited to the party.

He looked up. His expression went from patience to pleasure then he was on his feet, coming towards her. His hands grasped her elbows the moment he could reach her. 'Were you staring at me?'

'Little bit, yeah.'

They smiled at each other.

'How is she?' he asked.

Adaline shrugged. 'Good, considering, but she's got a list of problems that aren't going to get her out of here for a while. Jenny's pulling out and staying too.'

Her recount was interrupted by Jack appearing around the corner. He spotted them and joined them. Rory glared at him then looked away, and it startled Adaline to think that there were other, much smaller issues that could still cause trouble amongst this larger mess. The unwanted kiss. She'd told Rory about her morning jog yesterday morning, about mending fences and not holding a grudge. He hadn't liked it.

Just as they had been yesterday, his eyes were full of wariness and dislike. Jack's eyes, on the other hand, were bloodshot and glassy. His eyelids seemed heavy and his face seemed ... sagged, somehow. Less chiselled, more ... moulded. This tour group, with its mothers, thefts, thwarted affections and accidents, was putting him through his paces. He looked like he hadn't slept in days.

'How are you?' Jack asked.

Rory let go of Adaline's elbows and stepped back.

'Fine,' she said. Her hands came up to hold her own elbows.

'Have you been in yet?'

She nodded. 'I've just stepped out. We were just about to catch a cab back to the village.' She glanced at Rory and he nodded. She looked back at Jack. 'Are you coming or going? Did you want to share a ride back?'

Rory stopped nodding and scowled.

Jack looked between them. 'That would be good, actually, I've got a lot of calls to make and I don't have all the information I need here. Give me two minutes, I'll just say goodbye.' He stepped between them and walked into Claire's room.

When Adaline looked up at Rory, he had an expression akin to sucking on a lemon. His shoulders were drawn back and he looked ready to argue. Before he could say anything, called for or otherwise, she held up a hand and said, 'Please don't make this a thing, I don't have the energy to fight with you. Jack's been doing it tough since the accident and it wouldn't cost you anything to be nice.'

Incredulity answered her. 'You're making me into the bad guy?'

'No, I just know you can rise above it. You have no reason to feel threatened by him. Jack and I have settled our differences, so I'm asking you to be patient with a guy who'll never get what he wants from me, and who's going to get hell from his bosses because someone got hurt on his tour.'

Rory looked away and pushed his hands into his pockets. He didn't adjust his combative stance, but the crease between his brows lessened and his frowning lips returned to a neutral position. 'Jack told us what you did, you know. That you were the one helping her before the ambulance arrived.'

Now it was Adaline's turn to look away. Accidents were common, people got hurt every day. It was reported on the news, discussed over coffees and seen by those on the scene, but she hadn't been prepared for the exhaustion. The calcium in her bones had changed to something infinitely heavier. Even her thoughts were anchored down, beleaguered by the night. Physically, she'd done little more than roll Claire more securely on her side, but her limbs were barbells, and only isolation and silence had begun to recharge her. If Rory had come to her asking questions or speaking endless words of comfort, she would have retreated from him. From Rory, the only person in Europe who drew her to his side time and again, who knew what she wanted before she did and gave her patience beyond what she deserved. Even his words would have been too much. She'd need the quiet, because in that there had been recovery.

But the quiet was over.

He said, 'Did you really faint after you'd spoken to the cops?'

Adaline crossed her arms over her chest and gazed down the hallway. 'Please don't tease me.'

A beat of silence, then, 'I think it's incredible that you held it together for as long as everyone needed you to.'

Adaline turned to him. There was no humour in his eyes, only warmth. She gripped her arms tighter. 'I don't feel like I'm holding it together now. I said we should cross the road.'

She imagined he'd tell her it wasn't her fault – that was everybody's go-to line. Don't feel guilty. She was lucky you were there. Hollow words that didn't change how she felt and did nothing to assuage the sense that Claire should be sharing the blame between her and Jenny, and not leaving it for Jenny to shoulder alone.

But Rory said none of these things. He said nothing at all. He stepped forward, closed her in his arms and beat a slow, rhythmic heartbeat against her chest. She pressed the side of her face against his T-shirt, closed her eyes and listened to his soundtrack; pulse and breath and the brush of fabric on skin. He was the answer to a question she didn't have the words for, and however long they stood here like this, it would feel like a lifetime too short.

Jack sat in the front passenger seat on the way back to the village, checking messages and voicemails. Rory and Adaline rode in the back, faces turned to their respective windows, hands joined across the divide between them. Adaline watched the beautiful buildings slide past them.

She'd had such plans for Florence. There were still so many things to see, things that she wouldn't because time had moved strangely here. The tour would depart as scheduled, regardless of what she had or hadn't accomplished, and the clock would restart in the next city.

Would she stay longer were she free to? Adaline didn't know. Florence had been little more than alcohol, blood and water, part of her was happy to frame it in the back windows of the coach. But the Duomo … now that was something worth holding onto. Standing on the ancient mosaic tiles so close to Rory that she'd felt the warmth of his body against hers, staring up at the dome frescoes. And the water balloon fight. That was something worth remembering, something that would not have happened had Claire not fallen.

Gateway footed the bill for the fare when the cab arrived at the village. As they all climbed out, Jack with his phone still pressed to his ear, he reminded them to be at the coach at six-thirty if they were attending the group dinner and Space Electronic Disco.

Adaline's sympathy went with him when he walked away to his cabin.

There was no way she was going to either of those things, in fact, she was counting down the minutes until she could shrug off her bra and face-plant her pillow. But Jack had to go, and he had less than two hours to rally whatever scrap of energy he had in reserve. He would also be fielding a multitude of questions about Claire, and possibly about Jenny and Adaline, too. She hoped whatever he got paid made it worth it.

She turned to Rory. 'Thanks for today. For all the quiet then all the noise. Thanks for knowing what to do.'

Rory nodded. Instead of reaching for her hands, he pushed his own deep into his pockets. 'Do you want to have dinner with me tonight?'

Adaline opened her mouth but no words came. She thought of the pretty dress that he'd seen and liked at the Parisian dinner. It was the only fancy thing she had now. Of the delicate gold studs that she'd bought on the Ponte Vecchio – they deserved a night out. But with almost fifty people leaning over tables to ask her about Claire, and at a strobe-lit club that just thinking about now made her eyes hurt?

'Not with the group,' he added, again reading her correctly. 'I thought we could go into town with them then peel off, do our own thing. As fancy or as casual as you like.'

Infinitely better.

'Adaline!'

Adaline turned towards the sound of her name. Jack was hurrying back along the path. Something had changed. The muscles in his body seemed to be gathering at his centre – his neck and shoulders were taught, strained. There was focus in his eyes. The way he looked at her as he closed the distance between them filled her with disquiet. Her thoughts tumbled towards Claire, who'd been so stable and lucid, who'd found room amongst all her problems to care about how things turned out with Rory.

'It's your mother,' Jack said, reaching her side. He took her wrist and squeezed. Rory shifted, but Jack appeared oblivious to him.

The tension that had been spreading through her body like smoke left her in a rush of breath. She should have guessed, should have anticipated that Georgia would make her presence felt again.

The reprieve had been a blessing but everything had changed now. Things couldn't go on as they had been, Adaline couldn't ask Jack to keep fielding these interferences. Not when he was dealing with so much.

'I'll take care of it now,' she said, apology in her voice. She tried to ease her arm free but he didn't let go. 'I'll give her my number. I'm sorry that I've —'

He spoke over her. 'You need to call this number.' It was written on his palm; an Australian number, one she didn't recognise. 'Something's happened to your mum.'

33 PLANS

The room smelled of bodies and dirt. Sweat, soiled clothes and old food. Someone was carting something rotten from place to place and Rory was close to upending everyone's bags to find and destroy the thing. The Australian boys were more subdued than usual. A day on their feet in the sun, battling hangovers they never gave themselves enough time to recover from … the five of them were spent. Scott, Jonno and Matt were playing a lazy round of cards at the U-shaped kitchen bench. None of them had raised the stakes in over half a dozen hands. Chris and Pies were in the room they were sharing with Rory, having a conversation in furious whispers. Rory suspected they'd figured out he'd been the one who put salt in their drinks back in Venice.

He lifted his can of beer from the table, drank from it then leaned his elbows on his knees and held it against his chest. He was outside, his chair facing the long dirt path that led to the middle of the village. He'd told the others he couldn't stand the smell inside but really he was waiting for Ada.

All the colour had left her face as she'd copied the number Jack had given her into her phone. She'd walked off without a word, without a backwards glance, then she'd heard something bad. Rory and Jack had both seen it. Her back had gone very straight then all the air had seemed to flee her body.

Jack had stopped him going to her. Stopped him long enough that she'd wandered blindly into the mess of cabins and trees, phone pressed to her ear, and disappeared. So here he was. Thinking about dinner and space electronic discos, and wondering what her mother had done now. What had been so bad that Adaline had finally given over her international phone number.

He shifted. Thoughts of home came forward; of his mum telling his dad about the highlights of a documentary she'd seen, her voice high with excitement. Of his mum retaliating against one of Rory's pranks by concealing food colouring in his bar of soap. The way her hands were always seeking his dad's. The way her goofy impressions made Junk laugh and her worry made everyone dig for patience.

She'd never hurt any of them. Never make them feel the way Ads was feeling now.

Rory was going to hug her really hard when he got home.

'Frosty,' said a voice.

Rory turned. Pies and Chris were sharing the doorway, each with an expression he couldn't place.

'Boys,' he returned.

Pies surveyed the scene. 'You having a moment or what? You want a blankie and a cuddle?'

Rory held his arms out and Pies flipped him off.

They stepped onto the small veranda. Chris took the second seat and Pies propped himself against the balustrade, his back to the path. When they crossed their arms at the same time it felt choreographed.

'Jonno,' Rory said. Pies and Chris looked at each other then back to Rory. 'We're voting someone off the island, right?' Rory leaned back in his seat and lifted his can in a kind of salute. 'I vote Jonno.'

Pies grinned. 'Yeah, I'd vote Jonno too. Jonno and his festy bag. So listen,' his voice became abruptly serious, 'about Sydney.'

Rory raised an eyebrow. A glance at Chris gave nothing away.

'We're thinking we should do this.' Pies pointed at the floor and made a weird circling motion. 'Thing.'

Rory waited for more words.

'You know, the share-house bit. The three of us and your mates.'

Rory set the can down. 'You two want to live with me in Sydney?'

'And your mates,' Chris piped in. 'The more the merrier.'

Pies shook his head. 'The more the cheaper. We figure if they can put up with you, we've already got something in common.'

Rory smiled. 'How lucky.' He looked between them; Pies with his bloodshot eyes and a liver that could quit any day now, and Chris with his bitten fingernails, dirty sense of humour and relentless superhero references, and needed no more time to decide. He enjoyed them both. He said, 'Works for me. I'll start a group chat and you can all see what you make of each other. We'll be looking for a place the week after we get back.'

'Works for me,' Chris said.

Pies shrugged. 'I can go anytime.'

The three of them looked at each other.

Rory shook his head and smiled. 'God help us all.'

'He just needs to help you, I reckon,' Pies said. 'I know it was you who short-sheeted my bed.'

Rory held up a hand. 'You know, I'm not comfortable with the rumours going around about me. I worry for my reputation.'

'Worry for your eyebrows.'

Before Rory could reply, Ada brought the banter to an abrupt end. She appeared on the path before him, her eyes wide and over-bright, fussing with her hands, looking for all the world like she'd lost something. *Her mind*, he thought, rising slowly to his feet.

She said his name and the word was strangled. Full of gravity, torn from her. Pies and Chris went quickly inside and Rory had the curious sense of wanting to follow them, of not wanting to hear what was coming next.

He put his drink down. When she was close enough to touch him but didn't, something bright and fundamental deep inside him dimmed and shied away. He was too scared to reach for her, too scared to speak.

She lifted her chin, but couldn't seem to hold it up. When she spoke again, it was to her chest. 'I'm going home,' she said. 'I've come to say goodbye.'

34 THE ALMOST

Adaline sat in the eye of the storm. Clothes, words, bodies … she thought of a cyclone as her favourite roommates moved around her, sharing clothes, asking questions as they moved from room to room. The coach was leaving in twenty minutes and everyone was moving fast to be ready. Adaline's news had done something weird to time, compressed it somehow.

'If she's stable,' Rachael said, standing in the doorway to her room, the bra she'd shown off at the Chateau once again on display, 'can't your dad handle things himself for a few more days?' She worked her arms through the sleeves of her tight, lime-accented top then stretched the fabric into place.

Adaline was sitting in the middle of the U-bend bench. Her hair was bundled into a careless knot and she was wearing her favourite yellow jeans and a simple black top. She was riding into town too, but bound for a different destination.

'I calm her,' she said, 'and I want to be there.'

The lie filled her cheeks with a taste she wanted to spit out. Yes, Adaline calmed Georgia – having someone to bully and bark orders at had always had a cathartic effect on her mother – but as for wanting to be there …

Rachael didn't press her point. She stepped into the bathroom to share the mirror with Jenny. Jenny, dressed in tight pants and a burnt-orange strapless top, who'd insisted that Claire hadn't minded that she join them tonight. Jenny who smelled faintly of spirits and found an inordinate amount of excuses to step in and out of their little room.

With all that had happened since arriving in Florence, Adaline was inclined to ask her to share whatever it was that was putting that shine in her eyes.

It was a mercy that alcohol didn't play a big role in Adaline's life. To have to deal with that on top of everything else would be monstrous. Georgia had her vices, but hers were the kind that rattled.

Adaline imagined the sound. She pictured Georgia shaking the pills onto her palm. Had she counted them? Had she thought of Adaline? Adaline's father? Had she thought of anything beyond the oblivion that handful had promised?

Again Adaline imagined Georgia filling her palm with drugs, but this time she imagined red too. Streaks of scarlet braceletting her wrist. Had Georgia cut herself first and shied away from the pain, or had she pushed the knife into her skin once the painkillers had slowed the world down?

Did the order matter?

'Hey.' Maree's voice, soft and present. She reached across the table, curled her fingers over Adaline's and squeezed. 'You're on the first flight back.' She lifted her hand and tapped a finger against Adaline's temple. 'Try not to go back sooner.'

She looked different tonight. Beautiful but casual. Also in jeans, she wore a pretty top with an abstract butterfly pattern and silver teardrop earrings. It was a far cry from the glamorous dresses and jewels she'd opted for on previous nights. To postpone her building hysteria, Adaline remarked upon it. 'You look more princess than queen tonight.'

Maree sat back and smiled. 'And I feel more heroine than damsel.'

'Uh oh,' Adaline said, 'someone's made a decision.'

'Yes.' Maree considered her hands.

As Adaline waited, unsure whether or not Maree's was as inclined to share as she had been in Venice, Holly joined them on the bench with a compact mirror and make-up bag. She smiled at the pair, her eyes more pronounced tonight because of the eye-liner Rachael had applied in long, cat-like strokes beyond the outer corners.

She was going to miss it, Adaline realised: the big meet on the Spanish Steps in Rome. Only two nights ago Adaline had promised to walk Holly there, to wait with the others as Holly met Pete, as she touched him for the very first time and hoped everything fell into place from there. The thought further emptied Adaline's already depleted heart.

'I'm going to break up with him,' Maree said. Quietly, not including the girls in the next room in the news. Trialling it, perhaps. Sounding it out, feeling the words on her tongue with a small audience.

Holly froze, the stick of mascara halfway to her left eye. Adaline pulled her hands from the table and pushed them into her lap.

'Tonight?' Adaline asked.

Maree shook her head. 'When we get home. I wouldn't hurt either of us that way, it doesn't need to be now.'

Holly set her make-up down. 'I'm so sorry, Ree. You don't … want to marry Will anymore?'

'I do, but … not as much as I don't want to be around someone who's fine with letting me feel so uncertain. I don't think I'll ever stop thinking that he's strung me along. That he's … that he'll never commit but doesn't want to be alone.'

Adaline leaned forward. 'He's not keeping you around because he doesn't want to be alone.'

Maree attempted a smile. 'I don't doubt that he loves me. But I don't think I'm The One.' She considered this, as if the possibility had occurred to her only after she'd spoken it. 'I don't think he's waiting for someone else or something better,' she continued, 'but I don't think he has anything more to offer me, either.' She dropped her head into her hands and stared at Adaline through her fingers. Flesh and bone bars and wild, despairing eyes. 'Oh god,' she said, and the words were strangled now, 'I think he can't love me anymore than he does.'

Without consciously deciding to do it, Adaline opened her arms.

Maree scooted around the corner of the table and Adaline hugged her. Hair between their faces, their bodies twisted strangely, it was both awkward and infinitely comfortable. A curious sense of power blossomed in Adaline's battered heart. A strength that wasn't for herself, but for the girl at her side.

'Just promise me,' Adaline said, 'that you'll tell Will exactly how you're feeling when it's time. Don't assume he knows. You may end up losing something big over a misunderstanding.'

Or, she thought, Maree might be right. She might be a much loved placeholder, and she deserved better than that.

Maree nodded.

Holly moved around the bench to join them. When she was hip to hip with Adaline, she put her arms around them both.

Rachael stepped out of the bathroom, finished with her hair, and made a tiny yelp of indignation. 'Hey!' She slid hastily into the bench and crashed up against Holly's other side. 'They're having a moment!'

Jenny seemed to materialise on Maree's left side.

The five of them embraced and laughed. Adaline couldn't tell who she was touching anymore. The table made the five-way hug awkward but they somehow made it work, and when they pulled apart, the mood had changed. Maree looked bolstered, Jenny had laughed, which seemed like a kind of miracle.

Adaline looked at each of their faces as they disentangled themselves and felt a swell of sadness. This was one of the last moments she would share with these girls. These girls who, despite her initial detachment, had persevered with her. Who had reminded her that connections should be celebrated, not avoided. Yes, every relationship Adaline now had in this room came with some expectations and obligations, but they were tolls she was willing to pay now. Because they didn't want much; a willing ear, some kind words. Someone to share a moment with. Hardly the hefty fees she'd come to expect from people.

This trip may not have given her the amount of space she would have liked from her mother, but it had gone a long way to breaking down the walls she'd built around herself. She couldn't return to Adelaide and fortify herself again – not after this. The isolation would feel keener than it ever had before, and letting her mother be her whole world wouldn't be tolerable anymore.

Adaline was going to reach out to her old school friends. Reconnect. She was going to speak with her dad – things were going to change. He may have checked out on Georgia, but he couldn't quit his daughter. She'd ask for more support, more time for herself. The words were smoke at the moment, but she had the whole Indian Ocean to figure them out.

'Is everyone packed?' she asked, following the girls out of the booth and over to the door. Everywhere she looked hair was being adjusted and purses were being checked. It seemed cruel to schedule a big night on the town ahead of a 7.30 am departure, but that was life on the road – there were schedules to keep. Jack had promised everyone they could sleep most of the day away tomorrow, so no one had complained too much.

Maree grabbed the plastic bag on the floor by the door and they were ready to go. It was full of used books, pens and paper, and small gifts from each of them, destined for Claire. Maree, Holly and Rachael were going to the hospital before dinner to see her.

'Someone please make sure I'm on the coach tomorrow,' Jenny said, elbowing the door open and stepping through.

'Like Jenny duty?' Rachael asked. She looked over her shoulder at Holly and the pair shared a significant look. 'And the baton is passed.'

Holly said nothing. She closed the cabin door behind them and handed Adaline one of the keys.

Adaline took it. 'I thought Jenny was staying here.'

Holly glanced ahead. Rachael looked back, quickly read the moment and fell into step with the others.

'Claire and Jenny sort of … broke up.' Holly zipped her purse shut then let it swing from the strap around her wrist. 'Then I guess Jenny figured she shouldn't miss out on anything else for someone who isn't going to be in her life after this.'

'Oh. Wow.' Adaline floundered for something more to say. Poor Claire.

'I know.' Holly glanced at her. She looked wretched. 'Is it terrible that I can see both sides?'

Adaline watched Jenny's back. The swing of her long hair and the shakiness of her legs as she navigated the stone path in her wedge sandals. She laughed at herself, then with Maree. Her make-up was flawless and her confidence was boosted by booze. Her mood was inexplicable in light of this news.

Claire, alone in hospital, there because she'd been holding the 'Jenny baton' at the time. Jenny, guilty and unforgiven, but quick to move on. She'd chosen not to be a martyr – to not stay at the bedside of someone who'd cast her out of their life.

Adaline could see both sides too, but she didn't presume to know the whole story.

'I'll be interested to know what Claire says,' she said. She slipped the room key into her purse, pulled out her phone and followed Holly off the porch. There was free Wi-Fi throughout the village and Adaline used it to log on to Facebook. She sent Claire a private message – *I'm sorry about you and Jenny xx* – then put her phone and her questions away.

'In case I don't get a chance to say this tomorrow morning,' Adaline said to Holly, 'good luck with Pete. I bet it's wonderful for you both.'

Holly smiled. 'Thanks. I'm pretty nervous but mostly excited. I wish you were coming to Rome with us.' She hesitated. 'And to the islands.'

What Adaline had most been looking forward to. What – even amongst places as marvellous as Paris and Venice – she'd been counting down to.

Holly said, 'How's Rory handling the news?'

Adaline shrugged. 'He was quiet for a while and a little cross at my mum, I think, although he'd never admit that. We've got tonight at least, so I'm trying to focus on the positives.'

Her alternative was to curl into the foetal position and break – which seemed like a monumental waste of the little time she had left. The first available flight out of Florence was 11.30 tomorrow morning. She had to be at the airport three hours prior and by then the people she'd shared this adventure with would be within the outskirts of The Eternal City.

When she'd gone to Rory's cabin earlier she hadn't yet processed the details of her departure. She'd not long been off the phone with a nurse at the hospital her mother had been admitted to. The nurse had said she and Adaline's father had taken it in turns trying to reach her, that they'd both kept calling Gateway only to be told each time that her tour manager hadn't collected his messages yet. Because he'd been in the hospital, Adaline thought, dealing with another crisis.

She'd called Jack through Facebook after she'd hung up – numb with shock – and begged him to help her. He had, of course. He'd made all the necessary calls to her travel agent and her travel insurance provider ... he'd even booked a cab for her tomorrow morning.

When the storm passed Adaline was going to give Gateway the best feedback of its life.

'I hope you have a nice night,' Holly said. They were within steps of the larger group now. Dozens of people were crowded around the coach, once again dressed to impress. Lois commanded the most attention in an angelic white mini-dress and electric blue shoes. Lisa stood with her, more demure in a pale yellow maxi-dress. Adaline remembered what she'd heard in Venice, that Lois was lonely and desperate to connect, and Adaline hoped she'd found that connection in Lisa. The pair appeared to have hit it off following their room arrangements in Monaco. Adaline smiled in their direction.

Beth was standing with Daniel. She'd been ready long before anyone else and out the door to babysit her brother. He'd so successfully alienated himself from everyone on tour that if Beth wasn't with him, it was a fair bet he was alone. Adaline thought of her own family when she looked at the siblings. Theirs was a relationship out of balance, too. A relationship that drained rather than energised, that cost and challenged and isolated. Beth had put her life on hold for Daniel – she'd stepped away from a romantic relationship that, from the little Adaline knew of it, sounded like it needed TLC not distance. She'd used up the last of her holiday leave that she'd no doubt been saving for something else – somewhere else with someone else.

Daniel had taken all of these sacrifices without a scrap of gratitude. He accepted her company now with belligerence. When he looked at her he saw supervision, not selflessness. An authority figure to be rebelled against, not a sister who'd enabled him to travel.

He was unworthy of her.

Adaline curled her fingers around the fading bruise on her wrist.

She pitied Beth as much as she saw herself in her.

A few steps apart from the group, Rory stood with the Australian boys, his hands deep in his pockets and his brown eyes unfocused.

Seeing him magnetised her.

One of the boys saw her, elbowed him and he looked over. None of them appeared to take offense when he moved instantly from their sides.

Holly followed the line of Adaline's attention, squeezed her arm and stepped away.

Rory reached her and she was overcome with a curious sense of reunion.

If so short a separation could create such a sense of longing, the coming weeks were going to be brutal.

'Hey pretty girl,' he said through a smile. 'I'd have brought you a corsage if I'd been a little more resourceful.'

She grinned at him. 'This isn't a high school dance.'

'No, but it's a date. I'll just have to buy you one of those LED roses from one of the gypsies in town.'

Rory linked his arm through hers and turned her towards the coach. Danya had appeared and was making his way through the throng, keys jangling between his fingers.

'Your very noisy carriage awaits, my lady.'

35 WILL TO LIVE

They talked like long-distance friends reunited over coffee, like children who had to say it all before playtime was over. Their words tumbled into one another, rolled over the top of each other and were pushed aside for laughter.

There was a lot of laughter.

Over the course of dinner, Adaline and Rory discussed all things distant and local; their favourite holidays, cafes, beaches ... the places that made them feel connected somehow and the places they ached to see. They had a passionate debate about the proper way to cook eggs and couldn't settle on if it was card shark or cardsharp – each took a side and would not budge. They agreed that bacon should be so crispy it could snap and that the Harry Potter book series needed to be recreated in virtual reality. In fact, they agreed and disagreed on so many things that the restaurant closed around them.

Back on the street, hands entwined, they walked. For over an hour, down every laneway that caught their imagination and through every piazza that appeared before them. They bought the most absurd gelato flavours they could find and laughed through the taste experience.

They indulged every thought, every question and every topic except the one that loomed over them.

When their feet grew tired they showed a cab driver their accommodation business card and rode back to the village, hands still linked and the future still undiscussed. A single red rose lay across Adaline's lap. The red fabric covering the small light within it cast an unusual hue on the cab roof.

She watched the city through the small backseat window; the dark rooftops against the star-strewn sky, the ornate and the old beside the functional and new, and thought of Claire. Of how her night should have been more like this one. Florence had redeemed itself. It had stopped being all about blood and bad news, now it curled around her like a closing song in a beloved play. It had been the perfect host of a perfect night.

A night Adaline was going to soon ruin with goodbyes.

'Are you packed?' Adaline asked. She watched the village grow larger in the front windscreen, the shaped hedges like ticket booths on a freeway.

Beside her, Rory's attention was on his knees. 'Mostly.'

Adaline didn't reply. The cab driver stopped by reception and they pooled their loose change and small notes together to pay. They walked in together, their legs and backs lit by the headlights and their shadows long and close.

'I'll sit with you,' she offered. 'If you want to finish packing.' She smiled over at him. 'I wouldn't want you to miss the coach.'

Rory gave a short, unhappy laugh. 'Right.'

They were getting closer, she thought, to the moment they couldn't talk around for much longer.

He looked at her and smiled tightly. 'Yeah, all right. Better now than at the crack of dawn. I can't promise I won't tuck you in the top corner of my bag, though.'

She grinned. 'Just don't close the zip all the way so I can breathe.'

'Of course. I was even thinking of giving you a straw.'

Adaline doubted she could have found Rory's cabin again without his help. The first time she'd gone there she'd been given approximate directions, then she'd heard him speaking with Pies and Chris which had saved her from knocking on doors. Now everything looked different. The pines were cylinders of darkness, their leaves overhead blocking out the stars. The cabins – identical in design – no longer boasted indicators of the people inside; no towels hung over railings, no shoes cluttered up porches. People had packed their things away, maybe in suitcases ahead of their early departure, or at least out of sight whilst they turned and swayed to whatever kind of music played at a space electronic disco.

Rory put his arm around her shoulders and pulled her against him. They walked like this, tucked up against each other, until they reached a cabin that looked the same as all the ones around it, and Rory stepped up onto its porch.

He fumbled with the room key because no one had thought to put the outside light on. Adaline waited patiently by his side, listening to the insects and trying desperately to stay in the moment. Her mind kept trying to drag her forward, to tomorrow, to the end, to the moment when she would see her mother again. She didn't have the words yet – didn't know if she'd greet Georgia with relief or resentment.

Parasuicidal behaviour wasn't uncommon for someone with Borderline Personality Disorder. Doctors had warned her, warned her father: Georgia might hurt herself. And she had. A year ago. When Adaline's father Simon had walked out, done with the drama and the manipulation and the constant hostility, Georgia had been frantic. Phone calls, stalking – the things she'd said and done still made Adaline's skin heat when she thought of them. She'd been erratic, unstable. She'd threatened Simon then threatened Adaline. Simon hadn't listened and Adaline had been way over her head and largely useless, so Georgia had followed through.

There had been so much blood.

Dozens of cuts. Some deep, others superficial. She'd used the lovely coloured knife set they brought out for guests. Sat in the middle of the lounge room, staining the carpet. Adaline had been looking at her friends' leavers' holiday pictures at the time, imagining herself there, imaging her life was different – and had had to grow up really fast when she'd set the phone down

An ambulance. Towels. Tears – from Adaline, not from her mother.

Adaline had thrown out the pretty knives and rearranged the furniture to cover the stain. She'd vomited in the hallway and cried herself to sleep. Her dad had said nice things, but more than he'd wanted to spare her he'd wanted her to stay and look after her mother.

There's a good girl.

He'd escaped. Georgia's cry for attention may have distressed him, Adaline would never know, but it hadn't brought him back. If anything, it had pushed him further away. Slammed the door on their marriage.

Adaline had been standing in the proverbial doorway at the time, between them.

Now she was on the other side of the world and in more ways than not, responsible for this latest bloodshed.

Adaline's fingers curled into fists.

Her mother had applied a currency to freedom.

Rory opened the door then turned to block her path. 'Okay, so there's something I want to say first.'

Adaline tried to listen. She tried to keep her eyes on his face, but they were beginning to water. She screwed up her face and threw a hand up to cover her mouth and nose. 'Oh my god, what *is* that?'

Rory was serious. 'Jonno.'

'Jonno's in there? Rory, I think he's dying.'

'No, that's just your nose hairs and will to live.'

Adaline took a step back. She spoke through her hand. 'I can't go in there.'

Rory nodded. 'I know. It's bad.'

'Bad? I feel like it's *on* me. If I go in there I'm going to smell like that forever.'

'At least you'd get a row to yourself on the plane.'

Adaline crossed her arms over her chest and grinned. 'I'd get put in baggage.'

'Speaking of,' Rory said, glancing inside, 'are we abandoning mine?'

'You should burn it,' Adaline replied grimly. 'I'm not going in there.'

Rory shrugged and pulled the door closed. 'I'm mostly packed anyway.'

Adaline considered what could follow and wondered if they hadn't returned too early from the city. There had been distractions there; cafes, restaurants and music. Here there was only the night, seats under the stars and their cabins. The night seemed swollen with time. Which was curious, because in the bigger picture they had so little of it.

'We could go to mine,' Adaline suggested. 'If you don't mind the smell of hairspray.' She heard herself say it as if she were a spectator to the conversation. Dozens of movie scenes rolled through her mind. Femme fatales inviting tall, dark, broody types to their demise. Leading ladies seducing leading men. A hotel room key and all it symbolised, all it teased. Those long, torturous walks to the front door then to the bedroom beyond.

Was that what was going to happen? Is that what Adaline wanted to happen?

Yes. Without question.

He was wearing the same shirt he'd worn in Paris, the night they'd drank shots in darkened doorways and she'd ached to claim him but lost her nerve. It had been the first night her mother had called and Adaline had been a mess of contradictions. She'd wanted him close but not the obligation. The intimacy but not the expectation.

So much had changed in so little time.

Adaline had spent so long with her mother's manipulations and constrictions, isolated from friends and balance, that she'd come to despise intimacy and all it had come to represent to her. To need someone was to bind them.

Rory had contradicted all of that.

She needed him – his friendship, his humour, his touch – and that need came without restriction or cost. As did the need he had for her.

But it was building. The countless long looks, the mounting anticipation … the desire. Before all the horror of Claire's accident had driven the everyday from her mind, Adaline had thought of Rory and wanted. Wondered. She had trailed her fingers over his legs on the coach, plunged into deep kisses and reached for him – over and over and over again.

Now they were alone and she wondered still.

It was ironic then, that as Adaline contemplated ways they might not speak for hours, Rory decided it was time for deep conversation.

'So how's the life plan looking?' he asked. His hand was around hers, his stride in sync with her own. The deeper shadows of the night were passing over his face like thoughts entertained then discarded.

She shrugged and pushed her thumb over his skin. 'Vague,' she said. She moved her free hand in an arc before them, as if she were outlining words in the air. 'With moments of blinding clarity.' An idea had begun to form, a possible direction that seemed exciting and tangible, but without having had the time she needed to research the ins and outs of the concept, it wasn't something she wanted to talk about yet. 'I'm working on something. How about you? Your life plan looms.'

He squeezed her hand, and maybe it was Adaline's imagination, but his walk seemed to change – was that a sudden spring in his step? 'I'm actually pretty excited about it. I want to read everything my lecturers even mention in passing. I want to get to know other people who feel …' he pressed his knuckles to his breastbone, '*this*. And I get to meet patients in my first year, that'll be amazing.'

Adaline's gaze lingered on his chest – on the passion he'd suggested lived in there. She looked away and smiled. 'Kid patients?'

'I dunno, maybe. I don't get to specialise for the first few years, but that's good, because I don't know exactly what I want to do.'

Adaline looked back to him. 'What do you mean, I thought you wanted to do paediatrics?'

'I do, but I don't know what kind. There's general paediatrics; but there's also cardiology, medical oncology, neurology.' He shrugged. 'More than a dozen others. I'll learn what I like and dislike along the way.'

Adaline led the way up her cabin steps. The girls had left a light on, so it was easy to find her key and unlock the door. She stepped aside so he could enter first. 'I wish I had a calling like you. Specifics aside, you know what you want to do for the rest of your life.'

He stepped around her and turned the inside light on. 'You'll get there. You're fearless – that opens a lot of doors.'

Adaline laughed. 'Yeah, right. That's me.' Hadn't she spent most of this trip in varying states of fear? Fearing connection, fearing isolation …

Rory watched her cross the room to the kitchen bench. He remained in the middle of the room, hands in pockets now and expression earnest. 'It is. You are. I don't mean it in the sense that you don't fear anything, I mean it like …' He floundered. His thoughts weren't translating into the appropriate words and it appeared to be frustrating him. 'Like you're afraid, but you do it anyway. Like this trip.' He pulled a hand free from his pocket to sweep it about the room. 'You knew you had to do this for yourself. Putting yourself first can be a kind of bravery, especially if the people in your life are used to being your only priority.'

Adaline sat, settled her elbows on the table and leaned forward. She was acutely aware of the distance between them – of the table she'd hid herself behind and the closed expression on her face. She didn't want to talk about her mother. About the life that she'd escaped from for this short time. She wanted to laugh. And kiss. Discover him, and with each discovery, commit him to memory.

Rory was still talking.

'Don't get too hung up on not having all the answers already. You're not where you want to be, but neither are you where you used to be.' He paused. The grin that snapped across his face caused an immediate reaction low in her belly. 'Hey,' he said, 'that came out how I hoped it would.'

Adaline nodded sagely. 'It was very poetic.'

'Yeah, you go ahead and tease, you basket-case.'

She feigned offence and he laughed.

He said, 'Maybe we can google some inspirational quotes or something.'

Adaline rose from her seat and crossed the room to stand toe-to-toe with him. 'We'll create a Pinterest board,' she agreed.

He didn't respond. The mood had changed the moment she'd moved back within reach, and she reached for him now.

It occurred to her that the small room wasn't very well ventilated. There wasn't enough air. That, or Rory was using more than his share of it.

His skin was contained fire. Warm, devastating. He smelled of the country and the night and when she tasted him she thought of sugar and barley. She couldn't settle her hands – they roamed over him, ceaselessly searching, and every new curve was a curve to remember. Even as she lived this moment now, she knew she'd live it a thousand times again.

Adrenaline coursed through her body, electrifying her fingers and hastening her heart. She leaned in closer. Kissed deeper. Took more. The frantic pulse in her neck was a clock of sorts, marking the time left, pushing urgency deeper under her skin until it was cellular. In the marrow.

She pushed all of her need and hope to the fore, and imagined the pressure of his lips forcing her fear back into the deepest chasms of her consciousness.

Without breaking the kiss, he walked her backwards until her back was against the wall, then eased his weight against her, holding her there. She pushed her palms up his neck and into his hair. He dropped his hands to grip her waist. When his tongue slipped silkily into her mouth, her concentration shattered.

There was pressure from all sides; the wall, Rory's warm body, his big, grasping hands – but it wasn't enough. It wasn't nearly enough. How was it possible they hadn't done this before when everything felt so familiar and natural? He was perfect, and he was giving her everything she craved about him. His humour and kindness seemed to crackle in her mouth and roll into her belly. She wanted to both moan and laugh, so she started with the first, then fell helplessly into the second.

He eased back. His mouth a fraction from hers, their brows touching, he said, 'Please don't tell me you're laughing because this feels ridiculous.'

She allayed his fears by kissing him again, and this time he moaned.

Her hands behind his ears and her thumbs on his cheeks, Adaline pulled back and smiled. She felt punch-drunk and off-balance, and was glad she was supported against the wall. She never wanted to stop kissing Rory now that she'd finally started.

She trailed her fingers down to the button on his jeans and hesitated. She revelled in the hitch of his breath – in his scattered concentration. Then she plunged on, fearless.

36 PRESSURE

It was happening. The kisses were becoming more intense. Adaline's hands were on his pants. Assuming no one piked on the disco, he'd have the next few hours to rock her world. Or … give it a solid rumble at the very least. Rory didn't have a hell of a lot of experience to fall back on, but he'd make up for that with enthusiasm.

He moved his mouth down the length of her neck, buried himself in the warmth of her skin. Her hair tickled. It caught on his eyelashes and trailed between his fingers.

She tasted like … dessert – the reward for getting through everything else. She felt like home and something altogether foreign. Like something he knew and something he'd never know enough. She was colour and light and comfort and magic, wrapped around him kissing him like he was something special too.

Rory thoughts were a muddle of nonsense and need. Her fingers were clumsy on the button of his jeans and he found this cute without knowing why.

He thought to help her, but his hands got distracted on the way down. She wasn't busty, but there was enough. God, was there enough.

That sunshine smell was all over him. He thought of warm grass. Fresh fruit and the beach. Washing on the line, of all things.

The button popped free and her fingers moved down to the fly. She didn't struggle with this one.

Rory's pulse skipped.

He said, 'I've wanted … You're so …'

Oh god, shut up or she'll change her mind.

But she beamed up at him. His bumbling appeared to flatter her.

The room seemed to fill with the sound of the descending zipper. He dipped to claim her mouth, kissed her hard to distract himself.

Her fingers became less sure now that she wasn't watching their progress.

She pulled away. 'Should we …' She looked first at the front door, then at the bedroom door. 'Can we go in there? I mean, there's a bed and all,' colour was flooding the lovely skin of her neck, 'but it'll give us a minute if anyone comes back early.'

She wasn't stopping this. She was escalating it – bed, yes! – but being careful, private. He would have said yes to anything. He would have done a head stand if she'd really wanted it, but this was an easy request. He nodded and she led the way, their hands linked and smiles wide but shy.

Rory followed her up the bunk ladder. It was the second time he'd been here, but this would be nothing like the first. Shock and loss were here still, between them, lodged within her like shrapnel, but she was bearing it well.

Very well.

If anyone was at risk of losing their cool, he was.

He wanted to whoop, pump his fist in the air, swing her around in his arms. Instead, he settled down beside her and thrilled in the weight of her body on top of his. They didn't have much room to move – the ceiling was close and there was that press of time in the back of his mind, the worry that they may abruptly run out of it.

Also in the back of his mind was something more calculating. If he was good at this, memorable, generous … the answer to fantasies she'd not yet shared with him, it would improve his chances of seeing her again. If he could show her how compatible they were in this way, she might believe they could withstand the looming distance. She might believe that he was worth the wait between visits, that they were more than banter and friendship – that they were passion, too.

The pressure of it all made him feel a little sick.

Adaline settled her knees on either side of his and pushed herself up. He heard the soft scrape of her shirt against the ceiling and thought of the comfort of warm cotton.

She was beautiful. Stunning. Better than everything else he'd seen on this trip.

They smiled at each other.

Adaline's fingers curled into the pockets of his jeans and pulled. The denim gave way and began to slide down his legs. She followed them, shimmying down to his knees so she could pull off his shoes and wrestle his pants over his feet. It wasn't lithe. It wasn't anything close to a moment that would make it into a sexy movie, but he didn't care. He was pretty sure his jeans had never been more spectacularly removed.

She looked at his underwear, at the bulge in the middle, and seemed nervous. He didn't know what to say or do, so he just lay there mute in his shirt, underwear and socks.

Socks.

They had to go. Girls hated when guys left socks on, the internet was clear on that.

He eased her off him, rolled onto his side and drew his legs up. He peeled his socks off and tossed them on the floor far below them.

'Sorry,' he mumbled.

She leaned forward and kissed him, which went a long way to settling his nerves. He put an arm around her neck and drew her against him.

They really should have taken their pants off before getting up here – he had hers to contend with now.

But Adaline's fingers were already working on them. She dropped onto her back and lifted her butt in the air. Her jeans were half way down her thighs when she paused. 'Do you have a condom?'

Rory dragged his eyes away from the perfection of her legs.

She waited.

It was a simple answer. No. No he did not have a condom. No, he was not prepared. No no no. Shit.

Adaline lowered her butt onto the mattress and propped herself up on her elbow. She'd guessed his answer.

'Do you?' he asked hopefully.

She shook her head. 'Don't guys carry them around in their wallet or something?'

Rory dropped down onto the pillow and stared at the ceiling. 'Some guys do that. I've never been the type.' He wished he was now. He wanted to punch the Rory who'd once considered that presumptuous and arrogant. That Rory may not have thought there'd be a time when he'd suddenly have his pants off, but *this* Rory ... *this* Rory was about to lose out.

'Girls should carry them too,' he grumbled.

Adaline's face was a dance of pity, amusement and disappointment. She settled down beside him and trailed her fingers over his chest. 'You're right. It's never occurred to me to take responsibility for that, too.'

'Can we debate sexist presumptions later? I'm busy crying right now.'

Her sound of sympathy tailed off in a laugh.

'Do you know where you could find one?' she asked.

'I could root through Jonno's bag.'

She screwed up her face.

He sighed. 'No. Do you reckon they sell them at reception?'

'Reception's closed.'

'Crap.'

'Maybe there's a condom dispenser in the guys' bathrooms!' She sounded excited by the idea. Not a question so much as an epiphany.

Rory rolled his head towards her and arched a brow. 'Say what?'

'Like in the girls' bathrooms.'

He waited a beat then propped himself up on his elbows. 'There are condom dispensers in the girls' bathrooms? Then there it is – let's go!'

She frowned. 'No, they're tampon dispensers in the girls' bathrooms. I figured you lot would have condom ones.'

Rory dropped back on to the pillow. 'We don't.' He thought for a moment. 'We could go into town?'

Adaline grimaced. 'By the time we get in there, find a twenty-four hour shop and get back, the girls won't be far behind us. They might even be here by then.'

'Your roommates are soft.'

And now so was he.

He sighed and pushed his disappointment into the room.

Adaline watched him. Her mouth was moving, as if words were teasing against the inside of her lips but she wouldn't let them pass. She looked down at his underwear again.

He looked away, not wanting to see her reaction.

Her lips made him turn back. She'd moved in, folded herself over his shoulder and pressed a kiss to his jaw. She claimed his mouth when it was back within reach, and the kiss was bolstering.

'There are other things we can do,' she said softly. Teasingly. Her warm breath rolled down his cheeks and chased away the chill of anti-climax.

Her fingers dragged a fiery trail down his stomach and over his legs.

He kissed her harder. Roused by her flirtations, he tumbled back into the moment. Their explorations resumed. His heartbeat accelerated. Disbelief, rapture and something altogether more complex fuelled him. A single word rolled around his mind, behind his eyes, in his mouth.

Love.

In its infancy, but undeniable.

37 THE WALLS WE BUILD

Adaline opened her eyes. She'd been lost in dreams, warmed by skin on skin and memories that heated her belly and curved her mouth. Something had woken her: a sound, an intrusion. She was curled against Rory's bare chest, his arm under her neck and against her equally bare back. He breathed the deep, rhythmic breaths of sleep.

Not Rory then.

Another sound. Outside. It was the front door, she realised, and before Adaline could react, it swung inward.

She'd left the main room light on and the bedroom door ajar, so from her high vantage point on the top bunk, she caught a glimpse of blonde curls and the shine of a royal green dress.

Beth.

No one followed her inside. She'd come back alone. Perhaps before Daniel, perhaps with him and she'd since tucked him in. Either way, she didn't look in Adaline's direction. She pressed her palm over her eyes for a moment Adaline thought might never end, then went into the bathroom and closed the door.

Adaline glanced down at the man under her.

She imagined all the ways she might wake him and imagined all the noisy ways he might respond. It seemed simple then to simply kiss him into consciousness. His mouth would be covered, that way.

Her lips touched his – sucked and nudged.

After a moment his pliancy became response. Rory's lips rose to meet hers. His eyes fluttered open and fixed on her, and the immediate smile that accompanied his understanding made her feel as warm as the sheets and limbs around her did.

She pressed a finger to her lips.

The fatigue in his eyes cleared at once. He lifted himself from the pillow and glanced through the doorway. He looked back at her. 'Who?' he whispered.

'Beth.'

'Daniel?'

She shook her head.

Rory pushed the sheets down and uncurled himself from around her. She almost laughed as he hastened down the ladder, naked and rumpled from sleep. He began grabbing at the clothes that littered the floor. She followed him down and toppled into her underwear.

The toilet flushed.

Adaline and Rory looked at each other.

Very quickly, Rory closed the door further. It didn't latch, and thankfully didn't squeak.

They continued dressing. In the other room, the bathroom door opened. They heard heavy footsteps then there was a long pause. When Beth started walking again her footsteps sounded different – much lighter. She'd taken off her shoes, probably so as to not wake Adaline. She opened a cupboard in the kitchenette, ran the tap for a moment, then seemed to go to bed.

All was quiet.

Fully dressed now, Adaline and Rory watched each other as they waited. She strained to hear the soft click of a light switch or the creak of a mattress, anything that told her Beth wasn't standing in her doorway on the other side of the room.

Nothing.

Rory raised his brows in question. She nodded.

Adaline went first. Bent over, as if being closer to the ground might somehow make her quieter. Shoes in one hand, she stood by the front door and waited until Rory was in position. When he was ready – after pretending to throw his shoe at Beth's closed door – she pulled it open and he hurried out. She was close on his heels. The front door banged closed behind her, but they were already off the porch, half a dozen strides into the dark.

When they reached the cloak of trees, they turned.

The door opened again. Light spilled out into the night, broken by Beth's silhouette.

Adaline clapped a hand over her mouth and tried to suffocate the laugh that was bubbling up her throat. Her heart was racing. She felt alive and daring, cheeky and young. So young. So boundless and excited.

Beth stepped back from the doorway and closed the door, pitching them once again into the dark.

Rory took Adaline's hand and leaned close. 'Guess what …'

Adaline moved in to better hear him. 'What?'

'I've seen you naked.'

Adaline lurched away and swat his arm. They stared at each other for one long, loaded moment, then burst out laughing.

'I've seen you naked too, you fool.'

'And we've done naked things.'

'And learned naked lessons.'

Rory nodded sagely. 'Seriously, I'm going to start wearing condom packets on a necklace.'

Adaline grinned. 'I'm sure your pocket would do the trick. I'm going to pick up the habit, too.'

'No.' Rory's hand shot out to claim hers, so fast it seemed to surprise even him.

Adaline straightened. 'No?'

Rory's expression changed. He wasn't carefree any longer. His words no longer came easily, they seemed to grow in his chest and get stuck in his throat. 'I mean …' He held her hand tighter, as if afraid she might take it from him. 'You won't need to. I'll have it covered.'

Bam.

They'd burst into the clearing like a plane shot from the sky. The clearing was the conversation they'd been skirting around for days, and in Adaline's mind, it had been as big as Adelaide itself. It had been inevitable that they'd land there eventually – the only unknowns had been the pilot and the nature of the landing.

Rory had opted for a nose-dive.

Adaline pressed her free fingers to the bridge of her nose and closed her eyes. 'Okay, so this is happening …'

'The conversation or exclusivity?'

Her lips twitched. 'The conversation.' She opened her eyes and looked at him over their joined hands. He was made darker by the night; the shadows sharpened the angles of his face and made his eyes seem like something bottomless she could fall into.

'Which includes exclusivity,' he said. There was no laughter in his face now.

'You're about to go to Mykonos,' she protested.

His expression hardened. 'If you think I'm going to wave you off tomorrow then go hook up with someone else like this was nothing, then you don't know me at all.'

Adaline dropped his hand to press both her hands against his chest. 'You're right, I'm sorry. That was a stupid thing to say.'

He glowered at her then looked away.

She tipped herself sideways to catch his eye. 'I'm sorry,' she said again. 'I know this is … something.' Everything. *It*. All she would think about when she got home. 'But we're young. We've got a lot of changes coming up, a lot of expectations. Being together seems so easy when we're a meter apart like this, but when we're fourteen hundred Ks away from each other, it'll be too complicated. We won't survive it.'

Her response didn't appear to dissuade him, instead he looked inexplicably pleased. 'That's a pretty good estimation. Did you look it up?'

She straightened and angled her chin. 'So what if I did?'

His answering smile made her blood heat, part embarrassment, part pleasure – although which had the edge, she wasn't sure.

'Don't get encouraged,' she said, poking him in the chest. 'I can see what you're thinking, but it's not even about the long-distance thing.'

'It's not? Because seriously, what's a few flights between Sydney and Adelaide if it means making this happen?' He starting ticking things off on his fingers. 'There's video chat, messages, emails, Facebook – hell, the good old fashioned phone call. Technology *wants* to make this happen. There's deals on flights all the time. I'll get a double bed for my room so you can stay with me. I can stay at a hostel when I visit you and you can tell me how to make a good impression on your mum.'

The lovely world he was building in her mind fractured and crumpled.

She started shaking her head. It was so easy to imagine herself in Sydney with him, but just the mention of Rory venturing into her Adelaide hell …
'No,' she said. 'Trust me Rory, you don't want to be part of my world.'

Rory grabbed her arms and gave her a light shake. '*You* don't want to be part of your world! Whatever it is that I see when I get there won't be whatever you're going through now, because I know you're going to change it. I've been watching you – *you've* changed. You're not that damaged little girl trying to be invisible anymore, you're curious and worldly and you're too big for the life you've come to think of as a cage. I know you're going to go home and do things differently. I *know* that because you let me in. You let all of us in who wanted a part of you because you stopped believing we'd hurt you if we could.'

His hands moved from her arms to her face. Frustration turned to tenderness. 'Ads, don't push me away because you don't like everything going on in your life right now. No one ever likes everything they're doing. Gives us a chance.' He grinned. 'Dare to believe. Dream big.'

She raised an eyebrow. 'You're starting to sound like an advertising campaign.'

'Yeah, I thought things were getting a little heavy there.'

He opened his arms and she went immediately into them. He closed his support and strength around her, and she did dare. She dared to think that he was right, that she would go home and be brave enough to fix her life.

It was one thing to want change, but it was quite another to confront her parents and demand it.

She nuzzled her nose against his shirt and breathed in the soft, summer scent of him. The comfort of his closeness was strong but incomplete – incomplete because it would soon be lost to her. She thought of the ocean that would soon be between them, of the plane rides that could punctuate their futures. She thought of him being willing to cross half the country innumerable times just to be with her, and felt something deep inside her loosen, then give way.

It was an avalanche of feeling, one that almost reduced her to her knees.

Adaline grasped Rory's shirtfront as her mouth fell open and her eyes closed. She clung to him as all her reservations and assumptions tumbled away.

When she opened her eyes again and looked up at him, all she could think to say was, 'If you hurt me I'm sending you my therapist bill.'

For a moment he looked confused. Then when he understood, he looked ecstatic. 'I won't need to save a cent towards it.' He kissed her mouth, her cheeks, her forehead then her mouth again. 'Holy crap, I thought you'd never give in.'

They laughed unsteadily, dazed by the promises they were making to one another.

What was the point, she wondered, in getting in her own way? What reasons could she possibly have that were strong enough to end them before they'd even really tried? If they tried and failed, she could live with that.

She drew him closer. 'I'm starting to freak out that I'm running out of time with you.'

He laughed. 'I started freaking out about that the day I met you. But I'll come to Adelaide really soon.'

Adaline smiled. 'You have uni. I'll come to Sydney first.'

If the crazy idea rolling around in her mind got legs, that would be a very easy promise to keep.

Movement further down the path made them both look up in surprise. She'd completely forgotten where they were, clutching each other in the dark between a tight group of trees, mostly hidden from view. From where she stood she could just make out the twin beams of headlights on the main road and the disembodied sounds of laughter and remembered stories. Their tour mates were returning. As one set of headlights left, another set arrived. Cabs, she realised.

'Has everyone got their keys?' a familiar voice called, rising above the general bedlam that was moving closer to where they stood. Jack, ever the tour manager, always working. Although there was a clumsiness to his steps that suggested he'd enjoyed himself too.

There were shouts and giggles in reply.

Rory pulled Adaline further into the shadows of the trees. There was mischief in his eyes.

'Uh oh,' she said softly. 'What's going on in that head of yours? Another prank?'

Rory's face split into a wide grin. His cheeks creased in that way she loved, and she knew the moment he turned to her that she'd say yes to anything he asked of her.

'I've got an idea,' he whispered.

They glanced back at the revellers. Cabins lights were turning on, feet were stomping on porches. The night was coming alive.

She looked back to him. 'I'm in.'

What would he need – a diversion? Sleight of hand? Some sort of story to explain something possibly unexplainable?

'I need you to wait here.'

The smile building on Adaline's face dropped. 'What?'

'Just … right here. I won't be long. I need to get a few things.'

He stepped away and she reached for him. Her fingers snagged the sleeve of his T-shirt and he paused. 'I can help,' she said. There was a bit of huff in her tone.

He kissed her quickly. 'You'll be plenty of help in a few minutes. Keep low and try to spot a cabin where everyone seems to be back. We don't want to get interrupted half way through.'

Then he melted away into the blackest part of the black.

Adaline dropped into a crouch. She stared at the space where he'd disappeared, then gave her focus to the main path. The second group was close now, she could make out their faces. Maree and Will were amongst them. Adaline didn't recognise them at first because they were walking separately – Chris and Hamish were between them singing in a way that would make alley cats proud. Maree and Will were quiet. Chris paused, threw an arm up and dropped it on the shoulder of a fourth person who'd been walking close behind them – Pia, the Italian girl Adaline had had one or two conversations with.

In the low light Adaline couldn't be sure of expressions, but there was enough body language for her to begin to piece together the night. Things hadn't gone well for the New Zealand couple again. Arms were crossed, shoulders were up.

At this rate they'd be hashing out their relationship on the Greek islands.

The Canadian boys went left. The Italian girl went right. Maree and Will looked at each other for a long moment, then went silently into the cabin nearest where Adaline hid. Their light was off by the time Rory came back.

He returned empty-handed.

Adaline held her hands up in question.

He snagged one of them out of the air and tugged her in the direction he'd come from.

Fallen leaves crackled underfoot and all the mysterious sounds of the night followed them over to the next line of cabins. They stopped outside the most private one – nestled against the tree line with a lone pine spearing out of the ground near the front door, partially concealing it from its neighbours.

'This one?' she whispered, craning her neck to see if she could spy a line of light under the doorway.

'Yeah,' Rory murmured, 'everyone's inside.'

'So what's the plan?'

He grinned at her. His teeth were a pale line across his dark face. He inclined his head towards a shape she was standing near. She peered down at it.

An industrial sized watering can and two long plastic wrapped items.

Adaline ducked down to see them better. They were plastic cups, dozens of them stacked together. She frowned and looked up at Rory.

He held up a roll of masking tape.

'I'm afraid to ask,' she said, cataloguing his latest tools for trouble.

He chuckled softly. 'I reckon we'll only have time for one door. I would've liked to do two or three, but it's too risky.'

'What are we doing?'

'We're creating a second door.'

'I don't understand.' She narrowed her eyes. 'Where did you get this stuff?'

He grinned down at the things on the ground. 'Beside the maintenance shed and just inside the food tent.' Then in low voice, 'And the masking tape's mine, of course.'

'Of course,' she repeated, bemused.

'Okay, everything's about to happen really fast. You ready?'

'Not in the slightest.'

Rory handed Adaline the heavy watering can, grabbed the cups and led her onto the small porch. He quietly prised the plastic wrap open, then dropped to his haunches and began assembling the cups on the wood. 'Pour,' he whispered.

She struggled closer, angled the can over the nearest cup and poured. The cup toppled and water trickled between the slats. Rory righted it without comment and kept going. She tried again, this time managing to fill it two-thirds of the way to the top.

'That's enough,' he whispered. 'Next one.'

Adaline glanced at the door and moved the spout to the next cup.

When Rory finished setting up the first packet, he shifted closer to the door and began moving the filled cups onto the threshold. The first touched the frame and the door, and the second was two fingers-width along. He did this until he ran out of space, then reached for the roll of tape and pulled a length free. The sharp, sticky tearing sound made them both freeze.

Adaline's heart tripped and spluttered, and she gazed wide-eyed at the door, expecting it to open. But seconds passed.

Rory turned to her, held up a finger then darted around the side of the cabin.

She stared after him, horrified that he'd left her.

She looked down at the watering can, at the cups she'd filled and the many yet to do, and panicked. If someone found her here she would look like the mastermind and sole executor of a prank she didn't fully understand; and Rory – gone, probably laughing maniacally behind a bush somewhere, would have set her up perfectly.

Oh god, was the prank on her?

What a fine send-off – stitching her up and denying all involvement. The tour prankster unmasked – caught in the act.

Soft thumps made her look over her shoulder. Rory reappeared with long strips of unrolled tape stuck to an outstretched arm, flying behind him like ribbons off bike handles. He transferred the pieces to the cabin exterior then used two of them to secure the cups against the door and frame. He pressed the tape to each of the cups, affixing it, then began to build a second storey.

They were making a second door. His enigmatic response made sense now, in a terrible yet hilarious way.

For the next few minutes she continued to fill cups and Rory continued to balance and tape. When the water ran low he took the can from her and passed her the second packet of cups. She began to set these out on the porch as he went somewhere unknown for a refill.

He was away much longer this time, but just like before, he returned.

The second packet of cups went up much faster than the first; Adaline and Rory fell into a rhythm and she was able to help stack the last few rows once she finished pouring. Their last row consisted of three cups instead of the regular seven or eight, and were most securely fastened with the rest of the lengths of tape. They'd almost reached the top of the door. There was only a narrow strip of walnut above the crowning cups.

They stood back and admired their work. Rory snapped a picture on his phone, then they gathered the watering can and the torn plastic and ran like hell.

Rory ditched the can near reception almost without breaking stride, then they were out on the street, bitumen flying beneath them and their laughter making it hard to breathe. When they reached the end of the block they slowed, gasping and smiling.

Rory dragged Adaline into a clumsy embrace and almost toppled them both.

'Wow,' he panted over her shoulder, 'what a rush.'

She was still laughing, giddy from the adrenalin spike. 'Whose room was that?' she managed to say.

He pulled away. 'It's a surprise.'

'I helped you and you're keeping secrets?'

'I'm prolonging the enjoyment.' He planted a loud, smacking kiss on her mouth then turned her in a quick circle, as if they were dancing. The air rushed across her face and made her hair fly, then she was against his chest, arms around him.

'You're a bad influence.'

'I'm hilarious,' he returned, 'and you can't get enough of me.'

'True. What next?' she said.

Rory didn't answer.

Adaline flinched. Stupid, she thought. Stupid to mention time.

What was left for them? It was too late to go into town for anything other than nightclubs, their cabins were no longer places of privacy. There were only seats and low-lit paths. A few short hours before dawn and a million things unsaid.

She pitied her racing heart. Exhaustion, frustration, endless longing and self-abuse – the things she'd put herself through since meeting Rory, and the things she would put herself through yet. He would leave for the sun and she would return to the dark. This was all ending. This life on the road, punctuated by dreams come true. All the culture, all the food, all the people who'd made both better – soon she'd be back to waking up in the same bed every morning, surrounded by the same things, enduring the same psychological dance before she could retreat to her room and do it all again the next day. It would all be made worse by knowing everyone had continued on without her, that they were still together, still on a break from their real lives.

Just the thought of it made her want to cry.

Rory touched his thumb to the corner of Adaline's mouth, then kissed her again. Gentle, lingering, not playful this time.

Adaline tugged his arm around her again and stepped so close they were touching almost from forehead to toe. 'Thank you,' she said. His face was so close to hers that he was a blur, so she closed her eyes and spoke to the dark. 'For tripping on me in the ferry café line.'

He laughed. 'Yeah, anytime.'

They kissed again, a little desperately this time.

It was a little past two o'clock in the morning when Rory left her at her cabin door. In her bed, Adaline breathed in the scent of him on her pillow and dreaded the dawn.

38 JUST DANCE

The carpark looked like an obstacle course. Suitcases and backpacks leaned against the coach, against one another, and against legs. There were two less bags, Adaline thought, thinking of herself and Claire, but Danya wouldn't notice – there were at least a dozen more, bought on the road, stuffed full of souvenirs.

People were glancing at her curiously. Word had got around that she was leaving the tour early and those who knew her well enough were singling her out to say goodbye.

Lois and Lisa came up to her first. Not much was said, the goodbyes were brief and full of the generic things people say.

Adaline said goodbye to Will next, and despite all they'd been through together, Adaline found they had very few parting words. They thanked each other for the friendship, reminisced on a few of the highlights, got a photo together, then parted company for what Adaline was sure to be the last time in their lives.

Her sympathy went with him. He was about to lose the biggest relationship in his life because he was afraid of the next step. Only a few shorts days ago, Adaline had been where he was now. He'd hesitated when he should have stepped forward, and merely watched as a possible future had slipped out of reach. Or maybe it wasn't fear – maybe it was that there wasn't enough of a connection to prompt him to fight. Maybe Maree was right, maybe she wasn't The One. Either way, Adaline and Will's similarities ended today.

When Adaline looked forward, she saw a lot of white noise and a lot of questions, but in amongst it all was the tall, smiling prankster who'd wriggled his way into her heart. There was enough connection between her and Rory to warrant one hell of a fight.

The Australian boys approached her next, and these goodbyes were less cut and dry, all of them – especially Pies – said they'd see her again down under. She hugged them all, dodged Pies's attempt to lift her in the air, and she appreciated that they left Rory to wait quietly at her side without too much of a ribbing.

Her little group stood around her like a guard of honour. When it appeared that all her acquaintances had come and gone, the harder goodbyes began.

Holly was first. She'd gone all out this morning; her pixie cut hair was perfectly styled, her make-up was flawless and her hollow cube earrings drew the eye to the soft skin of her neck. She was ethereal in her moss coloured summer dress.

'You're going to stop his heart,' Adaline said, thinking of Pete. She held her fingers up, a fraction apart. 'For just one, unforgettable second.'

Holly beamed at her. 'Thanks. I'll tell you all about it, I promise.'

'I want all the best adjectives. The really visual ones.'

Holly laughed and nodded. Then she became serious. 'I'm going to miss you. I've really loved getting to know you.'

Adaline hugged her. 'Me too. Thanks for everything.'

'If you're ever in the middle of nowhere New South Wales, we'll catch up. And if I'm ever in Adelaide.'

'Of course.'

Rachael came to stand by Holly's elbow. She'd been the careful hand behind Holly's smoky eyes and had done just as nice a job on herself. Small gold Fleur De Lis dangled from her ears, a Florence souvenir. Adaline couldn't say what about them caused a clutch in her stomach.

'Speaking of nowhere New South Wales,' Rachael said, 'don't visit too soon, I might not be there.'

Adaline raised her brows as she accepted the girl's embrace.

'What do you mean?'

Rachael beamed. At her side, Holly beamed wider. 'I've decided to stay on a bit longer. I'm going to kick around in Athens for a while then do another tour in Turkey.'

Adaline gaped. 'But ... what about Sean?'

Rachael waved a hand. 'If I'm not worth waiting for, then I guess he doesn't love me the way I love him. I need to do this before I settle down. I need to do more and see more and *be* more, before I get swallowed up by a small town. I've invited him to visit, and when he calms down, he may come.'

There was a beat of awe-struck silence, then Adaline murmured, 'Hail Rachael.'

Rachael and Holly laughed. 'Yeah, well,' Rachael dropped her arm over the back of Holly's shoulders, 'someone inspired me to seize the day.'

Adaline grinned at Holly.

Rachael dipped forward to catch her eye. 'I meant you, Ada.'

'Me?'

'Of course you. I don't know what's going on with you at home, but the last few days you've been getting ready for it. Whatever you're going to do is going to be really brave, I can tell. You changed when you made whatever decision it was.' She smiled. 'I hope it all works out how you want it to.'

They hugged again. Adaline was speechless.

Rachael smiled over at Rory. 'I'll keep an eye on this idiot, and report back on how many times I catch him crying in a corner somewhere.' She accepted his playful shove with a laugh, and the girls left.

The next person who crossed Adaline's path was not a welcome one. Daniel – too lazy to walk around their little huddle. His eyes were bloodshot and his hair was sitting every which way. His lips were pressed into a tight, crooked line. Hung over, disorientated and cranky, he didn't pay much mind to who was standing where, or that he might be in the way. And he paid no attention to Beth, who was close behind him, dragging two suitcases.

Adaline's gaze dropped to the ground. The sight embarrassed her.

It didn't look like a sister taking care of a brother – nothing as balanced as that or as endearing as someone showing love for another. It looked like weakness. Like someone being taken advantage of and not being strong enough to demand something different for themselves.

Adaline looked up and the girls' eyes met.

Not embarrassment, she realised. It wasn't embarrassment she felt when she looked at Beth. It was shame.

Adaline and Beth played the same role in a similar play.

Adaline stepped away from the group and intercepted the Texan near the bag drop. Beth slowed to a stop and considered her warily. Her fingers curled and uncurled on the plastic handles. Her hair was bundled in a high knot but tumbled loose in some places. She wore no jewellery and no makeup. None of that mattered in the grand scheme of things, but in years to come Adaline suspected Beth would regret wearing tracksuit pants and a shirt Adaline had seen her sleep in before. She'd forever look at the photos of herself in front of the Colosseum or the Trevi Fountain and wish she'd taken more time for herself this morning instead of worrying about getting Daniel to the coach on time. Everyone wanted to look good in the really important pictures.

Adaline opened her mouth, then hesitated. Beth didn't need her advice. The wariness in her eyes had come about through too many people pushing their opinions on to her. Adaline didn't want to be the latest in a string of unwelcome criticism.

So she offered Beth what she wished someone had offered her when she'd been struggling. 'Do you need some help?'

Beth's eyes widened. She inched around Adaline with the bags, rolled them into the mess waiting for Danya, then wiped her hands on her pants.

'No, but thanks.'

Adaline nodded.

It was a shame that things weren't easier between them. They should have been kindred spirits on this trip, drawn to each other through shared experience and understanding. But Beth, like Adaline had been after school, was hard to reach. She was too wrapped up in obligation and worry, and she placed her needs at the bottom of a long list of priorities. Adaline looked at Beth and saw herself, and she felt what her friends must have felt: unimportant.

That was another thing Adaline was going to change when she got home. She was going to make a few long overdue phone calls and set things right. Prioritise some more people in her life.

'I'm glad I met you,' Adaline said.

Beth's face relaxed further. 'I'm glad I met you too, Ada.'

Adaline reached forward and squeezed Beth's elbow. 'Good luck with everything. I hope things work out with that guy.' The older one, the one she'd mentioned once at the Chateau and never again. It had been a rare insight into Beth's otherwise closed world, so it had been particularly memorable.

'Thank you.' Beth smiled then nodded over Adaline's shoulder. 'I hope things work out for you and Rory.'

'I hope so too.' Adaline turned to look behind her. He was lingering on the fringes of her small group, waiting for the moment he would get her alone. She craved that moment too, but he wasn't the only one she'd connected with on this trip – she was glad he seemed to understand that. She looked back.

Beth's expression had changed. 'I hope your mum's okay, too. It's awful what happened. It's really good of you to go back early for her.'

Adaline didn't have a response for this, so she instigated a hug. Arms around each other, each thinking a dozen unsaid things, they said goodbye.

They were just about to turn from each other when Daniel appeared between them. He glowered at Adaline, put out with her and put out with the world.

'Where's your boyfriend?' he snapped. He slapped two fingers against the crystal face of his watch then cast his hand out impatiently.

Adaline knew he wasn't talking about Rory, but it was Rory who appeared.

'Good morning,' he said, appearing at Adaline's side and winding an arm around her waist. 'I see the assassins continue to keep us in suspense.'

Daniel's top lip curled back from his teeth.

Before he could reply, Beth curled her fingers around his forearm and moved to steer him away. He resisted at first, but then Pies, standing nearby – who's voice had been a constant background to this conversation – stopped talking. He took a single step in Daniel's direction. The rest of the Australians looked over with interest, and Daniel appeared to quail against the numbers.

Daniel cast a look of deepest loathing towards Rory, then stalked away, Beth on his heels.

Alone together for the first time since dawn, Adaline looked up at Rory and smiled.

He kissed her forehead. 'If you're saving the best till last, I'm going to get very little time with you.' He said this lightly, but she heard the concern in his voice.

'I'll think we'll have more time than you think.'

Rory pulled back to look at her, his brows drawn together in question.

She rolled her eyes. 'Oh please, you think I haven't figured out who's door we blocked?'

The only people unaccounted for were the tour manager and driver. By choosing their cabin Rory had bought himself some more time, which impressed her no end.

His grin confirmed it.

'May I have this dance?' It was Maree, standing with Jenny, looking both happy and apologetic.

Adaline laughed. 'Of course.'

Rory squeezed her tight then stepped away again. Adaline heard the Australians greet him with sarcasm and laughter, and her smile widened.

'Sorry to interrupt,' Maree said, glancing towards Rory. 'I just figured we'd get our goodbyes out of the way and leave you two to it.'

'It's okay,' Adaline promised, 'I wanted to see you. Both.' She tacked on the last word after too much pause.

Jenny seemed far from a smiling mood, she looked like she'd been dragged through a hedge backwards and wasn't happy about it. She reeked of spirits and stale sweat, and was cringing away from the sun.

'Thanks and all,' Jenny began. Adaline couldn't see Jenny's eyes through her dark sunglasses, but judging by the way she was holding herself, Adaline could guess they were bloodshot. 'Sucks about your mum. Keep in touch. Invite me to the wedding.' She pointed between Adaline and Rory then slung her arm around Adaline's neck and squeezed.

It was one of the more uncomfortable embraces of Adaline's life.

Jenny pulled away and pointed a finger at Adaline's face. For just a moment, Adaline thought she was going to say something about Claire. Vulnerability flickered, then died. 'You're weird, but I like you.'

Jenny left as unsteadily as she'd arrived. She picked her way through the bags and backpacks then sat on the ground by the coach door.

Adaline and Maree watched her a moment, then Maree looked back to Adaline and shook her head. 'To think the party island is yet to come.'

Claire was lucky to be shot of her, Adaline thought. There was one relationship that wouldn't have the chance to get any further out of balance. Claire might not feel it now, being left behind in a hospital bed and short a friend – but she'd be relieved in the long run.

Adaline scrubbed her face and the thoughts tumbled away.

'I'm not going to say goodbye,' Maree said. 'Because we're going to see each other again. You're really special to me and I don't want this to be the last time I see you.'

Adaline nodded vigorously. 'I agree.' She threw her arms around Maree and pulled her close.

'Don't just say that,' she said into Adaline's shoulder. 'Mean it.' Adaline pulled away and Maree blinked quickly. She took a deep breath. 'I know I don't know your big stories – like what's going on with you at home and how freaked out you are about trying for long distance. But I hope you'll tell me them one day. Let's not just be girls who holidayed together once.'

Moved and humbled, Adaline took Maree's hands and squeezed them. She'd had no idea she'd made such an impression. Was it possible that she was leaving this holiday with more than she'd imagined? With a friend, a confidante?

'Thanks for listening when I needed to talk.' Maree swallowed. 'I don't have a lot of people who listen in my life, so I appreciate it more than you can know.'

Adaline's lips curved. 'And thank *you* for persevering with me.' She hesitated. 'I know I can be ... hard to get to know.'

Maree laughed. 'I still don't know you.'

Adaline grinned. 'Ah, but you're getting there. Which is more than I can say for most.'

Maree nodded. She said, 'I hate that you're leaving early. Let me know how everything goes when you get back.'

'And brag to me about Mykonos.' Adaline considered not mentioning it, but ... 'Let me know how things go with Will.'

Maree nodded again. 'Okay.'

'Sorry! Sorry, sorry everyone.' Jack exploded onto the scene. He had maps and papers clutched to his chest and his backpack was swinging wildly from one arm. Danya was close behind him, his backpack bouncing against his back as he ran. The pant legs on both of them were wet.

Years of practice told Danya to unlock the coach doors before the undercarriage – in doing so, almost the entire group flooded on board to sit and wait, effectively getting themselves out of the way. A few stayed outside to help load the bags, something that made Danya's typically stormy face soften in gratitude. Jack dropped his things on his seat then stepped off the coach again. He spotted Adaline and hurried towards her.

Maree grabbed Adaline, squeezed her tight then was gone. Adaline's arms were still singing from the pressure when Jack reached her side. She glanced over at Rory, who had his hands in his pockets and a downcast look on his face.

Her goodbyes had taken too long. By the time Jack had said his piece there would be no time to tell Rory all the things she needed to say. No time to listen to all the things he had to say.

But she needed to talk to Jack. It was important.

'You okay?' she asked him.

Flushed and harried, he laughed dryly. 'Yeah. It's a long story that I'm sure you already know.'

Adaline raised her brows in innocent curiosity.

'Don't give me that.' He laughed and shook his head. 'I'd apologise for standing you up this morning, but something tells me you weren't waiting too long.'

Now Adaline's brows came down. When she understood what he meant – that he'd assumed they'd go for one last jog together – she had to look away so he wouldn't see the guilt that flooded her eyes and pinched her mouth.

She hadn't given him a second thought this morning. Exhausted from her late night and wholly focused on Rory and home, there hadn't been much room in her mind for unspoken commitments. Even when she'd guessed whose door they were barring, she hadn't hesitated to continue. Hadn't thought to stop. She'd only thought of herself, of the extra time she and Rory were building themselves.

Her total disregard for the empathy that usually dictated everything she did surprised her.

It wasn't the best timing to ask for a favour, but Adaline had run out of options. It would have been better had they gone for a run – no audience, no ticking clock, no Rory dying by inches a short distance away.

She cleared her throat. 'Jack, when you said you were coming back to Australia, will it be as a franchise of Gateway?'

'No. I'm leaving Gateway at the end of the year.' He pushed his hair back and flashed her an odd look. She was bringing up something they'd spoken about during a moment they'd agreed to never speak of again – with Rory within earshot, no less. He said, 'I'm done with all this,' and shrugged.

She thought of the late nights, the endless kilometres and the ever-changing faces, and thought she understood why. But when he explained himself, he surprised her.

'I'm starting my own tour company. It'll be small for a while, but I've got a number of ex-Gateway people on board. We're going to take tourists to the highlights. Pitch the company in such a way that Australians want to see more of their own country.'

He wasn't destined for the quiet life, she thought. However exhausting, however lonely and isolating this life must be, Jack had no plans to leave it.

It was the perfect answer.

'That's amazing,' she said.

'Hey, if you want a job, I could hook you up. I'd love to have someone on board with your kind of passion for travel.'

Was it really going to be that easy?

She grinned. 'I'll keep that in mind. Would you mind if I … can we talk more later? Maybe I could email you?'

Jack tilted his head to the side. 'Sure. Of course.'

Adaline pulled her phone from her pocket and opened up her address book. Jack took it, typed in his details and handed it back. She saved the information and tucked her phone away again.

'I have to be honest,' she said, 'I'm going to ask you a favour.'

He smiled, his wide, full lips pressed together. 'Another one?'

'It's not about my mother.'

'Then I'm dead curious.' He hesitated. His eyes flicked to Rory and back again. 'I should leave you to it. We've got to leave as soon as possible, so be as quick as you can. I can't really give you more than a couple of minutes.'

She nodded. 'Thanks for everything, Jack.' If he were anyone else, she would have hugged him. A handshake felt too formal, so she was at a loss how to conclude the conversation.

Jack seemed to be similarly unsure.

In the end their half hug, half pat on the back manoeuvre would have made the Australians proud. They loved a good awkward moment.

The moment Jack turned away, Adaline ran into Rory's arms. The weight of her body knocked him back a step. His arms came around her and his lips were on hers. She heard the cheers of her tour mates on the coach, but didn't care. It was all coming to an end.

She was going to miss everyone. She was going to think of them often, and probably for the rest of her life. They would forever be the faces of her trip to Europe, and although she'd wish she could see them again, she knew that wish would never be as powerful as the wish to be here again, in this moment, in this time. Because every time she'd said goodbye to one of these people, she'd said goodbye to a little piece of herself. She was going to miss who she was when she was with them, and the end of this trip would mark the end of this Adaline.

She would return home, changed in more ways than she'd ever imagined, and she would remember; but this part of her life – this highlight, this yo-yo of joy and heartache and friendship and combat – was coming to an end.

This Adaline with this Rory.

The clock was ticking.

'I'm so glad you tripped over me in that line on the Dover ferry,' she said, so fast her words were tumbling over themselves. 'I'm so glad it was you and me through Europe. Thank you for being so patient with me and nice to me and —'

He cut her off with a kiss. Then he said, 'You don't have to thank me for being nice to you. You should thank me for not throat punching everyone who wanted a piece of you this morning, though.'

'Yeah, it was a close one. I know how much you like to throat punch.'

'It's my signature move.'

They grinned at each other. When her smile began to waver, Rory shook his head.

'No,' he said, 'none of that. I'll see you in a few weeks.'

She nodded. 'Okay. Start thinking of all the free things we can do in Sydney.' Between this holiday and a trip interstate, Adaline's cash situation was going to be pretty dire until her father had a bout of generosity again, or Adaline got a full-time job.

He drew her close again. 'I can think of one free thing we can do over and over again.'

Such a flirtation could have heated the moment, but it only served to make it tender.

It didn't matter that their intimacy hadn't extended to sex. Emotionally, Adaline was captured.

'You're my favourite feeling,' she whispered.

She could draw no comparison to it in her life. There was affection, then there was what she felt for Rory. There was need – the ugly, binding kind – then there was whatever this was; sweet and keen and beautiful at its core. He made her feel everything her family did not; adventurous, funny … free.

Rory was larger than life and in falling for him, she'd allowed herself to be the same.

Forehead against forehead, he countered her compliment. 'You're my favourite place to be.'

Life would never be the same. Not now that he was in it.

The coach engine rumbled and it felt like Adaline's heart dropped into her stomach.

'Rory.'

They both turned. It was Jack, standing on the bottom step at the front door, leaning outside looking sorry to have spoken. He waved a hand in a helpless gesture. 'I'm sorry,' he said. 'It's time to go.'

Rory nodded and turned back to her. In the measure of two heartbeats, a thousand unsaid things seemed to pass between them in a look. He pulled her into his arms and closed them around her for the last time.

She had to remember this – this exact feeling, the way it elevated her and empowered her. The way it made her feel both fragile and all-powerful. She would need this memory back home.

He pulled away before she could memorise it.

His lips touched hers at the same moment that she slipped off the final rung of the ladder. When he pulled away, she was in love with him.

Rory stepped back and his hands trailed down her arms. They slipped into her hands, squeezed, then trailed down her fingers. The connection broke, and he turned away.

The day song began to play. Its familiar opening chords rolled out the door and overwhelmed her with nostalgia. She could hear some people singing along to it, and see others – her friends – waving down at her through the tinted windows. She waved back.

Jack had been right: the people had made this trip more than she ever could have managed to herself. Rory, most particularly, but all the people she had raised a glass with, shared a room with or stood in the shadow of a monument with – they'd given her more precious memories than any building or art piece had. She'd come to think of the coach as a kind of home, and in that home during the many hours on the road, she'd heard so many of their stories. There had been so much to know and share. There was so much they would all share still, and things she would never know now that the journey was over for her.

Adaline worked to bury her jealousy.

The coach began reversing before Rory had sat down. He walked to the back and dropped his knees on one of the back seats. She hurried to her left to better see him, to stand apart from the site reps who were waving the group off, and they stared at each other through the yellow semi-transparent film on the back window.

She held up her hand.

At the back, she thought, where he might have spent the whole trip had he not met a culture vulture determined to hear and see everything she could. She smiled. He'd asked her on the ferry which traveller category she most identified with, and she hadn't known at the time. Now she finally had her answer. She'd chosen the world. More than food and parties and hair-raising adventures – history and culture had been her siren call.

It felt wonderful to know herself just that little bit more.

The coach stopped reversing and began to roll forward. Within moments, she could no longer see the finer details of his face, just the outline of his head and shoulders, and the one arm raised in farewell.

The coach turned the corner and took all the sound in the world with it.

Adaline stood there in the quiet and slowly dropped her hand to her side.

It was over.

39 THE THREE C'S

Adaline's anxiety had grown steadily worse as she'd crossed time zones, disembarked, then begun the last leg of her journey home. She'd text her parents on the shuttle bus and received no reply from her mum, which was ominous. Her dad had sent her a simple 'welcome back', which was marginally better than his standard, 'ok', but just as unhelpful. She had no idea what she'd be walking into, and her imagination had had plenty of time to assault her with terrible scenarios.

Plenty of time. Over twenty-three hours in flights and just shy of fifteen hours in lay-overs. Oddly enough, it was this last half hour on the bus that was likely to break her.

Maybe it was because everything was familiar now. The local bus was rolling down the street she drove to get to her local supermarket. It was passing houses she'd been in for sleep-overs and pool parties. There was nothing foreign about this place. All the adventure and discovery was long gone, a world away with people she hadn't been able to stop thinking about.

The bus eased into the stop before Adaline's and she began to gather her things. It took two tries to hook her fingers through the handle of her suitcase, and a moment for her to search everywhere for her sunglasses before she found them balanced on top of her head. She'd been on the move too long.

Hypersensitive and overtired, Adaline had been convinced that the Melbourne to Adelaide in-flight safety announcement had been lecturing her. In case of an in-flight emergency, put on your own oxygen mask before helping others. Georgia was the emergency, of course. And for years now, Georgia had got her oxygen mask first. Help yourself before you attempt to help others. It was such an obvious, common-sense statement that was so easy to forget in the heat of the moment.

Adaline wanted to sleep, but the chance of that happening any time soon was slim – it was only 10 am and her mother would be waiting to have it out with her.

Georgia had been discharged. She was home, and as far as Adaline had been able to determine from her dad's too-brief email received when she'd been killing time in Dubai, unsupervised. The cuts had been shallow. Superficial. The drugs Georgia had taken only marginally more than a prescribed daily amount. It had been a cry for attention, which her dad had no doubt promised the hospital staff he'd give her.

He would have changed his mind in the car when Georgia had said something horrible to him. He would have dropped her at the curb and kept going, and told himself that behaviour was okay, because Adaline would be back the next morning.

Back.

Adaline sighed. The bus reached her stop and she tumbled off with her assorted things.

It was a short walk back to her house, two blocks without a footpath, so Adaline dragged her bag along the road, causing an almighty racket, and used her last moments alone to run over her plan in her mind again. Be friendly. Listen patiently. Do not apologise.

Do not apologise for daring to have a life outside of her mother and her mother's illness.

Do not accept blame for her mother's actions and behaviour.

Set boundaries and don't back down.

The last was going to take some time. A lot of patience and a lot of unpleasantness. Patience to even find the moment to broach the conversation about boundaries, let alone ride out the subsequent fall-out. But that was what they would be working towards now. Georgia was going to have to get on board.

The house, when Adaline came close enough to see it, looked the same as it always did, except there was a lot of mail hanging out the front of the over-stuffed letterbox and the hanging plants looked thirsty. All the curtains were drawn, blocking out the beautiful morning. It was possible her mother wasn't even awake yet – there had been many days when Georgia hadn't seen the point in going through the motions of another day, so she simply hadn't. Maybe this was another bed day.

It would make it easier to walk away from her if that was the case.

Adaline fumbled for her key and let herself in.

The house smelled stale. There hadn't been a window open in weeks, nor a broom pushed around. Dust bunnies rolled along the floorboards in the hallway, disturbed by the breeze through the front door. There were more wilted plants.

Adaline glanced into the front bedroom, her mother's room, but it was empty. The bed was unmade and there were pyjamas on the floor.

Not a bed day, then. Maybe a happy day because Adaline was back?

She rolled her suitcase behind her as she searched the other doors off the hallway. When she reached her own, she wheeled the bag in and parked it by her cupboard. Everything was by and large how she'd left it. Her bed had been slept in and there were a couple of glasses of water on the desk and bedside table, but otherwise it looked the same. Comfortable and colourful, full of trinkets and books and countless magazines about history and travel.

She hesitated. No, not the same.

Adaline set her day pack on her desk as she stared at the pile of books beside her reading lamp. *The Essential Family Guide to Bipolar Disorder: New Tools and Techniques to Stop Walking on Eggshells. Understanding the Borderline Mother: Helping Her Children Transcend the Intense, Unpredictable, and Volatile Relationship. Surviving a Borderline Parent: How to Heal Your Childhood Wounds and Build Trust, Boundaries, and Self-Esteem.* She'd covered those with a hoodie before she'd gone, which was now on the floor. The pile was askew.

Something coiled around her stomach, hot like boiling treacle.

She crossed to her bed and shoved her hand beneath the pillow. Nothing.

Slowly, she straightened and turned. Her eyes searched the room for anything else out of place, and after a moment, she found it. Another book. Opened on the floor, its pages bent under its own weight, partially concealed by the door. Thrown against the wall, no doubt.

Adaline crossed the room and stooped to pick it up. She ran her fingers along the title, *Divorcing a Parent: Free Yourself from the Past and Live the Life You've Always Wanted.*

She closed her eyes.

Today was going to suck.

Her awareness shifted to her feet. Just as they had done at the departure meeting in London, they itched to run. Not home this time, but away. Away with no view to return.

This book had been the catalyst to Adaline asking her father for money and booking a trip overseas. The paragraphs within, the case studies and the practical tips – they'd all given her the courage to put herself first. In her hands, this book had been liberating. In Georgia's, this book would have been an assault. One long accusation. Heartbreaking.

Adaline held it to her chest and tried to divorce her emotions from the facts. Georgia had seen this. At the very least she'd read the title, at the most read something that had affected her so adversely that she'd thrown the book across the room. She been feeling vulnerable at the time, as she'd been in here, not her own room. She'd found the other books, perhaps read their titles too.

Had the experience been constructive? Was it possible that Georgia had calmed down enough to ask herself a few hard questions? BPD suffers typically exhibited low empathy and capacity for guilt, it was a common hallmark for them to demonstrate a reduced ability to grow from feedback. So it was unlikely anything good would come from this, but Adaline could hope … Maybe Georgia had done some soul searching?

It was her inability to step outside of her disorder and accept she had a problem that was the real sticking point here. Adaline couldn't fix her, Georgia needed to want to help herself.

Adaline set the book down on the desk and carried her hopeful thoughts back out into the hallway. Georgia wasn't in the kitchen. A quick glance in the fridge told her Georgia hadn't gone shopping recently. So was she there now? Stocking up for Adaline's return, buying a dinner they could talk over?

Adaline glanced into the empty lounge room. Her eyes dropped momentarily to the recliner which covered the blood stain from the incident a year ago. Where had Georgia cut herself this time? Adaline had been faintly surprised to not see a pool of dried blood in the middle of her bedroom – Georgia's revenge for Adaline leaving her alone. The bathroom this time? Her own bedroom?

Adaline pressed a hand to her stomach and turned away. She hoped there wasn't a grizzly discovery waiting for her somewhere in this house.

An ugly, sharp anger pitched itself in her father's direction. He should be here. Never mind that her parents were separated, it wasn't for Adaline to be the one happening upon pools of her mother's blood. What had Adaline done to him that he would sacrifice her this way?

She sometimes wondered if he would come in the middle of the night if one of Georgia's rages got violent. Did Adaline have to bleed or bruise before he'd see the girl he'd thrown to the wolf? What of all the bruises that didn't show up on the skin? What of the welts on her heart and the psychological damage that had cut her apart from the world?

If he thought money fixed such problems, she was going to hit him with a shrink bill he'd need to take out a second mortgage for.

That'd show him.

Adaline was about to return to her room to wait for her mother to come home when a sound outside caught her attention. The back door was open, and beyond it, the door of the small metal shed in the far corner of the lawn was open too.

Adaline hesitated on the back step. She pushed open the screen door and stepped down onto the narrow crushed gravel path that led to a neglected fishpond. The concrete basin was typically dry as a bone save for the rain, but today it was full. The water was clear and bubbling playfully out of a small aeration device. Small water lilies had materialised, and a quick flash of gold and white told her the Sharp population had gone up.

There was another bang, similar to the one that had drawn Adaline outside. It came from the shed, and a moment later, a tall woman in a floral print shirt and black tracksuit pants emerged. The floral print shirt was Adaline's, and it hadn't been intended for the garden by any means. Soiled beyond repair, it was as good as rags to her now. Or something she might wear to paint the house.

Georgia saw her standing there and stopped. She carried a potted plant in one hand and a garden spade in the other.

A minute passed as mother and daughter regarded each other.

Adaline hadn't been sure what she'd feel upon seeing her again. Now, in the moment, she realised it wasn't any one thing. It was a dozen things, all vying for the lead. Relief. Apprehension. Resentment. Pure, unshakable love.

Adaline hadn't really missed Georgia, the distance between them had been too welcome for that, but now that she was home, she was glad to be.

'Hi Mum,' she said.

Georgia narrowed her eyes. 'Excuse me if I don't drop everything.'

The smile building on Adaline's lips fell away. She held her arms around herself and nodded towards the pond. 'This looks good.'

Georgia grunted and stepped around her.

Adaline watched as she dropped to her knees to balance on a foam board, then set about burying the potted plant amongst the water lilies.

'It's good to see you,' Adaline ventured. 'You look good.' A lie – Georgia had dark circles under her eyes, wild hair and dry, cracked lips – but it didn't cost Adaline anything to say it. There were wide adhesive bandages on the insides of her arms covering her cut wrists and forearms. She had bruises under her right ear. In all, she was a bit of a mess, and those bandages weren't going to last long after being submerged in pond water.

'Do we have spares of those?' she asked.

Georgia looked up then followed the line of Adaline's gaze. She shook her head and laughed. 'Oh please, spare me.'

'Spare you?'

'Don't swan in here and start acting like you care. Fussing and complimenting and what-not. I'm not interested. You can't just take it on and off like a hat.'

Adaline tightened her arms around herself. 'Okay.' She buried her natural instinct to defend herself. In the long run it just wasn't worth it.

'I suppose you're going to want to know what when, how much, what they do.' Georgia's shoulders had drawn together. She was becoming agitated. Her pills, Adaline guessed. She was talking about what the doctors had given her. Obviously enough that there was a kind of regime to get through each day.

Adaline shook her head. 'We can talk about that later. When did you start this?'

'I know it looks bare, I'm not *finished*.' She slapped at the water fern. One of its fronds slipped below the surface then came back.

Just like Adaline.

She held her hands up. 'I'll leave you to it. I'll be inside when you're ready to talk.' She didn't want to leave, but this conversation was circling the drain.

Georgia was in a mood, and nothing Adaline said was going to be interpreted correctly.

Georgia said nothing.

Adaline waited. She dropped her hands then turned away.

Just as she reached the back steps, something blurred past her ear and crashed into the side of the house. There was a metallic squeal, then a crash as whatever it was fell to the ground. Adaline leapt back from it. She was bleeding. There was blood on her face, her neck. Her hand shot up to cover it, wipe at it, but it was only pond water.

Georgia had thrown the spade at the back of Adaline's head.

'You raging *bitch*!'

Adaline turned, eyes wide and heart wild, to see Georgia on her feet and advancing on her.

'You leave, you hurt me and ignore me, and now you come into my house and mock me? How I look, what I'm doing?'

Adaline put her hands up between them, shielding her face. Her mum had never struck her before, but she'd never thrown something at her head either. This outburst was a level Adaline didn't know how to navigate.

'I suppose you're hungry?' Georgia continued. 'I suppose you want to eat and wash your clothes? Tell me about all the fun you had when I was in the hospital? Or what you were doing when I was calling you and calling you, and you didn't have any time for me? So that's the end of my day, then? The rest of it's all about you and what you need?'

It was nonsensical. It was always nonsensical. Everything Adaline had been told and read stated that people with Georgia's condition struggled to express themselves in words. Their thoughts would come out jumbled, which only served to further agitate them. Adaline knew this, but it didn't help her. How was she supposed to respond? What did she address, what did she ignore?

How did she get her mother out of her face so that she wasn't so goddamned scared?

Don't apologise, a small voice reminded her.

This wasn't her fault. She'd gone on a holiday. People went on holidays all the time. She didn't owe her mother any kind of servitude, her life was her own to live as she wished.

But these were new thoughts. New truths that orientated her. She hadn't thought this way two months ago. Even a month ago when she'd been memorising her Gateway itinerary when she'd decided she had the right to travel, she hadn't changed her behaviour towards her mother. Georgia had no idea Adaline felt completely different about their lives now. To her, this was all so sudden, so out of character. The reliable daughter had left her in the lurch, adopted a new attitude and gone.

Abandoned her.

Georgia was feeling abandoned, and she finally had the chance to fight about it.

'You should see what you made me do,' Georgia hissed. Too close, her breath hot and awful on Adaline's cheeks and mouth. She tore at one of the sodden adhesive bandages. It came away easily.

Raw skin. Angry red lines and butterfly stitches pulling cut flesh together. More bruises.

There was a horrible clutch in Adaline's stomach. She closed her eyes and turned away.

'No, you *look*! These are your fault – as good as you'd cut me yourself!'

'Please stop!' It was more shriek than beg, a strangled, high voice that Adaline didn't know she was capable of. Every cell in her body wanted to shove her mother away. She curled her hands into fists and stepped back. One step. Two.

'Don't you walk away from me!'

Adaline opened her eyes. 'Stop shouting at me.' Another voice she didn't recognise. Abruptly level and no-nonsense, completely devoid of emotion. Where had it come from when her body was so rattled?

Georgia hesitated.

'I'm going inside,' Adaline said in that same voice. 'Don't follow me. We both need some time to calm down.' She moved another step back, then hesitated. 'And don't ever throw anything at me like that again.'

She hurried inside.

Or what? she thought. Boundaries needed consequences. She hadn't been thinking straight, hadn't been quick on her feet.

Granted, she hadn't imagined needing to prepare a consequence for being attacked with a spade.

She threw open her door, ran inside and slammed it.

Adaline sank to the floor, her back against the door, and drew her knees against her chest. She wrapped her arms around them and dropped her face into the dark space in the middle. 'I didn't cause it,' she whispered. A tear slipped from her eye, trailed along her nostril, then fell away. 'I can't cure it.' She tightened her arms as little tremors rocked her body. 'I can't control it.'

The Three C's, a mantra she'd learned from an online community.

How many times had she repeated it to herself? How many times had she believed it? All the research she'd done, all the forums she'd visited and advice she'd sought – they'd all agreed on one thing: loved ones were not at fault. The person with BPD was responsible for their own actions and behaviours.

But what would these experts say if she told them she'd fled the country and left her suicidal mother behind? Would they still encourage her to be selfless? Or did they have another word for daughters like her, another category?

Adaline began to cry, and she didn't stop until she slumped sideways onto the carpet and exhaustion claimed her.

She fell asleep with tears on her face.

40 CONSEQUENCES

The thief was unmasked. According to email reports, Lois had been caught stealing from Lisa's handbag. She'd eventually confessed to the Chateau theft, and had been held to account for the unpaid international phone charges. It was all very dramatic.

It was also unanimously confirmed that Pete had proven himself better than anticipated. Not only had he been prompt and handsome, but he'd bought Holly a dozen long-stemmed roses and fashioned a makeshift backpack for him to carry them in – thereby adoring her *and* keeping her arms free. Rachael had observed a flattering degree of nervous trembling (how close had she been?) and Maree had declared him well-groomed and romantic. Jenny didn't write to Adaline, but Maree said she'd been there and hadn't hated it.

No one had a cheeky photo of the big meet, so Adaline was forced to be content with her imagination.

There were, however, many photos of her friends in Rome. The Colosseum, the Roman Forum. The Trevi Fountain, where Pies had taken a picture of Rory throwing a coin over his shoulder. Rory had been wearing the first shirt she'd ever seen him in, the one which read 'I've got more issues than Cosmo'. He'd looked good. Happy.

It had hurt like a swift kick to the ribs.

She'd wanted to share the moment with him, write to him and ask him if he'd thrown the coin over his left shoulder so he'd return to Rome – but then she'd worked out the time difference and hadn't wanted to wake him. That had been hours ago.

Not only were they a day's travel apart, but they were out of time. He was in the past, approaching a day she'd mostly lived.

They wrote often, but she was already lying to him. It wasn't the best start to a long distance relationship, she knew, but in the long run she was sparing him. He didn't need to know that she was walking on eggshells, pushing her way through a sluggish silence that became a one-sided rage as fast as a leap into freefall. He would want to comfort her. He'd let her misery become his.

He deserved to be as free as she'd been that night in Paris before the first call. That, and she never wanted him to dread hearing from her. When they spoke, she would bring him joy.

She stared at his last message for so long that her phone screen dimmed, then locked. She unlocked it again and pressed her lips together.

Show me where you are! Show me your life!

Adaline glanced around her bedroom. She was cross-legged on her bed, her back to the small window that overlooked the street. It was a far cry from the backgrounds he could manage, but that wasn't a problem, really. She was happy for him. She hoped the next photo he sent her had St. Peter's Basilica in the background. She'd live vicariously through him, and it would be enough.

She switched the camera on her phone to selfie mode and fixed a grin on her face. One, two, three attempts, then she finally managed a picture where she didn't look grim.

She didn't feel grim. Just isolated and a little envious.

Adaline added a caption, *You aint got nothing on Paxton St!* and sent it. It was after lunch in Adelaide and just on dawn in Rome. She hesitated, then added, *Good morning.*

She looked across the room at her door. It was time to stop hiding. She'd eaten lunch and dinner in her room yesterday, and spent most of this morning grocery shopping, jogging the streets and obsessively checking Facebook.

She had to face her mother. Set some boundaries, threaten consequences.

She thought of Beth dragging Daniel's suitcase alongside her own and Adaline's resolve strengthened. Beth trailed after her brother like hired help and made herself responsible for someone who refused to take responsibility for themselves. For her efforts, she was rewarded with disdain.

Adaline recognised too much of herself in the other girl.

She pushed off the bed, pocketed her phone – her lifeline now – and stepped out into the hallway. Georgia hadn't sought her out yesterday after the backyard incident, except to throw a box of tissues at her door. Adaline stepped over it, determined to leave it there. A small consequence to throwing things – they were no longer going to be magically cleaned up by the resident slave.

Things were worse now. Georgia was a thrower, she liked to emphasise her point with a pillow or a magazine. Once she'd thrown a mug of coffee across the kitchen, but never something sharp before, never something directly at Adaline that could hurt her.

Adaline touched the hair the spade had whizzed past, and kept her head down until she was in the kitchen.

Georgia was there; perched on a stool, one elbow on the counter, a steaming mug of coffee nearby. She was leafing through a magazine, her reading glasses too far down her nose to be helpful. She glanced up as Adaline walked in, stared at her for the measure of two heartbeats, then continued reading.

The kitchen was small and in dire need of a makeover. It had been fashionable in the mid-eighties but was now too ugly to ever be considered retro. One fun weekend a long time ago they'd replaced the cupboard handles and begun re-tiling the dated splashback. Simon had said something Georgia had taken the wrong way, a fight had ensued and the tiling bucket and tools had sat in the bottom of the pantry ever since. Adaline looked at the incomplete job and considered all it had come to represent.

It was a shame, because when things were going well her mum was wonderful. She had a dirty sense of humour, she loved puns. She had a laugh that built for ages before it broke. She even thought Adaline was funny. Some of Adaline's favourite internet memes had been sent to her by her mum. They even liked the same music. On particularly good days, she called Adaline 'Lynn', on all the others she called her 'You', or the hated 'baby'.

Was the darkness made worse because the light was so wonderful? Would Adaline have fled too, just like her dad, if she didn't have so many nice memories anchoring her here?

Her mum wasn't a bad person. She was sick. Sometimes she said and did hurtful things because she was desperate – because she'd do anything to stop the pain she herself was drowning in.

That didn't make it okay, but Adaline took a small degree of comfort in knowing it wasn't all completely senseless.

Adaline crossed to the mail tray and leafed through the unopened envelopes. Bills. Junk mail from the travel agency Adaline had booked her trip through, product brochures from the nearby shops. She opened the one from the bank and sighed.

'What have I done wrong now?' said Georgia.

Adaline chose her words carefully. 'I think we should switch to online statements. Maybe automatic deductions.'

Georgia turned a page. 'Fine. Do that.'

A tickle of irritation slowed Adaline's response. 'Actually, you're the primary card holder. You'll need to make the call.' She didn't know if this was true or not, but it was time for her mother to start taking some responsibility for the finances in this house. 'We may even be able to do it online. I'll sit with you and we'll figure it out together. We can pay this while we're at it, Dad transferred some money over again.'

Georgia closed her magazine and straightened in her seat. Adaline knew immediately that she'd misspoke, but she couldn't think how. Georgia's lips pressed into a thin line and her brows lifted a fraction.

Adaline spoke quickly, anxious to head her off, to disarm her somehow. Distract, distract, distract.

'I was thinking of going and seeing him tomorrow. I mean, I haven't checked if he's free, but I'm free all day so I'll work around him.'

It wasn't working.

'Did I mention a girl I was travelling with got hit by a car in Florence?' No, Adaline thought wildly, of course she hadn't mentioned it – mother and daughter had barely spoken in weeks.

The skin around Georgia's mouth was white now, and her eyes were wild.

Adaline wrapped her arms around herself and stiffened. 'Please don't yell at me.' She said it so quietly, so … pathetically, really … that it got through to Georgia as nothing else had. Consequences, she reminded herself. 'If you start shouting I'm going to leave. I've made new friends, I have places I can go now. If you need a time out, that's fine. We can talk later.'

This was a strange, muddled world. A child teaching her parent manners, boundaries, respect. Everything was reversed. Surreal.

Terrifying.

Georgia gripped the edge of the counter so tightly that her knuckles turned white within seconds. She seemed to be grappling with her breathing, working to steady it – steady herself.

After a seemingly endless moment in which Adaline almost apologised and took everything back, Georgia unlocked her lips and colour flooded back into her face.

Adaline had seen a thousand mood swings, but she'd never got used to the speed of them.

A moment ago, Georgia had been set to detonate. Now she was composed.

The boundary and consequence had worked! But there wasn't time to congratulate herself: Georgia was stepping around the kitchen counter and advancing on her.

It shamed her that she cowered.

Her mother stopped within arm's reach and bent forward at the waist. When she spoke, quietly and full of drama, it was as if she were sharing a secret. 'Who the hell do you think you are? Threaten to run away again and I'll do worse than yell at you.'

The last of Adaline's childish innocence tumbled away into nothingness. All that remained was fear.

41 PROVIDER

The scrappy little inner-city apartment was more modest than Adaline remembered. Perhaps she'd seen it through a lens of envy before now, but today it spoke of a man stretched to financial breaking point. Adaline's father was still paying the mortgage for their house in Gawler. Doctors, specialists, medication and insurances, they were all billed to him, and somehow between rent, two lots of bills and two lots of general expenses, he'd managed to find the money to send Adaline to Europe.

It was a good thing he was taking so long to make tea, it had given Adaline time to smother the angry words she'd carried over here. She'd been set to rage and blame, but looking around, she felt only gratitude and a grudging understanding.

If Adaline could be here instead of down the hall from Georgia, she'd live off toast and second-hand furniture too – in a heartbeat.

A breath of effort then a rattle, and he was back in the room carrying a loaded tray. Adaline fell on the sweet biscuits hungrily. It had been too toxic to chance breakfast this morning, so she'd skipped it and hoped for something here. The sad turn of his mouth showed he guessed as much.

'I'll put some two-minute noodles on in a bit – you like those. I got the chicken flavour.'

Her favourite flavour. She accepted the humble meal with a nod.

'And I've got some raisin toast. A better breakfast than biscuits.'

'Maybe a healthier breakfast, but not a better one.' She took another biscuit and smiled.

He sat opposite her on a couch more at home in an old lady's house, and opened his arms wide in welcome. 'Tell me about your trip.'

She did. The highlights. The struggles. The friends she'd made, the things she'd seen and what that meant to her. Claire. The amount of times Georgia had rung.

Some of the light went out of Simon's eyes as he listened. He shook his head. 'Let's not talk about your mother.'

Adaline moved forward on her seat. 'Actually … we need to talk about her. That's why I wanted to see you today.'

Adaline had spent half of yesterday reading articles on courageous conversations; how to have them, how to listen when the person responded against your expectations. She'd practiced in front of the mirror, murmuring confessions to herself and schooling the accusation out of her eyes. And she'd been calm. Until her mother had stopped the washing machine mid-cycle and hauled Adaline's sopping clothes onto the floor. She'd put her own clothes in, restarted the machine, and Adaline hadn't realised until much later when she'd stepped in soapy water as she'd passed the laundry door.

She'd grabbed her things, told her mother she didn't know when she'd be back, and stormed out.

Two bus rides and a short walk had gone a long way to calming her temper, but she'd started blaming her dad for all the bad things that were happening to her – thankfully Adaline hadn't shared those thoughts when he'd opened his door and hauled her off her feet in a bear hug.

The duality confused her. How could he love her this much, yet leave her to carry such a burden alone?

Adaline took a deep breath. 'Some things need to change.'

Simon reached for his empty mug and cradled it between his hands.

'I don't want to be a full-time carer anymore.' She paused. 'I don't want to be responsible for a grown woman. A woman who doesn't respect me and who … frightens me. Dad, I'm scared of my own mother.

'She's worse than ever.' Adaline paused, then reconsidered. 'No, she's as bad was she was when you left.'

A trigger word, she thought, one she'd been trying to avoid.

Simon looked miserable. His shoulders had dropped and his mouth had sagged. The fun father-daughter reunion was over, things were back to being hard.

'They … they punish the ones they love the most,' he said. 'They' was his way of referring to those who suffered Borderline Personality Disorder. 'Punish them and test them. When you went to Europe you failed.' He swallowed. 'I should have warned you she'd behave this way.'

I've read all the books, Adaline wanted to say, I lived with this woman during the fall-out after you left – you're not telling me anything I don't already know. She looked at the floor until she was sure these thoughts were no longer crowding her tongue.

'I can't keep doing this.' Adaline looked up and met Simon's eyes. 'I won't.'

She could see the rising panic in him, the confusion and the horror that his precariously balanced life was changing again.

It was so hard not to blame him. To blast him with accusations and judgement. He deserved it: his freedom had come at the cost of his daughter's. But that was a conversation for another time. Right now she needed something from him and she was willing to frame it as his chance to make amends.

'I want to make a deal.'

The words hung between them like bait. There were so many strings attached, and he knew it.

'I'll give you three months,' she said. 'Three months to sort out a different situation for her. Therapy, somewhere else to live, whatever. I'll continue looking after her, but I'll start getting her ready for whatever comes next.' She waited. 'It's going to be hell for me, you know that.'

Simon licked his lips and pressed his fingers to his temple. 'What happens after three months?'

'I get a full-time job and move out. But in the meantime, I want this.' She pulled a folded sheet of paper from the handbag at her feet and held it over the tea set.

He took it and read.

She supposed he read it twice, because it took a long time for him to look up.

'I can't pay for it,' she said. 'I was hoping you would so I could get started in the industry.'

Simon squinted at the page. 'A certificate two in tourism.'

Adaline nodded. 'There's an online component and a couple of classes in the CBD. A Gateway tour manager is going to be my reference when I start applying for jobs.'

'I didn't know you wanted to work in travel.'

'I didn't either until I went travelling.' She leaned forward. 'I'm going to be good at this, Dad. Aren't you pleased? I had no idea what I wanted to do when I left school. Heaps of my friends have gone to uni and I've become an expert on product placement in my local grocery store. I've finally got a direction.'

Simon handed the page back and returned to cradling his empty mug. 'Of course I'm pleased, I'm just … this is a lot to take in.'

You owe me, she thought. And he seemed to know that, because he began to nod.

'Of course I'll pay,' he said. He glanced around the room as if the answer to his new financial burden was somehow within reach. Adaline couldn't worry about that – she'd have to trust that her father could find a way to make it work.

'Thank you,' she said.

He nodded. 'Of course,' he said again. He stared into his mug. 'Three months. God, she's always resisted therapy.'

Adaline nodded. 'It's probably time Mum stopped getting her way all the time. She needs to do this for us.'

Mostly for her daughter. Simon could finalise the divorce at any moment, they'd served their time apart. He'd always be in Georgia's life because of Adaline, but Adaline and Georgia's relationship could go either way. Georgia needed to make an investment. She needed to better herself if she wanted any chance of removing the fear and disappointment from Adaline's heart.

Simon and Adaline talked about Georgia for a long time. They made plans. They agreed on responsibilities and timelines, consequences and acceptable behaviours. He paled then flushed when she told him about the spade incident, and Adaline suspected he'd be on the phone the moment she left.

Much later they spoke about all things Simon, then Adaline told him a little about Rory.

He had a lot of questions, but she dodged most of them. He wanted answers to things she didn't know herself.

He made chicken noddles for lunch and they had more tea, then Adaline paid for the course using Simon's credit card. By the time she left, she was enrolled.

Out on the shared lawn in front of the apartment building, Adaline hugged herself and grinned at the sky. Things were changing.

She fell out of her daydream when her phone started ringing. It was a Skype call, and she almost rejected it in her haste to answer. 'Hi.'

'Okay, my morning's made.'

Her grin widened. 'You're easy pleased.'

She checked the time on her phone. It was dawn in Rome. If she had the schedule right, the group would be on the coach soon heading to the Athens ferry. Inarguably the most brutal start time of them all.

'We're off to Greece today,' he said, confirming it. He yawned. 'Meet me there?'

'Sure. I'll grab the next bus over.'

'The next airbus?'

'No, the next two twenty-two.'

'In that case I might have lunch while I wait.'

She nodded. 'That's smart. Tell me about Rome. Tell me everything. Tell me how much you miss me and tell me who you've terrorised since I've left.'

'Were you this needy when we were together?'

She laughed.

She listened to his stories hungrily. Wanting to give him her full concentration, she sat in the middle of the lawn and pulled her legs up to her chest. He spoke fast, and when she was all caught up, she shared her good news.

Rory's delight made her drop her head against her knees and smile in a way she hadn't since returning home. His enthusiasm filled her; it pushed against her lungs and squeezed her heart, and in that moment, nothing could touch her.

'I wish you were here,' he said.

'Not as much as I wish I was there.'

'Nu-uh,' he said. 'Pies keeps calling himself Ada and trying to hold my hand. Trust me, my wish trumps yours.'

She grinned. 'Aw, he knows you miss me.'

There was a pause, and Adaline's heart sank. He wasn't coming up with a pithy come-back, he was being hurried along.

When he spoke again, he sounded put-out. 'I've got to go. Everyone's boarding and my bag's still in the room.'

'Hurry!' she said, as amused as she was disappointed. 'They can't wait for you!'

'But you can?'

Adaline smiled and closed her eyes. 'Yes, I can.'

42 LOVE LOCK

Just being within the Sydney University Camperdown campus made Adaline feel smarter. It was as if the air was fragranced with potential and the coffee flavoured with facts. The cafes and walkways were teeming with students on their lunch breaks and as Adaline waited, she imagined all the ways they would change the world.

She sat against the external café wall – not in one of the metal chairs that would soon become so important, but on the low concrete wall, inconspicuous. From here she could see a familiar face. She couldn't hear his laugh, but his mouth seemed constantly open – telling a joke or receiving it, Pies had a presence that people around him couldn't help but notice. He definitely had Rory's full attention.

The would-be doctor had his back to her. He was slouched in his seat, drinking the last of a beer. There were empty plates on the table and his backpack was tucked beneath his seat, doubtlessly full of textbooks.

It was the first time she'd seen him in person in five weeks. He'd come to Adelaide twice over the last three and a half months, but she hadn't been able to return the gesture until now. She'd explained her reluctance to ask her dad for more money and he'd understood, but it had been hard. Hard to wait, hard to keep this secret. They had spoken every day, without fail. Mailed each other things. Texted each other photos of their world and their experiences. In all of those conversations, she'd not so much as hinted of this day.

She pushed her fingers through her hair and checked her reflection again. For what had to be the hundredth time, she wondered what he'd think of her shorter hair. Of her clothes. She'd dressed with care this morning; she wore her Florentine earrings for luck, which he'd recognise, but the black pants and smart pinstriped blouse ensemble was nothing like anything she'd worn on tour.

When she looked back, Pies was staring at her significantly. Rory was standing. Turning.

Adaline shot to her feet at the same moment that Pies held a hand up, urging her to wait. She hesitated.

Rory walked inside.

Pies watched him go, then waved her forward.

They embraced when she reached the table, but broke apart quickly. There wasn't much time. She dropped to her haunches beside Rory's empty chair and thread the material handle through the metal bars of the chair. She folded it back on itself and secured it with a small green padlock.

'You look shit-hot,' Pies said when she stood. 'If Rory turns you down I'm available.'

She grinned. 'I'll keep that in mind.' She held the small silver key out to him. 'Here. I'll be too distracted to use it.'

He took it, glanced over her shoulder then waved her away. 'Get going, it was just a piss.'

She was out of sight less than a minute before Rory returned from the bathroom. Pies was back in his seat and he'd pulled out his phone to feign waiting.

Rory didn't sit again. He said something that made Pies laugh, then Pies was standing. Rory reached down, grabbed one of the straps of his bag, and hauled it up, intending to swing it onto his back. The chair flipped. Its legs shot towards his legs, and he was too surprised to move quick enough. They crashed against him. He dropped the bag and the chair fell.

Rory stared down at the mess. He glanced around, then pointed at Pies in accusation.

Adaline moved from her hiding spot. The laughter and general bedlam meant she didn't have to be quiet about it.

Rory was laughing. Pies was denying it, his hands up, and the moment was almost upon them.

Rory dropped down to inspect his bag. He found the padlock immediately, but it wasn't until he turned it over that Pies was completely absolved of blame. He'd seen them. Her initials above his initials. The heart that enclosed them.

The padlock from Verona that she hadn't secured onto the gate behind Guilietta.

He shot to his feet and turned.

Eyes lit with hope and amusement, he saw her, and the world beyond them ceased to exist.

She was in his arms before she'd fully taken in the joy on his face. He pulled her closer and closer against him, until she was gasping for breath. He released her only long enough to claim her mouth. They kissed. Held. Laughed against each other's mouths.

People around them murmured, but in Adaline's mind they were so far away.

It was the camera click that made her pause. She prised herself away from

Rory and narrowed her eyes at Pies.

He scoffed. 'Don't look at me like that. You think all that subterfuge was free? I'm posting this on Facebook. Eye-witness account. How many people were on our tour – forty-eight? I'll get at least forty-eight likes.'

'Forty-eight including us,' Rory pointed out.

Pies raised an eyebrow. 'If the pair of you don't like this status then it says bad things for your relationship.'

Rory laughed. 'Would you please shut up?'

Pies pointed at Rory's face. 'You should be buying me a carton right about now for how much I had to talk to your girlfriend to set this up.'

Adaline said, 'Hey!'

Pies grinned. 'I'd do it again.' He paused. 'For another carton.'

Rory and Adaline continued kissing as Pies set about freeing Rory's backpack from the chair. He departed immediately after, stating he could only bear so much 'reunion suck-face' in a day.

Rory and Ada walked. Hand in hand, they talked fast about everything they'd done and thought and wanted since they'd last spoken on the phone. He chided her for keeping her visit a secret, but then lapsed into stunned silence when she shared her news.

'I moved out.' She squeezed his hand to reanimate him. 'Don't be too impressed. It's with five other people in a converted brothel. It's got some odd features but we all get our own bathroom, which I hear is pretty rare in the rental market.'

'I'm jealous,' Rory said. 'I share a single bathroom with four other guys and Pies is the absolute worst.'

Adaline wrinkled her nose. 'Ew.'

Rory bumped his forehead against hers, his smile wide and face wrinkled with happiness. 'I love that you surprised me. And that you pranked me. That was good.'

The little padlock was still secured to his bag, and Adaline wondered if it would be a permanent accessory now.

'Let's walk this way,' he said, pointing. 'You'll love the old quadrangle, it reminds me of Hogwarts.'

She did love it. They entered through a stone arch and walked the path that intersected the brilliant green grass in the middle. There was a Jacaranda tree in the corner, a flame of purple colour that kept drawing her eye.

She tugged on his hand and they stopped walking.

'I need to tell you a few things,' she said. She wished she had prompt cards, something she could fidget with and be led by.

Rory's smile dipped. 'Sounds ominous.'

She filled her lungs and covered their held hands with her free one. 'I haven't been honest with you about the last three months.' She swallowed. 'About what it's really been like living with my mum and sorting things out with my dad. Truthfully, every day was worse than the last, and there were days where you were the only thing keeping me sane.' She looked up as his serious face. 'You were the only thing that made me happy. Those times you visited me, I … pretended to be okay. Every time you called I … well, I wasn't honest about how much I'm struggling.'

It seemed apt that they were having this conversation within the embrace of such a prestigious building – it reminded her of all the beautiful places they'd seen together.

Rory's free hand covered the knot of fingers between them. 'Look, honestly, I knew you were struggling but I didn't want to force you to talk about it. But I've got to say, we can't be together properly if you compartmentalise your life. I'm in this for the lot – good and bad.'

She nodded. 'I know. I'm sorry I lied to you.'

He pulled her into a hug and spoke into her hair. 'It's okay. Is she doing okay with the therapy?'

Georgia had finally begun speaking to a professional about her illness. It had taken three tries – she'd hated the first two therapists then held the process up with a rage that had lasted over thirty-six hours, but the third therapist had gotten through to her. Now Georgia was undertaking Dialectical Behaviour Therapy twice a week, and there had been enough improvement that Adaline had been able to follow through with moving out. This had of course set everything back and the fights had been horrendous, but her dad had helped her pack the small amount of stuff she'd wanted to take with her, and managed to keep the worst of Georgia's moods away from her.

Adaline nodded. 'Yeah, and in the long run I reckon we'll see a big difference.'

Experts estimated a two year course of this particular therapy – it was anything but a quick fix but it was the best treatment she'd had to date. Georgia had even spoken positively about it over dinner one night. Adaline had been so terrified of saying the wrong thing that she hadn't responded well. Georgia had gone quiet and not spoken of it again.

Adaline hoped she got another chance one day. She'd love to hear more about how her mother felt she was progressing.

'Thanks for telling me,' Rory said. 'And please keep telling me, okay?'

She nodded.

'While we're confessing crap,' he went on. He lifted his hand to his face, pushed at it then rubbed his neck. 'I've kind of lied to you too. You know, through omission.'

Adaline's brows flew up. This surprised her, as Rory was usually so candid with her. So open, like a book she was welcome to read over and over again.

'I was going to tell you last time I saw you but I kind of lost my nerve. I guess I thought … I thought if you came here to see me, then I'd tell you.

Because then it wasn't all me being all desperate and doing all the travelling.'

The lovely certainty that had been warming her skin from the inside began to cool. She pushed her bottom lip between her teeth. 'I'm sorry I didn't come to you first like I said I would. My dad was really struggling financially because of that course – I couldn't ask him for more money on top of that. He's living off toast and noodles, you have to believe that.'

He ducked his head. 'I know. I do.'

'I came as soon as I could.'

'Okay. I know.'

'So tell me whatever it is now. I came.' She pointed at the ground and he laughed. 'I'm here.'

He nodded. Their eyes met and she felt burned. The heat within her body was back, but it wasn't the comfortable warmth it had been a moment ago, it was fire.

'I love you,' he said.

A bird landed in the Jacaranda tree and purple tumbled soundlessly to the ground. They stared at each other, firmly in a moment that seemed to defy the natural progress of time.

She smiled. 'I know. I love you too.'

'You do?'

'Duh.'

Rory blinked. 'Duh?'

Her smile widened. 'Yes, "duh". Of course I love you. Of course we love each other!' She poked him in the ribs and he laughed in surprise. 'I was going to tell you today. You know, get it out of the way.'

'Get it out of the …'

She kissed him. 'I love you,' she said when they parted. She brushed her lips over his again then stepped back and straightened her top. 'How do I look?'

His eyes were hungry. 'Devastating.'

She lifted her chin and patted her hair. 'Thanks.'

'I meant to tell you that earlier. I love your hair.' He stared at her. 'I love you. I really, really love you.'

She dropped her face into her hands and giggled. Delirium, she thought. Giddy, blissful delirium. When she looked up he was smiling, but shy.

'I'll stop.' He reached for her and she went to him. 'It just feels good to say it after all this time.'

'It does feel good.'

'Do you want to see my place? Where's your stuff? How long are you here for?'

Adaline answered the first question because it most suited her. 'I would love to see your place, but I might have to meet you there later.'

His brows came together.

'In fact,' she pulled her phone from her little handbag and checked the time, 'I have to get going.'

'What?'

'What's the quickest way to Town Hall?'

Rory was blindsided. 'What's at Town Hall?'

Adaline blew out an exasperated breath and rolled her eyes. She was having a brilliant time messing with him, it would almost be a shame to finally deliver the punchline. She said, 'My interview.'

Rory's already rounded eyes boggled. 'What?'

Adaline nodded. 'Yeah, when I finished my course Jack hooked me up with someone he knows through Gateway. A manager at Flight Centre. At Town Hall.' She made a show of smoothing her shirt again. She met his eyes and feigned innocence. 'Didn't I tell you?'

Rory shook his head. 'I'm confused.'

Adaline touched her fingers to her forehead, as if she'd just realised her mistake. 'Oh, I'm so silly. That room I'm renting? Yeah, that converted brothel is thirty minutes from here.'

It was the most delicious silence of her life.

They stood there, surrounded by learning and history, as a new future unfolded before them. One that didn't involve checked baggage, long stretches of time between touches, and fourteen hundred kilometres.

He had changed her. Europe had changed her. It had emboldened her, challenged her, and ultimately set her free. She didn't fear this new relationship, nor all the obligations it promised. She felt as wild as the bird that had leapt from the Jacaranda and launched into the sky. As anchored as the grass beneath their feet. And she felt so full of hope, she was sure it would spill from her body and colour the way forward.

THE ROAD SERIES CONTINUES

The Road Less Travelled
Elise K. Ackers

Dana Ryan can make even the most seasoned of travellers feel like day-trippers. She's got scars from Machu Picchu, tattoos from the Greek islands, and more stories about the world than the average Facebook newsfeed. Dana is led by and lives by her wanderlust, until an invitation to attend her kid sister's elopement changes her priorities.

She has to stop that wedding.

Dion Houghton has never been this far from home before. The Cook Islands is beautiful but disconcerting. There's a chicken wandering around the international airport and the customs are strange – it's like an alternate reality to the small country town he's known all his life. And then there's Dana, his high-school girlfriend and first love – looking like she's seen it all, and looking ready to tear his best friend's vows in two.

He has to save this wedding.

Dana is adamant: there's too much her sister hasn't experienced, and so much she doesn't know about herself and the world. Dion is immovable. He's never seen two people more in love.

Is it fate that Dana should be reunited with her family at this important milestone, or is Dana just full of opinions that no one wants to hear?

Faced with the life that could have been hers had she stayed in rural Australia, Dana discovers she has more to learn than teach. It turns out life back home has gone on without her – infinitely more complex than she could have imagined – and her nomad ways have cost her more than foreign currency.

Visit www.elisekackers.net to buy now.

ABOUT THE AUTHOR

Thanks for reading *One for the Road*. I hope you enjoyed it. I did a trip much like this one, and I knew when I was singing in a gondola and sampling the best of the Bordeaux wine region, that I would write about it all one day. This book is the first of many adventure stories to come.

If you'd like to know more about me or my books, or you'd like to connect with me online, you can find me on Twitter, Instagram, and Facebook. You can also subscribe to my newsletter for exclusive content, giveaways and release news. Visit my webpage www.elisekackers.net for information and social media links.

If you liked this book, please write a review. Good reviews are like chocolate to authors, and like French martinis to me. You can post a review on Goodreads or on the website of your favourite book distributor.

Made in United States
North Haven, CT
25 September 2022

24555160R00168